Urban Rain

Urban Rain

AN ODYSSEY THROUGH THE DARKNESS OF NIGHT

a novel by
David Dane Wallace

iUniverse, Inc.
Bloomington

URBAN RAIN

An Odyssey through the Darkness of Night

This is a work of fiction. All of the characters, names, incidents, organizations, and dialogue in this novel are either the products of the author's imagination or are used fictitiously.

iUniverse books may be ordered through booksellers or by contacting:

iUniverse
1663 Liberty Drive
Bloomington, IN 47403
www.iuniverse.com
1-800-Authors (1-800-288-4677)

Because of the dynamic nature of the Internet, any web addresses or links contained in this book may have changed since publication and may no longer be valid. The views expressed in this work are solely those of the author and do not necessarily reflect the views of the publisher, and the publisher hereby disclaims any responsibility for them.

Any people depicted in stock imagery provided by Thinkstock are models, and such images are being used for illustrative purposes only.
Certain stock imagery © Thinkstock.

ISBN: 978-1-4620-7181-4 (sc)
ISBN: 978-1-4620-7182-1 (hc)
ISBN: 978-1-4620-7183-8 (ebk)

Library of Congress Control Number: 2011962416

Printed in the United States of America

iUniverse rev. date: 12/19/2011

In memory of the best friend that I ever had. My Dog Hunter.
I will always love you, and forever keep you in my heart-Daddy.

**Thomas Edward Sheridan Halsburth Wallace.
My Uncle and My Dear Friend. Love Always.**

This Book is also for THE ONTARIO STREET ORIGINALS.
You know who you are.

Introduction

Several years ago, in the city of Montreal, I got involved in something. This is our story . . . mine, and a girl you'll come to know as Lilly. It's about a place called Ontario Street, a place with an ambiance of sinister addiction so thick that it exists like a rolling fog. A place whose evil will haunt you for years to come, if not forever, and have you in some cases waking from fitful sleep, either trembling or in tears. A place where dreams become nightmares. A place where the regulars drug themselves to sleep, or to stay alive. A place with characters so unique and intense that you will find it impossible to forget even years after you've read this book.

But this is not just a story about drug addiction. It's much more than that. It's about the middle of night, and an order of people who live and breathe amongst the rippling blackness that they so embody.

And so, as I said at the beginning of this introduction, this is our story. Mine and Lilly's. So step inside our world one time. Step inside, of Urban Rain.

Dedication

In memory of the best friend that I ever had, my dog Hunter. I will always love you, and forever keep you in my heart-Daddy.

My Beloved Uncle Thomas Wallace Passed Away Before Ever Having The Chance To Read This Book. I Love You, Dude. This Book Is Also For You.

As well. This Book is for The Ontario Street Originals. You know who you are.

I'd also like to thank my idol, mentor, and friend "The Rico Suave Bad Boy" Chris P. for his teachings in Boxing aswell as for teaching me everything that I know about style and pinache. There is only one. Truly. I love you my friend.

I'd like to thank my Parents, MaryAnn and Paul for their continued support throughout the endeavor of Urban Rain. I love you both.

I'd also like to thank Robert and Richard Gray for their teachings in Bodybuilding and for always treating others with the same respect. You are my friends and my mentors. I'm proud to know you.

PART 1

Chapter 1

David Dane, twenty-five years old, walked briskly down the shadowy streets in a city that was as unfamiliar to him as a midnight T.V. series that was sporting its pilot episode.

He had been in town for one week.

Dane's long-time friend, Bobby Troy Edmonds, had hired Dane on to be the head trainer in one of his Iron Gym's, a business long owned and successfully developed by Edmonds, who had become a millionaire overnight making huge profits off of the clientele that had come through his doors.

Dane glanced at his watch. The hour nearing was two.

Already the suns rays had evaporated and the cloud cover was now heavy, its shades echoing an ominous gloom that threatened rain.

Bodybuilding, Dane's lifelong passion, had occupied the better part of his soul for the past nine years. Moderate success at an amateur competitive level had been his reward, and he did not use performance enhancing drugs, nor those of the recreational kind either, although he had been offered cocaine on countless occasions by other heavy lifters who liked to mix the effects of coke and steroids to give them a boost. Dane had always spurned the offer with extreme prejudice.

David Dane had no interest in drugs. None.

As Dane began to walk downhill towards Ontario Street, his eyes turned upward toward the sky.

A dark and sinister rain had begun.

The shiny treetops above swished and sloshed above Dane's head, and the cold damp air was beginning to penetrate his flesh, searing him to the bone. He was not properly dressed for this weather, having worn only a thin brown workout sweater and blue jeans. The rain was attacking the streets and rooftops of the surrounding area now blowing in gusts that looked like a series of miniature hurricanes.

A Police cruiser rolled by him and stopped at the curb. At the same time, an out-of-control drug addict was screaming as he wielded a knife, his long raggedly cloaked arms flailing about in the dampening air. The two cops exited the car, approaching the forty something year old man who quickly dropped what he was carrying.

Ontario Street, an older area, had become a problem for the police over the past eight or nine years. The area itself, full of sleazy taverns and miniature after-hours clubs had always been rough. Only now the dealers had moved their business into the streets selling high volumes of coke and heroin to the local regulars. This change of business location had also brought its share of prostitutes and riff-raff into the neighborhood, as well as other undesirables. Dane looked up into the shade as he heard the sad winds blowing through the billowing treetops above him, as if Mother Nature was crying out and wanted him to hear her.

The rain had accelerated, but not by much, and he hadn't brought a jacket with him. However he had come this far in his exploration of this place and he wasn't about to turn back now, even as seedy as he recognized this locale to be. Neighborhoods like this did not faze David Dane. For even though he was raised by a mother who was a politician and a father who was by and large corporate, he had had a different upbringing outside of this home; one with an exterior far more harsh than the one he had received at the hands of his parents who bordered on upper middle-class.

4

Dane glanced over his shoulder as a woman dressed in a blue top with black fishnet stockings walked passed him. She reeked of liquor, and judging by her speed, she was probably on her way to her fix—whatever and wherever that may be.

As he turned away from watching her, there was another female standing in the rain before him.

"Hi," she began, dancing back and forth from one foot to another without music. "I'mmmmm Lilly," she said, hands clasped behind her like a soldier. "And you are?"

"David Dane," he replied.

"So, are you looking for something?"

He knew what she meant but he played along anyway.

"A raincoat".

"I don't sell raincoats," she quipped. "I sell something else."

Lilly Chicoine, one year Dane's junior, was the product of a Portuguese mother and a Salvadorian father. Together, they had produced a daughter who resembled a Latin supermodel, who now, due to heavy drug use sported only traces of that original beauty. There was something else about her too, something forlorn and abandoned, like a quiet street in the middle of the night, empty and dark.

The rain was blowing in gusts now, making rippling laps around them.

"Why are you dancing?" Dane asked Lilly.

"Probably too much coke. And I haven't slept, so that's probably contributing to it too."

"Do you live in the area?" he asked.

"Sometimes. Not right now though."

She was still dancing.

"Are you a cop?" She asked.

"No way". Dane said.

They were standing outside a tavern with a solid silver door and the rain had begun to fall. She looked at him for a moment, her long brown hair wet and dishevelled, as if she had fallen overboard and had just been rescued. She wore a brown sweater with long sleeves and a pair of blue jeans. She was as thin as a rake.

"Wanna come inside the bar with me? They kicked me out before, but I'm allowed back in now." She waited for a response.

He wanted to put his arms around her. She had that effect on him, and his eyes reflected that emotion. He did not know if she saw it or not. Lilly opened the door and the two stepped inside. The place at first made Dane uneasy, but it wasn't out of fear. He did not know why he felt this way.

She looked back at him. "You have to buy a drink if you want to sit here or they'll get mad. I don't have any money because I haven't made a client yet. Soooooo . . . I guess you're buying the drinks."

He wondered if she did this often. Dane wondered if alcohol might also be one of her problems. He would later find out that it was not.

As he approached the bar he noticed someone wearing a camouflaged baseball hat glaring at him from the far corner of the room.

Dane made eye contact and then looked away.

Lilly was sitting in front of one of the gambling machines when he returned with the drinks. He set her orange juice down as she took a pull from the machine in front of him. Neither one of them drank alcohol.

Lilly pushed down on the glowing red button and watched as cherries, apples, and treasure chests overflowing with gold rolled simultaneously into place before her eyes.

"I thought you said you had no money," he said. He didn't mind paying for the two drinks. It was being lied to that David Dane did not like.

Her demeanor changed slightly. "I just found twenty bucks in my pocket."

He did not care. He was happy to have her there to keep him company. And besides, outside of Beautiful Bobby, Lilly was now the only other person in town that he knew by name.

Beautiful Bobby was what Dane called Bobby Troy Edmonds. It was a nickname that Dane had bestowed upon his friend once many years ago after finding out that Edmonds had at one time been a Chippendale dancer. David had found out about Bobbys second occupation one night when they'd gone out to a club and Edmonds had bumped into an ex female client of sorts, that had paid Edmonds and another dancer to have sex with her and six of her friends. Bobby was good looking. And it didn't hurt that he had also made it big out in California as a professional bodybuilder before returning home to open up a string of work-out clubs he that he called "Iron Gym". Then he had moved a franchise out here and offered Dane a job, for which David would be forever grateful.

Dane himself was not huge. Not like Edmonds. He stood five eleven, weighing about two hundred and twenty pounds with a shaved head and a handsome pinch that fit him like the glass slipper fit Cinderella. He had a look that could be thug or puppy-dog, depending on his mood. His roots were Irish and Scottish, but he had been raised in Canada. He was the first of two sons born to Jonathan and Marilyn Dane. Both of them had been raised in poverty but worked hard to fight their way out and achieve success.

Jonathan, his father, had been the son of a farmer who grew crops and drove a tractor to feed his family. There were five of them. Jonathan and four others, all of which were girls. Dane bore no resemblance to his Fathers side of The Family in character, having forged a completely different path for himself in life.

"Is it still raining?" Lilly asked.

Dane turned to look at the two windows at his back. Silver outside, and the cloying minions of smoke were making his eyes burn. They curled and swirled about his head in a fuseless batallion.

She had lost track of the answer to her question as she pounded away furiously at the glowing red button on the slot machine. She wasn't paying any attention to him now, or, if she was, she wasn't showing it, her eyes glued almost menacingly to the screen.

"You got a quarter?" she asked sticking out her hand without watching him for a response.

He stood up, fumbling around in his pocket for loose change.

"Here," he said, handing her twenty-five cents.

She took it and did not say thank you.

There was a pay phone on the other side of the room by the hooded glare of the Budweiser sign. She was on it now.

"Okay. How long? Fifteen minutes?" She had a cigarette in her hand which she had bummed from a skater while he wasn't looking. Dane had not watched her when she walked away from him.

"Okay. Okay," Lilly chirped into the mouthpiece before hanging up."

"C'mon, we gotta go," she said, making a mad dash for the door. With him or not. Dane followed her.

"Where are we going?"

"I have to go meet my dealer. He's fronting me for a half-point."

"What the fuck is that?" He had never heard the term before.

"Heroin," she said without hesitation. "But try and stay a few feet behind me because these guys are fucking paranoid. If they see you they won't serve me, and I'm already asking for a front."

So now he was traipsing down the street, eight feet behind this girl that he had just met, so that her heroin dealer would not believe him to be a cop. And he was getting soaking wet. She kept asking him for the time, which he provided for her.

They were obviously in the inner city,but other than the two or three prostitutes they had passed the area appeared unremarkable.

The wind howled through the green treetops now.

"Fuck. I'm getting sick," she said.

"What?" He had not heard her.

She came to the corner and stopped. "I need another quarter."

Dane gave her one.

The chilling rain was blowing in gusts now as the wind cried out in soulless collusion. He was freezing. And he felt like an idiot. The treetops were bent as if giving way to the will of the afternoon current.

He waited there shivering as Lilly crossed the street in search of a pay phone.

"Tell me if you see a green car," she called out with her back to him.

Just as she said this a small green Toyota rounded the corner and stopped just shy of the payphone where Lilly was standing, her dance still vaguely apparent. He could not make out the face behind the wheel, nor did he try to.

"Meet me in front of the bar at the stone park," she whisper-yelled before getting in with the driver. The lights of the car blazed through the afternoon gloom as the two of them drove off.

Dane complied with her instructions, although he did not know why. He liked her. There was no other explanation. He went back and waited in the park across from the tavern where they'd been earlier. They called the park the "The Stone Park" because it was made of bricks. It had two pay phones to the left of where he was sitting that many of the girls in the neighborhood, be they prostitutes or not, used to call their dealers. To his back was the west side of a building called Chantal's and across from him was the tavern where they had been earlier that he would soon come to know as the The Black Domino.

As he sat there, Dane wondered why the guy in The Bar had been staring at him. Why had he been glaring at Dane from beneath the shadow cast by his camouflaged cap? He did not like Dane. That was for sure. And in return, Dane did not like him either.

Cars whizzed past, their tires forming ditches in the fallen downpour. One of them had been a police cruiser, and the driver had inspected Dane as if wondering how he know him.

Suddenly, the little green car returned and Lilly hopped out. About ten minutes had passed. She was holding something tightly in her clenched hand.

"Let's go," she said as the Toyota sped off.

"Fuck! If this gets wet, I'm fucked."

"Why?" he asked, walking by her side.

"Because the paper sticks to it and then the smack is no good. You have to keep it dry."

Dane had only just learned that 'smack' was one of the many street names for heroin. There were also others, such as Downtown, Brown, Junk, Skag, or the simple abbreviation H.

Several years earlier, a lethal brand of Heroin called Black Death had hit the streets of both New York and Vancouver, killing a record number of addicts in only one day. The brand, also known as Black Tar, had twice the potency of regular heroin and it killed its obsessors like an assassin.

". . . Fuck, and I'm out of new ones. I have to go get some from Guardian."

"New ones?" he asked.

She had stopped, and was looking back and forth now as if she couldn't decide what to do next. They were standing in front of a church with a wrought iron gate around it, its gray cement darkening in the rainfall. It had a high clock tower that loomed overhead like a guard post as the two stood there like drowning rabbits. The hooded vapor lamps from the street, now on, were glowing through the coiling dusk, giving ominous presence to the area.

He thought that these streets had an energy. One that he was unfamiliar with, even in concept. They watched somehow. As if everything that the two of them did was monitored and recorded by a nocturnal eye that swept over the area and kept track of what went on. The vapor lamps seemed to brighten as the rain pounded the cement, illuminating the alleyways between the shops across from where they stood.

From where he was standing, Dane noticed a beautiful blond girl in an alley tying a *garro* around her arm. A *garrot*, pronounced simply 'garro' was a junkie's term for the strap, string, rubber tube or whatever else a junkie could find to tie around their arm to make the veins pop.

The sight of it made him wince.

"Hey Jillian," Lilly the Latin girl called out as she reached into the air, waving for attention. She had just noticed her friend.

11

The blond girl across the street stopped what she was doing as she saw Lilly Chicoine heading towards her.

"Jillian!" Lilly called out again, making sure that she had the girl's attention.

"Lilly!" the girl exclaimed, rolling up her bloodied sleeve and heading across the street, the needle still in hand.

Dane stood by, watching as the two females embraced.

"I was in therapy for four months, . . ." the blond with the bloody arm began.

"It's so good to see you," Lilly said genuinely. "Hey. Do you have a clean one I could borrow?"

The blond reached into her purse and handed Lilly a fresh syringe wrapped in clear plastic with a white backing.

"Hold on. I just wanna do my hit," Lilly said, rolling up one of her own sleeves. "And do you have a condom I could use as a *garro?*"

Jillian nodded, handing her a packaged Trojan—not normally the brand carried by street hookers, but somehow, that was what she had.

"And that's . . . David Dane," Lilly said pointing over her right shoulder.

The three of them were now soaked.

"Fuck. I need to find somewhere to do this," she exclaimed. Again, looking back and forth.

All of the shops were closed. Not that it mattered to her dilemma.

"I was pregnant, but I got an abortion," Jillian said. "Tiny baby boo-boo."

Jillian had been a drug addict for fifteen years, and had had open-heart surgery twice by the time she was twenty-one. She had done so much coke that her heart finally gave way and now she only had half of it left. None the less, she was beautiful and had managed even through her drug-induced Hell to keep most of her looks. Her naturally light hair and big brown eyes had made her a hit with many of the local barflies, not to mention men everywhere else in the neighborhood whose eyes often followed her down The Street or to wherever else she happened to be going. She had a piercing in her nose, a hoop ring, and also one in her tongue, and she sported a small tattoo on her neck. She did not have a boyfriend, but she lived with a man named Jean Paul, who was more of a sugar-daddy than anything else. He took care of some of her financial needs, plus he put a roof over her head, but she did not like living with him for two reasons. The first of which was the considerable number of years between them. She was twenty-seven and he was sixty-one. The second reason was that he would become angry and jealous and occasionally beat the living shit out of her. Years ago, and towards his own daughter, Jean Paul might not have been a violent man, however in her eyes, he had proven to her to be a monster on several occasions. Once she had come home from work ten minutes later than she said she would and he had given her two black eyes, raped her, and then tossed her out in the middle of the night. And he had done worse. The previous August he had chased her around the house with a coat hanger that he said he would use to disfigure her and destroy her ability to have children.

"I need to duck in somewhere to do this little thing," Lilly said. "Are you coming?" she called back to Dane who was still standing in the downpour. Without answering, he followed the two girls behind a row of houses through a playground into a small park with a canopy and bird baths.

Silence and the rain drumming against the ground.

He still did not know what he was doing here. After all, this wasn't his world. He didn't even use drugs. But he was lonely and it had been a while since he'd been paid attention to by a woman. Especially one that he thought to be as beautiful as Lilly.

"I'm gonna do it here," she said, emptying the contents of the small wrapper into her syringe.

All three of them were now under a canopy, the rain attacking the metal roof above them. Across the street from them was the edge of a building that housed a medical clinic, its small carport shielding about fifteen or sixteen cars from the darkness and downpour.

Lilly wrapped the condom tightly around her arm twice and searched for a vein.

"Fuck! I can't find one," she fussed, hammering the middle of her arm with two fingers. Even with the Trojan condom *garro*, she still had trouble locating a place to put her needle.

With the sleeve of her brown shirt pulled back, Dane could see that her arm was badly mutilated and all but a tiny portion of flesh was still maintained beyond a mess of cuts and bruises that had obviously come about when she had missed her vein or didn`t get her hit. The sight made him wince at first. And here he was. Fucking crazy, diluted, insane. But somehow, for some reason, he stuck around.

Chapter 2

Bobby Edmonds stood in an office surrounded by pictures of himself, each one demonstrating a different muscular pose. They ranged from a left or right tricep display to a most muscular, and back again. Most of them had been taken by the same photographer: Carol Edmonds.

"Carol is very sick, David," he began.

Bobby Troy Edmonds, forty-four years of age, was born in Trinidad and later moved to southern California. He was African American and spoke with an accent which was native to his place of birth.

David Dane had wandered into Iron Gym about seven thirty that morning and had been sitting with his close friend ever since.

"Look at these pictures," Edmonds said, focused on the wall behind him. "She took all of them."

Carol Edmonds, Bobby's wife of five years, was the love of his life, and the only woman he had ever met who made him want to settle down. She had captured his heart in seven months and they were married in eight. The two had met at one of Bobby's competitions where Carol was working as a photographer, shooting photographs from the edge of the stage as Bobby and four other competitors posed down.

Carol, who knew the judges well, told one of them that she thought that Bobby was cute and could she be introduced to him. Later that night, after the introductions were made, the two of them went out for a late dinner, and continued dating steadily for about six months after that.

In their seventh month, Bobby told her that he loved her and proposed. She had said yes, and the two of them had eloped.

David Dane sighed. "Carol's always treated me like a younger brother. I love her. I love both of you. If there's anything I can do to make any of this any easier on you, let me know".

Edmonds just shook his head.

Dane felt a tension building in the air.

Edmonds was still facing the photographs.

"Her health is worsening. She can't even walk by herself."

"I thought her cancer was in remission," Dane said.

Edmonds turned to view his own reflection in the small mirror that hung on the wall. He looked drained and the whites of his eyes were veiny and red.

"You want some coffee?" he asked. "It's still fresh."

"I'm fine," Dane responded.

He had first heard of Carol's illness when he was back home, when Edmonds had called to tell him about the job. Things were not so good then, but now it seemed, The prognosis had worsened.

Edmonds poured coffee into a glass mug that read: Blond girls and barbell curls.

"She saw a specialist last week," he said. "They didn't like the way that the x-rays looked. It's all over inside her now. Tumors everywhere."

Dane felt nauseous. He himself had at one time been a hypochondriac, and his irrational fear of diseases had to be treated through a psychiatrist as well as with medication. He had been young then. Younger than the average age of a hypochondriac, maybe fourteen or fifteen, if memory served. So talking about disease made him feel un-easy.

A buxom red-head with a dark colored shirt marked "Personal Trainer" strolled across the gym floor toward the open door of the office. Outside, the clanging and banging of weights mixed with the odour of lime protein shakes.

Edmonds turned to face the open door as the red head appeared on its threshold. She was sexy. About five six and a half with big brown eyes and a pristine smile.

"Kristen, this is David Dane. Our new addition," he said, looking her up and down as if for the first time.

"Hi," the girl with brown eyes said offering her hand.

"Hi," he replied in return. "David Dane," he said as he stood up, extending his hand.

Bobby walked around them and closed the open door, his enormous shoulders dwarfing them both. He had been doing steroids for years. Pills, injections, etc.

"I heard about Carol. I'm really sorry . . ." the girl said.

Dane thought she was superficial.

"There's money missing from the till," Edmonds launched.

The female trainer offered no expression.

"David. Would you mind leaving us alone for a few minutes," Bobby asked, turning his attention to his friend.

"No problem". Dane responded, closing the door behind himself on his way out. Dane thought nothing of being asked to leave the office. He would later hear rumors of Bobby and Kristen having an affair. Dane did not know whether to believe them or not.

Night time on Ontario Street. Quiet, dark and vapor lamps a-glare. David Dane lifted his head and walked across the street toward the Black Domino Tavern. He could vaguely hear the chants of the song "Stupify" by Disturbed echoing from within the bar giving memorable ambiance to the otherwise quiet night. This neighborhood. Dane had noticed, had a surrealistic feel to it that he hadn't experienced anywhere else before, one that made you feel as if you were dreaming although you were awake. It was a feeling comparitive to being entranced.

At his back, two prostitutes paced the sidewalk in front of The Stone Park. There seemed to be solitude as far as traffic went at this hour, broken sporadically by a few misfit cars, occupied for the most part by perverts or johns who were cruising the area for action. The clientele around here was always looking for strange. A pattern that repeated itself over and over twenty four hours a day.

"Honey, can you grab my water from out of my purse?" Lilly began, upon seeing him.

He obliged her after making certain that no exposed syringes were protruding from her leather handbag. You could never be to careful.

Water was what drug addicts mixed in their needles along with coke or smack to make the powders liquid. The park they were in was small, surrounded by three walls, two of which were covered in greenery. At its entrance was a small lattice canopy painted beige with flowers at the bottom.

"I made seven hundred bucks tonight," she said cheerfully. "Fuck, I think that's pretty good for only four hours of work."

He winced at the thought of how she made her money.

"There's a guy in the bar. Green hat. He doesn't seem to like me."

"Steven," she said, pulling the leg of her pants back down. "It's not that he doesn't like you, baby, it's that he probably thinks that you're a dealer."

"He's wrong". Dane said.

"Steven sells smack," she went on. "He probably thinks that you're moving in on him."

"What would he do about that"??

"Try to scare you," she answered. "But I'll talk to him. I know his girlfriend."

"Do it soon. I don't want him calling anyone that might have the same wrong idea that he has".

Just then a blond girl with tattoos entered the park. Dane recognized her from the other day. She had been shooting pool with the skater punk when he had first walked into the bar with Lilly.

"Hey Chiquita Banana," Lilly said to her. She called her this because of her light blond, almost yellow hair.

"Hey. Do you have a cigarette?" the girl asked. "I'm dying for a smoke."

Lilly fished into her bag, offering her friend the pack she had bought herself earlier. The girl took one and returned them.

"I'm Star," the blond girl said, introducing herself to Dane.

"You have a very beautiful name Star." Dane replied.

"Yeah. Thanks." Star said. "That's what I am."

She was both sweet and sleazy in her demeanor. She wore a black cocktail dress with fall-away straps. And she was covered in tattoos. However. She was still pretty.

"He's worried about Steven," Lilly said.

"Why?" Star questioned with an expression that was half scowl, half frown.

"I think Steven thinks he's selling around here," Lilly responded.

"Either that or he's spoiling for a fight. One or the other. I can't tell".

"He just looks fierce, honey. He doesn't wanna fight you," the tattooed blond said.

Star, thirty-two years old, had almost died four times, three of which were OD's, and the forth was a car accident brought on by her own drinking. She'd made four babies, and all of them had been taken from her by the authorities. Her life from day one had not been a bowl of cherries, but she was still a nice person, in spite of her problems.

When Star was ten, her mother's boyfriend Jack had tied her down and raped her repeatedly for two days. And the worst part of it was that her mother had allowed it, ignoring her cries from the blackness of the basement. She had been upstairs in her bed, drunk out of her skull and ignored it when she heard Star crying out for help. Indifferent.

Now she was thirty-two years old with four children of her own that she could not take care of due to her IV drug use. She loved every one of them, but still could not be with them.

She used needles, but her arms were not scarred. Most of the time she found veins in her legs to shoot her drugs into. It beat having arms that would be scarred for the rest of your life.

Lilly Chicoine finished her hit, her irises rolling back into her skull so that only the whites of her eyes were visible for seconds at a time. She took Dane by the arm, the way a blind person would, although she could see. Her mood and demeanor had changed now. It had become much softer than before.

"Wanna go back in the bar, baby?" she asked, eyes closed now as if asleep. Like she was dreaming.

"What did you do?" he asked.

There was a surreal look on her face.

"Two points," she answered, sweet as sweet.

Lilly smiled, eyes still shut. She was looking up at him from behind closed lids. She put her arm around him as they entered the bar through the side door. Steven's eyes locked on him as the two sat down in front of the slot machines. This time Dane did not avoid his smoulder.

There was mild shock on the drug dealer's face at Dane's resistance, surprised that he wasn't looking away.

"Come here," Steven said.

"Steven . . ." Lilly protested.

Dane stood up and approached the smack dealer's table.

"Sit down," Steven said, ushering Dane in the direction of a chair. Dane obliged.

"Listen, what's your name?" the dealer questioned.

"I'm David Dane."

"My name's Steven. I do business here," he said. "You can't do business here."

Lilly was still in front of the machines. She appeared too baked to know what was going on. Eyes still tightly shut. Steven raised slightly from his chair, confrontationally.

"Sit down," Dane warned ominously.

"You can't do business here."

Just then Jillian came in through the side door.

"Hey, hey. I know him" she said to Steven. She had heard a portion of their exchange from the street because the side door had been open to let the night air blow in. "He's Lilly's boyfriend," the girl vouched.

"He thinks I'm here to do business. I'm not," Dane said to her, his eyes never leaving Steven's.

Lilly had come out of the oven. No longer baked. She was standing at Dane's back now.

"Steven, he's not a dealer," she said. "I know him."

"He better not be doing business," Steven finished.

Dane stood outside now, across from The Stone Park. A police cruiser moved past him at a crawl, its headlights on. There was a vacant expression on his face.

"Fuck! Cops," she said.

"Do you have any warrants?" he asked.

"No. Not anymore, but I have conditions. I'm not supposed to be in the area."

"Let's go for a walk," Dane said.

The two began to stroll along the quiet street with very little traffic.

"Lilly? Do you have a boyfriend?" David Dane asked.

She paused, drawing a cigarette from the pack in her purse. She lit up, smoke trailing into the dark around her.

"No. I'm single" She said amisdt her puff.

He was glad that she didn't.

A car drew close to the curb, the driver, about forty, ushered Lilly over to him.

"Okay, I have a customer," she said. "I have to go."

She pecked him on the lips before leaving his side to get into the car. David did not see her again that night.

Chapter 3

Mathieu Logan stood underneath a stone footbridge gazing into the darkness above him, a small pond glistening hypnotically at his feet. To his left, two ducks glided smoothly along the surface of the water as if out of a dreamscape and disappeared into the blackness on the other side of the pond.

He was in a large park just off Ontario Street, searching for his girlfriend. He had not seen her for three days and he needed to find her.

Mathieu Logan needed money. He needed to get high and he was joansing for coke or for crack, whichever came first. He had become an addict at the age of fourteen and heroin was his drug of choice (DOC). Tonight he was joansing badly. He needed his girl to go to work and make money. Maybe he would find her soon. Maybe she was already on Ontario Street, working the corner.

Fuck. He wanted his shit. She would have to give him twenty bucks from the first client that she got. If not, there would be trouble.

They had been together for three years, since he was twenty-one. They had met at a rave. She was so beautiful and he had seen the potential in her right away. And so he had lured her away from her fiancé, and away from her infant daughter, and he had used heroin to do it.

A rave was the name for an all-night party with loud dance or techno music with a stream of drugs flowing through the place. Everybody, or close to it, would be high on ecstasy or on something else.

He had not told her that he was an IV drug user when he first met her. When she'd found the bag with the used syringes in it, he had told her that he only shot up the day following a rave. He had lied. He had lied about a great many things. He had, at the time, been using heroin steadily for years, not to mention pushing it. Outside of Lilly, he had no other way of supporting his habit.

It was 9:00 P.M.

David Dane sat on a barstool at The Black Domino with Lilly Chicoine's leg draped over his. It was Halloween night. It was the first time in two days that he and Lilly had seen each other. Lilly leaned over to lip-lock with Dane as Steven watched them out of the corner of his eye.

She liked David Dane. He was cute and she like his bad-ass looks.

Smoke rolled into the air from the multiple dreads who were puffing away their fix in the bar. Two prostitutes sat at Steven's table dressed to the nines. He was serving them from a bottle that he was hiding in his hand below the table. The door to the bar opened. Dane did not look up.

Mathieu Logan stood inside the Tavern now, looking straight across the room at Lilly Chicoine. He could not see David Dane who was hidden from sight by one of the bar's patrons.

"Lilly!" he called out, walking across the room toward her. She did not hear him over the loud music which was blasting out over the speakers. When he reached her, he cupped her elbow with his hand.

"Hey, whoa!" Dane said, standing up to confront him. "Who the hell are you?" David Dane asked.

"I'm her boyfriend . . ." Mathieu said.

"Lilly told me that she didn't have one," Dane said scornfully of Chicoine.

25

"Yeah, well, she does," Mathieu said matter-of-fact.

Steven noticed the encounter and was raising from his seat. This type of altercation could bring heat. That would not be good for business.

David ignored Steven. He walked toward the door in anger and then returned.

"How long have you two been together?" Dane asked. He was wondering if it was worth it to throw a punch.

"Three years," Mathieu responded.

"Off and on," Lilly said with her back to David Dane.

"Fuck You Lilly". The Nova Scotian said before exiting.

Had a fight broken out, David Dane would have killed Mathieu Logan. Mathieu was not the all-around badboy that David Dane was.

Six months later, the sun burned hot over Ontario Street. It was a Sunday morning and almost no-one in the neighborhood was awake. The streets were close to empty and the heat was blistering. The kind of heat that you felt inside of dreams, as if the whole earth was an oven.

David Dane strolled about seven blocks past The Stone Park, walking into an area known as Frotenac named after the street and subway station that Ontario Street closed in upon. As he neared a cross street, he noticed a familiar looking figure dressed in black, back turned to him.

"Lilly!" he shouted.

It was her.

Where are you going?" Dane asked as she turned to face him, her bag dangling, half torn, from her shoulder.

"Nowhere," she responded.

She looked burnt out, drugged-out, and un-slept.

"You look tired," he said. "Where's your boyfriend?"

"Long gone," she said. "I'm sorry. I didn't mean to hurt you."

Dane nodded, squinting in the sun's glare.

"Where's my hug?" Lilly Chicoine asked.

"Back at my apartment. Have you slept?"

She shook her head, full of messy brown curls.

"I slept in the pizza joint across the street for a while. They gave me a piece of pizza and an Orange Crush, but then they kicked me out."

He felt sorry for her, and he didn't like the way people treated her. He gave her her hug. They embraced for a long time.

"I missed you so much," David Dane said honestly looking up at the big clock that was mounted on a smoke stack made from orange brick. There was a brewery with a series of loading docks at its feet enclosed by a chain link fence. Four trucks were parked in front of it.

"I'm dope sick," Lilly said.

"Isn't that when you need your fix?" he asked out of inexperience. She nodded, pouting at the same time.

"I have an apartment maybe ten minutes away by metro," Dane said. "If you want you can sleep there."

She was smiling and nodding now. She was happy.

"Mmm-hmm," Lilly said. She looked like an orphan, and she had been one.

He was happy that she was happy.

"Have you eaten anything. I mean besides pizza?"

She shook her head. "I'm starving."

Dane looked across the street at the small unlit pizza joint that was not yet open.

"I have groceries," he said. "My cooking will put you in the hospital, but it won't kill you."

"Okay," she said. "But if I'm gonna go to your house, then I'll need to make a customer first because I don't have any money for smack and I'm sick. And they won't front me because I owe money."

He couldn't stand the thought of her leaving with a customer and not coming back. He had her here now and that's where he wanted to keep her.

"How much do you need?" he asked.

"It's twenty bucks for a half-point and thirty for a point," Lilly explained.

He reached into his pocket and pulled out three tens.

"So can we call?" Lilly asked.

"Where's the nearest payphone?"

"It's in the metro."

Frotenac was the closest metro station to them. It sat at the base of two cement stair casings just before a tiny strip mall that housed a grocery store, a restaurant, a vacuum cleaner outlet, a cigar shop, a McDonald's and a bank. And just beyond the mini-mall loomed an eighteen-story high-rise with glassed off balconies.

"Let's go," he responded.

The sun's heat burned against the side of the bodybuilder's face as they walked towards the silver structure that housed the entrance to the neighborhood's underground transit system.

"I'm so tired," Lilly said. "After I call, can we lie down for a while? There's a field near here. I can tell them to meet us there. Then we can go to your place".

"Suit yourself," he said.

Inside the metro station Dane reached into the pocket of his blue jeans and handed Lilly a quarter for the phone. The turnstiles at this hour were still. One attendant occupied the glass booth where they sold tickets, and she took sharp notice of Lilly as the girl made her call. It looked like recognition, Dane thought. And not of the good kind.

"So can you meet us at the field behind the Community Center" Lilly asked the person on the other end of the line.

"Okay. Okay," she said cheerfully. "How long?" A pause. "Twenty minutes? . . . Okay. Bye." Lilly finished, hanging up the receiver.

"Let's go," she said, taking Dane by the hand. She led him across the street past a large square building with a gymnasium and an aquatic center inside that could not be seen from the street. Walking onto the sidewalk, Lilly led David Dane onto a large open stretch of grass with no trees that spread out for a mile.

"Mmmm . . ." She made a sound pointing to Dane's legs.

"What?" he asked, surveying his pants.

"I wanna lie down on you while we wait."

Somewhere in the distance, "Everybody Wants To Rule The World" by Tears For Fears blasted over the speakers of somebodies radio.

He sat down on the grass, obliging her. Lilly wrapped her arms around Dane's thigh, resting her head on his leg."

"They won't be long. Then we can go."

"How long have you been up?"

"Two, maybe three days," she said.

Dane looked across the street at the rows of two-story condos with no space between them. They were brownstones and most of their windows were open onto the street.

Lilly sat up on the thin grass beneath her.

"Fuck. I thought that was them," she proclaimed as a red Ford Tempo drove by. "Oh wait, it is them, but they're stopping further up."

She waved, standing up. "Okay, I'll be right back," she said, turning to Dane who was still sitting down.

He watched her walk into the distance and get into the back of the car.

Dane sat there waiting for about five minutes before the red car, which had done a once-around-the-block, came back into view. The car's brake lights came on just before the back door opened. In seconds Lilly was walking toward him.

"Let's go," she said. "How are we getting to your place?"

Dane stood up, his muscles rippling beneath his shirt.

"The Metro," he said, pointing toward the Metro terminal that they had come from only moments earlier. Dane fished into his pockets looking for change. He only had a twenty.

"Never mind," he said. "Let's get a cab."

Lilly took Dane by the hand as the two walked slowly toward the taxi stand at the end of the street. When they came to the first car, the cabbie eyed Lilly from behind the wheel with baited curiosity. He folded over his newspaper, setting it on the seat beside him and ushered David and Lilly into the back seat. Inside the car, Lilly rested her head on David Dane's shoulder and shut her eyes.

"Two thirty-five Leopold Heights," Dane said.

The cab driver nodded.

"You okay, baby?" Dane asked. Lilly murmured in the affirmative.

They were headed out of the area now, going uphill through the city.

"East or West Leopold?" the driver asked.

"West," Dane responded.

Soon they were stopped in front of a large high-rise apartment complex that spread out into three sections. The address by the big glass doors read 235.

Dane handed the cabbie twenty bucks for which he got back eleven.

"Baby, we're here," Dane said, kissing the top of her head.

She shook feverishly with her eyes still closed. This was her enigmatic way of waking up.

"We're here?" she asked. She was looking around, still half asleep. They got out of the car, Dane closing the door behind them.

Lilly Chicoine looked up at the balconies of the big high-rise. The height made her dizzy in her almost comatose state.

What floor do you live on? She asked.

Eighth, Dane answered, as the two entered the air conditioned lobby with mirrors on either side. Ceiling fans churned above their heads.

"I wanna do my hit," Lilly said as the elevator doors opened.

"C'mon," Dane said, leading the way into the elevators.

When they reached the eighth floor, Dane took a set of keys from his pocket.

"Fuck! I have no cigarettes!" Chicoine cursed.

"There's a store downstairs," Dane said, unlocking the door to apartment 802.

"'Cause I wanna smoke a cigarette after I do my hit," she said.

"I'll go down in a few minutes," he exclaimed. "What's your brand?"

"Player's Light. King Size."

"Oh yeah!" Lilly said as she walked into the living room of Danes one-bedroom apartment. "Yes, sir!" She was impressed. Obviously.

Dane had never been that taken with his surroundings. It was a modest one-bedroom apartment with a living room, kitchen, bedroom and bathroom, however spacious.

"You like the apartment or is your sudden jubilation a delayed reaction to my company?" Dane quipped.

"This place is *fucking* awesome," she said.

"No, it's 802. Fucking awesome is three floors up," he said.

"Can I do my hit in there? Lilly asked. Dane eyed the bathroom which sat to his left in an un-lit alcove.

"Go ahead, I'll get you some smokes," he said, heading for the door.

Outside in the hallway it occurred to Dane that she might steal from time to time. He hoped that this wouldn't be one of those occasions.

The orange light above the elevator glowed as the big old-fashioned doors opened and Dane stepped inside. He hit the button marked G. On his way down he thought about Lilly. How could someone put themselves in this predicament? She was as severe a drug addict as he had ever seen, however beautiful. And she was in his apartment.

The big green elevator doors slid open onto the shadowy lobby full of ceiling fans that whipped and whirled away at the warm air. To one side of the entrance was a bank of mailboxes with numbers engraved on them, and further inside to the left was a small walk-in convenience shop. Its offerings were cigarettes, chocolate bars and four or five bouquets of flowers, just behind the cash. Dane wondered how they stayed open. The man who ran the place, who now stood before him, was named Ahmed. He was from Moroco.

"Today, me twenty-seven times!" said the imposing Arab.

Dane knew that Ahmed was referring to the number of times that he had had sex that morning. A running joke.

"I don't know how you do it," Dane responded dryly to the big man's quip. Dane like Ahmed. He made him laugh.

Ahmed made a pumping gesture with his hand, recognizable as the sign for fucking.

"You see? You see? Garage." Ahmed said, recklessly fishing a porno magazine from behind the counter and randomly flipping it open to a picture of a naked woman with her buttocks spread.

"Garage," the Arab exclaimed through a thick accent. "For plane. Truck," he said, poking the photo.

"I need some cigarettes, brother." Dane said and gave him the name of Lilly's brand.

Ahmed regarded Dane intently for a moment before dropping the open magazine on the floor.

"Here," he said fishing them from an open box to his right.

"Thanks Dude". Dane said, forking over seven fifty.

"Matches?" Dane inquired.

Ahmed went back into the box and retrieved what Dane had asked for. He handed Dane the matches. Dane turned to take a chocolate bar from the rack.

Now Ahmed had a box of rubbers in his hand. "Raincoat, no good," the Arab proclaimed, before tossing the box of condoms over his right shoulder.

"Herpes is worse". Dane responded.

An elderly woman passed by the entrance to the store and paused when she heard the conversation.

"Christ, Ahmed, why don't you make a little more noise?" Dane said.

"Old," Ahmed responded. "No good," he made the sign for fucking again. The elderly woman huffed before walking off.

"Ciao, bro," Dane finished.

Back upstairs, Dane unlocked the door to his apartment. Inside he found Lilly sprawled out on the floor sound asleep. He tossed the pack of Players onto the counter, found his way to the big, black leather couch and himself fell asleep.

When Lilly Chicoine awoke fourteen hours later, there was darkness and rain at the windows. The apartment was cool, the result of the blowing current from the open window. Dane was lying on the couch sound asleep, however she suspected that he had been up a few times throughout the night because he had changed his clothes. She thought she had remembered someone kissing her on the forehead while she was semiconscious.

"Fuck, I need a cigarette," she said to the darkness before standing up to look around. Her eyes immediately found the pack of Players that sat atop the counter, with a book of matches next to them.

"Yayy"!!!!! she quietly celebrated as she tore the cellophane off the package and retrieved what she had been craving.

"You're awake," Dane said from behind Lilly, who was now puffing away on a death-stick.

"Thank you for the smokes," she said leaning over to kiss Dane on the forehead.

"You're welcome Baby", he said as the refrigerator switched on and began its nightly hum.

"Lilly? Do you have any family?" Dane inquired.

Her expression changed slightly.

"I don't speak to them. But I miss my brother. Well, fuck, the one I know, that is," she said. "I left home when I was two months shy of my fourteenth birthday."

"What's his name?" Dane asked.

"Julian," she said. "I don't really like to talk about these things."

Dane nodded.

"My mother's a bitch. That's a story and a half. 'Oh, what will the neighbors think?'"

"Yeah, my parents tend to be a bit wrapped up in the opinion of our neighbors back home sometimes, too. When my family fights, we fight," Dane said, stretching.

"Where are you from?" Lilly asked.

"Halifax, Nova Scotia," Dane replied. "Back East. And you"????

Lilly blew smoke into the air.

"I'm from TO," she answered. "You know, Toronto."

Later, Dane would find out that Lilly was from a suburb of Toronto, one whose name Dane was not familiar with.

"Why'd you come here?" the brown-haired girl asked.

"I'd been everywhere else, or damned close to it," he said.

"Cigarette?" she asked, offering him the pack.

"Nah. I don't smoke. Those things'll kill ya quick"!! He exclaimed.

"Fuck, I'm getting sick. I should go back to work."

Dane couldn't understand how the hell she could live like this.

"What. Now.? It's fucking three a.m., for Chrissakes," he said.

"Yeah, but if I wake up sick, there might not be anyone working who'll front me." She paused for no reason. "And I don't want to get sick in the morning. It's harder to work."

She thought for a moment. "What day is tomorrow?"

"Monday," Dane answered.

"Maybe Max will be working. I don't owe him anything. Maybe he'll help me out."

Lilly was resolved that she would not go to work tonight. She would wait for morning and get a front. She was also hungry and she asked if Dane could make her something to eat. He agreed that he would.

When morning came, Lilly went back to sleep and Dane was on the phone with his friend and boss over at Iron Gym.

"What time will you be in, David"?? Bobby Edmonds asked.

"Later. I'll be in later," Dane said, resting the phone back on its cradle.

David Dane turned to look out the window. It was raining outside. He wondered what time Lilly would wake up.

Dane picked up the channel selector and turned on the TV. The news was on. Dane took sudden notice of what the local anchor woman was saying. He had vaguely remembered seeing this woman in a restaurant someplace once before.

". . . Police recovered a second prostitute's body behind an apartment complex on Ontario Street this morning, the second in as many weeks. So far, no identification has been made of the victim other than the name that she was known by to the regulars in the area: Torrid. Police spokesman Daniel Wilson reported that her throat had been cut in the same manner as the first victim, Mandy Cohen, a week and a half ago. Police are not saying whether or not they believe this to be the work of a serial killer."

"Lilly!" Dane said, shaking the brunette who was passed out on the floor in front of the TV that was now muted.

"Mmmm?" she murmured aggressively, rolling in the opposite directions of Dane's hand.

"Fuck," he said.

The rain was pounding the wet cement and iron railing of Dane's eighth-floor balcony. "Coming down in sheets," he thought.

There was a knock at the door.

"Who is it"

"Concierge," the Frenchman answered.

The knock had awoken Lilly, who was now dope-sick and feeling it.

"Fucking Jacques," Dane said to himself, walking briskly to the door. He didn't want any staff members seeing Lilly like this. They would know something was wrong. "What's wrong amigo"??? Dane asked through the door.

"I have to fix the shower," Jacques replied.

Dane thought for a moment and then, unlocked the door, and let the maintenance man in. He knew that if he put him off, it may be forever before the repair was ever made.

"Go ahead, Jacques," Dane said, ushering the short man with the white hair and beard toward the bathroom. He hardly seemed to notice Lilly Chicoine, who had taken refuge underneath the big blue blanket that Dane had thrown over her a few hours earlier.

The morning news report kept flashing through Dane's mind. He hoped that Lilly would take this warning seriously, and maybe even consider rehab. She would have to be insane not to.

Dane was squatting down next to her blanket now. "Lilly?" he whispered in her ear.

She did not respond, still dead to the world.

Dane stood up fully and stuck his head around the corner so that he could see what was going on in the washroom.

Jacques, a former biker associate, was leaning over sideways as he reached into his toolbox to retrieve a wrench.

"How long will this take?" Dane asked.

"Maybe twenty minutes. I have to replace the washers. They're fuckin' fucked."

"No problem."

Lilly moaned from below the big blue comforter.

"You need to watch for the two Italian women next door!" Jacques exclaimed through his heavy French accent. "They make fucken shit for everyone. Hey! What sound do a woman's cunt hair make when it hit the floor?

"Tell me Jacko".

Jacques made a dry spitting sound with his mouth.

"Have you met Ahmed, yet?" Dane questioned.

"Ahmed?"

When Jacques was finished, he closed the lid of his toolbox and gave Dane a rundown of what he had done. Dane liked Jacques. He was down to earth, and, like Ahmed, he made Dane laugh.

Lilly was waking up now. Dane could see her shifting beneath the covers.

"Okay. It's fixed. That's it," Jacques said.

"Thanks Jacques," Dane said, patting Jacques on the back of the shoulders as the maintenance man walked out the door.

"Baby?" Lilly managed to say. "I'm sick."

Dane walked toward the phone. Lilly was perspiring badly and her pupils looked like two black saucers. She was sitting up now with the blanket just covering her legs.

"Can I have that?" Lilly motioned as Dane handed her the phone.

The girl quickly dialed a number.

"Yeah, it's Lilly. Can you help me out this morning?"

Dane could not hear the person on the other end of the line.

"Oh please, Max? I'll pay you back tonight! Please!" she was starting to cry now.

Dane couldn't believe how desperate she was, and he didn't have any money.

"Okay-okay. Where?" she asked.

The bodybuilder tossed her pack of cigarettes into her lap. He figured she could use one, or more.

"Champlain Metro? How much time?" The person on the other end of the line answered her.

"Forty-five minutes?" she asked her dealer. "Okay. Okay. I'm coming," she finished, before hanging up the phone.

"I have to go to Champlain station," Lilly said tossing aside the blanket and standing up. "Will you come with me?"

"Okay," Dane answered. "I have a pass. Do you want money to get on the . . ."

"I'll sneak on. I'm good at it," Lilly said, pulling on a pair of jeans that she had retrieved from her kit bag.

"Fuck! Where's my sweater?" she asked, her eyes darting all over the room.

"This one?" Dane asked, holding up a dark green pullover.

The girl responded by taking the article of clothing from him and pulled it on.

"Can I wear your sneakers? My feet are too sore. They won't fit into mine."

Dane tossed Lilly his white Nikes.

"I just have to put on a pair of jeans." Dane said.

"Well, hurry up! I'm fucking sick. I wanna go," Lilly scolded.

Dane did not respond to her tone. He knew what frame of mind she was in. He changed into a black Nike sweater with gray stripes on the arms and a pair of blue jeans and black running shoes.

"Let's go," he said, and the two of them headed for the door.

In the lobby of Dane's building, Lilly asked him if he had a quarter for the phone so that they could call her dealer when they got to Champlain station.

Dane passed her a quarter. Outside the rain fell in cold light drops. The sky above was gray. The traffic at this hour on Leopold was heavy and the street was abuzz with the sound of car horns and motors.

"Which subway are we close to?" Lilly asked, looking back and forth in front of Dane's building.

"It's Leopold," he answered.

"Which way do we go?"

"Down," Dane responded, leading the way past a grocery store, a gas station and a technical school.

In the distance, past a set of traffic lights, Lilly could see a square structure above which there was a sign for the subway station.

When they got there, Dane pushed the weighty glass doors open so that Lilly and a tall black man could walk inside. The man seemed to know Lilly.

"Hey," she said in greeting.

"Do you have any filters?" the stranger asked Dane.

He wanted a filter for smoking crack. They looked like small glass tubes, or thin cylinders.

"No, we don't," Lilly answered. "I've got to go."

Lilly and David made their way down the long cement staircase toward the turnstiles that led to the subway tracks. Dane did not ask who the man was.

"Okay, You go ahead and use your card. I'll sneak on," Lilly said, eye balling the man in the small glass booth.

Dane went ahead, not watching back for Lilly. He didn't want to attract any attention to her. There was a sea of people flooding the gates, and for a second, he lost sight of her. This made Dane panic. He did not know why.

"See? Piece of cake," Lilly said, appearing out of nowhere.

They could hear the sound of the subway train approaching. David and Lilly ran for it. The metro was packed. No room to sit down.

Lilly hung on to David's waist, wrapping her arms around him. Dane enjoyed having Lilly close to him. He tilted his head back to lean against hers. She did not move.

After four or five stops, they reached Champlain station. Inside, the two ascended the three steep flights of stairs that led back outside into a barren cement park. It was perfectly square. Right away Lilly noticed a small group of people to one side of the park.

"They're waiting for the guy, too," Lilly said. The word "GUY" was code for "Dealer".

Right away, one of the waiting persons approached her. He was about Dane's age, with a moustache, and not bad looking. Lilly hugged him.

"Hey, I waited in McDonald's for two hours last time, but you never showed up," she said.

Dane already did not like this conversation and his eyes reflected his dis-content.

"Yeah, I got arrested that morning," the guy said.
Danes adrenaline was beginning to pump.

"So I figured that you stood me up," Lilly went on.

David Dane's fists were clenched now, and his eyes smouldered like two fused diamonds. Just then a red car stopped at the curb attracting almost as much attension as Brad Pitt and Angelina Jolies Limo rolling up at The Grammy's.

"Fuck. That's them," Lilly said, leaving her purse on the ground next to Dane.

The guy with the moustache made himself scarce. Dane was fuming. If the conversation resumed Lillys friend with the moustache would be sorry.

Her friend did not return and the conversation never resumed. Dane would only see this guy once more in his life.

Soon Lilly returned with a smile on her face. "Let's go!" she chirped. "I have to find somewhere to do this."

Dane led the way back into the metro.

"No wait. I want to do it in the mall across the street," she said, halting suddenly.

"Jesus Christ. You're gonna get us fucken pinched. Can't you find a safer place to do it than in there"??

She was looking around now, eyes shooting back and forth.

"No, I wanna do it in the bathroom," she said. "I don't have any water and I need water to do my hit. 'Cmon, baby," she said as she began to cross the street with Dane in tow.

"Who's your friend?" David Dane asked as they entered the market mall and walked down the small ramp into the dimly lit food court.

"A guy I almost went out with," she answered, nonchalant.

"It took balls for him to try to move on you in front of me like that".

"Don't be like that," Lilly said, placing her handbag on top of the railing. "Fuck! Where are my new ones . . ." she cursed.

"In your other pouch," Dane said. "I saw you shove them in there."

He was now cooling down. The pressure was off. No more competition today he hoped.

Lilly fished into her pouch which was strapped to her waist and retrieved two fresh syringes, still in their packaging.

"Okay, I'll be right back," she said, disappearing into the ladies room at the far end of the shadowy food court.

Dane found a table and sat down. There was an A&W, a Mr. Frosty, a Burger King, and a Treats behind him. Lilly had been gone now about five minutes. Dane knew that it was his nature to be jealous when it came to members of the opposite sex. It had been his nature since puberty, a trait that he had inherited most likely from his mother's side of the family. Some believed that jealousy was a sign of being insecure, but Dane believed that to be bullshit. If you loved someone, how could you not get upset watching another person take an interest in them, or vice versa? Whoever associated jealousy in romantic relationships with insecurity had obviously never had feelings for anyone in their life. Period. It didn't make you weak or a bad person, as some would have you believe. Dane had often wondered where those notions had come from, because to him, they made no fucking sense. None.

Lilly strolled out of the ladies room about seven or eight minutes later, her eyes at half mast, as if she were nearing sleep. However in truth, it was the heroin that was making her act this way. She was nodding.

"Okay, baby, let's go," she said taking Dane by the hand.

"Where are we going?" Dane asked.

It was raining hard outside now, and somewhere deep in the distance there was a hint of lightning followed by the faintest rumbling of thunder.

"Let's go home until the rain stops, but then I have to go to work. My half point was small," she said.

They waited by the mall doors in the foyer for about another five to six minutes before the rain stopped. Dane suddenly remembered what he had heard on the news that morning about the slain prostitutes.

"Honey, do you know a Mandy Cohen?" Dane asked.

"Mmm-hmm," Lilly responded. "She got murdered."

"Yeah, and they found another girl this morning behind an apartment. Torrid," he said.

Lilly froze.

"Did you know her?" Dane asked.

There were tears streaming down Lilly's face. "I did."

"Come here, sweetie," Dane said, drawing Lilly Chicoine into his arms. She was sobbing hard now against his chest.

"I'm sorry Baby. I didn't mean to surprise you like that."

"I saw her two days ago. She gave me these jeans and ten cigarettes. And a teddy bear named Bart," Lilly said, her cries stiffening.

"It was on the news this morning, before we left the house. I tried to wake you but you were sound asleep . . . You were sound asleep," Dane repeated now holding the back of Lillys head with one hand as she sobbed into his chest.

When she was done crying and the rain had completely stopped, Lilly fired up a cigarette and stood at the entrance of the mall with Dane. Her mood had changed.

"Baby, it's too dangerous for you to keep doing this . . . ."

"Well, fuck, whaddya want me to do? Just Quit? I could die from withdrawals".

Dane looked up at her quizzically. What, was she fucking nuts? Hadn't she heard any of the things that he had just said?

"I don't wanna hear anymore about it," she scolded, dropping the remains of her cigarette, and crushing it with one of Danes white Nikes.

"Look, Lilly, withdrawals are not all that you could die from here. There's a Mad Man on the loose who's killing sex trade workers".

She was walking away from him now, and with his hundred and fifty-dollar sneakers on . . .

"Where the fuck are you going?" he asked loudly.

"To work. I need to make money."

Dane was on her trail.

Lilly headed down the street they were on and crossed another at the intersection which led onto Ontario Street. Dane was two feet behind her, wondering what the hell to do about this situation. However no solution in this wicked predicament came to mind.

"Lilly, maybe you could check yourself into a hospital. They could help you go through your withdrawals with medication or an IV. At least you wouldn't have to be out here."

Already Lilly was scoffing. It was as if she understood no concept of reality. They were walking through a neighborhood just off Ontario Street now, with a series of two-story brownstone condominiums lined up row upon row with no space between them. Across the street, Dane noticed a sandbox and a playground that were squeezed between two community centers, the windows of which were covered in wire mesh. The Play-Ground was empty this soon after the rain. In the center stood a big yellow slide with three curves that now had rainwater snaking down its length.

"Baby, two girls are dead. Do you want to be the third?" Dane asked.

Lilly ignored him and kept walking, picking up the pace.

He had never in his life met anyone who was this stubborn. If there was a title, she'd be the champion.

They were back on Ontario Street now, standing in front of The Black Domino, across from The Stone Park. Lilly looked up and down the length of the street, which was almost silent at this hour.

"I don't know if I'm going to be able to make any money. There's no customers. Fuck!"

This was really unbelievable. He wondered who was crazier, Lilly for being out here or him for being with her. After all, he wasn't on drugs. Then again, maybe this was a good example that he didn't need them.

A block away from them, an orange pickup truck slowed and then came to a halt on a side street.

"I have a customer. I gotta go," she said, giving Dane a farewell peck on the lips.

"Lilly, . . ." Dane called out as the brown-haired girl climbed into the cab of the truck and disappeared.

Dane would not see Lilly again that day.

Chapter 4

Bill Ramirez, thirty-one years of age, loved movies. As a matter of fact, he a had a house full of them.

At this early morning hour, Bill stood in the horror section of a local video rental club called Santino Video, owned by a gentleman whose name was also Bill. Ramirez, whose father, Therius, owned a local restaurant which he had run ever since coming to this country, had spent many a morning standing just where he was now, pouring over one movie jacket or another, reading synopsis after synopsis. Sometimes he would get there at one or two a.m., and not leave for eight or nine hours. This was his hobby. Many mornings he would mull over so many films that he did not know which one to rent, so he would leave with the store's quota of six. Bill had given the store so much business that the staff permitted him to hang out behind the counter, along with a small handful of other VIPs, which included David Dane, who, on this day, had not yet come in.

On this morning, the store was all but empty except for its one regular early-morning employee whose name was Jeff; a medium built, shaggy blond-haired drummer from just outside of town.

"Hey Jeff, you might be closing early this morning. I wanna buy all of the previously viewed horror movies," Ramirez called out from the back of the store.

Jeff smiled before responding. "That's okay, I'm anxious to go home anyway," he said.

"But there's two or three without the cases, man. I wanna get a better deal than eight bucks. Last week I bought some used DVDs that were supposed to be Sci-Fi Films man.

Bill Ramirez always said 'man' or 'you know' after almost everything he said.

"What were they?" Jeff asked of the films.

"Fucken Foreign Films. I hate that. They take the labels off of the tapes and then put the wrong damn ones back on".

Just then an exhausted looking David Dane came through the door, which rang whenever it opened. He had drifted in and out of sleep all night, worrying about Lilly who had not yet come back.

"What's up David"?? Jeff greeted coming out from behind the counter to hug the street-savvy bodybuilder. Dane looked like he was about to collapse.

"Where's Bill?" Dane asked, speaking of the owner of the establishment.

"He'll be here at nine," Jeff answered.

The hour was now four.

Bill Ramirez, who had never before met Dane looked up.

"Oh . . . David Dane. This is Bill Ramirez". Jeff said, making the introductions.

"What's up, man?" Ramirez said, extending his hand.

"David Dane," he said, doing the same.

"I think I've seen you around the neighborhood a couple of times before," Ramirez said. "Maybe at our Restaurant".

"Where's your restaurant"??

"The Silver Dollar. It's just up the street."

"I've eaten there a few times".

"Yeah. That's why I recognized you. My Father owns the place". Bill said.

"Tell him I say Hi. I like your food."

"When did you start coming in here"??

"Recently. I usually wander in here in the middle of the night. I keep odd hours".

"Okay. That's why I haven't seen you."

It was four fifteen a.m.

The buses at the Terminus Voyageur were lined up in rows, the glare from the overhead spot lamps bouncing off of their smoked windows and landing softly on the automatic doors that, when opened, led inside of the terminal.

At this hour the Bus Terminal was quiet and the convenience store windows asleep. A night janitor with a thick beard and a shaggy mop pushed garbage along the edges of the wall towards a pile in the middle of the floor leaving streaks of dust and dirt behind in his wake.

Outside, in the coiling blackness, a tall man whose work had been on the news earlier the previous morning watched from his sports car as Lilly Chicoine pushed a needle full of heroin into her left arm. She waited for a moment to feel the effects of her hit before standing up and brushing herself off.

The man in the sports car was not idling his motor, for fear of being detected. The sound might attract attention and cause the brunette who had just shot up to look his way. He wanted her badly. He was going to hurt her. He'd slide his hunting knife in a curve around her throat the way that he had done with Mandy Cohen and Bethany 'Torrid' Katman.

A police cruiser moved at a crawl past Lilly Chicoine who ducked for cover into an alcove between two buildings. She was across from a motel on St. Hubert Street, its high steps leading up to its front doors. A lot of girls in the area took their clients to such motels which rented rooms by the hour and often gave out clean condoms or fresh needles at the desk.

The man in the sports car, whose eyes were bloodshot from using drugs himself, stepped out of his vehicle and closed the door. His footsteps made almost no sound as he approached Lilly Chicoine, whose back was now turned to him as she sat sideways on the steps of a motel.

It was four forty a.m.

Bill Santino was just waking up. He leaned over and kissed his wife Phyll. on the cheek before he crawled to the edge of the bed. It wasn't often that he woke up this early, but on this morning for some reason he could not find it in himself to sleep. As he rose he rubbed his eyes and reached for his glasses that were on the nightstand by his alarm clock. Bill placed the glasses on his face and reached for the remote control for the television set at the foot of the bed. He pressed the on button. In seconds the image of a local news reporter, Samantha Harrington materialized. He pressed the arrow that read Volume Up. He caught the reporter in mid-sentence.

". . . the brutal murder of a local prostitute. The twenty-seven year old prostitute's name was Bethany Katman."

"Oh my God . . ." Bill said, his stomach churning. She had been his daughter's friend and schoolmate many, many years earlier, and he remembered once having met the parents at his store. She had been a good kid. Even his sons Tony and Enzo had known her. How the fuck had she gotten involved in a world like that?

Bill stood up and walked into his living room to sit down in the darkness.

*   *   *

David Dane stood behind his client, in front of the lateral pull-down machine at Iron Gym. It was half-past nine in the morning, and Dane was tired. He hadn't gotten that much sleep the night before and he had spent the better part of the morning talking to Bill Ramirez and Jeff. He was worried about Lilly. If he hadn't heard from her by later tonight, he was going to take a trip to Ontario Street and see if he could find her, however long it took.

Dane looked up from what he was doing and noticed Bobby Edmonds and his wife Carol. He was rolling her towards him in a wheelchair. Carol looked gaunt and as sickly as Dane had ever seen her.

"Hi guys," Dane said in a friendly voice.

"David." Carol said, fussing as she threw her arms around him.

Bobby laughed warmly, happy to see her reacting to him that way. David Dane and Carol Edmonds were like brother and sister.

"I can take your client later if you two wanna leave," Dane offered, over Carols shoulder.

"It's up to you, David". Bobby said.

"You look good, hunny," Carol said, holding Dane's face in her hands.

He managed a humorless smile, but what he really wanted to do was cry. Dane couldn't stand to see her like this, knowing that she was going to die. He loved her and he would give anything to see her healthy again.

Dane's client pulled the bar down to his pectorals and slowly raised it back up again.

"Ohhh," Carol said, reacting to the anguish on Dane's face. She held him by the shoulders for a moment before embracing him a second time.

He could feel the love in her arms.

*   *   *

Nine forty-five p.m. on Ontario Street. Cars moving at a crawl and gathering darkness. David Dane made his way past The Stone Park and walked two block east underneathe the ominous glow of the vapor lamps. There were three girls working at this hour but Dane did not recognize one of them. He was looking for Lilly amidst the panic that he was feeling in his chest, and his worried anxiety was growing. As he made his way toward Frotenac Metro Station he saw a lone girl working on the corner across from the brewery. He stopped to ask her if she knew or had seen Lilly.

"I know Lilly," she said. "My name's Angela. Everyone here knows me!" she exclaimed with a heavy French accent. Angela would go on one day to become almost a sister to David Dane.

Angela O., twenty-nine years of age, was French-Italian with dark brown hair and blue eyes, and she had a kind of way about her that Dane took to immediately.

"I'm David Dane".

She noticed right away that his mind was somewhere else.

"I saw Lilly tonight. She was fucked up though, you know? Dancing around because she did too much coke and didn't sleep."

"Yeah, I've caught that act once before," he said.

"She's a stupid bitch, sometimes. I'm not trying to give her a bad rap, but it's true."

"Do you know where she is now?" Dane asked.

"Maybe with a client or getting high."

"Thank you, sweetie," Dane said to the girl in the black leather jacket who would go on to become his close friend.

He was beginning to get thirsty. Maybe he would go into the pizza joint with the revolving pattern lights around the window and get a drink.

Inside the pizza joint, Dane bought a Coke and sat down at a table. Except for two customers, the restaurant, with its yellow walls, was quiet at this hour.

Through the window Dane could see the corner of a local tavern and the side entrance to Frotenac subway station.

Suddenly the door opened and Lilly Chicoine danced in, dressed in a three-quarter length black leather jacket and matching slacks. She had a needle in her hand and it didn't appear that displaying it made her the least bit uncomfortable.

"Hi," she said, joining him. "I want pizza."

The two customers by the window looked alarmed.

Dane was smirking. He was humored by Lilly's behavior, and their reaction.

"What the fuck are you on?" Dane asked.

She glanced below her. "A chair."

Dane laughed devilishly. The guys behind the counter were watching them now, and Lilly was aware of it.

"Well, fuck! Am I that interesting?" she asked, straining her neck to look at them.

"What kind of pizza do you want?" Dane asked, his tone defying the onlookers.

"I'll pay for it," she offered. This would be the only time during the course of their relationship that Lilly would offer to pay for anything.

"Where's my purse?" she asked, looking below her seat in both directions.

"You didn't have a purse when you came in," Dane answered honestly.

Lilly was crying now. Completely out of it.

"I must've left in the customer's car," she said, rising to her feet.

"Lilly," Dane said, for no reason.

And with that she went out the door and disappeared for the rest of the night.

*   *   *

Dane would not return to Ontario Street until around ten p.m. the next night. His first stop in looking for Lilly was The Black Domino Tavern, but before he could make it inside, the big silver door opened and an irritated looking Jillian was standing before him.

"Where are my clothes?" she asked.

"What?" Dane had no idea what the fuck she was talking about.

"Lilly said that you stole her purse," Jillian said. "And the key to the locker at the bus station where my clothes are was in that purse."

Dane was baffled.

"I don't have your key and I didn't steal Lilly's fucking purse," he said.

"Where is Lilly now?" Dane inquired.

"Behind you, in the stone park," she said.

Dane turned about to see Lilly Chicoine and a girl that he would later come to know as Tiffany, whose-ID-read-Dale-Frost, sitting on the edge of a planter in the stone park. He crossed the quiet street to greet them, a point of light from one of the street lamps extending and then burning off in the darkness.

Lilly and Tiffany were both wearing denim suits and white cover-up.

"Hey," Dane greeted them.

"What did you do with my purse?" Lilly asked.

Tiffany-whose-ID-said-Dale-Frost, did not look up.

"Your purse?" Dane questioned. "How the fuck should I know where your purse is?"

"Well, you're the one who stole it, aren't you?"

Dane felt like kicking the shit out of her. He did not believe that she thought that he stole her purse. He remembered the scene in the pizza joint and thought that maybe she had lost the purse and wanted to blame it on him. He couldn't believe this. Not her side of it anyway.

"Alright . . . I was just asking," Lilly said in a sheepish voice.

"This is Tiffany," Lilly said

Dane greeted the girl with a nod and a hello.

"So, what are you up to?" Dane asked, letting bygones be bygones.

"Work," Lilly answered flatly.

Jillian had disappeared into the bar. Dane thought that he should go in and try to explain the situation to her, after all, she had lost all of her clothes.

Inside The Black Domino, "Somebody's Watching Me" by Rockwell was blasting over the loudspeakers as two trannies (transsexuals) put on a floor show that included kissing, groping, fondling and touching each others genitals.

Jillian was sitting at one of the gambling machines. There was a flower in her hair. Across the small tavern that was awash with disco-style strobe lights, Dane saw Jean Paul, Jillians so-called boyfriend.

"Hey," Dane said into the girl's ear.

"How are you?" Jillian asked.

"I'm alright. Listen, I talked to Lilly. I don't know where your clothes are, but I didn't take them," he said. "If anyone lost your stuff, it was Lilly."

"It's okay," she said. "Just talk to me."

Jean Paul, who was now The Black Domino's designated dealer, could not take his eyes off of David and Jillians conversation as he watched them menacingly from behind his wire-rimmed glasses. Behind him, one of the trannies leaned over and asked for something, to which he responded verbally, his words inaudible below the Bars sound system.

Seconds later, the front door of the bar opened and Lilly Chicoine walked in, her high heels clicking against the floor. She had a twenty in her hand, outstretched, which she gave to Jean Paul, whispering in his ear at the same time. Now both of their eyes were on Dane and Jillian.

David Dane was returning their look as he wondered what the fuck they were up to. His blood was starting to boil now, his pulse rising. He didn't like being watched, especially in this manner. If they kept it up, he was going to confront them and there would be an uproar. He knew who Jean Paul was and he didn't like him, as a matter of fact. He loathed him.

"So what do you do?" Jillian asked Dane.

"I train people," he said.

"For what?"

"Weights, cardiovascular, boxing."

"You're a boxer?"

"Was," Dane said.

"How did you learn"??

"I was trained by a guy from back east named Chris Markem. He's a very dangerous man"

Jillian was impressed. She liked boxers. Maybe one day she would go out with one. She liked Dane and she wondered if he felt the same way. But he was Lilly's find, although she had a funny attitude toward him. And tonight she believed that Lilly had pissed him off.

Dane turned to look over his shoulder. Lilly was joining them, her expression nothing less than sinister. She was playing the machine now, her eyes fixed on the strawberries and treasure chests that were rolling down behind the screen in front of her.

"I was just telling Jillian that I didn't take your purse, or her locker key."

Lilly hit the glowing red button again.

"Well, you were the only one there, weren't you?"

Exactly. She was trying to pawn it off on him, and he believed that she knew better.

Jillian, who was sitting between Dane and Lilly, was now silent.

"Lilly, I didn't take your fucking purse," he said, hardly able to control his anger toward her. He was wondering what she had been saying to the evil bastard with the wire rimmed glasses on the other side of the room. Dane could not see him now.

"I mean, who else could it have been?" Lilly taunted.

He was going to knock her the fuck out. Lilly got off the stool and stood up. Dane watched her as she grabbed her handbag and headed out the door.

Several minutes later, and eight blocks over, Dane caught up with Lilly. She was getting out of a cab. He was fucking fuming, ready to hyper-boil.

"What the hell was that about?" he asked, three feet away from her.

"Fuck, leave me the fuck alone," Lilly said, rolling her eyes and sucking in her lips in a gesture that made Dane want to throw her on the ground and kick her in the face. She had an attitude, if not an ego problem.

"What?" He did not understand her behavior.

"You're a fucking psycho, my friend," she said, flipping him off over her shoulder. She then disappeared into the night.

David Dane and Lilly Chicoine would not see each other again for fourteen days.

Two weeks later, David Dane walked into the Frotenac area and saw Lilly Chicoine standing on the corner by the pizza joint, waiting for the light to change.

The sun had just risen and its deep orange reflections were everywhere.

Dane looked at Lilly but did not call out to her. By chance he had found her, standing there in a pink-orange skirt and a black blouse buttoned to the collar that flared out at the wrists and neck.

He had missed her, and he hoped that she would feel the same. At first he did not approach her, but he kept up with her until they reached the mini-mall's dimly lit entryway. To the left of the doors was the entrance to an IGA grocery store, and on the right, a brown brick wall that opened up onto the glass storefront of a pharmacy.

"Are we still fighting?" he asked.

Her eyes were almost closed and he could tell that she had just done her hit.

She did not respond verbally, but answered by raising a finger as if to proclaim something and then gently shook her head.

"Noooo . . ." she said. "Breakfast."

She was funny, sometimes. Like a bunny with brown hair. The very funny bunny. That's what he would come to call this character.

"Where?" he asked.

"Ronald McDonald," Lilly said, heading in the direction of the restaurant.

"Okay," Dane agreed.

Two minutes later they were standing in the Egg McMuffin line waiting to order breakfast. Lilly had just that and Dane had a Coke. One of his favorite food groups. Caffeine. A healthy breakfast indeed, especially for a bodybuilder.

As they were finishing, a black woman wearing a plaid top over spandex biking shorts approached their table and greeted Lilly. Dane thought that the girl looked a bit like a very thin Whoopie Goldberg but with short hair.

"I don't wanna interrupt you guys," she said.

"No, no. Sit down," Dane said, inviting her.

Sheryl, thirty-four years of age, had been working these streets for many years. Her boyfriend, Claude "The Man With The Moustache", as Dane had heard him called was someone that Dane would one day come to know as a seasoned street fighter and a good friend. But it would be over a year before the two met.

"So, you guys are just chillin'? Just hangin' out . . . or what?" she asked in a way that was both humble and self-conscious.

Sheryl was a sweetheart and everyone in the area loved her.

"So you're the guy that Lilly's been telling me about," Sheryl said.

Dane looked around. "Me?"

Lilly nodded, still asleep, but eating.

"And I told her that you were taking care of me," she said softly.

He did not know what to say.

The hour was eight.

*   *   *

Two days later Dane walked onto Ontario Street which was under siege by a blistering heat wave. He had not seen Lilly yet, but he was in search. His first stop, per usual, was The Black Domino Tavern. It's front window was opened onto the scorcher. He looked in through the opening. No Lilly.

Across the street, he saw Tiffany who he greeted with a wave. She called him over for a hug.

"I haven't seen Lilly today, honey, but I saw her last night. But I'll tell her that you're looking for her if I see her," she said.

Tiffany-whose-ID-said-Dale-Frost was beautiful. She had long brown hair and big blue eyes, as well as a voluptuous figure that would make any man drool. And aside from that, she had terrific personality.

Dane did not stop for long. He hugged Tiffany and pecked her on the cheek before he continued his search for the elusive Lilly Chicoine.

At the intersection of Ontario and Duluth, Dane was halted by the sight of a young girl, no more than twenty four years old, who bore a remarkable resemblance to Sandra Bullock. She was hollering at someone who was standing on the other side of the street.

"What? Can't you see that I'm trying to work? I'm not out here for the sun. Fuck, I'm here to make money," the girl said.

Her name was Carolyn and Dane would one day come to know her very well.

As he entered the Frotenac area, Lilly Chicoine was on her way down the street, arms outstretched, eyes closed, and taking very big steps.

"Oh Christ," Dane exclaimed under his breath.

"Nooo . . ." Lilly said to no one. "Hmm-hmm. And you thought she didn't know that . . ."

Who the fuck was she talking to?

"Lilly," Dane said, but she walked right past him and kept going.

Suddenly about a block up, she stopped. Then she answered him. "Yes?"

"Holy fucking shit," Dane said quietly, squinting with one eye.

And so Lilly stood there for a moment in pause. Dane squinted in the sun's glare.

"Baby, are you okay?"

"Pizza," she answered. "Two slices."

She was hungry. Dane reached into his pocket. He had a twenty.

"Let's go," he said.

She stuck out her hand as if she was waiting for him to take it. He stood there for a moment looking at her. She had on a sky blue T-shirt and black dress slacks that were accentuated by a pair of navy blue gloves with the fingers cut off. She had made them herself from a pair of nylons. Her face was shiny with perspiration.

He took her hand and they began walking toward the pizza joint which was offering a two-for-one special.

Inside, Dane approached the counter and placed their order. Lilly had seated herself at one of the booths, sliding down underneath the height of the seat every few seconds.

When he came back with the pizza, her eyes were closed and her face wore a mischievous smile.

"Bon appetit," he said.

Lilly gripped the paper plate with the slice of pizza on it with both hands and began to nibble away on the crust.

"Wrong end," Dane exclaimed, just now becoming aware of the table full of people who had been watching Lilly and him since they had come in.

With only her head now visible above the table top, she had stopped chewing, although she was still holding her slice of pizza. As if frozen in time.

"Can I help you?" Dane asked the four people who were watching them.

They did not answer, visibly unimpressed with Lilly's behavior. Dane didn't give a shit. It was none of their fucking business anyway, and if they continued to stare, Dane would tell them as much.

"Baby, you're falling asleep," he said, turning his attention back to Lilly who now had a mouthful of crust that she was not chewing.

"Do you want a drink, sweetheart?" he asked.

She nodded with a mouthful of food behind her smile. She was chewing now.

"Orange Crush," she said happily, oblivious to the mocking glare of the three guys and girl across the room by the sun-glazed window.

Dane stood up, fumbling around in his pocket for change. "Orange Crush," he called out as the soda jerk behind the counter looked up.

"You want a pop?" the Lebanese pizza boy asked.

"One Orange Crush," Dane answered. He was returning the glare of these people now. They looked away.

Dane approached the counter and handed the pizza clerk a dollar for the Orange Crush. Lilly would try to drink the soda before opening the can.

"Doesn't work," she said.

Without questioning, Dane cracked open her can of soda. "Try again."

She did and this time it worked.

"Ahhhh, good," Lilly said, then abruptly set the soda down, spilling some of it onto her slacks. Dane saw that her shirt and arm-warmers—things like Madonna wore—had absorbed more of the soda than she had.

"What do you want to do now?" he asked.

"Picnic," Lilly responded.

"You just had pizza," he said.

"Pizza picnic," she said, smiling devilishly. "Nnnnooo . . ."

"Have you . . . ?" Dane began, then he wondered how the hell he was going to get her home.

"How about if we have a pizza picnic at our apartment?" Dane asked, finding a compromise.

She smiled, eyes still closed, happy with the deal she had struck. Then her smile evaporated.

"Laundry pizza picnic . . ."

Dane raised an eyebrow. "Okay," he agreed. And that was that.

Her smile reappeared as she took him by the hand and stood up. They were headed for the door when Lilly very nearly collapsed.

"Honey, you need to sleep," Dane said, carrying Lilly over his shoulder like a POW. But she was determined, and there was a field just past a section of houses and down a short alleyway. So that was where she was headed to go to sleep. Dane put Lilly down. On her way there, she was stopped by a golden lab who put its paw out to greet her. Lilly paused, hovering over the canine. She giggled softly as she gave the friendly lab a hug, and then was on her way. Dane her constant shadow.

As soon as Lilly Chicoine saw grass, she knelt down and stretched out an arm for her weight to fall on.

"Here," she said, pounding the patch of grass next to her, as if motioning for him to lie down beside her.

He had no other choice. He obliged her.

The two of them slept there for about four hours, and when Dane awoke his arm had gone numb from the pressure of his head that was now aching like a tooth. It was past nine p.m. and the sun had already disappeared below the horizon. Ontario Street was about four blocks ahead of them and, on this black night, it made no sound.

Dane's eyes were glassy and he could hardly see, suffering from the effects of his head feeling like it was seemingly inside out.

"Lilly?" he called to her softly, but she was still dead to the world, as she would be for the next six hours. He made no attempt to wake her. The word 'sundown' invaded Dane's mind with ominous overtures. He did not know why. He was hungry, but he could not leave Lilly alone like this. Not with a fiend wandering the grounds, stalking hookers.

Soon they were not alone. A tall, slender girl with a brown corduroy jacket had come to sit beside them.

"Oh, hi," she said, greeting Dane.

"Hi," he managed.

"I'm Laura." she said.

"Pleased to meet you," Dane said, extending his hand.

She noticed that he looked exhausted. "Is that Lilly?" she asked, pointing to the sleeping beauty.

"The one and only," Dane replied. "You two know each other?"

"Just from working the area. I'm from Boston. I haven't been here for long. But, like everyone else on these streets, I do know Lilly".

"So what brings you to our little town?" Dane asked, a grin on his face.

Laura's expression was more subdued now.

"School. But then I ended up back on drugs and the school thing went to hell. I was clean for over four years. Then I came here to get my degree and that's when I started chipping."

Dane understood 'chipping' to mean 'chipping away,' or only using drugs now and again.

67

"How did you find this place?" he asked.

"I met a dealer through a friend at a party and he told me that there was a stroll out here for girls who wanted to work". she said.

"Helluva friend," Dane said.

She responded in the affirmative, widening her eyes.

"So, whadda you do? Coke? Smack? E? . . . what?" Laura asked.

"I don't," he answered.

Laura looked surprised.

"So what are you doing with Lilly Chicoine?"

"What can I say. Opposites attract."

"You don't do dope at all?"

"None," he said.

She hadn't gotten over it yet and Dane could tell.

"So, how did you two meet?" Laura asked, curiously.

He paused, baiting her. "She walked into my living room with a syringe in her hand," the bodybuilder said.

"You're kidding?" Laura asked, her face a mask of shock.

He laughed lightly and then let it die. "I'm kidding."

"Hey, do you have a cigarette?" she asked, striking a match in the darkness.

There was silence and sulphur between them in the day that had turned to night.

Lilly might have one in her purse, but I don't have any. And I'm afraid to reach in there for fear of sticking myself," he said.

Just then a police cruiser drove by, shining a blinding spotlight on the three of them.

"Who's that?" a voice called from behind the warm blaze. The cruiser had halted.

"I'm David Dane and this is Laura." he said, not motioning to either female.

"Who's the one sleeping?" the lady cop asked.

He hoped they wouldn't become aware of his girlfriend's conditions, if he told them who she was.

"That's Lilly," Dane responded.

"Lilly Chicoine?" the cop asked.

"Yeah, Lilly Chicoine," he replied.

"Is she okay?"

"Far as I know," he said, trying to end the conversation. The blinding white glare was extinguished.

As soon as the cruiser evaporated into the engulfing absence of light, Dane resumed his conversation with the girl from Boston.

"Do you talk to your parents?" he asked.

"Not that much. They would fucking freak if they knew what I did. I mean they know that I'm on drugs, but they don't know that I'm a prostitute," she said.

"What do you tell them"???

"That I'm on drugs."

"Don't they ask how you pay for them"?? he asked.

"Student loan, and I lie," she paused. "I tell them that I have part-time jobs that I don't really have."

"They don't find out"??

"Well. They're back in Boston and they know they can reach me on my cell," she said.

Dane nodded understandingly.

Laura extended her hand. "It was nice meeting you," she said. "Good luck with Lilly."

"Thanks," he said. And with that, Laura from Boston walked away into the night.

Dane looked around, stretching before he assumed his position next to Lilly, holding her in his arms. He went back to sleep.

At three a.m. Dane and Lilly awoke together, blinded by their own surroundings. He had been holding her in his arms and now his left arm, which his head had been resting on, had stiffened and would not move.

Upon waking, Lilly's pupils had become like to black saucers, occupying the entire whites of her eyes. She could feel the effects of the dope withdrawal coming on in her stomach and in her head.

Dane's stomach was growling with hunger. He had not eaten for over twenty-four hours and his system was letting him know it.

Behind them, in the distance, was a cab stand, the lights from each car burning hypnotically through the night like the eyes of druid demons in the dusk.

"Fuck, I'm sick," she said.

"We'll get a cab back to my place. It won't cost much."

"You have money?" she asked. "I could use a half-point."

"We'll call the guy from our house."

"Yeah, but it'll be quicker from here," Lilly half whined.

This was not what Dane was in the mood for, but he didn't want to fight either. Especially not in his present condition.

"If I call Max from here, he'll be at the house by the time we get there," she said. She started to stand up. "You got a quarter?" she asked. She knew she'd get her way.

Dane was also beginning to rise to his feet. "Let's go," he said, starting toward the cab stand.

Dane was in the lead with Lilly in tow. When they reached the row of cabs, Dane paused in front of one of the cars, its shining headlights bathing him in cylinders of bright yellow dust. He handed Lilly Chicoine a quarter which she took to the pay phone across the street and called her dealer. She returned in moments, her mouth now in the shape of a smile.

"Okay," she chirped. "Let's go."

"How long?" Dane asked, hustling into the back seat of the cab with Lilly piling in behind him.

"Ten, maybe fifteen minutes," she said, and with that they were off.

When they reached Leopold Heights, Lilly followed Dane out of the taxi and slammed the door shut. The two walked across the sidewalk and into the complex. The air produced by the ceiling fans sailed around them like a breeze off the ocean as soon as they were inside, as if

71

welcoming them home. The lobby was silent at this hour, and only one person passed by them on their way to the elevators that were standing bright and open.

"He's gonna call from downstairs as soon as he gets here," she said.

"I hope he won't be long. I'm exhausted," Dane said.

"At this hour, they should be fast."

"Yeah. I hope so."

Dane and Lilly rose to the eighth floor on the elevator and stepped out into the humid hallway that led to Dane's apartment. Seeing 802 on the door, Dane turned his key in the lock and the two went inside. There, Lilly made one more call to her dealer, waited for him to arrive, did her hit, and fell asleep next to her boyfriend who followed suit.

Chapter 5

"When I first got into bodybuilding and boxing, I had four idols: Chris and Jack Markem, who were the ones that trained me and oversaw my training in boxing, and Robert and Richard Gray, that we affectionately call "The Brothers from the Ghetto." Chris Markem is kind of a fashion plate / playboy / hustler who's also one of the best fighters that I've ever seen, both in the ring and out. His brother Jack is all porn star good looks with a well-chiseled physique and cool demeanor. Very relaxed. Laid back. He trained in kick-boxing while his older brother Chris became a boxing champion in Alberta. Robert and Richard Gray are identical twins. African American bodybuilders to whom the word 'RESPECT' is synonymous. You will not find better people anywhere on the planet. They're a credit to their race. Without the four of these guys, I'd be nothing," Dane said to Lilly who was lying next to him on a mattress.

"I love you, baby," Lilly said, pecking Dane on the cheek. "Can we watch a movie?"

"Whaddya wanna watch?"

"Aliens," Lilly answered.

Just then there was a knock on the apartment door.

"Who is it?" Dane asked.

"Dominoes," the voice responded.

"Yay! Our pizza's here," Lilly exclaimed. Dane had the DVD in his hand now.

"Fuck, I'll get it!" Dane said, racing Lilly to the door.

"Ten forty-five," the delivery guy said.

"Thank you," Dane said, handing the guy a ten and a five before closing the door behind him.

Lilly had been stoned for six days. She had not slept and her eyes looked as though they were attempting to escape their sockets. She wore a green velvet bathrobe with her brown hair tied up in a scalp-tight pony tail.

"Ooooooh! That's what you think!" Lilly said to no one.

"Baby, there's no one on that side of the room," Dane said to Lilly who was staring into space.

Just then there was a knock at the door.

"Oh Christ," Dane said expectantly. Lilly had been screaming earlier, and this visitor, whoever it was, was the likely the result of it.

Lilly moved very quickly to the door and flung it open. She had an exposed syringe in either hand and her fists, now clenched, were pressed hard into her hips.

"It's the neighbors," Lilly exclaimed, her posture unflinching.

"What's all the screaming for?" the younger of the two Italian women asked.

Dane had left his spot on the sofa and was now pacing back and forth behind Lilly who was taking matters into her own hands.

"There's always noise over here. Why?" the older of the two Italians asked.

"Oh I see. So you're saying, that we're not normal?" Lilly inquired. Dane was laughing devilishly now, about a foot behind Lilly.

"Ahhhhh . . . !" the younger of the two women uttered, throwing up her hands in resignation.

"Um-hmmm . . ." Lilly finished off, slamming the door shut in their faces.

"Who needs neighbors like that?" Lilly demanded to know.

Dane was laughing uncontrollably now.

Five minutes later there was another knock at the door. This time it was the police. Dane quickly opened the door before Lilly could get to it. Lilly's form of tenant management would not work with the cops.

"Yeah, what can I do for you?" Dane asked guardedly.

"The neighbors called us. What's wrong with the girl?" the youngest of the three cops—two males and a female—asked. He was short and chubby.

"Oh . . . so this is about me?" Lilly asked, forcing her way in front of Dane.

"Why were you screaming? Is it because of all the drugs?" the taller male officer asked.

"I was having a nightmare," Lilly replied.

"For over two hours?" the female officer broke in.

"Since when is it illegal to have a nightmare in your own house?"

"Okay, listen. We gonna call an ambulance for you," the tall cop said.

"I'll just refuse treatment and then you'll have to go back to the station and do paperwork."

"Jesus . . . Lilly," Dane cautioned her, trying to fight off the urge to laugh.

"You are the tenant?" the female officer asked David Dane.

"Yeah," the fighter responded.

"What kind of drugs is she on?"

"Bad ones," Dane responded.

"Okay. We gonna leave her here. But if she keeps screaming and we have to come back, we gonna arrest her," the female cop said.

"Good night," Dane said closing the door behind them.

Soon Lilly would be asleep.

The next morning, after a brief drizzle, Dane followed Lilly to work at Frontenac. She wore a blue denim jean jacket over skin-tight blue jeans and black stilettos. Dane wore a black sports sweater over blue jeans with black leather cut gloves and matching Nikes. Neither looked appropriately dressed for the harsh current that would soon be upon them.

"Fuck, I don't know if I'll be able to make a customer. There's no traffic," Lilly said.

"Yeah, well, make one as fast as you can. It's getting cold out here, baby."

"I'll try," Lilly promised.

Dane wasn't just cold, he was also hungry. He had given Lilly his last twenty bucks that morning so that she could get a half-point.

Soon a red Ford Tempo rolled up and Lilly got in. When she hopped out, ten minutes later, she had a jar filled to the brim with twonies. Hedia had now arrived on the scene. She looked in pretty rough shape.

"Hey," Dane said in greeting.

"Hey baby," Hedia responded. "How are you two?"

"Lousy," the boxer said. "I'm freezing."

"I'm gonna call for coke," Lilly exclaimed.

"I thought we were going home," Dane said.

"I wanna do a hit," Lilly said.

Are you at least gonna give me some money for food outta that jar?" Dane asked.

"Get your own food money," Lilly answered. "I suck dick for my money."

"Yeah, and I gave you my last twenty bucks for a half point this morning."

"Too bad," Lilly said. "If you don't like it, you can just *leave*," Lilly said, emphasizing the last word in her statement.

"Jesus, what the fuck is wrong with you, Lilly?" Dane yelled.

Lilly flicked her hair, standing there holding the clear jar with the red top.

"You should give him some of those coins, Lilly," Hedia said.

"FUCK! And EVERYONE SIDES WITH HIM!" she shouted in a voice that was all bitch.

She then retreated down a side street alone and left Dane and Hedia standing there.

"I tried, baby," Hedia said sympathetically.

"I know". Dane said, tossing a crumpled receipt to the ground.

The biting cold wind was growing stronger.

Bianca Robitaugh was forty-two years old. She was also a criminal and, if you were looking for someone to buy drugs from on Ontario Street, then Bianca was the person see.

Bianca was what street-level dealers called a Portion Person, or a supplier. Someone who purchased narcotics in bulk and sold them in smaller quantities to the local runners, or peddlers. And, on this afternoon, she was about to meet David Dane for the first time.

David Dane turned to see Bianca standing on a street corner in the rain and gloom behind him. He had been out searching for Lilly Chicoine all afternoon, and he had not yet found her. Raindrops fell from the green leaves on the trees as Ontario Street turned to silver in the growing darkness of the day, leaving everything awash in the rain's silver light. Car horns honked and windshield wipers slashed away at rain soaked windshields as many of the locals returned home from leisure or work.

Bianca, who was also a prostitute, wore a white sweater over skin-tight blue jeans that hugged tightly to her thick thighs and butt, her house keys hanging idly from her waist, signaling to those looking that she was a dealer. She was not smiling.

"Where's your little bitch?" she called out to Dane, who stopped abruptly.

"Who the fuck are you?" Dane shot back, giving the Portion Person an intense eyeballing.

"Should I know you?" he continued, making a slow but threatening approach. She was shady-looking, and he couldn't remember seeing her here before.

She turned her head, giving him her profile before answering.

"Your fucken' little bitch owes me big money."

"Lilly owes you money?"

"She stole from one of my employees," she snarled.

"Who?"

"It doesn't matter."

"Really?"

"The next time she decides to go sticking her hand in someone's pocket it better not be one of my runners, let me fucking tell you," she said.

"You know what hell is?" Dane asked. "You go anywhere near Lilly and I'll fucking show you," he retorted.

She was eyeballing him now, looking straight at him.

A car swished by in the rain.

"Put your eyes back in your head. You'll live longer," he said.

"We'll see if you can back up your big mouth. She's not worth it," Bianca warned.

"Go fuck yourself," Dane said in parting. He had said what he had to and now he was leaving.

Finally, after roaming the parking lot of the strip mall at Frotenac, and walking up and down the street forty times, he had found Lilly Chicoine. She was sitting alone on a bench in front of a local bar called Nightlife. She had a shopping bag with her and she was rummaging through it.

"I found these," she began, dragging an old worn-down pair of Reeboks from the bag. "And this . . ." she said, producing a blue jean jacket. It looked like stuff that she had fished out of the trash. This was probably how she had been surviving, and he felt sorry for her.

"Have you been out here all day?" he asked, taking a seat on the bench next to her. At first she did not answer.

Dane noticed that her eyes were buggy and weird, like a zombie. She had probably been doing coke for the past two or three days. It was why her eyes looked the way they did. He also noticed that she had lost a tremendous amount of weight. Coke addicts didn't eat or sleep for days and weeks at a time, and that's what had likely produced these effects in her.

"No, well. Not really. I went to the day center for a couple of hours and then I—I . . . I went to work," she said, stammering.

She was wearing a little yellow baseball cap and a tight-fitting gray sports bra with spandex pants. Dane thought that she looked cute in the outfit.

"You can come home whenever you want," he said. "I like having you there."

She kept rummaging, sitting sideways to him.

Lilly didn't seem to be focusing on him, too busy with the results of her scavenger hunt. He didn't mind. He was just happy to be sitting here with her, even in the rain, which had started to slow down to a steady drizzle.

He didn't want to mention his conversation with the woman to her, but now seemed like as good a time as any.

"Baby?" he began.

She still wasn't focusing, face peering into the bag.

"Go ahead, I'm listening," she finally said.

"I just got stopped by a pretty freaky looking person who says that you owe her money."

The bag made a rustling sound. Cardboard moving.

"Was sheee . . . older? Like forty?"

"Yeah, something like that," he said.

"Fucking cunt! That's Bianca. And I don't owe her shit! She keeps telling me that I owe her money because someone ripped off Yoko while he was sleeping on some stairs. I wish I knew who it was so I could go kick their ass. Huh! I'm the one who got blamed for it." She said.

He didn't know if she was lying or not.

"Who's Yoko?" Dane asked.

"A fucking asshole. Well, he used to be really nice until all of this happened."

"What does he look like?"

Remember that guy that I bummed a smoke from at Frotenac subway the other day? The fat guy with the chunky gold rings? That was Yoko."

Dane had no memory of him.

Just then a man stepped out of the bar and joined them on the bench. His name was Brando and he was from Venezuela. One day, he and Dane would be the closest of friends.

"I'm sorry to bother you," he began politely, "but what I mean to say is, I'm looking for a friend of mine. Her name is Ann, and she works out here, like your girlfriend. I'm very worried about her. She was supposed to come back days ago to my house, but she never showed up.

Ann. The name did not ring a bell in David Dane's head.

Brando was about 40, very slender and had black hair and brown eyes. Dane would one day come to think of Brando as one of the most honorable people he had ever had the pleasure of knowing.

"I don't think that I've met an Ann out here," Dane responded. "Lilly, how 'bout you, baby?"

She had returned to her scavenging in the afterglow of the rain, which had now stopped, leaving only greyness in its wake.

"Ann from Cape Breton?" she asked.

"What I mean to say is, that sounds like the same one. And she has long brown hair and blue eyes," he said.

"It's the same one," Lilly said, still pouring over the shopping bag. "I think I saw her yesterday at the hotel. She was with a client."

"Well, I'm glad to hear that you've seen her. That makes me fell a little bit better," Brando said.

"I don't think we've met," Dane said politely.

"My name is Brando," the man from Venezuela said, extending his hand to the bodybuilder.

"David Dane," said the Scotian, doing likewise.

"I've seen the two of you around before," he said to Dane and Lilly.

"I think the neighborhood is getting to know us," said Dane.

"Well, what I mean to say is, I see a lot of people around, but I don't always get to know them all by name."

"Pleased to meet you, Brando," the Scotian said kindly.

Lilly lifted her bag from the bench.

"Okay, I have to go back to work," she said.

Dane's heart sunk a little inside. He didn't want her to leave him so soon, but he knew that no good could come from arguing with her. Plus, they had company. He kissed Lilly on the lips and watched as she disappeared around the corner.

Four days later, David Dane, Lilly and a wino named Luc were standing on a back street in front of a cargo door with a short loading dock. Lilly had been up for almost a week, and the drugs, coupled with sleep deprivation, were taking their toll on her. Lilly was out of her mind. She had reached the point of no return and Dane recognized it. Although he was still doing everything that he could to reach her, his attempts were in vain.

"Lilly?" he said, grabbing her by the elbow.

She pulled away, telling him to fuck off, to leave her the fuck alone.

"Lilly? Let's get a cab . . ."

Luc, five foot fuck all, was laughing like a mad man. He handed Lilly a fistful of twenties and Dane wondered where in the hell the little bastard had gotten that kind of money.

Soon Lilly was leaving, heading out to the nearest street which was Ontario. Dane, who hadn't slept, was following two feet behind her with Luc trailing two feet behind him. Lilly was high, Luc was drunk, and Dane was now in the middle of all this, which, in his own mind, made him crazier than either one of them.

Now Lilly was sitting down, right in the middle of the road on the yellow line where she proceeded to dump out the contents of her shoulder bag. Needles, both new and used, condoms, alcohol swabs, plastic vials of water and Kleenex fell all at once to the ground before her, and she was laughing.

Soon sirens could be heard coming from everywhere, and all around, their loud incessant whining ricocheting off Dane's eardrums as he tried to deal with this situation best he could. They had called out everyone, because everyone was here. Dane wondered if they had called the FBI and the Marines.

Police and fire department vehicles were flooding the street. What the fuck had the caller told them—that we were at war? There were even two ambulances now racing to the scene, wailers on.

Dane was speechless. How the fuck could this have happened?

Lilly Chicoine danced around on her ass and eventually fell over backwards as policemen wearing rubber gloves tried to take hold of her.

"Hold on, hold on here," Dane said, trying to save the day and at the same time save Lilly Chicoine from going to jail.

"Do you know her?" one of the policemen asked.

"I'm her boyfriend."

"You're her boyfriend?" The cop asked in disbelief.

"Yes," Dane answered

"Can you take her home?"

"I can damn well try," Dane said.

"Do you want to go with your boyfriend?" an officer standing closer to Lilly asked.

Luc had found a spot on the sidewalk and now four other cops were trying to deal with him.

"Boyfriend, . . ." Lilly responded.

"Do you want to go home with your boyfriend??" the lady cop attempted to confirm.

Lilly nodded childishly.

"Okay," the lady cop said, looking up and towards Dane. "Go with him," she said.

Dane did not flinch. How was he going to get her out of here? She was baked.

All at once Lilly stood up and walked wobbly-legged toward him. Everyone in the neighborhood had come out from wherever they were. They were on balconies, porches and looking over fences, watching this drama unfold. Some were sitting behind the wheel of their cars, others on their front steps.

"We don't want to see you two here again," one of the cops said to Dane, who was now leading Lilly away from them.

"Jesus Christ, Chicoine, you've gotta find another hobby," Dane muttered.

"Hobby . . ." she said, taking him by the hand.

Helluva day.

When Lilly Chicoine awoke the next morning in Dane's apartment, she was very dope-sick and had no money. Dane, who had brought her home, was in the bathroom, shaving around his pinch with a disposable razor,and at the same time getting shaving cream all over the floor. Outside, the sun was up, the birds were chirping and the air was warm.

"Baby, can you pass me twenty bucks?" Lilly called out from the living room.

Oh fuck. He hated this with her. Dope was her responsibility, regardless of the circumstances. He would not enable her.

"I don't have twenty bucks," he replied, running his razor under the tap and then returning it to the skin of his neck.

"Please, Baby! I'll pay you back double when I go to work tonight."

Dane had heard this before and she didn't pay back.

"Lilly, you don't pay back. And it doesn't matter anyway because I don't have twenty bucks."

"Oh c'mon . . . I'm fuckin' sick. Why did you bring me home then? You should have just left me downtown. At least that way I'd be closer to work."

She was behaving irrationally now. A common trait that drug addicts displayed when they were without their fix.

"You wouldn't be downtown, baby, you'd be in jail," he responded, entertaining her.

"Fuck!" Lilly hollered, tossing back the covers and rising to her feet. "Where's the fucking phone? I wanna call someone for a front," she said, heading across the room.

He could hear her dialing, her fingers angrily pounding the keys on the phone.

"Fuck, I can't believe this. I'm sick and you can't even loan me twenty fucken' bucks. I'm not coming here again," she threatened.

"Hi Max. It's Lilly," she said. "No wait . . . please don't hang up. Listen, can you help me out this morning? Yeah, yeah. I have money."

Dane looked up from the blue towel that he was using to dry his face. A memory from the previous night popped into his head. Hadn't Luc given her money?

"Okay. Okay," she chirped. "How long will it take you to get here? Half an hour? Okay. Perfect," she finished, setting the phone back on its ears.

"You have money?" Dane questioned her, curious himself. He had come out of the bathroom now, wearing a pair of jeans, no shirt, and he was barefoot.

"No, I don't have money, but if I tell him that, he won't come,"

"What happened to the money Luc gave you?"

"I don't know, . . ." she said. "Fuck! I better call back Max and tell him to call me when he's downstairs. I don't wanna stand around waiting for half an hour."

The phone was in her hand again. "Max . . . . yeah. So you'll call me when . . . . ? Okay, okay. Bye," she said and returned the phone to its cradle.

"So, can we watch some TV while we wait?" Lilly wanted to know, bouncing up and down on the edge of the mattress where she had slept. She was like a hyper child waiting for her Christmas present. That's what she looked like. Dane turned the television on but paid no attention to it.

In a moment Lilly had the channel selector in her hand and was flipping through channels when she heard a familiar name.

". . . Bethany 'Torrid' Katman and Mandy Cohen. The third body of a girl was found yesterday morning by a street cleaner who was on his break. The body at this time has not been identified and police are still searching for clues as to who the girl may be. For News One, this is Wendy Whalen."

Dane froze, having taken notice of the TV as the news broadcast came on.

Suddenly there was a knock at the door.

"Who is it?" Dane asked, raising his voice.

"Max," the dealer responded.

Lilly got up and unlocked the door.

"Hey what's up, David?" Max greeted walking in.

The two had known each other for a while and Dane liked Max because he had fronted Lilly out of sympathy for Dane's on-and-off again predicaments with her.

Max unscrewed a small plastic jar and fished into it for a half-point. Lilly clasped her fingers together uncomfortably. She knew that the shit was about to hit the fan.

"I . . . I don't have any money," she confessed.

"Aw, no Lilly!" he said, returning the half-point to the jar. "I'm not gonna work like that," Max said with an accent.

"Please, Max! I pay you back as soon as I go to work. I make my first customer, I call you." she was crying now. "Pleeeease . . . Don't leave me like this," she begged.

Max looked at David Dane who was standing silently on the other side of the room. He knew that Dane did not want to be involved.

"You know what, Lilly? I'm gonna give this to you, but only for your boyfriend's sake," he said, handing Lilly the half-point of smack. "You know that your have to tell us on the phone if you don't have money. This is the *last* time."

"Thanks, Max," Dane said sincerely.

"It's okay," he said addressing Dane. "But in future Lilly, you have to tell us. From now on, if you don't pay us, then no-money-no-funny." And that was that.

Chapter 6

He stood rigid amongst the rippling blackness behind the community center, and there was nothing in his eyes. Nothing. Not a single trace of human emotion. No hint of kindness, or reason, or love. He was but a single existing shape, with a mind of coiling madness and twisted fantasies that exhibited themselves when he slit the throats of his victims. Tonight would be no different. He would do it again, bringing the end to the sin of another prostitute. He would sever the cord of her life blood and listen as the air exited her body. He would take from her as they had taken from him. He would take as many as he could.

As he heard footsteps, he moved deeper into the midnight black shadow that engulfed the field where he was standing unseen. One orange light burned dimly underneath a white canopy across the street.

The footsteps had faded and now he stepped forward, the rhythm of his breathing even and unchanged, as if hollow.

Soon he would choose her, the one whose time would end on this night. The endless night. There were more footsteps now. He did not move, the shadow blending in with him, as if taking him in, accepting him home.

Now there was silence.

The hour was one.

David Dane and Lilly Chicoine were walking down a hill on the sidewalk through a neighborhood that led to Frotenac metro. There, they bumped into Lilly's friend Isabelle who was walking in the opposite direction. She did not look happy.

"You still owe me two points . . ." Isabelle began, upon greeting Lilly who was wearing a long-sleeved crimson top over form-fitting black dress slacks.

I know, I know," Lilly responded, intertwining her fingers uncomfortably. "I'm going to work now. I'll give you whatever I make from my first customer. I'll try and do a blowjob for sixty so that I can pay you back all at once," she said nervously.

Dane winced at Lilly's last comment. He fucking hated what she did, but he loved being with her and, at that moment, Dane thought that this was probably the worst predicament that he had ever been in.

"This is David. My boyfriend," she said, gesturing toward him over her shoulder.

"You can play with him later," Isabelle said, looking at Dane standing there.

Isabelle La Roche, twenty-seven years of age, ran a shooting gallery near Frotenac, a place for addicts to go and get high, as well as a place to buy drugs. Lilly Chicoine had once lived there, a privilege Isabelle had afforded her, for being a good steady client and at the same time helping her line her pockets in money.

"So, then, . . . I'll see you later?" Lilly asked.

"I want my fucking money tonight, Lilly!" she said aggressively. She was fed up with hearing Lilly's excuses. This was it, if she didn't pay up tonight, she was going to get a beating.

"Let's go," Lilly said, looking over her should at David Dane.

They walked about two more blocks together before a customer approached Lilly on foot and asked her if she wanted to trip with him back at his place. A "trip" meant "dope trip," to get high together, for whatever period of time. Usually these clients didn't want sex. They would normally ask the girl to get naked and do drugs with them, sometimes for days at a time.

Dane hated these fuckers and, if he had his way, he would give them all a blindfold and a cigarette and shoot them in the back of the head. This one in particular had pissed Dane off by approaching Lilly right in front of him. Dane felt like blinding him. Nonetheless, Dane watched as Lilly and the dope trick walked five blocks before entering his building through the front door.

She had told Dane what apartment she would be in, from having been with this guy before, so Dane waited and then walked the five blocks, parking himself on a bench in front of the tricks building.

About five minutes later, a round, heavy set male wearing a denim suit and chunky gold rings approached the brightly lit lobby of the three-story building where Lilly and her client were. This had to be . . . .

"Yoko," he answered, after Dane asked. He had a French accent and, to Dane, he came across as a nice guy with a big, burly voice and a solid handshake.

"Do you know who I am?" Dane asked the twenty-one year old.

"You're the guy who go out with Lilly," he said.

"Word travels fast around here. Then again. It's an exclusive community".

"I am go give the coke to Lilly and her client," Yoko explained, a bit nervous.

Dane felt bad for him and he didn't believe that he had it in him to hurt Lilly.

"Lilly owes you money?" Dane said, remembering what Bianca had told him days ago about Lilly ripping off Yoko.

"I am go and come back," Yoko said.

Dane looked up at the churning ceiling fan through the third-floor window of the apartment where he knew Lilly to be.

"Fucking Jesus Christ," he muttered under his breath.

Yoko went inside the building and came out five minutes later. He took a seat on the bench next to Dane.

"So, you are da boyfriend?" he asked.

"I've had simpler tasks," Dane said. "This isn't exactly an easy lifestyle."

Yoko nodded appreciatively.
"You ask if she is owe money. She fuck up Bianca's whole house."

"I thought she robbed you," Dane replied.

"She did. And she destroyed Bianca's house."

Lilly did have a tendency to leave a mess behind.

"How the fuck did she do that?" Dane asked.

"Bianca feel sorry for her, so Lilly was sleep there. Then, before she leave, she fuck up her house.

Just then a loud scream exploded from the alleyway across the street. It was shrill and horrid.

Dane bolted from the bench where he had been sitting and stood up, his eyes glaring into the shiny dream like blackness between the two buildings where the sound had come from. Yoko, back on his feet, was standing shoulder to shoulder with David Dane. They waited for another sound, but none came.

Dane's heart was pounding so hard in his chest he thought that it might come through his shirt. In the pit of his stomach, something was telling him that the noise they had just heard might have signaled the fourth murder. Another slaughter in this fiends grisly series.

"It's him. I can feel it," Dane said.

Yoko's pulse was now doing laps.

"You read about the guy who's killing girls?" the dealer asked.

"We better go and see what that was," Dane said.

Two minutes later they were standing over the blood soaked corpse of Lisa Bruno, her body red with blood and glistening in the absence of light.

"I know her. She was buy the coke from me yesterday," said Yoko.

"The police should be notified. What was her name?"

"Lisa. We call her Lisa B," Yoko said.

Somewhere in the distance a yellow porch light glowed softly through the middle of night.

"Are you carrying a cellphone?"

Yoko responded by handing him one. Dane dialed 911 and reported the slaying, telling the dispatcher that he had found the body.

"The police are on their way. You might wanna leave," Dane said to Yoko.

"It's alright. Already they know me and I'm not carrying drugs," hc said.

"I can hear sirens," Dane said.

In minutes the streets were jammed with official looking vehicles and an ambulance, and one of the officers was questioning Dane.

"About what time did you find her?" the surly looking cop asked, scribbling notes on a pad.

"About five minutes before you got here. It didn't take you guys long."

"Were you alone when you found her?"

"I wasn't alone. The guy over there with the big gold rings was with me," Dane said. The cop looked over his right shoulder in the direction that Dane had glanced.

"Yoko. Yeah, we know him. Good kid, but he's got alotta problems."

Yoko stood a couple feet away with another officer and was being interviewed.

"You live around here?" the cop asked David Dane.

"I live in Leopold Heights". Lilly Chicoine's boyfriend answered, looking around as if distracted by something.

"So what are you doing in the area?" the cop asked.

Dane did not want to tell him about Lilly.

"Visiting a friend," he said.

"Yoko? Was he the friend you were visiting? You were buying drugs?"

Dane laughed. "I don't even use aspirin," he said.

"Do you have a number where we can reach you?" the cop asked, seeing no point in going further with this interview.

Dane gave him one, looking at the digital read-out on his own watch. The hour was two.

A day later at eight a.m. there was a knock on David Dane's door.

He rushed to open it, praying that it would by Lilly on the other side, but stopped.

"Who is it?" he hollered, before touching the knob.

"Fuck! It's me! Now open the door," she said.

Dane turned the round handle, seeing for himself that Lilly had not been without drugs since he had last seen her.

"I wanna call for smack," she said, walking right by him and heading for the phone. Her eyes were wide and her hair was standing straight up on top like a rooster. Dane would later find out that her hair looked like this because Lilly would attack herself whenever she did coke. (It was) A horror show that he would be privy to many times in the future.

"Fuck, I hope that they're open because sometimes they leave their phones off at this hour," she mumbled.

"Lilly," Dane said, as if trying to slow her down to get her attention.

"Fuck! They're not answering," she said, slamming the phone down on the receiver, then picking it up again. "Fuck. No one's answering . . ."

"LILLY!" he finally yelled.

"Your buddy Yoko and I . . . We discovered a body," Dane started, "right across from your client's building. They think it's the same guy."

Now he had her attention. "Who was it?" she asked, her weight shifting as her hands fidgeted with the receiver.

"Her name was Lisa Bruno."

Lilly's weight shifted again, caused by her coke stimulant.

"I know a Lisa, but her last name's not Bruno," she said.

Lightning pulsed in the distance outside the window.

"I don't know, maybe *you* knew her," Lilly said, her eyes bugging out of their sockets.

Dane knew that Lilly was fucked up, so he didn't pay her responses any strict attention.

"Baby, you gotta stop working or they'll be pulling you out of an alley." he said.

She was dialing again.

Dane wondered if she had even heard a word he had said. Probably not, he decided, and he knew that his warning would probably have gone without consideration anyway. The drugs controlled her, not the other way around.

A light rain had begun to fall.

Chapter 7

David Dane could not find Lilly Chicoine. It was Saturday evening and the pale sun was beginning to set in a stretching pink glow over Ontario Street. It was about seven-thirty, and the sound level was low. Above, the street lamps were just starting to burn florescent silver in the day that was turning to dusk.

A few cars and cyclists drove slowly past Dane who was headed down the street toward the Frotenac area, in search of Lilly. She had gone to work the previous night and had not called or returned home. This was not unusual but, given her state and the danger level, Dane was more than mildly concerned.

In the distance Dane saw a street hooker that he knew as Stephanie B climb into a car and close the door. The car proceeded down the street about ten feet, made a u-turn and headed back in Dane's general direction. Only seconds passed before the four-door Chrysler stopped at a corner.

Dane paused.

Stephanie was getting out on the passenger side. She slammed the door shut before beginning a tirade at the driver through the open window.

"Fucking PERVERT!" she yelled as she kicked the passenger door.

As Stephanie turned to walk toward Dane, the driver's door swung open and a massive man of about three hundred pounds stepped out. He was obviously drunk. He had a thick beige moustache and his shirt, which we wore with a tie, was hanging out.

"Watch your back!" Dane said to the girl, eyeballing the man who was following Stephanie toward him.

"I'm telling you, buddy, don't!" the man warned Dane who was now walking towards them. He had grabbed hold of Stephanie's coat.

"Dane!" she pleaded.

"Hey!" Dane growled, separating that man's hand from her coat.

"I'm telling you, buddy. Don't!" the man in the blue shirt and tie repeated coldly.

His head was the size of a watermelon, Dane thought. He looked like the type of person that you'd hit square in the face and he'd laugh at you. He had grabbed Dane now and Stephanie was moving away.

"Get your fucken' hand off me," Dane said sharply, striking the man's wrist so as to break his grasp.

I'm from the east end," the man threatened. This end of town was known to be rough.

Just then a police van rolled up, occupied by two male officers wearing gloves. Dane was backing away from the inebriated suspect. He had been involved in an assault earlier that evening outside a local bar, and in minutes the two sixes (cops) were loading him into the van without incident. Dane had never been so glad to see the police in his life.

"Thank you!" Stephanie B said. She was sweet and caring, and she pecked Dane on the cheek.

"Where's Lilly?" she asked.

Dane was squinting in the pink sunset now.

"I don't know," he said, trying to catch his breath. The confrontation had winded him. "That's why I'm down here. I was trying to find her."

Just then a skinny, scruffy-looking drug dealer on a stolen ten speed bike stopped on the curb next to where Dane and Stephanie were standing. His name was Jesse, and he would one day go to jail for stabbing a man to death on a bus in a fight over his wallet.

"Are you looking for Lilly?" he asked. Dane responded that he was.

"She's on Havre with the ambulance boys," Jesse said.

"When's the last time you saw her?" the ex-boxer asked.

"Five minutes ago," Jesse said.

"Thank you, man," Dane said.

"Okay, give me a hug and a kiss," Stephanie said, putting her arms around Dane. She kissed him on the forehead and then on the lips. "Thank you," she said, backing away.

"Stay outta trouble," Dane warned.

"Which street is Havre?" he asked Jesse.

"Over there by the school," Jesse answered, leaning forward on the pedal of the ten-speed bike before driving off.

Two minutes later in the silent dusk, Dane walked onto Havre where he saw a large yellow ambulance sitting by the curb in the dying sunlight. Its only attendant, a driver, was jotting something down on a clipboard that leaned against the steering wheel.

"I'm looking for Lilly Chicoine," the fighter called to the ambulance attendant whose window was open onto the warm evening.

"Up there. Pink shirt," the driver said pointing toward the slightly risen city park that was adjacent to them.

Dane climbed the small embankment, his heart racing underneath his shirt.

Lilly Chicoine was sitting at a picnic table with her back to him, her head resting on folded arms. She wore brown cowboy boots and a flamingo pink sweater that matched the sky.

"Lilly!" Dane exclaimed, now standing over her.

She looked up as if she had heard the voice of an angel calling.

"David," she said, starting to cry. There was dirt in her hair and under her finger nails, as if she had just clawed her way out of a grave. Dane suspected that the ambulance attendant had tried to help her, but that she had refused.

"How long have you been here?" he asked.

All day and part of last night. I'm hungry, I'm tired, and I'm sick," she sobbed. "Can we go to your place?" she begged.

"Yes, baby. We can go home," he responded, draping her arm over his shoulder like a POW as she stood up.

"Can we get something to eat at McDonald's?"

"No problem," he replied.

They were headed away from the field and onto the side walk by the road. The cab stand by Frotenac mall was a close distance now. Lilly could already smell the hamburgers. She was walking with her eyes shut, cradled by Dane's arm.

"I'll call for a front before we get on the Metro. That way, they'll be there by the time we reach home," she muttered.

Inside the McDonald's, Lilly sat down while Dane ordered the food. As soon as the four hamburgers, two large fries, and two Coca Colas were on the tray, David carried them to the table and began hand-feeding them to Lilly.

She was starving, and it showed.

Normally when she'd come home after being out for days, she'd raid the cupboards and the refrigerator, putting away almost ten days worth of groceries, forcing Dane to go out and stock up again. Sometimes he could not keep up with her.

"I'm so tired," she said, trying to fight off the advances of sleep.

"Nor am I a bit surprised," he said.

"Can we watch a movie when we get home?" she asked.

"Which one?"

"Halloween," she decided.

Dane leaned across the table and kissed Lilly Chicoine on the forehead.

"We can watch whatever you want Baby." he said softly. Her eyes were closed now.
"I love you Lilly".

David Dane and Bill Ramirez sat in a sports bar about three miles from Ontario Street. It was Monday night and the five or six monitors that were suspended from the ceiling around them roared with the sounds of football.

"What are you drinking, Billy?" Dane asked, as the bar's pretty blond hostess loomed over them. Bill fussed a bit, unable to make up his mind right away. He could be slightly indecisive at times, however beyond that, Bills resume included being a stock market whiz who worked on and off as a Bouncer on the local club scene aswell as a savvy business entrepreneur with a sharp mind for numbers. He had once attained a "Gold Award" in Commerce.

"I'm not sure yet, man. I keep thinking to just have a beer and some pizza, but then I know that in two or three hours I'm gonna be starving again," he said.

Bill made an impatient sound with his mouth. "Man!" he said, following it.

"So order Pizza then." Dane suggested.

"Can we have a few more minutes?" Ramirez asked.

Someone on the other side of the room dropped a glass. It didn't break.

"I'll come back," the hostess said.

"Jesus Christ, Billy. You're not buying a house," Dane said with light-hearted impatience.

"I know that! But I work hard for my money man. Fuck" Bill said. "I already ate out once today, but now I'm thinking that I'm gonna have to eat again. Eating's a pain in the ass man, i'm tellin yah."

Once more he fussed, shifting his weight, arms folded.

"Mannn . . ." he said again, becoming further agitated.

"Bill, you ever been to Ontario Street"?? Ramirez turned his attention to Dane's question.

"Yeah, I think so. There's a lot of drugs in that area." Bill said, briefly glancing up at the score on one of the monitors. "Why?" he asked.

"I met someone down there. A woman," Dane said.

"What's her name?" Bill asked, his focus on his close friend now.

"Lilly . . . . Chicoine". Dane said separating the words matter of factly.

"So you're dating her, seeing her, or what?"

"It's more . . . I don't know how to explain it. It's not a simple matter."

"Well, is she good looking at least?"

"Yeah. She's an attractive person."

"Well, what does she do?" Ramirez asked.

"That's the part that's not so easy," Dane said.

"Well, why not?" Bill asked, humored.

"She's a street girl," Dane answered in a plain voice.

"Street girl?" Bill questioned, half anticipating the answer.

"She works. She has a drug problem."

"A hooker?" Ramirez responded out of both shock and affability. He knew that David Dane had a street background, so this didn't come as any enormous bombshell to him.

"How did you meet?"

"Outside a bar, on a wet and rainy day," Dane said, dragging out his response.

"Holy shit, man . . ."

The waitress had now returned. "Are you two ready to order?"

"Yeah, I'll have a steak," Bill said.

She turned her smile toward David Dane.

"And I'll have a steak as well, and two baked potatoes with no dressing," he said.

"Anything to drink?" she asked, pen poised on her notepad. Dane glanced at Bill Ramirez.

"Yeah, I'll have a beer."

"And for you?" she asked the ex-fighter from Nova Scotia.

"Coke."

And with that she walked away.

"Bill. Watch my jacket. I wanna go call my mother from a payphone," Dane said.

It had been about a week since Dane had phoned his Parents in Nova Scotia. He had been busy with Lilly and hadn't had a chance to call much of anyone. Right now they didn't know about Lilly, but when the time came he would tell them, even if it meant a screaming match or an all-out war, which it probably would.

Dane stepped into the stairwell outside the bar, away from the noise and inserted his calling card into the payphone. There were a series of instructions that Dane followed.

Marilyn Dane removed her earring before she answered the phone.

"Hello?" she said in her best aristocratic voice.

"Mum?"

"Where are you?" It was always the first thing that she asked him. She wanted to know where he was.

"I'm at a sports bar."

"Well, who are you with?"

"I'm with Bill. What are you up to?"

"I'm just writing up an offer for someone. I've got a woman coming in from Vancouver tomorrow to look at a house and i'm not even half done my preparation yet."

His mother, Marilyn, the former Deputy-Mayor of Halifax, was now a real estate agent, a broker, or something. He wondered what it was that she had broken.

"Where's Dad?" Dane asked.

"Oh, please don't bother him, he's doing his bills," Marilyn Dane said.

"Mum, I need to talk to Dad. I don't have time for the Miranda act tonight."

"Just hold on," she said.

Dane heard footsteps nearing the phone and his dog barking in the background.

"Hello?" Jonathan Dane said.

"Dad?"

"Yes. Go ahead," he said, slightly agitated.

"Yeah, listen. I ordered a steak and two potatoes that I can't pay for. Can you put some money in my account?"

There was a long pause at the other end of the phone. Dane was now waiting for all of Hell to be unleashed.

"I have your phone bill here," Jonathan began, now ill-tempered.

That was the equivalent of David Dane's father storming the beach of Normandy.

"Oh Jesus," David Dane said in an I-know-what's-coming-next tone of voice. "How much was it?"

"Two hundred and forty-five goddamn dollars. You know how much your cable bill was this month?"

"Too much," Dane answered with a lump in his throat.

"You're goddamn right it was too much. Three hundred and twenty bucks," he said.

"Yeah, that's a lot," Dane said in a sophomoric voice that intended no disrespect.

Jonathan and Marilyn Dane had been stricken with paying their eldest son's bills for a great number of years and it sometimes appeared that there was no end in sight. For even though Dane had employment off and on in gyms, or with fly-by-night telemarketing operations, he could never seem to find a way to adequately support himself.

"So, how much is the meal?" Jonathan inquired, his voice still fueled by anger.

"Thirty bucks," David Dane said.

"I'll go put it in your account, but from now on, you have to get by on what we give you."

"I'm sorry," the younger Dane said genuinely.

"Do you want to talk to you mother again? I have to get back to work."

"Please."

"Hi," Marilyn said, returning to the line.

"Yeah, I asked Dad to put some money in my account for a steak. I don't get paid until later this week and I'm broke."

"What did you do with your last pay check?"

He did not want to tell her that he had spent part of his check on Lilly Chicoine. Tonight was not the night to raise that whole issue. Dane wanted to be armed for combat when that happened.

"I, ah, I had to buy some shirts because I was running low on clothes," he said. "How's Hunter?" he then asked, wanting to change the topic.

Hunter was David Dane's dog. He was a mix of German shepherd, lab and collie, and he had the kindest heart of any canine that ever lived. Hunter had never met a human being that he didn't like. Never. And if you were sick or lonely, Hunter was the one soul on this earth that would never leave your side.

"He's fine. He's into everything. I made your father a ham and cheese sandwich earlier and Hunter stole it off the counter and ate it."

However Hunter did have his vices, and apparently ham and cheese sandwiches were one of them.

"I hope he enjoyed it," Dane said. "Can he come to the phone"??

"You should have seen the look on his face when you father walked into the room. His head was down, eyes turned up toward the ceiling, just like a human being. As if to say, 'I'm sorry, I couldn't help it,'" Marilyn said.

David Dane was smirking on the other end of the line.

"You talk to my little brother?" the Scotian fighter asked.

"Oh, . . . Andrew's working seven days a week from morning through noon and tonight," she said.

"Yeah, apparently, because he hasn't bothered to call me," said Dane, irritated.

"Well, that's because he's so busy," Marilyn tried to explain.

"That kid has more fucken excuses than an evangelist in a whore house." David Dane said.

"Hey, mister, you watch your mouth," said Dane's mother.

Christ, he hated it when she started to make up stupid fucking excuses for people's behavior, especially when that person was his younger brother. Here was a guy that you could leave forty-seven messages for and he might call you back once in six weeks. Maybe he was busy, but no one was that busy, no matter what their workload was.

Andrew Dane, David Dane's younger brother by five years, was studying to be a lawyer, an aspiration of Andrew's that had started before the younger of the two siblings was even out of high school.

"You need to be more respectful of other people," Marilyn said, chastising him.

"Jesus fucking Christ," David mumbled. She was already starting in with her shit and they hadn't even been on the phone for ten minutes.

"Alright, alright. I gotta go. My steak's probably been sitting on the table for twenty minutes."

She hung up on his last word.

Back inside, the noisy room was full of screaming sports fans and buzzing television monitors and Bill Ramirez sat alone watching the game as he waited for David Dane to return.

"Man!" Ramirez said, gesturing toward one of the monitors. It was obvious that he didn't like what he saw.

Across the room, David waded his way through the tightly gathered crowd.

"Fuck, man, it looks like I'm gonna lose a hundred bucks on this game," Bill called out as Dane took his seat at the table.

"No steaks yet?" Dane asked.

"Bill shook his head.

On the screen a large man wearing a white helmet and a red jersey ran the length of the gridiron with the ball and scored a touchdown, causing the packed house to come unglued. Dane turned his head as he saw the waitress nearing their table in his peripheral vision. Dinner, and the ball, were served.

The crowd roared.

Marguerite Blankenship was running for her life in an alleyway just off Ontario Street. The black curtain of night had opened up, and now the man driving the car behind her, whoever he was, was trying to kill her.

The chase had started two blocks over, on Fullum Street, when she had noticed him watching her and, when she had tried to run, he had followed, the headlights of the car that he was driving never letting her out of their beams for a second.

She had heard about the four girls who were murdered, and she did not want to be next. If only she hadn't wanted to get high tonight. If only she had been content with staying clean the way that she had been for the past two months, at home with her sister and their father. Only no such good fate had befallen her. The drugs had had their way, as they had so many times in the past. They had brought her back to Ontario Street and into their clutches of, whoever it was that was stalking her.

Tonight, at first she had thought that he was just a client who was cruising her, but when she looked into the man's eyes, there was a smouldering there like something from hell. His eyes were demonic, and they had been all over her, up and down, like a cheap suit. That's when she knew.

Marguerite turned the corner, running into the flaring shadows of the brewery parking lot that, at this hour, was vacant. Her heart was pounding and she could feel her pulse drumming within the walls of her head. Oh, Christ! He was right behind her. Oh sweet Jesus in Heaven. She didn't want to die this way at only twenty-three years of age.

As she turned to look once more over her shoulder, she collapsed, falling to her knees.

Right away, the man who had killed Mandy Cohen, Bethany 'Torrid' Katman, Paula Wilson and Lisa Bruno stormed out of his four-door vehicle and came toward her with his silver knife drawn. He slashed open her face and then took out her eyes and throat with the point of his blade. In seconds, Marguerite Blankenship lay dead on the pavement, the fifth victim of the Ontario Street Killer.

The next morning at around eight a.m., David Dane woke up to the sound of someone knocking on his door. When he went to answer it, he found Lilly Chicoine on the other side, tired and in a horizontal position on the floor.

What are you doing down there?" he asked.

"Sleeping," she said. "I've been knocking for an hour. I guess you didn't hear me," she explained, rising to her feet and making her way inside.

Dane had not heard her knocking until now. Sometimes he slept very soundly and, apparently, this morning had been one of those occasions.

"I brought us some food from Guardian," Lilly said, setting two plastic bags containing groceries down on the counter top.

"We have Kraft Dinner, Ritz Crackers, chocolate pudding, Reeces Peanut Butter Cups and some granola bars," she said, looking toward him for a reaction.

Dane had tears in his eyes. Lilly did not know why. It was her small sentiment that had touched him. He loved Lilly and sometimes he thought that she would never know how much.

"You got onions in that bag?" he asked, wiping tears away with the back of his hand.

"Nope. No onions," she said. "They don't give away onions at Guardian, but I suppose I could ask."

"Do I get a hug this morning?" Dane asked.

Lilly responded by obliging him. She was a bit high, he could tell. She had probably been doing coke for the past couple of days. This was the first time that he'd seen her since the morning after he found her in the field and brought her home. That had been about three days ago.

"Do you want me to make some macaroni now?" she asked, their hug coming to its end.

He wondered if saying yes was wise. The whole fucking building could burn down. He remembered the last time that she made grilled cheese. He had had to use the fire extinguisher.

At that moment, there was a knock at the door.

"Who is it?" Dane inquired, loudly enough that the person on the other side of the door could hear him.

"It's Bill."

Dane let him in.

"I'm sorry to bother you," Ramirez said upon noticing Lilly sitting on the edge of the couch.

"Hey. No problem. You're always welcome here." Dane responded genuinely before going ahead with the introductions.

"Well, it's nice to finally meet you," Bill said, shaking the girl's hand.

"Likewise," Chicoine answered.

"Bill, we're just about to cook some Kraft Dinner for lunch, if you're interested in joining Lilly and I. There's plenty to go around if you wanna stay."

"No, no, I don't want to intrude," Ramirez said politely.

"Bill. What, are you kidding me? You're fucking family," Dane insisted enthusiastically.

"Well, since you have plenty to go around."

"Then it's settled. I'll set three places," David Dane said.

"Kraft Dinner at eight a.m. in the morning. I think that's a first for me," Bill said smiling.

Lilly sat on the arm of the couch now, wearing a light blue denim jacket over black corduroy pants. She had shifted her attention and was now watching a comedy on TV.

Bill moved more closely to Dane who was standing in the kitchen close to the cupboards in search of a pot. He had something to tell his friend and, out of fear of upsetting anyone, he did not want Lilly to hear about it.

"I watched the news this morning," Ramirez began, his voice low. "They found a prostitute with her throat slit in a parking lot off Ontario Street. It's not the first one either . . ."

"Yeah, I know. I mean, I know that it isn't the first. It's at least the fourth or fifth. Did you hear about the one in the alleyway? Here name was Lisa Bruno," Dane asked inquiringly.

"Yeah, I might've," Bill answered, hands on his hips and frowning inwardly, as if he were trying to call up the memory.

Dane turned around to face his friend. He was wearing a pair of gray sweat pants and a black and silver Gators Gym sweater. It read, "No

Chrome, No Pool, No Music, Just Iron." It was the same sweater he had worn over blue jeans the day he met Lilly.

"I was like ten feet away when Lisa Bruno got cut. I was with one of Lilly's dealers. We found the body," he confided.

"Well, how come you didn't tell me before now?"

Dane had turned on the stove and now the top left burner was glowing orange.

"Cause I just told you about Lilly last night,"

"Remember, I think it was the first or second one? Bethany something..." Bill asked, unable to remember the girl's last name.

"Bethany 'Torrid' Katman..." said Dane, filling in all the details.

"Yeah, I think that's it. I guess that Bill Santino and his kids knew her, or at least I think he said that Tony and Enzo went to school with her, man."

Dane had opened the faucet and was now filling the pot with water.

"Have you had a talk with Lilly?"

"Had a talk with Lilly about what?" Lilly asked, having heard the last part of the sentence. She was looking toward them now.

It had to be reopened, sooner or later, for her safety, Dane thought. He hesitated for a moment.

"They found another prostitute today, Baby. Someone cut her throat."

"Where?" Lilly Chicoine asked, her voice possessing only a hint of alarm. And now she was just realizing that Dane must've told Bill what she did for a living. That pissed her off. She hated it when people went around blabbing about what she did, especially when it was to people that she didn't know. And Bill was a total fucking stranger.

"So, you told your friend here that I'm a hooker?" she asked spitefully.

Oh Jesus Christ, Dane thought. Now she was gonna start a fight, and the discussion that they needed to have, would go nowhere. And of course, because she was high, that would make things that much worse. The coke would amplify her emotions.

"So, what else have you told your friend?" she asked, standing up wearing an animated smile below wide eyes.

"Baby. We need to talk about something important," he said.

Bill wondered where this was going. Maybe he wouldn't be staying for macaroni after all.

"Let me guess . . . that I might get murdered?" she sneered.

Dane thought that it was probably him that was going to be murdered. Luckily Bill was here.

"Can I make a suggestion?" Lilly asked sarcastically.

Dane responded with a single nod that almost made Bill laugh out loud.

"Why . . . . don't YOU stay the fuck out of my business?"

"Oh Jesus Christ," Dane sighed. There was no winning with this woman.

"I have a better idea," he began, "why don't I call the hospital this afternoon and see if I can get you a doctor? Maybe one who prescribes methadone."

Dane glanced at the boiling water on the stove. Maybe he could still interest her in dinner.

"Apparently you didn't hear my first suggestion," Lilly said.

"I'll have to take that one into consideration," he said.

She pivoted on one foot and landed on the other in the opposite direction, arms out behind her. This little spin was one of her coke habits, especially when she was angry.

"Do you still want dinner, or not?" he asked, noncommittal.

Lilly paused. "Yes," she said.

"Good. Bill, you want cheese on your macaroni?" David asked. "Because I don't take any on mine."

"Yeah, I'll have a bit, but not too much, man. Cheese doesn't really agree with me," Ramirez said, taking a chair at the table.

"Lilly?" Dane asked.

She was still moving around from the stimulant she had injected earlier.

"What?" she asked.

"Do you want extra cheese on your Kraft Dinner?"

"No, I'm having ketchup on mine."

Dane winced. "Ketchup?" he asked.

"Yes. It tastes better. And I want salt on it, too."

What was she trying to do? Pump her own stomach? Her diet was proof positive that the drugs were infecting her brain.

Dane took the steaming pot off the stove and strained the macaroni by holding the lid on the pot and letting the water run out while the pot was upside down. He then took three plates from the cupboard and divided the pasta onto each one before setting the servings down on the table top.

Lilly was on her way to the refrigerator now to retrieve the ketchup that was on the inside of the door. Her walk was a slight march, as if she was taking part in an invisible parade, one that no one else could see. She soon returned, ketchup bottle in hand.

Dane handed Bill the packet of cheese that came with the Kraft Dinner.

"You guys want anything to drink?" Dane asked.

"I'll have a Pepsi," Lilly answered, drowning her macaroni with enough Heinz to sink a small ship.

"I'll just have some water, man," Ramirez said.

In a moment Dane had returned. He handed Lilly a can of soda and Bill a glass of water. He then sat down, reaching behind where he was sitting to grab the can of Pepsi that he had set aside for himself.

"Where's the salt?" inquired Lilly.

Dane stood up once more and returned with the salt shaker.

"So, Lilly," Bill began. "Are you from Montreal?"

"Toronto," she said.

Dane spooned a bite of macaroni into his mouth, washing it down with a pull from his soft drink.

Bill had a friendly nature about him and it came through in the smile that he wore during this conversation.

"So how did you and Dane meet?" he asked. Dane was what Bill used as a nickname for his friend.

"Hmmm, well, I'm a drug-addicted prostitute, so not very many people are nice to me," Lilly said. "Wherever I go, I usually get thrown out, most times."

Bill's smile diminished slightly, out of respect for her plight. He could see why Dane liked her. She had a certain charm.

"A lot of people don't like street hookers. Hmmm? Especially when they're drug addicts!" she suddenly exclaimed.

It was times like this that Dane loved her more than ever, somehow, knowing that he was one of the few people in this world that she could count on. And it gave him a feeling of importance, because he was needed. He would do whatever it took to help her and get her off the street, no matter what the cost, and now not only was she at risk from the drugs and the clients, she was at risk of meeting a knife-wielding madman.

"Have you been in Montreal for long?" Bill asked.

"Maybe four years," she said, swallowing a mouthful of Pepsi. "I came here with my fiancé and our daughter."

Dane froze. He did not know anything about this.

"You have a daughter?" Dane, the muscular fighter asked, turning his shaved head towards her.

"Mmm-hmm. Her name is Lilianna. She would be about five years old now," Chicoine said, her eyes welling up with tears. "I miss my little girl."

Jesus Christ, and on top of it all she had a five year old daughter, Dane thought to himself.

Lilly had broken down now and was crying.

"I'm sorry. I didn't mean to . . ." began Bill.

Dane looked in Bill's direction, then to Lilly. "It's all right," he said, understanding, before standing up to put his arms around her. "I love you Lilly," he said. "I love you."

Ontario Street had many small parks that were tucked away between buildings, inside alcoves away from the street, and on this foggy morning, Angela O sat in one of them preparing her hit. It was about five a.m., and most of the girls who worked the area had gone back inside, having already made enough money the night before. On this morning, it was not money that was keeping Angela outside. The fact was, she had nowhere else to go. Just the day before she had been at her mum's house for a couple of days, watching television and sleeping it off. Unfortunately her mother lived in an apartment at the other end of town away from Ontario Street. She could've gone back there if she had wanted to, but she did not want to show up there while she was tripping. And certainly not while she appeared to be fucked up or as high as a kite.

In a matter of minutes a familiar figure appeared before her. His name was Nick, and he was a street worker from one of the local needle exchanges. They called it Cactus. It was at least five years earlier when she and Nick had first met and she had had a crush on him ever since.

Angela believed that she was not the only working girl in the area that like him, because to her and to many others, Nick looked like a movie star. He had short blond hair and chiseled features and his arms, right now hidden beneath a long tight shirt that hugged his toned frame, were covered with tattoos.

"How are you?" Angela asked in a high-pitched, sad voice.

The fog between them was growing now.

Nick's hands were on his hips and he was squinting, even thought there was no sun.

"I'm fine. And you?" he asked.

"I'm alright," the French-Italian girl answered, her blue eyes full open.

"Christ, I hate this fog," Nick said.

"Yeah, it was warm the past few days, but now it's starting to cool off," she said.

Around the corner, a dog was barking.

Nick felt badly for Angela. He could see the sadness in her eyes. This was more than just a job to him, it was his mission in life. This and his band called Union Main.

"Have you had anything to eat this morning?" the band leader asked.

"I ate yesterday at my mom's house. She was happy to see me."

A small green car drove past the park, its muffler making a racket.

"Are you going to eat something today?" he asked.

He was going to offer her breakfast at McDonald's, if she was hungry.

"I don't feel like eating," she said. "You know, when you do coke, you don't feel like eating food."

"Do you need any clean ones?" Nick asked, removing a leather knapsack from his shoulder. His job as a street worker entailed counseling people who wanted or needed someone to talk to, giving out pamphlets on the dangers of drugs and the diseases that came with them, as well as distributing clean needles and condoms.

"Sure. I could use a few," the girl said.

Nick reached into his bag and pulled out a handful of fresh syringes which he gave to her.

It was five fifteen a.m.

Later that day, after dark, David Dane entered The Black Domino to the sound of "Down with the Sickness" by Disturbed. The thrash metal music he loved was booming over the big black speakers which were hung from all four corners of the room. He was alone. Lilly had gone to work half an hour earlier and had not yet made a reappearance. To one side of the room, Dane saw a familiar face watching him from beneath the shadow of a camouflaged ball hat. A face that he knew all too well.

Steven stood up from behind a table and approached David Dane, wearing a smile amidst a stubble beard. His mood appeared light.

"Man, I'm sorry," Steven said, embracing Dane and with one arm. Steven led Dane back to the table where he had been sitting with his girlfriend Danielle. Jillian was there too.

Dane was in total shock. He had not expected this and in the back of his mind he was wondering what the hell was going on.

Jillian shuffled over to make room for David Dane. "Hi," she began, her soft lips pecking his cheek.

"Hey," Dane replied. "How you doin"??

"I made a big mistake about you," the dealer said. "I thought that you were selling in the bar."

Dane shook his head, his eyes full of reflections from the candle flame that danced on the table top before him. Now he was wondering what in the hell made this guy tick. Why had he picked now to change his tune? That was the strange thing about guys like this. They could stop and turn on a dime, but you had to be careful, because they could turn back too.

"What are your drinking?" Steven asked.

"Orange juice," Dane said, leveling his eyes at Steven.

Danielle, who was twenty-three years of age, leaned over and kissed Jillian on the cheek. The candle's flame swelled.
The music droaned on.
The hour was nine.

Two minutes later David Dane walked out into the dark, sinister folds of Ontario Street. The quiet was all around him tonight. Engulfing him.

A tall beautiful girl with an hour-glass figure appeared out of nowhere and greeted Dane.

"Do you know who I am?" the girl asked, stepping out from the golden brown shadows.

Dane shook his head, somber.

"I'm Alyssa," she said. "I'm a friend of Lilly's."

"Yeah, me too. Except for the Alyssa part," the boxer replied in a low, gravelly voice with a hint of sarcasm.

"I just got off the bus from T.O. yesterday. Your girlfriend was the first person that I met when I came down here."

"We have that in common," David Dane said.

"I recognized you from her description," Alyssa told him. "She's right. You are handsome."

"My reputation exceeds me."

"I've heard a lot about you. She told me that you were a bodybuilder and a boxer. How long did you Box for?"

"Long enough". Dane said in a straight forward voice.

Alyssa was sweet and she had a beautiful smile, not to mention the singing voice of an angel, as Dane would one day find out. You didn't meet people like her every day. She could bring sunshine into a room just by entering it.

Dane looked into Ontario Streets limitless black distance.

"You know that it's dangerous around here? We've got a fucking fiend on the loose," Dane said.

Alyssa's smile faded, her features darkening. "Yeah, Lilly said something about that," she said. "But I still have to work."

"What's your vice?"

"I'm on the pipe. Strictly. I can't stand shooting. I don't know how Lilly does it. Lilly's fucked in the head anyway."

They all talked like that about each other, Dane thought.

"Have you seen my girlfriend in the past hour?" David Dane asked.

"Yeah. Down there," Alyssa pointed with her finger in the direction of Frotenac subway. "But I want you to hang out with me for a while until Lilly comes back up here," she said, finishing her thought by giving Dane a massive hug.

Attention and affection were Dane's drugs of choice. He was an addict. Incurable.

"Let's go sit in the park behind the church," Alyssa said invitingly.

Dane followed his new-found friend two blocks over and into the silent park behind the church. There they found Lilly Chicoine. She was already seated alone at a picnic table, syringe in hand. Her neon pink blouse was glowing in the darkness and she was higher than the clouds that Heaven rested upon.

Alyssa looked mildly disappointed to see her. This would take away from her evening with Dane.

"Hey, Baby," Dane said, wrapping his arms around Lilly from behind. She didn't seem to notice him, fidgeting back and forth on the bench, her needle being guided recklessly through the air by her right hand, the way a child would wave a paper plane.

She was baked. Fried. Sizzled. There was no way around this finding.

"Hi, Lilly," Alyssa greeted her, hugging the wide-eyed Chicoine the same way Dane had. She felt a bit sorry for her.

"Mmm-hmmm. I see you've met Alyssa," Lilly said, the motion on the ocean continuing.

Alyssa hugged Dane again. This time in front of Lilly.

"I like your boyfriend. Can I keep him?" Alyssa asked.

"Nope. He's mine," Lilly replied casually.

"Damn straight," Dane said, giving Lilly a full hug from behind followed by a peck on the left cheek.

Lilly smiled.

Open displays of affection were part of hanging out on Ontario Street, and Dane's relationship with Alyssa was no exception. Things on Ontario Street were different from the everyday world. People reacted differently to each other. More open. And affection was handed out freely.

It was nine forty p.m.

Chapter 8

One week later on a Wednesday night, David Dane was looking for Lilly Chicoine. He found her standing in a pool of yellow light that was pouring out through the glass door of a convenience store that stood across the street from Frotenac metro station. She was wearing a white blouse tied up Daisy Duke-style above her navel, a beige skirt that reached her ankles, and a pair of brown dress boots with square heels. Dane thought that she resembled actress Madeleine Stowe.

"Lilly!" he called across the street. She did not look up, too busy scavenging after her hit.

"Scavenging" was the street term used in the same context as the dictionary term, only that she was fidgeting, fussing and looking around at unseen people or things. In short, sifting through and mindlessly searching.

Lilly's eyes darted back and forth over the sidewalk before her as if she had lost a contact lens, although she had not lost anything. This was normal behavior for addicts who had just done their hit.

"Lilly!" he called again.

She raised her head briefly. He thought that she had noticed him this time. It was drizzling now. Soft silver.

Dane crossed the desolate street to meet his girlfriend. "What are you doing?" he asked her.

"I'mmmm searching. Looking . . . . I guess I mean. I don't know, from your point of view."

It was coke talk. She had just done coke. The words 'Blue Wednesday' entered Dane's mind and faded away for no reason.

"I miss you," he said honestly.

"I miss you, too," she replied, eyes still on the hunt.

There was no traffic at this hour.

"I want to . . . You know, walk through the cinder-block park, now that I have you with me for protection. I haven't been there for a while, and I feel like going there," she said.

Dane gave Lilly a lingering kiss on the cheek. She smiled a quiet smile.

Soon Lilly was walking in front and Dane following behind as they headed up a gentle slope through a park that was littered with dark colored cement brick blocks. They were spaced out all over the place, underneath big shadowy oak trees that billowed and sighed dreamily in the wind, some of them rising out of the earth as if half submerged in it.

Dane thought of an old song called "Emotion in Motion" by Rick Ocasek, from nineteen eighty-one.

"Are you cold?" David Dane asked Lilly.

She did not answer immediately. She was still scavenging.

"Not really. How about you?"

"I'm fine," he said.

They were trudging uphill through the darkness now, walking deeper into the rain-glazed night. The sky above was a mass of swollen black storm clouds that threatened a violent downpour with thunder and lightning that neither Dane nor Lilly was dressed for. If the couple continued walking, they would hit a clearing and then a road.

Dane's eyes were badly blurred. He did not know why. Greyness in the distance.

The bruised sky was suddenly ripped open by a blinding burst of static electricity, the voltage of which was so high that Dane could feel its heat on his face. It was followed by a deafening concussion of thunder.

"Christ that was close!" he said

The park seemed to quiver now, like an image from a nightmare. Somewhere in the dungeons of Dane's psyche, there was a morose cackling.

"Baby? Are you okay?" Lilly asked.

Dane nodded, the look on his face confused.

Soon they were back on Ontario Street and the storm and tumult had moved on. The sun was coming up.

"Are you going to come home now?" Dane asked Lilly, who was still walking two feet in front of him now with her head down.

"Nope. Nope. I think I'm gonna go to work. I wanna call for some smack soon," she gestured with her hand, eyes wide. The gesture held no real meaning. "And you?"

"I'm tired, but I can't stand for you to be out here alone. I wish that you wouldn't stay out here without me, or at all, for that matter," he said.

"Yeahhh, but I can't . . . I mean, fuck. It's not like I don't know the risks," Lilly responded, preoccupied by whatever the coke was doing to her.

"And I'm not on anything, which makes it nearly impossible for me to keep up with you," David Dane said.

"Well, you can go then. I mean, I'm a big girl."

"Uh-huh?" Dane's comprehension skills in this matter were nonexistent. How could someone put themselves in this position? Someone was around here slaughtering girls as if it were a pass time and Lilly was reacting as if it were a day at the beach. You had to be fucking insane, and he didn't care what she was putting in her needle.

"What's that supposed to mean?" she asked of Dane's last response.

He didn't want to argue with her. "Nothing," he said.

In a moment a car pulled up to the curb and the man behind the wheel, who looked to be in his forties, ushered Lilly inside.

"I have to go. I have a customer," she said, giving a peck on the lips to a down-looking Dane.

Love had a way of trapping you, Dane thought. If it didn't, then he would not be in this situation. He stood on the curb and watched as Lilly and her client drove away.

It was 6:57 a.m.

* * *

Bianca Robitaugh wanted her money and, on this day, she was in no mood to play games with respect to getting it. She had seen Lilly go into the coke house near Frotenac a few minutes earlier and now she was on her cell phone trying to reach whoever it was that was selling that day. She would tell whichever runner that was working to delay Lilly, at least for a few minutes until Mark showed up with the car.

Mark Halogen was Bianca Robitaughs boyfriend. They had been together for the past ten years, including five of those years when Mark had been inside for trafficking. On this day, it would be Mark that Bianca would use to discipline the little bitch as well as to get money from her.

In moments Bianca heard the sound of Mark's red Ford Tempo out back beneath the fire escape. She grabbed her black leather jacket off the love seat, turned off the apartment lights, and headed outside. Downstairs, her tall, brown-haired boyfriend, who was in his late thirties, sat behind the wheel of the car with the motor running. His face was unshaven and his hair long.

"Where is she?" Mark asked as the car's exhaust pipe produced puffs of white smoke that drifted high into the sky with the cold morning air. It was turning from fall to winter and there were traces of compacted snow on the ground beneath the wheels.

"She's in seeing Eric right now. He'll stall her for a few minutes. Let's go," Bianca said.

The red Ford Tempo made a U-turn in the small parking lot behind the three-story building where Bianca lived and headed out onto the street to Frotenac Metro. They drove half a block and then stopped directly in front of a four-story brownstone with bars on the first-floor windows.

Mark Halogen killed the ignition and the two went inside.

On the first floor they found Lilly on her way out. She had two quarters of coke in her hand. Mark grabbed Lilly by the hair and slammed her head first into the wall, creating a blood smudge on the darkened white paint. When she was down, he kicked her in the ribcage twice with the tip of his steel-toe boots before Bianca got her own licks in.

"I want my money, little bitch!" she said, huffing and puffing. "By tomorrow night. Hear me. No more delays. I mean business"!!!!!!!!!!!!!!!!!!!!!!

It was 9:45 a.m.

That night, the whispering wind over Ontario Street seemed askew as Lilly Chicoine sat on a wooden divider by the road, waiting for customers to come and pick her up. She would have to pay Bianca back now. There was no other choice. If she did not, not only would she probably end up getting her throat slit, but no one would serve her anymore either. And, as it was, she was dope-sick.

Around ten p.m., David Dane appeared from somewhere out of the unlit nowhere and gave her a hug and a kiss. He wore a black Nike sweater, blue jeans and a pair of black cut gloves that were used for lifting weights. They had been a trademark of Dane's for years.

"What happened to your face, baby?" the boxer asked.

Lilly Chicoine knew that if David Dane had found out about what Bianca and her boyfriend had done to her, it was likely that he would have executed them both.

"I got a bad client," she lied.

Telling Dane what had happened would bring more trouble and, right now, she couldn't afford that.

Somewhere in the distance, Stephanie B was on a payphone trying to call someone. The area and the night was otherwise deserted.

Dane wondered what was really going on. He sensed that she was lying, and her face was awfully mangled, but he knew that line of questioning would only make Lilly mad. He stayed out of it.

"I love you Lilly," he said, kissing her softly on the forehead.

She gave him a warm smile. "I know," she chirped."

A car pulled up, the driver flagging Lilly inside. In a moment they were gone.

It was 10:05 p.m.

The following night David Dane was standing in front of the huge mirrors on the second floor of Iron Gym, doing a set of lateral raises.

It was an exercise used for isolating the shoulders, focusing mainly on what is known as your interior deltoid group, in the middle of the shoulders.

During his workout, Dane met a man by the name of David Jacobs. He was from Detroit., and he would be dead within a year.

The conversation began when Dane put his weights on the floor and did a short shadow-boxing session in front of the mirrors. It was for the amusement or benefit of no one in particular. Jacobs approached Dane and shook his hand.

"What's up?" the black man said.

"Nothing," Dane replied, killing the routine and turning to face the stranger who was wearing shorts and a sweater.

"You know how to throw your hands. I can tell!" Jacobs exclaimed. "You were a fighter?"

"Once upon a time maybe."

"I did some boxing back home in Michigan, before my partner died."

"It's a dangerous sport". Dane responded.

Jacobs was still out of breath from his own workout. "Nah, nah . . . Drug deal gone bad. He got shot."

"I'm sorry to hear about your partner. I've never liked guns. Were you there when it happened"??Dane asked pulling a straight bar from the rack.

"I walked in with him. I didn't walk out with him. They just hit me and left me there. Kind of cold-cocked me," he said.

"And when you woke up?"

"Total adrenaline rush. Like, I didn't really know where I was. I've had people point guns, but that doesn't really change my attitude any. It just means that the other guy's scared or that he doesn't have any guts."

"I used to run with gangs, but we never had guns. It wasn't like that back home. If we had a problem, we solved it with our fists, never with firearms. The penalty's too heavy. I've always preached abstinence when it comes to guns. From when I was just in to when I was a captain," Dane said.

Back home in Nova Scotia, gangs were the exception rather than the rule, but they did exist. Dane had been recruited by a friend of his named D-Knight, short for Daniel Knight. He was a white easy-mic rapper turned gang leader and gang recruiter who had appeared once on MTV. He had recruited Dane due to his popularity as a boxer as well as for his reputation on the streets for being a cold hitter, which meant knock-out man. If they faced David Dane, they wouldn't last long.

The gang had existed for about seven or eight years and brought in over a hundred members. Now, they weren't the Bloods or the Crips, but for a small city like Halifax. They had momentum. They were known as D.P., named after D's rap group "Dynamite Productions". They even sold their own logo on T-shirts, ball hats, long leather coats and bumper stickers. The slogan was "Bad is in the Blood." A David Dane creation.

"I'm gonna go up and get a couple of shakes from Andre. It's on me". Dane said.

"Yeah. Anything . . . strawberry. No chocolate."

And with that, Dane disappeared into the stairwell.

It was 11:10 p.m.

*   *   *

Ann Marilyn who was born and raised in a mining town in Cape Breton stopped before the brewery at Frontenac. The early morning light was blinding and her blood shot eyes were sensitive to the heat. However, as early as it was for Annie, it was nowhere near as early in the eyes of her best friend and canine companion "Princess" who stood happily on all fores wagging her tail.

"Sit". Annie ordered the black K-9 who was one hundred percent pure pitbull.

"Good morning Princess". David Dane greeted.

"Are you talking to her or me"?? Annie asked smiling.

"I guess that goes both ways".

"Do you have a cigarette"?? The brown haired girl asked.

"You never remember that I don't smoke".

"Oh. That's right. I always forget".

"I'm hungry". Dane said.

"You could have breakfast at Mc-Donalds. It's twenty four hours."

"I've never been a big fan of breakfast".

"Me neither. I usually don't get up until around supper time so it's not an issue for me".

Princess stood up fully and turned her strict attension to David Dane as if she were a student watching a Professor give a lecture.

"I don't suppose that you've seen Lilly today". Dane inquired.

"Um . . . . Yeah. I think so. But it was much earlier".

"If you see her . . . ."

"I'll tell her that you're looking for her . . . . Love you".

"Love you to sweetie". Dane said kissing Annie on the forehead before walking off.

It was 7:43a.m.

"They're going to think that you're a pimp if you keep standing there. Fuck. It's hard enough to make money this early in the morning," the girl who looked like Sandra Bullock said.

It was nine a.m. and Dane was still in search of Lilly Chicoine, whose involvement down here was of mounting concern to him. And the worst part of it was that he couldn't stop her. Both Lilly and the drugs had a mind of their own, and neither one could be changed.

"Pimp?"

"Yes, pimp. Are you deaf?"

"What?" Dane asked. He had heard her just fine.

"Now go, so I can work," Carolyn said.

"What? I really can't hear a damned thing that you're saying," he said.

"Fuck, are you stupid? I need to make money."

"Tell me something," Dane said, straightening from the hint of a grin to stark seriousness. "Do you think you're funny?"

This time the wicked stepsister attempted to slap him. She was not successfull Dane had stepped backward and Carolyn had missed her target. Soon they were joined by a young man wearing French braids and a pair of camouflage shorts. His name was Silva, and he was Carolyn's boyfriend.

"Hunny. Are you misbehaving again?" asked Silva who was a guitarist for a local metal band.

Dane thought that Silva looked like a reject from the Red Hot Chili Peppers.

"Fuck! This guy . . . he won't let me work!" Carolyn exclaimed.

"You don't own the street, hunny," Silva said. He turned to Dane. "How are you?" he said, extending his hand.

"I'm good. Who the hell are you?"

"My name's Silva," he said affably. "And you are?"

"David Dane," the Scotian redneck answered, his face hard. He did not know Silva. He would get to know him. Dane was not being rude. Just sizing him up.

Silva thought that Dane looked like someone who would wire your jaw shut if you gave him a reason.

"Your girlfriend has a strong sense of entitlement."

"See, he's being a fucking smart ass," Carolyn said, seriously.

"What the hell you got in here?" Dane asked, fishing into Carolyn's purse. She tried to pull it away but David Dane would not let her.

"Condoms," he said, tossing two red packets over his shoulder.

Silva stood frozen.

You got a compact mirror. I'll bet it hates your damned guts." In truth. Carolyn was gorgeous. It, too, went flying left over Dane's shoulder.

"You got a damned G-string with little red hearts on it," he said, tossing out the piece of lingerie. Carolyn looked appalled. Dane looked like he was having a good time.

"And I'm truly impressed," Dane said, fishing a children's book out of her handbag. "You know why I'm impressed?"

Lilly was standing nearby now. She could not stand Carolyn. They had fought many times before. So, to her, Dane's antics were more than amusing.

I'm impressed by the fact that you know how to read, regardless of the fact that this is a Dr. Seuss book," he said. The book went flying, exiting stage right.

"Fuck you . . ."

"Not a chance in Hell," Dane replied.

"Hey, Carolyn, c'mon," Silva said, trying to lead her away by the shoulder. He knew that Dane was probably right, and besides that, he didn't want any trouble with the bald-headed badass who was standing just feet from him now.

The traffic light on the other side of the street turned green.

"Let's go," Silva said.

"That's the best damned offer that you're gonna hear today," Dane said darkly, his eyelids at half mast.

"Little bitch," Lilly said, tauntingly.

"Shut your mouth, you fucking cunt," the Bullock look-alike retorted.

"Aye—aye," Lilly snapped back, stabbing four fingers in Carolyn's direction.

"Kill it," Dane said flatly to both of them. He didn't want a fight to break out.

"Maybe someone should kill you," Carolyn retorted.

"Yeah . . ." the Scotian replied with a hard drawl. Miller was leading his girlfriend across the street now, as Dane and Lilly watched them vanish into the morning sun.

The digital read-out on Dane's watch read 9:12 a.m

Chapter 9

In David Dane's dream there was a blackout on Ontario Street. The only light in the dream, which existed as a rising haze, engulfed an Esso station at the corner of Papineau and Ontario street, and all who occupied its grounds. There was a dealer with a flock of regulars standing around him. Squeegees, ravers, and four street hookers out long after their shifts, not to mention a local collector who worked for a shark named Jack stood in a semi-circle. Two gas station attendants were manning the pumps, dressed in uniform.

The neighborhood was otherwise paralyzed by a surreal blackness that made the upper stories of the buildings look like asylums rising out of the darkness of a dream.

Somehow Dane's nocturnal eye inside was letting him see past the opaque windows that were oily with the nightshine from the dreamily lit fueling station, and into the living rooms and alcoves of Ontario Street's surrounding structures.

On the first floor of a two-story apartment complex, Dane saw a prostitute of no more than fifteen years old fixing herself with a *garro* and a syringe full of heroin. She wore a black top and a pair of blue jeans that were stained with drops of blood from her arms, but there was something else going on. There was a droning like the motor of a furnace, tuning up, and then there was someone else there. Dane could not see the face of the man who was standing to the left of the girl. The room was too dark.

In a moment the pretty blue-eyed girl looked up. She could see him now. There was something in his hand. Shining. The droning hummed on.

Dane rolled over, outside of unconsciousness.

There was a bursting silver glare like a flashbulb going off and, for a second, Dane could not see what was going on in the room inside of his dream.

When his vision returned, there was blood everywhere. It shouted at him from the walls and floor of the little room, like a soft cry from beneath the depths of the ocean. Dane's inner eye shifted again to the body of the fifteen year-old junkie who lay dead in the center of the room. Her eyes were gone and her throat had been cut by the demon who had been in the room with her. The figure whose face Dane could not make out.

There was another flash and then he could see what was going on in another non-descript area.

This time he saw Lilly, and she was down on her knees getting ready to have sex with a group of faceless men who were standing around her. They were naked, using their hands to work themselves up as her eyes ran up and down their forms.

Dane moaned in his sleep.

Soon the men were gone, having used Lilly to satisfy themselves, leaving the room in single file. She was alone now, and then the droning began again.

The dream figure with no face reappeared, as if from nowhere.

He was upon her now.

"Dream a little dream," a raspy voice echoed.

It was 2:04 a.m.

* * *

The next evening the sky over Ontario Street was a deep shadowy blue and the lingering remnants of last night's dream were still with David

Dane, somehow invading his consciousness. It was around 7:45 p.m. and, as he was on so many other nights, David Dane was in search of Lilly Chicoine. But as he climbed to the top of Frotenac, David Dane met a short, bald-headed man who looked like a bank robber. His name was Joe, and he said that he knew where Lilly was. She was in his car, where she had been sleeping for the past two hours.

"Is this her?" Joe asked, opening the passenger side door of his blue Chevrolet Impala to reveal Lilly Chicoine.

"It is," Dane said affably.

Lilly lay sleeping, her seat reclined. There was drool running down her face from the right side of her mouth.

"Thank you, man," Dane said. "You just saved me a lot of walking."

"No problem. I just got out of jail this morning. You guys need a lift some place?"

"Can you drive us to Leopold Heights?" Dane asked. "I can pay for your gas."

"Sure," the short, dangerous-looking guy in the denim suit said. "Get in."

Dane walked around to the rear of the car and got in behind Joe.

"Say, you mind if I take a bath when we get there?" Joe asked.

"Yeah, why not?" Dane answered. It was a strange request. But why not?

When they reached two thirty-five Leopold Heights, it was dark outside. Joe parked the car and then the three of them got out and walked across the street into the main lobby of the building. Dane was convinced that Lilly, even though she was on her feet, still did not have any idea what the fuck was going on.

"Is that blanket keeping you warm, Lilly?" Joe asked.

Lilly nodded vaguely, pulling the knitted quilt that Joe had given her more tightly around her frail shoulders. She was sucking her thumb. When they were inside the apartment, Lilly went directly to the big black leather sofa and fell back asleep.

"You got a towel I can borrow?" Joe asked.

"Yeah. Top shelf, by the bathroom," Dane responded.

The bathroom door closed and then the water ran for about the next twenty minutes. Having this guy in the house was making Dane slightly nervous, but he owed him something* for taking him to Lilly and driving them home. And besides, he seemed all right.

Dane sat still for a moment, pausing. What a strange situation he was in. I mean, here was Lilly, curled up on his couch sucking her thumb. He had met her in the rain, standing in front of a bar in a bad neighborhood. She was a prostitute and a drug addict, and she was also the love of his life. David Dane had had other loves, but none that measured up to Lilly. Lilly was special. The enigma of his soul, he thought. At around eight twenty, the bathroom door opened and Joe walked out, fully clothed.

"Boy, that was a good bath," he said.

"How much do I owe you for the gas?" Dane inquired.

"You don't owe me anything. Lilly got any cigarettes lying around here?"

"I doubt it. She's usually all out by the time she leaves. There might be some in her bag, but I'm not gonna stick my hand in there and find out. I don't wanna get stuck."

Joe lifted his ball hat, rubbing his bald head with his free hand.

"So, how long have you guys been together?" Joe asked.

"Close to a year," Dane answered.

"You do drugs?"

"Nope, that's Lilly's thing."

"So you two aren't even on the same level, then?"

Dane was wondering if Joe had the hots for Lilly. First asking her if the blanket was keeping her warm, which to Dane seemed like a term of endearment, and then his last statement which Dane had decided not to respond to. Hopefully Joe would get the message.

"Are you from around here?" the Scotian boxer asked.

"I'm from Ontario. Lilly said that she was from Toronto."

What the hell did the two facts have to do with each other? Joe was trying to make a point. Dane was tiring of Joe, and he was also tiring of Joe being in his house, but that fact alone was the exact reason that David Dane did not want this to become heated. Wrong locale.

"Say, you mind if I sleep here til morning?"

"Listen, dude. I have nothing against you," he lied between his teeth, "but I don't know you, and now I don't owe you. I wouldn't be comfortable with it. Listen, it was nice meeting you," Dane said, on his feet with his hand extended.

Joe shook Dane's hand. "All right," he said.

If Joe had noticed Dane's demeanor, he gave no sign of it. Soon Dane was following the short, bald-headed man to the door.

"Thanks for the bath, eh?" Joe said.

"Don't mention it," David Dane said, opening the door to the hallway.

"Goodnight," the boxer said.

It was 8:31 p.m.

"My father molested me. He used to find excuses to come into my room after work," Lilly said sadly. "He'd say that he just wanted to watch my T.V., or that he needed a few minutes of quiet away from everyone else. I tried to tell my mother, but she would never listen. She always took his side over mine when he said that he had never laid a hand on me. She's a fucking cunt, my mother. I hate her. That's why I left. I don't want anything from either one of them. They can go to hell."

It was three a.m.

Dane took a cigarette from the pack that he had bought for Lilly hours earlier and handed it to her. The apartment was dark, and there was a cool breeze blowing in through the open window, pleasantly ventilating the living room where the two of them sat, Lilly on a mattress that was sprawled out on the floor, and Dane sitting on the edge of the couch. They were both up past the witching hour, Lilly was slept out, and Dane not able to sleep at all.

"How long has it been since you spoke to either one of them?" he asked.

"Years. I was two months away from my fourteenth birthday when I ran away from home. It got so bad that my brother and I wanted to leave."

"Hansel and Gretel," David said.

"Yeah, Hansel and Gretel," Lilly said flatly.

"So what did you do after that?"

"I met a guy on a bus and he gave me money. It was a special set of circumstances. That was the night that I turned my first trick."

Dane could not understand how two parents could put their daughter in that horrible position. Sometimes the relationship between parent and child could be bad, but allowing things to get to this point was unconscionable.

"And then?"

"They placed me with a foster family until I ran away again. I mean the courts did. For a while I lived with my brother until he couldn't afford to keep me, so I left. That's roughly when I met my daughter's father. My little girl, Liliana was born and he took her from me. I was on drugs and I wanted to come home and see her." Lilly's eyes were welling with tears now. "But when I came back, the apartment was empty. I called first, maybe a week before. He told me that he already had one baby and that he didn't need another. I told him that I just wanted to come home and see her. I asked him if he would bring her to see me if I went to rehab. That was the last time that I ever spoke to him."

"And you have no idea where he might have gone?"

Lilly shook her head.

"He's from here?" Dane asked.

"He's Yugoslavian," she said.

"What about the other guy? The guy from the bar that night?"

"Mathieu. He introduced me to heroin."

"Where did you meet him?"

"I met Mathieu at a rave. I was with two of Liliana's Father's friends. He sent two of his friends with me as bodyguards, in case I met someone . . . and I did. Mathieu and I slept together the same night we met, and then the following day we were sitting in a park together by the bus station. The one just off Ontario Street . . ."

"Terminus Voyageur," Dane said.

"Yeah . . . And he went to buy cigarettes, and that's when I found his bag of used needles. When he got back, he told me that he only got high on days following a rave. That was bullshit. That's when he introduced me to the junk."

"How?"

"He knew about my personal problems with my kid's father. He told me to sniff H. That it would make me feel better. Then, after about a week, I started to get sick. Headaches, cramps, vomiting, whatever . . . I asked him what was wrong with me and he said that was the drawback. You get sick when you have no more heroin. So I went to work. I think he knew that if he could get me hooked, I would pay for everything, and by that time I was shooting, so I didn't give a fuck."

"I should do 'em the next time I see him," Dane said under his breath.

The breeze coming in from the window was beginning to stiffen now, drawing lines around them.

"I love you, Lilly. I'm sorry that all this happened," he said, leaning in. He put his arms around her from behind. "I'm right here," he said. "And I aint never going away".

It was 3:22 a.m.

The next morning, David Dane stepped out of the elevator into the lobby of the building, two of the overhead ceiling fans whirled and churned about him, forging a path through the morning air.

Joe sat in the foyer between the two main doors, head down with his hands on his knees.

"You mind if I come up?" he asked, pushing the inside door open just enough to be heard.

Dane felt a bit bad for him, but he could not afford to have an ex-con getting comfortable in his house, especially not with Lilly around. Dane already had his hands full.

"Listen, man. I can't do that. I'm sorry."

Joe just nodded, and then he started dry sniffling.

Dane was sure that he was on something.

It was 9:17 a.m.

Hedia, who was born in Germany, was sitting on a bench in Park Copal. It was nine twenty-one in the morning, and Hedia was just preparing to do her first hit of the day. She had bought coke from the dealer over a half-hour earlier, but what she had really wanted to do was smack.

She heard the sound of footsteps as she drew a needle and some water from her purse. The last thing that she wanted to do was to attract any attention to herself from people walking by, and if, God forbid, Six were making their early morning rounds, she would likely end up spending her next eight weeks in jail.

Someone came into the park. Hedia looked up. Half of the park was surrounded by walls but there was still the main entrance that opened out of a chain-link fence. And it was there that you had to watch your back.

"Hi," the intruder said.

"Shhhhh. Fuck! Someone's gonna hear us and they're gonna call the cops," said Hedia. The other female, who was about ten years Hedia's junior, was Sheryl.

"I don't think we need to worry too much. I mean, there's no cops here. At least none that I can see."

"You're already high. I want to get high. Do you have a condom that I can use as a *garro*?" the German asked.

"Yeah, I have one." Sheryl fished into her handbag and pulled out a rubber wrapped in red.

"Thanks," Hedia said, taking it from her. "Do you know why no one's answering the number for smack?" she asked. "I mean, they're such liberal minded bastards, and I think that that goes without saying."

"Fuck, Sheryl, hunny. You're too high."

"Can someone share their hit with me?" Angela O. asked, walking up out of nowhere.

"If you have ten bucks, I'll split with you," Hedia said.

"I haven't make a customer yet, so I don't have any money," Angela said. "C'mon, Hedia. Don't be a selfish bitch."

"Look, girl, I did a customer just to make twenty, so I'm not sharing with anyone."

"I'm gonna remember that next time that you don't have any money," Angela said, her voice high-pitched but raspy.

"Please, Hedia. I'm so sick."

"Coke is not gonna take care of that. You need smack," Hedia retorted.

"Never mind. Fuck you, Hedia. I'll go back to work."

It was 9:28 a.m.

Chapter 10

The lush setting of Bobby Edmonds' office opened up with a series of rubber plants and greenery that led to a huge aquarium full of exotic sea life. The room was small and its many shadows were mostly shapes from the bubbling fish tank that was set on a stand by the east wall.

The hour was late, and the gym outside Edmonds' office was dark, deep and quiet.

At around eleven forty-five P.M. Bobby stepped inside from the outer area and sat down behind his desk. He wore only a yellow Speedo and a sheen that went from head to toe. He still maintained the build of a pro bodybuilder, keeping up with a special diet and his training regimen not to mention a shot of anabolic steroids whenever he needed them administered by one or more of his staff.

Bobby used a key to open the top drawer of his desk. Once opened. He retrieved a rubber *garro*, a small bag of heroin, another small bag with coke inside, a syringe, a pair of black leather driving gloves and a shiny black knife, the same knife that he had used to stab out Marguerite Blankenship's eyes. The same knife that he had used to become known as the Ontario Street Killer.

Edmonds rose from his desk and fastened the *garro* around his arm. One speedball and he would be zoned out. Then he would find another victim and do her.

Soon, he would be ready.

That same night, around midnight, David Dane accompanied Lilly Chicoine to work. It would be the last time that they would see each other for the next four months.

David and Lilly got off the metro at Frotenac at around twelve o two. They walked onto the brown platform and then up four flights of stairs to the outside into the evening air.

Lilly wore a denim jean suit and Dane a black Nike sweater, cut gloves, blue jeans and running shoes that were also black. His look, non pattened, had become trademark around here.

The night air was cool, but not so cool that you needed a jacket. It was still above freezing.

Lilly stopped to hold up her compact and put cover-up on, not that she needed it. Lilly's skin was perfect, like pure silk. Most addicts had blemishes. Lilly did not.

Dane pecked Lilly on the lips. He fucking hated all this shit, especially waiting around for Lilly to make a reappearance after she left with a customer. Sometimes the wait could be long, or even take hours.

"Okay, I'm ready. I'm gonna go to work now," she half said, half chirped.

"Uh-huh". Dane muttered.

Lilly walked up the street into the blue nocturne as Dane watched ·her go. He felt emotion tighten up in his chest as she walked away. He wondered if she knew how much this hurt him. Her occupation was for Dane like having demons rip away his soul.

There was a familiar smell in the air. Dane could not place it.

Soon the wind was blowing and Lilly had disappeared into a customer's car and vanished around a corner.

About forty minutes elapsed without Lilly's return. She usually spent no more than ten to fifteen minutes with one trick. This was typical Lilly behavior, if not typical addict behavior. When they wanted to stay out and they knew that you didn't want them to, this is what they did. They didn't come back.

David Dane looked up the street toward the glow of the phone booth on the corner. Still no Lilly.

The sidewalk stretched out and so did the hours. There was a two-level apartment building with a stone porch across the street from the corner where Lilly usually worked. Someone had graffiti-ed the word CRACK in bold lettering on one of the outside walls, white lettering against brown brick.

Dane went to the divider by the pay phone and sat down. No rest for the wicked, he thought.

A car stopped by the curb and a brown-haired girl got out. It was Angela O. She came over and gave him a hug.

"Hey baby, I'm happy to see you," she said, seating herself down next to him. "How are you?"

"Mentally or physically?"

"Both," she inquired.

"Broken. Lilly pulled another one of her vanishing routines. Same shit, different day. There's no rest for the wicked."

"I saw her at Isabelle's earlier."

"How long ago?" Dane asked.

"Mmm, maybe two hours ago."

"Was she alone?" Dane's suspicious mind was kicking into high gear.

There was a short pause.

"Yeah."

Dane did not believe her.

"Well, if you see her, you be sure and tell her that I'm looking for her," he said. Why the fuck was Angela lying to him? If it had been only a client, she would have told him that. There was something else going on. Something more sinister and less along the lines of working and getting high.

Dane stood up and kissed Angela on one eyelid then the other. They were very close, like brother and sister. If Angela was not telling the truth, it was to spare his feelings, but from what?

He started to walk east, in the direction of Frotenac metro, where he immediately ran into Isabelle and her boyfriend Steven who went by name "Blast."

"Hey. You see Lilly?" Dane questioned.

Blast was silent.

"Earlier, she was at my house. Mathieu came to see her. He just got out of jail," Isabelle said.

Dane was going to fucking explode. Jesus fucking Christ, this little French bastard was going to get it when Dane saw him next. The French wanted to separate from Canada? Dane was going to give Mathieu a head start. He was going to separate Mathieu's head from the rest of his torso. FUCK!

"You tell Mathieu that life's short, but for him I'm gonna make an exception. He gets to leave before everyone else does."

"Look, don't freak out. He was around here earlier," Isabelle explained, "but he wasn't with Lilly. He was with Irene."

"Good. Then she can help him write his fucken eulogy."

"Hey! He's a friend of mine," the girl said.

"Was. Was a friend of yours," Dane said.

Blast tried to stifle his laughter.

"Where's Lilly now?" Dane asked.

"I saw her around here too, but that was well over an hour ago," Isabelle remarked.

"You tell her I'm around," he finished.

Dane shook Blast's hand. Then he watched Blast and Isabelle walk off into the wee hours of the morning.

Another hour of walking and searching went by. It was almost sun up and Dane hadn't slept yet. He was exhausted and his feet were covered in blisters, making it almost impossible to go on any longer. He waited by the curb for a cab appear, got in the back seat, and went home. David Dane would not be able to locate Lilly Chicoine for the next four months.

David Dane Wallace A.K.A.-Von "The Icon"
"The Ontario Street Original"

This Book is dedicated to the best friend that I've ever had.
My Dog Hunter. I will always love you, and forever keep you in my heart.
Daddy

The Infamous Group Of Bears, and one rabbit of "Ontario Street".
A very shady bunch!!!

PART TWO
Urban Heat

A hot sun was rising over Ontario Street. It was six a.m. And almost no one moved through the downtown streets yet. The day promised to be ablaze with temperatures in the mid-thirties, eventually climbing to nearly forty.

Lilly Chicoine had just been released from the hospital where she had spent all of the previous night under supervision and now all that she was looking for was her hit.

The big cement park at the foot of the highway stood practically empty with only the odd vagrant or addict passing through to get high or to take a piss. Litter blew about the streets making rustling sounds as it scuttled along the pavement in the temperate morning breeze, most of it finding a home in the alleyways or gutters off Ontario Street.

Lilly wandered around for a few minutes longer before dropping into the twenty-four hour mini-mart to buy a Freezy. She was starving and the only money that she had on her was small change. As a matter of fact, that was the only money that she had at all. It wasn't, after all, as if she'd been out working all night. Lilly Chicoine was all alone in the world these days and it was beginning to hurt her both emotionally and financially. She was beginning to miss having someone to take care of her the way that David Dane had. For a while she had lived with Mathieu, but then he had done something stupid and ended up back in jail again. His typical pattern.

Working would be hard at this hour, but she would try. There would soon be lots of traffic, but most of the commuters would be on their way to work, not looking to stop for a blowjob.

When she stepped back outside into the morning air, she saw a familiar figure strolling down the street. Holy fuck, it was him. It was Dane, as if God had heard her prayers and had for once decided to answer them.

"Hey, hey," she called out, snapping her fingers above her head to get his attention.

He had seen her immediately, despite her short hair and her long black leather coat that would kill you in these temperatures.

"Lilly!" Dane called out, crossing Ontario Street to meet her. They embraced right away.

"I've come down here so many times looking for you. Someone told me that I just missed you last time."

"I know. Nadia told me that you were trying to find me. She said 'there's some big bald guy in a leather jacket looking for you.' I knew right away that it was you," Lilly said.

"What about Mathieu. Where is he . . . and don't lie to me."

"I don't wanna talk about Mathieu," she said.

"Mmmm," Dane muttered, almost comically. He wondered why she hadn't called. Was she living with him?

There was a loud, vacuous whistle as a large bus went by, its chrome glinting in the early morning sunshine. It drove two more blocks before its brakes squealed to a halt at a red light.

"So what now?" he asked.

"I'm tired. I wanna lie down."

"Where do you live?" the glare was in Dane's eyes now, pun intended.

"I don't have a home."

"Yeah you do," he said welcomingly.

Lilly smiled. "Yayyyy!"

Dane embraced her again.

"I just wanna make a customer to get some money for smack. I've been in the hospital all night," Lilly said."

"Why?" he asked.

"Because I had been up for days doing coke and the ambulance boys decided to take me to the ER. That's why." Lilly was not mad. It was just the way she spoke.

"Unless you can pass me twenty bucks," she said bringing the conversation back to the issue at hand.

"I don't have any money," Dane said. And besides, he wasn't going to give her any money for dope. Providing funds of that nature would have long standing consequences. He knew better.

"Okay then, I'm gonna try to work. Can you sit over there so that the customers won't think that you're my pimp?" Lilly was pointing to a stoop in front of an apartment doorway. Dane turned away and sat down. He fucking hated this.

Now the morning sun was growing hotter and it was becoming harder to breathe the air that smelled of yeast from the brewery near Frotenac. Across the street, Lilly stood on the corner of the big park where two fountains ran, foaming over at the brim of their pool. The heat wave had begun.

Chapter 11

Angelica: This One's for you.

Two nights later, at around 8:30 p.m., David Dane was standing on the sidewalk in front of the Travel Lodge Hotel. As he peered through its window into a stairwell, he saw a voluptuous blond beauty who he would soon come to know as Angelica and, as it turned out, David Dane would be one of the last people to see her, just twelve hours before her death. So this chapter is a dedication.

Angelica, this one's for you.

"I am Claude," said the man sitting on the sidewalk beneath the pizza parlor window.

"I am the boyfriend of Sheryl," he went on in a French accent.

The air outside was warm and Claude was dressed for it wearing only an open black track jacket and matching pants. On his head he wore a black ball hat that was mirrored above the rim in gangster rap-fashion that fit well with his hardcore image, and, although he hadn't trained in years, the chiseled physique beneath Claudes jacket left little to the imaginations of the women in the area who often thought of him as sexy.

"So you saw Lilly today?" Dane asked.

"I see her earlier with Sheryl, but then I don't see her again for maybe three hours," he said.

"She's really starting to turn it up with this vanishing shit," Dane said. Lilly had disappeared again, which to Dane was nothing new. Old habits died hard.

It was a Friday afternoon, and Dane had not seen Lilly in over two days. Her disappearing acts were beginning to frighten him more and more every time she pulled one of them. Dane feared that one day he would find her in a dumpster, dismembered, or behind a building with her throat slit like so many of the other prostitutes around there.

"Alright. Thanks dude. I'm gonna try Frotenac," the Scotian said.

Dane continued walking for about four blocks until Hedia halted him for a hug. They embraced in front of a small shadowy tavern, inside of which were four slot machines, a pool table and two pay phones. Opposite the bar was a small confectionary machine with an ATM in the basement.

"Have you seen Lilly today?" David Dane asked.

"No . . . but she stays up there sometimes," Hedia said, pointing to the upstairs window of the two-story building with the work CRACK spray-painted on it's wall.

"That's where she stayed part of last winter," Hedia explained.

"With who?" Dane asked with concern.

"Claude . . . He's Haitian." She was not speaking of the Claude that Dane had just left.

"Haitian?" Dane replied.

"Haitian," Hedia echoed.

Dane was fixated. Who was this guy and what was his relationship to Lilly? Dane would stick around if he had to in order to find out. He loved Lilly, and he did not like other men being in her life. Period. There were clients, which was bad enough, Mathieu, himself, and now this guy? What was this The Fucken Dating Game??

Dane walked about twelve feet and parked himself on the raised wooden divider across from the two-level apartment complex. He sat unmoving as the day melted into night. Still no Lilly. No sign of her whatsoever, and there was a growing cocoon of butterflies in his stomach.

Two girls had come to work the corner next to where David Dane was sitting. He did not pay them any mind, too transfixed on the upstairs left-hand window to which Hedia had pointed earlier.

Finally at around eight p.m., as dusk was growing, a small hunched-over black man with a beard and dreadlocks exited the stairwell of the apartment building via the front door. Dane crossed over Ontario Street to greet him.

"Where's Lilly?" Dane asked, more out of jealously than out of belief that Claude really knew her whereabouts.

"I am Rastaman, and me name be Claude, mon. And I am no afraid for police," he said in a barking, tribal tone.

Rastaman was short for Rastafarian. Dane had no idea what the fuck that meant.

"Rastaman?"

"Rastaman!" Claude barked in return to Dane's question.

"So, that means fuckin' what? You're like the Haitian version of Superman?"

"How you know that I am from Haiti?" the barefoot man asked. "I no give money for taxes. Lilly? Why? Why you are look for Lilly? You lose your time," he said.

"Yo Voodoo man. Listen up. Lilly is my girlfriend. That means that I don't want her staying at your house anymore. Capiche?"

"You lose your time," Claude said. Then he turned, went back in his house and closed the door.

It was 8:05 p.m.

Later that night under a black sky, David Dane walked into Nightlife to find Lilly Chicoine sitting on a stool talking to a guy named Josh. They were playing the gambling machines. The bar around him was noisy and almost completely white with cigarette smoke that was rising to the roof from its many patrons who were puffing away on cigarettes or cigars. The music that was selected by the evening's DJ was mostly hip hop mixed with R&B. The selection playing as Dane approached Lilly Chicoine was a song called "Around the World" by ATC. Dane had heard it before.

"Where were you?" he asked. No time for games.

Lilly hit the glowing pad on the slot machine twice, turned, and looked straight at Dane who was visibly pissed.

"I wasn't around," she retorted.

The guy next to her was getting on Dane's nerves. He was interjecting himself into their conversation and he wouldn't shut the fuck up. If he continued. Dane would make sure that Josh stopped interjecting himself.

"Hey Lilly," the college boy began, "you wanna come home with me tonight?"

The slot machine chimed as it began to dispense silver. Lilly had won.

"What?" Dane said sharply in reply to the college boy's request.

"You know I used to be a football player?" Josh said.

Lilly was not responding, too busy collecting her winnings.

"I don't know where Lilly's going tonight . . . What's your name?" Dane asked.

"Josh," the twenty-three year old answered sharply.

Dane's eyes were like black slats full of coal now. He clenched his fists, his jaw muscles tightening. He was starting to sweat.

"But you know what, Josh? You're going to the emergency room, motherfucker," Dane said, his left fist connecting with Josh's right jaw. There was a cracking sound and then Josh hit the floor with a thud so loud that it could be heard over the music.

"Hey!" the bartender hollered, noticing what had happened.

Dane grabbed Lillys hand and ran out of the bar and down a side street. Even in his panicked state of mind, Dane still noticed how beautiful Lilly looked in her white blouse tied up Daisy Duke-style and her skin-tight blue jeans that finished out over white pumps.

"Hey, you don't own me," she scolded.

"I'm sorry. I love you, baby. You're all the way in my heart now," Dane apologized.

Lilly's expression softened. She wasn't really that mad at him. She knew that he had a jealous streak and that he couldn't help it.

"Can we go home?" David Dane asked.

"I just wanna make enough money to do one quarter," Lilly said.

There was no such thing as just doing one quarter and Dane knew it. If you did one, you followed it with another and another and another. A coke trip. He didn't want to lose her now.

"What if I buy it for you?"

"You have money?"

"Yeah, I have twenty. Exactly," he said.

"Okay! Let's go," Lilly said happily.

"Can we call now?" she asked.

Dane handed her a twenty. He would later realize that he'd made a stupid mistake.

"Wait, wait, wait," he said. "Where's the money that you just won in the machine?"

"I dropped it on the floor on the way out of the bar," she responded.

"How much was it?"

"Probably twenty bucks," she said.

"Unbelievable . . ."

"I'm sorry. Are you mad?"

Dane just shook his head.

"Where are you gonna call from?" he asked.

There was a darkened park ahead of them under the black sky. It was silent.

"Maybe from Nightlife," she said.

"So, are you going to tell me about your Haitian friend?" Dane asked as they began to walk back in the direction of Nightlife.

"I lived with him while you weren't around. Fuck. I was living at a bus stop."

"So why didn't you call me?"

"Because I thought you'd be mad and I didn't want to deal with you."

"So instead you went to sleep at a bus stop?"

Lilly was speechless.

They were standing in front of Nightlife now, where Dane noticed Blast sitting outside, below the window. He greeted him and then followed Lilly inside.

"Can I use the phone?" Lilly asked the tall, lanky bartender with the moustache. He responded by placing the house phone on the countertop.

The music in the place was almost deafening. This was one more place on Ontario Street where you could hardly see your hand in front of your face because of all the smoke. The room was blue.

"Okay. Okay. How long will it take you to get there? Thirty minutes? Well, fuck. What are you gonna do, crawl there?"

Lilly was in the midst of her conversation with her drug dealer and she cursed very loudly, and then her conversation came to an abrupt end.

"Let's go," she said.

Dane followed Lilly back out the front door and onto Ontario Street where the two of them began their journey uphill toward Lafontaine Park, which was set in the middle of a residential neighborhood made up of houses, condos and apartment complexes. They were on their way to meet Lilly's dealer with Dane's twenty bucks. On their way they passed by a large hospital and a family courthouse with huge Roman pillars.

At the park, Dane stared into the big black pond that seemed to sparkle with sinister intentions. He seemed drawn into a trance for a moment, as a swan glided gracefully across the reflection created by an overhead streetlight that stood by the sidewalk.

Lilly was pacing back and forth as she anxiously awaited her coke dealer.

"Fuck. Are they coming or not?How long has it been?" she asked.

"Dane looked at his watch. "Relax. It hasn't even been ten minutes," he said.

"Fuck! I wanna do my hit."

"I know that," Dane said sympathetically.

Twenty more minutes went by with Lilly pacing. The dealer did not show.

Jesus Christ, where are they?" she demanded.

Dane shook his head.

"Fuck, I wanna call them again," Lilly said. "Give me a quarter."

"I don't have one," Dane said. You're gonna have to break your twenty."

"F-u-u-u-ck! Where?" She was being irrational now. "There's no store around here," Lilly said.

"We'll find one. Let's go."

Soon they were back on the sidewalk heading further away from Ontario. They crossed two streets and walked onto the same block as Iron Gym, stopping at the lights.

"There's a 7-11 . . . there," Dane said pointing to the brightly lit convenience store.

Lilly reached into the pocket of her blue jeans and found the twenty. She looked over her shoulder at Dane who was following behind. They walked into the store.

"Can you make change?" Lilly asked the female counter attendant.

The girl obliged her and soon Lilly was on the pay phone outside.

"Well, fuck, where are you? It's forty minutes I'm waiting already. Okay." The 'okay' was sarcastic. Lilly hung up the phone, stepping out of the booth.

"They're coming here. Where's my new one?"

Dane reached for her purse. "In the outside pouch. I saw it hanging out," he said.

In two minutes a red sedan rounded the corner and stopped just shy of Lilly who was already headed for one of the rear doors. The driver looked up at Lilly from behind the windshield. He was thin with brown hair and a five o'clock shadow.

Lilly got in and they drove away.

Dane waited outside the well-lit store for five minutes which seemed like an eternity before the car reappeared and Lilly got out.

"Let's go," she said, hurrying right past him.

"Where are we headed?" David Dane asked.

"Somewhere I can do this."

Dane looked around. "I don't think it's a good idea to do it around here. I don't wanna hear any wailers tonight," he said.

They were walking again, with Lilly taking the lead. They went back the way they came and ended up in Lafontaine Park under an oak tree.

Lilly squatted in her pumps, reaching for her syringe and the water that was in her purse. She took out the bottle of Evian first, unscrewed the cap and then removed her needle from its package. These rituals were followed by Lilly emptying half of her quarter of coke into her syringe, pouring in some water, and shooting up.

Dane turned away. He could not watch Lilly literally destroy herself. The horror show began with Lilly's face contorting in such a way that it appeared as if her jaw was being dislocated. She then began to use her hands, clenched into a ball, to rip the hair out of her head until the blood was pouring down her face. This was how she punished herself.

"Lilly! Lilly!" Dane said, turning to face her.

She was gouging herself with her needle now, her face a mess of hair and blood.

"Stop!" Dane said, taking the needle from her.

Lilly began to cry, her inner pain rising to the surface. He hated to see her this way.

Soon she began to come down.

"I'm just doing' my little . . . . I don't know," Lilly said, eyes wide. "You have a Kleenex?" she asked, pouring some Evian water onto her hands.

"No, but I think there's some in your purse," he responded.

Lilly fished into her leather handbag. "There's none here," she said.

"Fuck! I'm a mess and I have nowhere to clean up."

"You're bleeding," Dane said, staring into the open gap on top of her head.

"Okay, turn around. I'm going to do the rest of my quarter," she said.

"Fuck, Lilly . . ." Dane did as he was told. It was going to happen with or without him.

He turned away and she went at it again, mutilating herself. She was a bad trip, plain and simple. When she was through this time she dumped the entire contents of the bottle of water over her head. Streaks of blood ran down her cheeks and onto her white blouse.

"Baby," Dane said. He did not know what else to say.

"Can we go home now?" he asked.

Lilly paused, knowing that Dane would not like the coming response.

"I just want to do one more quarter," she said.

Dane was ready to snap.

"I promise just one more," she said. "Then we can go home."

"Holy fuck!" Dane said in response to his predicament.

"I just need to make myself look pretty so I can catch quickly."

To 'catch' meant to pick up a customer.

Dane was crushed. He hated this lifestyle with a passion. Nonetheless he followed Lilly back to Ontario Street where she used a car mirror to put on her makeup. As he watched this, Dane was sick to his stomach. Here she was, having nearly destroyed herself, and now she wanted to go and do it all over again. And it would cost her twenty bucks.

When Lilly was finished with her makeup, she went to the corner of the stone park and stood on the curb in the fallen darkness. One other girl stood next to Lilly. her name was Marie André. She was petite, sexy, and had shoulder length auburn hair. It was close to one a.m. and the streets were all but silent. Soon a Dodge Caravan covered in rust spots stopped and the portly, white-bearded driver ushered Lilly inside. She climbed into the passenger seat, closed the door, and the two drove off.

Dane hoped that Lilly would come back fast. She did not, and now he stood there waiting and waiting. Minutes became hours and Lilly did not return. The shadows deepened and so did David Danes anxious fear.

Soon Dane began to walk. Maybe she had gotten out and then gone to do another customer. It was growing later and later. He walked down the long street past the stone park, past Guardian, and kept going. In the distance Dane could see Sheryl. He stopped and asked her if she had seen Lilly. She had not. He continued on. At the end of four more streets he ran into Angela O.

"Have you seen Lilly?" he asked

"No, why?" Angela replied.

"I can't find her. And every time this happens it terrifies me a little more." he said.

Angela put her arms around him, melting into him. Dane loved Angela. She was one friend who was always there for him.

"Lilly needs to grow up," Angela O. said. "C'mon Dane . . . you deserve better than that," she said genuinely.

"This is definently Lillys sideshow." he said, looking over her shoulder.

"I'm gonna give her fucking shit when I see her". Angela said.

"You just tell her that i'm looking for her". Dane said, ending the conversation. He kissed Angela's forehead. His mind was pre-occupied with to many horrors for a standard conversation. What if the bearded driver had done something with her. What if she were lying in a ditch with her wind-pipe severed. These images sent cold chills down David Danes spine.

Almost sun-up. The air over Ontario Street was growing warmer. Still no sign of Lilly. Dane stopped at the corner of Logan and Ontario. Angelica now stood before him like an urban angel on the corner. She greeted Dane with a warm smile, the humid morning air gliding around her.

"You want me? You can have me for free," she said, touching Dane's chest with one hand. She was so beautiful, her blond hair falling across her massive chest in the early breeze.

"You see that patch of trees by the highway?" she asked, leaning into him.

Dane's resolve was weakening and Lilly hadn't seemed to care enough to come back.

"I could take you over there . . ." she finished the sentence in his ear.

They walked into the small field by the highway that led to the bridge, Angelica taking Dane by the hand. She unbuttoned her white blouse and looked into his eyes. Her blue eyes were so soft.

"I want you so bad," the urban angel said. She unfastened the button on Dane's jeans.

"Yeahhh," he whispered softly.

Soon he was in her mouth, hard as a rock. She moved her tongue up and down over his shaft until he shot a load of sperm down her throat and over her tonsils. She closed her eyes as he came.

When Dane was spent, he zipped himself back up and looked around. A car and a van passed by on the highway.

"Did you like it?" Angelica asked.

"What?" Dane asked quietly, responding with a mesmerized expression.

"You're so cute," Angelica said, standing up, eye to eye with him in her heels.

"Are you still with Lilly?" she asked.

"Yeah." he said, looking off into the distance. "I gotta go. You're Gorgeous angel."

She ran her hand across his chest as he began to walk away.

Back on Ontario Street, Dane heard a voice call out from behind him. It was Lilly calling his name. He turned around.

"Lilly," he said, his voice emotional. He was happy to see her.

Lilly's white shirt was speckled with blood and there were red dots on her forehead as if she'd been struck on top of the head with a hand held axe.

"What happened to you? I've been here all night waiting."

"My client hurt me. He was into the pain thing," she answered. Dane would one day find out that Lilly had been lying and that she'd been sitting in a shooting gallery getting high all night.

The warm air sailed about around them now.

"I have enough to buy you a point this morning," Dane said. "And we'll still have fifty bucks left over for groceries."

"You really love me, don't you?" Lilly said. Dane had never known what to read in the way that Lilly asked him that question.

"Let's go home," she said. "I wanna go home."

It was 7:25 a.m.

The suave-looking dope dealer who was shining a laser out the window of a parked car was J.P. He was thirty-seven years old, and dealing was the career that he had chosen. He sat poised, expressionless, aiming the red beam that resembled the laser sighting of a high-powered rifle at pedestrians as they walked by.

In seconds David Dane put in an appearance, crossing the street to meet his friend as two of Ontario Street's younger runners were taking exception to be targeted by the glowing red dot.

"I can't find Lilly," Dane said.

"Get in. We'll go look for her," he said.

J.P. pulled the car away from the curb, looking out of the window in the direction he was turning. He made eye contact with the lane and kept going. It was early evening and even though it was just past rush hour, traffic was not heavy.

Dane had met J.P. through Lilly. She bought coke from him when he was selling out of Nightlife bar.

"I saw her earlier," J.P. said. "Around three, maybe four."

"I just woke up. I haven't seen her since last night."

Valerie does the same fuckin' shit. All the time. I hate it," J.P. said.

Valerie was J.P.'s girlfriend. She had long brown hair and a hot figure. Valerie was also a prostitute and a drug addict. She had always done drugs but she started shooting only after one of her kids was tragically crushed to death in a horseback riding accident, leaving Valerie heartbroken. The accident was not her fault and Dane had told her that many times. Nonetheless she blamed herself and heroin was the end result.

"The other night I walked into the bathroom in our apartment and there was sperm floating around in the toilet. She didn't use a condom with the client," J.P. said.

"What do your initials stand for?" David Dane asked.

"Jean Pierre."

"Oh, fuck! Watch out!" Dane yelled, pointing at two pedestrians who were crossing the street at the crosswalk. "Are you high?" he asked alarmed.

"No. But I will be soon," J.P. said. "I have a quarter in the glove compartment."

"You're gonna do it now?" Dane asked. "Who's fucking car is this, anyway?"

"Client's."

"Whose client?"

"Mine," the dope dealer said, swerving to avoid another car. They were headed east on Ontario.

"You drive better on coke?"

"When I don't crash," J.P. said.

They passed The Stone Park and ran a set of lights.

"J.P.!" Nadia called from the street.

"Okay that we pick her up?" J.P. asked.

"I don't see why not."

J.P. pulled the brown Oldsmobile over to the curb and reached behind himself to open one of the rear doors.

"Hi," the cute blond said.

Dane knew Nadia, but not that well. He had met her one morning in the stone park.

"You have a cigarette, J.P.?" the girl in the tight dress asked.

"Valerie took my cigarettes," he responded. "I have to buy some."

"Where the fuck is Valerie"?? David Dane asked.

"J.P. shrugged lightly. "She's been gone since last night. Someone said she was with Junior."

"Aww . . . Christ," Dane reacted. "Have you seen him?"

"This morning."

"You say anything to him?" the Scotian asked.

J.P. shook his head.

"He shouldn't be around her," Dane said, pausing. "I can't stand that fucken sleaze bag".

"I can't do much about it," J.P. said.

Dane turned his head in J.P.'s direction. There was darkness at the windows now.

"I'll talk to Junior."

Junior, whose real name was Richard, was a crack slinger and lately he had become a little too friendly with J.P.'s woman. Dane could not understand it. J.P. was suave, he had good looks and charm, and Dane found him very likable and trustworthy. Junior was a piece of shit.

J.P. turned a corner and began driving uphill past a church and some houses. They were headed for the nearest convenience store that was about a mile north.

"J.P., what does J.P. stand for?" Nadia asked.

"Jean Pierre," replied both Dane and J.P. simultaneously.

"Can you loan me twenty bucks, J.P.?" Nadia asked, almost lamenting.

"I don't have a twenty," Jean Pierre said.

"Yes you do, J.P., c'mon. Please. Please! I wanna get high," she said.

"I only have a ten."

Dane was laughing now. He knew how persistent Nadia could be.

Soon they had stopped and Nadia was running around outside the car after J.P. who kept changing directions. Dane was laughing even harder now at the show that the two of them were un-wittingly putting on.

Soon they disappeared into the mini-mart together; J.P. in front followed by Nadia. Dane thought that Nadia would probably get herself arrested before they left the store.

In minutes J.P. and Nadia returned, J.P. tearing the cellophane off a package of smokes, the cover of which read Players Light King Size. Dane recognized the label. He had bought the same brand for Lilly many times in the past.

"I need a cigarette, J.P.," Nadia whined.

"Hold on," Jean Pierre said, fumbling around in his pocket for the keys.

Dane looked over at J.P. who was back behind the wheel now. He had found his keys and was beginning to start the car.

"C'mon, J.P., I need to smoke."

"Alright already," J.P. Said

"And give one to Dane. I like him," Nadia said, rubbing Dane's bald head from the back seat.

"That's okay, honey. I don't smoke," the ex-fighter said.

"He fucks, though," Nadia exclaimed.

"C'mon, J.P., I wanna smoke," she continued.

Finally he passed her a cigarette. It was already lit. The orange flame at the end of it was growing.

"I want to get high. Can you drive me back to work, J.P.?"

"Not right now. Dane and I have to go somewhere."

Dane had no idea what the fuck J.P. was talking about.

"Please, J.P.!"

"Alright, alright," the dealer said passively. "Fuck, she never quits."

J.P. drove eight blocks and dropped Nadia off on a side street. If she walked another half block, she would reach Ontario Street. It was just after dark and she would be able to catch quickly.

J.P. watched her go and then he pulled away from the curb, checking the lane as he went.

"You want coffee? Food?" he asked.

"No, I'm fine," Dane answered. They were back on Sherbrooke Street now.

"Can you fish that quarter out of the glove box for me?" Jean Pierre asked.

Dane opened the glove compartment door, retrieving the small bag of white powder.

"Here," he said, handing it to J.P.

"I have a clean one in there too."

Dane stuck his hand back in the glove box and came out with a wrapped needle that he handed to the driver of the car.

"You need water? There's an Evian in there."

"Yeah. Give it to me," J.P. said.

Dane obliged him and then slammed the glove compartment door shut. Reflections danced over the windows of the car. Jean Pierre held the steering wheel with one hand while he fumbled around with the other.

"We're gonna have to stop. I need both hands," the dealer said. "We'll stop at the stone park."

They drove over two more streets and made a left, turning down. The car passed a series of houses and the park behind The Black Domino Tavern before coming to a stop by the curb on Wolf Street. J.P. killed the engine.

"Okay," he said turning his attention to his drug and the tools that he would need to intake it.

J.P. placed the syringe plunger between his front teeth while he emptied part of the quarter of coke into the syringe with his right hand. He then placed the remainder of the quarter back in the glove compartment.

"Water," he said.

Dane unscrewed the cap on the Evian and held it as J.P. put the needle back together. He hoped that J.P. did not trip the way Lilly did, or they were both going to get killed tonight.

J.P. dipped the needle into the bottle of water and drew back on the plunger with the thumb of the hand that held the syringe, watching closely as the water mixed with the coke.

"There we go," he said, handing the bottle of Evian back to David Dane.

183

"Now, I just need a vein," Jean Pierre said, rolling up his left sleeve. He quickly found one and inserted the tip of the needle in his arm. Only a drop of blood came out. It did not fall on anything.

"Done," he said, pulling the point out. "Here. Put the cap back on this."

Dane took the small orange cap that J.P. handed him and pushed it onto the needle.

"What do you want me to do with it?" Dane asked, taking the syringe from between J.P.'s teeth.

"Glove compartment," the dope dealer said.

"Can you drive like that?" the Scotian questioned.

"I drive better like that. More alert," J.P. said, glancing over the back of his seat. This was not a side effect of the drug. This time he was actually checking for traffic.

"Where are the keys?" Jean Pierre wanted to know.

"Same place as the needle and the Evian."

J.P. leaned over and opened the glove compartment, retrieving his keys. They jingled for a minute before Jean Pierre found the right one and inserted it in the ignition.

"Let's go," he said, pulling out. There was no traffic on the rest of Wolf Street. The streets were dark and silent. Soon they were back on Sherbrooke Street headed in the opposite direction. J.P. did drive better on coke after all.

It was 10 p.m.

Later the same night, after J.P. had dropped him off, David Dane found Valerie and Junior sitting together on a bench outside of the Travel Lodge. They were in each others arms.

"Can't you find someplace else to sit? And maybe someone else to sit with?" Dane asked, his eyes fixed angrily on Junior.

"J.P. doesn't fuck me, so I take a man to fuck me," Valerie fired back.

"J.P. doesn't fuck you? I find that hard to believe."

"For sex, he's not my style," Valerie said.

"Fucking clown," Dane said, directing his comments at Junior.

"Are you her boyfriend?" Junior asked.

"No, and neither are you. If I catch you around Valerie again, you're gonna spit blood."

"I don't want fuckin' J.P.," Valerie yelled.

"Yeah . . . ." Dane said, walking away. "He just loves you, that's all."

"Shhhhhit," Valerie hissed, ending the conversation.

It was 10:29 p.m.

"I don't need a man telling me what to do!" Lilly yelled, slamming the bathroom door in David Dane's face.

"Hey, fuck you! If it wasn't for me, you'd be living in a shithole."

"Fuckin' motherfucker. I'm not coming back here, I'll go back to Mathieu."

"I'll put you in a fucking box!" Dane hollered, his foot connecting with the bathroom door.

"Put me in a fuckin' box? C'mon then! Put me in a fucken' box," Lilly shouted, throwing open the bathroom door and lunging at Dane who was eyeball to eyeball with her now.

"Fucking cunt. I'll fucking kick the living shit out of you," Dane said, shoving Lilly onto the floor.

"I'm not gonna let you do this for a living anymore!"

"It's what I was doing when you fucking met me mother fucker"!!!!!!! she screamed, raising a boot to connect with Danes inner thigh. "Fucking cocksucker!" she yelled.

Dane grabbed a handful of her hair and shoved her backward onto the floor.

"I'm never fucken' coming back here!"

"Get the fuck out, then!" Dane yelled." I don't need a whore for a girlfriend anyway"!!!!!!!!!!!!!!!!!!!!!!!!!

"No!"

"What?"

There were candles burning on the edge of the bathtub, their flames dancing, casting yellow shadows on the ceiling and all over the tiled bathroom.

"You want me to go? You want me to go? You can't even be alone, Fucking Bastard!" Lilly screamed, grabbing her makeup kit off the countertop in the kitchen and shoving it into her purse. She had been getting ready for work and now she was vexxed.

"I'll go," she said.

"If you go, you don't come back!" Dane warned.

"Fuck you!" Chicoine said, flipping him off. "Eat shit, BASTARD!"

"Why don't you show me how?" Dane said, calming down, tracing the edge of the dining room table with his fingertips as Lilly walked out and slammed the apartment door shut behind her.

"I love you," Dane said to the empty room. There were tears in his eyes.

It was 12:01 a.m.

Before dawn the next morning, David Dane crawled out of his bed and went to sit in his rocking chair.

His body was under emotional and psychological attack because of the outburst that he had had with Lilly the night before. The apartment was dead and silent around him. Still and quiet. Nothing moved, but inside Dane was a bundle of nervous energy. He felt bad now and he wanted Lilly to come home. He was starting to miss her. Last night's fight was worse than usual. He'd become so mad that he had gotten physical with her, and that was usually her schtick. At around eight a.m. there was a knock at the door. Dane lept from his chair, his heart racing. When he got to the door and opened it, Lilly was standing on the other side with her knapsack over her shoulder.

"I'm sorry," she said, stepping inside and wrapping her arms around him.

"I'm the one who should be sorry. I love you," Dane said, throwing his arms around her. "I love you." He repeated.

There was sadness in Dane's eyes and pain in his heart. No matter what she did for a living or how much they fought over it, he loved her with his whole heart.

It was 8:02 a.m.

The next night, around midnight, David Dane and Lilly Chicoine were standing in front of Nightlife. Just then, Angelica appeared out of nowhere and threw her arms around David Dane. There were racoon-like black circles around her eyes, and it seemed as if all of her weight, what little of it as there had been, was gone. She wore red slacks and a blue jacket over running shoes. This had been her way of saying farewell, because she would never see another daybreak. AIDS would claim beautiful Angelica's life before sunrise. She had given up hope and had stopped taking her medication. So, as I said at the start of this chapter, Angelica: this one's for you. God bless you, my Urban Angel. May you rest in peace.

Chapter 12

Bobby Troy Edmonds stepped out into the courtyard of his huge estate. It was six a.m. and the birds were beginning to chirp loudly on this tangerine morning, giving heightened sound to the calm breeze that blew about over the empty tennis courts and golfing area behind Edmonds' house.

Bobby was all alone on the front driveway, his pulse drumming in his head. He had just done a couple of lines of coke and now he was feeling the effects of it. Behind him stood three of his cars, a Jag, a Mercedes Benz and a Land Rover. The third of which he used more often than the other two, for its convenient storage space.

Last night he had killed another girl. No big deal—and there would be more to come. Still another and another, until he had finished what he had set out to do.

Helaina, Edmonds' housekeeper, had the morning off, so he and Carol were alone on the grounds. Carol, whose illness was in remission, was still sleeping soundly with the help of the battery of drugs that had been ordered by her Doctors.

Bobby, whose left hand was wrapped in a bandage from a cut that he'd received during last night's stabbing, walked to the rear of the Land Rover and retrieved a round leather bag that contained bloody clothing, a pair of gloves and the murder weapon: a standard, razor-sharp hunting knife. He took the bag along with its contents and tossed them into a steel garbage bin by the street. Today was garbage day, so Edmonds was not concerned about his things being detected. Still. He knew that there were those who would be looking for him. Not directly, but as an indirect result of his handy work. They would be fiercely investigating every lead and persuing it to its end.

After disposing of his wares. Bobby Edmonds took stock of his crecent shaped driveway and the house that lay beyond it. He was considering his options with respect to keeping un-wanted guests or intruders off of the property. Maybe he would install an electronic front gate with a buzz box that would be used to buzz the welcomed in. That idea pleased him. He would contact his Security Company about it by the end of the day.

It was 6:14 a.m.

A few minutes later, on the other side of the city, David Dane was walking past a convenience store on Ontario Street when he saw a blond girl wearing a red leather jacket and grey ski pants step out onto the sidewalk. She resembled a young Michelle Pfeiffer, David Dane observed. She had light colored hair and aqua-blue eyes that were accentuated by high cheekbones and pale skin. Her soft demeanor only added to her beauty.

"You look a little familiar," she said. "Aren't you Lilly's friend?"

"Without a doubt," Dane said.

"How come you're out here so early?"

"That very reason," he said in response.

"Do you have a name?" she asked.

"David Dane" he said. "What's yours?"

"Jenny," she said, extending her long white fingers. "Pleased to meet you."

Likewise.

So you don't use, eh?" There was a pause. "Some of the dealers think you're a narc because you never buy anything."

Dane regarded her for a moment. He had heard this rumor before, and now, even as high stakes as it was, it didn't bother him any.

"So, you take care of Lilly? That's awesome. I wish that I had someone to take care of me like that," Jenny said.

"It's rough stuff. It's not exactly twenty-four hours of entertainment," he said.

"But you do it?"

"I'm afraid so," Dane said, a panel of orange light from the rising sun falling across his face.

"Would you do it all over again?"

"If I had insurance,"

"Insurance?" Jenny looked puzzled.

"From her fucking dealers. Whatever I pay out for her dope when she's too sick to go to work."

Jenny rocked gently on her feet. She looked amused.

I don't think that they issue policies for that," she said.

"No, eh?" he asked, glancing over his shoulder at the empty street, a slow breeze blowing around debris. The window pane across the street that looked onto a fast-food establishment was glazed in orange from the sun's early birth. The sign on the door read Closed in bold white lettering.

"Fuck, I wanna get high," Jenny exclaimed. "I'm not a pro, though. I don't do that."

"It's an expensive habit. You don't sell yourself"?? Dane asked.

"I flirt with men when they stop their cars. It's easy."

"Watch," Jenny said, walking over to a car with a male driver that had stopped at the lights by the Travel Lodge. She leaned into the open window for a moment, speaking to the middle-aged driver. She was smiling. In seconds the light changed and Jenny had a five dollar bill in her hand.

"Pretty good, huh?" she asked, walking back toward Dane who was waiting on the sidewalk in front of a tattoo parlor that stood adjacent to the convenience store from which Jenny had originally appeared.

"What did you say to him?"

"I hustled him."

"How"?? Dane questioned, looking for a more elaborate explanation.

"I made him cum."

"You never touched him."

"I don't have to," she paused. "Look into my eyes."

Silence, and the whispering wind between them now.

It was 6:42 a.m.

The next morning at sun-up, Lilly Chicoine walked to the corner of Wolf and Ontario Street to find David Dane standing on the sidewalk in front of the stone park. She wore a gray and blue striped sweater with long sleeves over blue jeans and white runners. It was warm out, but not so warm that one would want to wear shorts or a t-shirt to ventilate the heat. The early morning blaze, as though still contained, was just beginning to peak above the black horizon.

"Fancy meeting you here," she said.

"Likewise," Dane responded calmly.

"Have you been out here all night?" Lilly asked.

"The better part of it, if there is one."

"Fuck. I can't wait for smack to open. I'm starting to get sick."

A blade of darkness crossed Lilly's face.

"I want to make a little money before they open," she said.

"It's quiet. You can't make money from pavement."

"Yeah, no shit," she said.

"Where were you all night?" he asked.

"I wasn't around." This was a standard Lilly answer. Dane had heard it about a thousand times.

"Being out here with you, is special sometimes. Even considering the circumstances," he said.

"Yeah, well . . . . I'm getting sick. That's not special."

"Are you hungry? I could grab us some breakfast," he offered.

"I'm never hungry when I'm sick. You know that".

"Rain check," she said.

"I think I'm gonna try to work," Lilly said, distancing herself from him by a few feet.

"I love you Baby Bunny." Dane said.

It was 6:05 a.m.

Later that night, around eleven thirty, David Dane and Lilly Chicoine fell asleep in front of the glow of the television set. They had been watching a movie called Session Nine. Now its menu screen was playing a sinister droning hum over and over again as it waited for a command to be shut off. About an hour later, when David Dane awoke on the mattress that had been placed on the floor, he turned around expecting to find Lilly on the same place on the couch where she had been. She was not. She was gone.

Dane's stomach was suddenly flooded with butterflies and his pulse, now racing out of panic, was pounding between his ears. He stood up, eyes still unfocused, full of cobwebs and dreams.

Lilly?" he called out.

No response.

"Oh fucking Jesus!" Dane swore, his vision darting to the balcony door that stood open onto the cool night air and the abyss of darkness below.

Had she fallen off the balcony in her drugged-out state? Oh God. He was afraid to go out there and find out.

"Lilly?" he hollered. If she had been in the bathroom or the bedroom she would have already called out to him. He stuck his head around the corner. His suspicions were confirmed. She was not there. Not in either of those places. He walked out onto the balcony, daring himself to peer over the iron railing. He pushed himself to look. She was not down below. His pulse relaxed. No cops. No police tape. No crowd of curious onlookers. Just the calm breeze sailing through the darkly shining treetops that swished and rattled in the night winds below.

So, where the fuck was she, then?

Dane went to the door that, in his state of mind, he had not noticed had been left unlocked, likely by Lilly on her way out. She didn't have a key, which was necessary to lock the door from the outside. He looked around for a moment, eyes in search of his shoes. There they were. There was no dressing to be done because Dane had fallen asleep wearing clothes. He had been overtired and just passed out. He sat on the edge of the leather sofa, pulled on his black Nikes and hurried out the door into the bright hallway. At the elevators, Dane pushed the bottom button and waited for the lift to rise to his floor. In moments the elevator arrived and Dane stepped inside.

On the first floor, Dane got out and walked through the big glass doors that led onto the night outside. Where the fuck was Lilly? Chances were that she had gone down to Ontario Street to get high but, just in case, he would try Santino Video first to see if she had gone in there to bum a smoke off one of the night staff. She had never done it before, but there was a first time for everything.

Dane walked half a block and stopped at the lights, across from which stood a gas station that wreaked of fuel, its fumes enveloping the night air.

When the light turned green he crossed the street, walking across the drive-up of the service station before coming to the front door of his friend's establishment. Locked after dark. Nick, one of Dane's close friends, was working behind the counter inside. He let Dane in.

"Nicky!" Dane called out as he came through the door.

"What's up Dane?" the short brown-haired Rhodes scholar with the glasses asked.

"Have you seen Lilly?"

"No, man. She doesn't come in here. Why?"

"She disappeared while I was sleeping." Dane's eyes were shooting around like a man possessed.

Nick fucking hated Lilly. She was always doing rotten things to Dane and he knew that Dane didn't deserve it.

"Did you check Ontario Street?"

"Not yet. Call me a cab."

Nick picked up the phone and did just that. Its ETA was about five minutes at this hour. When the silhouette of the cab appeared at the curb, Dane bid farewell to Nick and headed out the door.

"Where to?" the driver asked as Dane shuffled into the back seat of the car for hire.

"Ontario Street."

"No address?"

"Any corner will do."

As soon as the cab's wheels were in motion, Dane began to wonder where exactly he might find Lilly. It would be silent on Ontario Street at this hour. Not much traffic. Maybe he would tell the cabbie to let him off on Wolf in front of the stone park. Lilly had spent a lot of time working that area lately, so much so that Wolf and Mont Calm was where he usually found her.

When they arrived at their destination. Dane paid the driver and stepped out into the warm night air. In the distance a traffic light flashed in and out of the darkness like an instrument of hypnosis. Night's ambiance at play, Dane thought.

"Thanks," Dane said, slamming the cab's back door as he looked around. He took two steps away from the curb and headed west on Ontario toward Saint-Hubert Street that was three blocks away. When Dane came to St. Hubert and Ontario, he made a sharp left and began walking down the desolate street toward Cactus. The needle exchange would be in full swing at this hour. Lots of traffic going in and out. Maybe someone had seen Lilly. When he reached Cactus, Dane pulled the glass door open by the handle, stepping inside with the golden brown light that seemed to be powered by a dreamlike fusion. Down three stairs to his right was a desk, a couch, two well-hooded desk lamps and a counselor sitting at the far end of the room in a chair.

"How you doin?" Dane greeted the young hippy social worker with the frizzy hair.

"I'm fine. What can I do for you?" the young man asked.

"I'm looking for my girlfriend."

"I'm sorry, we can't give out any information. We're bound by confidentiality."

"I understand that, but this is an emergency."

"What kind of emergency?"

"My girlfriend is missing. He name is Lilly. She comes in here a lot," Dane said frantically.

"For how long has she been missing? Not that it would make a difference. We still can't . . ."

"About an hour. She . . . we were sleeping, and when I woke up she was gone."

"So she's missing from your house?"

"Yeah. Yes, but she left behind an entire pack of cigarettes, which Lilly wouldn't have done, plus a half-point of smack. It's not done. Ever. At least not by her." Dane had noticed these things on his way out of their apartment. "I've never known Lilly to go anywhere without her cigarettes," he said. "She's a goddamn nicotine fiend."

"Does she have a councilor here? Someone she sees?"

"Yeah. Yes. His name's Nick."

"What's your friend's last name?"

197

"Chicoine. Lilly Chicoine."

"Okay, just hold on."

The guy with the frizzy hair disappeared behind a door for a moment. Dane heard the hollow rolling of a filing cabinet being opened and then closed.

"Okay," he said, returning with a file folder with Lilly's first and last name at the top. "She hasn't been in here for about a month. Nick's away. She's seeing Serge now and he's not here."

"Fuck". Dane said under his breath.

"I understand your frustration," the councilor said. "I could call Serge at home."

"No. No, that's not gonna do any good."

"I can leave a message for her if you want."

Dane shook his head more out of exasperation than refusal.

"Just tell her that her boyfriend's looking for her."

"Your name?"

"I'm David Dane."

After exiting the needle exchange, Dane went back to Ontario Street to begin his search. He started by walking five blocks east to Papineau where he ran into Barbie. She was blond-haired, busty and beautiful. She lived up to her name, and Dane would come to find out over the next few minutes that beneath that beauty was a heart of gold.

"Hey, what's wrong?" she began sweetly, recognizing the emotion in his eyes.

"Lilly took off while I was sleeping."

"Christ. She should know better than that," Barbie said sympathetically. "I saw her walking out here about five minutes ago."

Dane loved Barbie. She was awesome, both physically and in her personality.

"Look. There she is," the thirty-something blond said, pointing across the street.

Lilly, who was with someone, had seen Dane and Barbie right away.

"Hey, yo!" the boxer called out.

Lilly and the guy she was with were coming toward them now. Her friend, who looked to be a bit on the effeminate side, was around twenty. Dane did not balk at his presence.

"I'm sorry . . ." Lilly began. Barbie had already disappeared into a row of nearby condos that were comprised of brown brick and siding.

"I woke up and you were gone. You scared the shit out of me," said Dane.

"Lilly appeared to be taken aback. "I figured that the door slamming shut would be it."

"At one point I thought that you had met your end at the bottom of the balcony."

"I'm sorry."

"Next time, wake me first or leave a note," Dane said dismissively. "Who's your friend?"

"Oh. This is Roger. He's gay."

"I'm gonna leave now," Roger said uncomfortably.

"No. Hey, that's fine," David Dane said genuinely.

"I have to go anyway," Roger said, walking away. "See you later."

"Bye," Lilly responded, knowing that the farewell was intended for her.

"So, what are you up to now?" Dane asked of her plans.

"I'm gonna do coke," she answered. "And you?"

"I'll hang out with you for a while."

"Okay," she chirped. "I have a quarter on me. I wanna do it."

"Where?" Dane asked, knowing that it would require privacy.

"Let's walk," Lilly suggested.

About two blocks and one side street over, Lilly stopped.

"I think I'm gonna do it here," she said drawing the necessary evils from her bag.

Dane looked around to make sure that no one was coming. Somewhere nearby a light went on behind a window.

"Bad locale. I think we should move". Dane said.

Lilly looked up from what she was doing.

"No, wait," Dane halted. The brief illumination had disappeared. "Go ahead."

Lilly had her left sleeve rolled up above her arm which was bleeding now. Dane fucking hated having to watch this. It gave him nightmares. She was dragging her hair out by the roots now, and there was blood all over her face and down her arms. The Devil's wickedness in technicolor.

The light returned behind the window.

"Baby, we gotta go," David Dane said.

Either she was not paying any attention to him or she did not hear him. One or the other.

"Lilly!" he whisper-yelled.

She responded by picking up her stuff and moving around the corner of the building.

"We should move further away," he said.

Lilly paused and then kept walking. Dane halted her and kissed her softly on the cheek.

"I love you so much," he said.

She gave him a quiet smile.

"Here," Lilly said, stopping in front of a series of parked cars, their shiny paint reflecting in the nocturnal shadow. She drew her needle and again found a vein.

"Lilly," Dane called. He had noticed that someone was watching them.

"Fuck!" Lilly said, scrambling to put her things away.

"Who's there"?? Dane called out to the shadow, his words echoing as if from a dream. He was trying to look above the shroud of darkness that was covering the man's face but he couldn't make out the features of the looming specter.

"I don't know who the fuck that is, but he's watching us." Lilly responded.

In seconds, the shape moved back underneath the curtain of night and vanished.

It was 2:47 a.m.

The next morning, after Dane and Lilly had been out all night, they were walking uphill toward Sherbrooke Street when a police cruiser pulled up before them. The black and white carried two male officers. The first to get out was the driver, followed by his partner.

"Lilly Chicoine. We have a warrant for your arrest. You have the right to remain silent . . . ." the elder of the two officers said while the other of the two hooked Lilly up and loaded her into the back of the police vehicle. Lilly looked pissed, Dane thought.

"What are you charging me with?" Lilly demanded.

"Breach of conditions. You're not supposed to be in this area," the younger of the two cops responded before closing the door behind her.

"Where are you gonna take her?" Dane asked them.

"Tonight she'll got to the station and tomorrow she'll go to court," the elder officer said.

In a way Dane was relieved. Lilly would be off the street and out of harm's way. She had been lucky up until this point. The killer hadn't come upon her, or Lilly hadn't come upon the killer. Either way, she had been lucky.

It was 9:21 a.m.

* * *

"This is the operator. You have a collect call from . . . 'Lilly!," the recorded voice said. "You may press one now to accept the charges, or answer the following questions with only yes or no. Will you accept the charges?"

"Yes," David Dane responded.

"Thank you. Please go ahead."

"Fuck, I'm sick!" Lilly said, coughing into the phone.

"Yeah, I know."

"Are you coming to court tomorrow?"

"Yeah, I'll be there."

"Are you gonna bring me money for canteen when I go to jail?"

"Canteen?" Dane asked. He had never heard the word associated with prison before.

"It's once a week. It's every Wednesday, but you have to bring the money on Tuesday night or it won't go through."

"What are they selling?"

"Toothbrush, toothpaste, soap, chocolate bars, Pepsi, Coke, cigarettes, yadda yadda yadda."

"And how much is all this gonna cost?"

"I don't know yet. I'll call you when I get there."

"Are you still at the police station?"

"I'm here until tomorrow," she said.

"Okay, I guess I'll see you in court."

"Okay. I think I'm gonna take a nap on the fucking bench," Lilly fumed.

"What? You don't have a bed?"

"Nope. There's one toilet, one sink, one phone, and a bench, and it sucks," she said.

"Holy shit." Dane said, feeling sorry for her.

"I'm gonna go now. I'm fed up."

"Lilly?"

"What?"

"I love you," Dane said.

It was 1:04 p.m.

The next afternoon David Dane sat on a bench in a courtroom at the municipal courthouse. It was around three p.m., and court had already been in session for five hours. The judge, who was currently busy with another detainee, would later on preside over Lilly's case. Right now there was a man with long shaggy hair standing before Judge Aaron Milo in handcuffs as he gave testimony about an assault that he had committed earlier on in the week.

In moments his trial was over and the police officers on court duty that day escorted him back behind closed doors to take a seat with the other detainees. Soon there was another and then another brought in to stand before the white-haired judge. Finally, around five p.m., just before the court was scheduled to close, a familiar face came wobbling in wearing handcuffs. It was Lilly Chicoine. Her lawyer, whose name was Philip, approached her quietly and spoke in whispers. Dane could not make out their conversation.

"Mister Laroche, how does your client plead?" the judge asked.

"Guilty, your honor."

"Alright. Miss Chicoine is sentenced to two weeks at the women's correctional facility."

"Thank you, your honor," Philip said.

Philip Laroche, who had a tempered, suave look about him, would one day come to be a respected aquaintence of David Dane's, both due to his professionalism and his loyalty, not to mention his consistently compassionate nature toward Lilly and her plight. His attitude and demeanor had impressed David Dane right from the start. He was a stand-up guy. He was also a mans man having competed as a mixed martial artist in his free hours away from the court room.

"Court is adjourned," Judge Milo said.

Outside in the hallway, David Dane and Philip Laroche came together for a short conference.

"So, she'll get two weeks. She's lucky that the judge didn't give her a stiffer sentence. With her record, she could have gotten at least two months," Laroche said.

"Has Lilly done time for this before?" Dane asked.

"Oh yeah. And then some."

"Thank you," Dane said, extending his hand.

"Don't mention it. I'm glad I could help". Laroche said closing the handshake.

It was 5:09 p.m.

"You may press one to accept the charges . . ."

There was a momentary bleep on the line as Dane responded to the automated operator in the affirmative.

"Thank you. Please go ahead."

"Hey baby," Lilly said.

"Where are you?"

"We just got back from court half an hour ago."

"Are there many girls in your block?" Dane inquired. He could hear a lot of noise in the background.

"Yeah. It's full. There are even girls sleeping in the gymnasium."

"Can I come and visit you while you're there?"

"I'll put my paper in tomorrow morning for the window visit," she said. "You have to have two window visits before they'll let you have a contact visit. It's called a conjugal."

"Yeah, I know."

"Hey listen. Can you bring me some money for canteen?"

Dane paused. "How much do you need?"

"Forty or fifty, for my first one, and thirty-five for my second."

"Okay," Dane responded. This would come to be the beginning of a long and expensive habit.

"Alright, listen. I gotta go. Someone else needs the phone. So you're coming to bring me money when?"

"When can I come for the visit?"

"Maybe Sunday night."

"Then that's when I'll bring your money."

"Okay."

"I love you, Lilly."

"You too," she said.

"Bye," he responded.

It was 8:45 p.m.

When Sunday night came, David Dane had butterflies in the pit of his stomach. He had traveled twenty-two metro stops and walked a mile to come and see Lilly Chicoine. At the foot of the prison's circular driveway, Dane paused for a moment, fishing into the pocket of his blue jeans to make sure that he had Lilly's forty bucks plus two pieces of ID. After confirming that he did, Dane approached the steel door at the front of the fenced-off building and rang the buzzer. In seconds someone permitted him entry via the electronic device.

"Thank you," Dane said to the butch-looking female who was sitting behind a plexiglass window. She was surrounded by live monitors that detailed the building's perimeter from inside to out.

"Please take off your jacket and place it in a locker. Then remove your keys and loose change and put that in as well."

"No problem," Dane said, following her instructions.

A small bank of lockers stood against the wall to Dane's back. He chose number fourteen, removing his leather jacket followed by the silver at the bottom of this pockets. The key to the locker's padlock was already provided, along with a plastic tag with the number fourteen on it.

"Now what?" Dane asked, squeezing the lock shut and removing the key.

"Go upstairs and pass through the metal detector."

Dane walked up two short flights of steps until he found himself standing in an alcove facing an airport-style metal detector.

"Can I see your ID?" the heavy-set male behind the window to Dane's left requested. His name tag read "Stephan."

"No problem," Dane said, slipping the "screw" his medical card along with a copy of his birth certificate through the opening in the glass. "Oh and I have forty bucks for Lilly's canteen," he added, giving the big man two twenties.

"What is the name of your friend?" Stephan asked.

"Lilly Chicoine."

"Okay," the screw said, stapling the twenties to an envelope.

"Just pass through the metal detector," Stephan said, guiding Dane toward the device with his eyes.

Dane walked through the rectangular magnet. It made no sound. He waited for a moment now, staring into the room across from him. There was a long window with plastic chairs on either side. Soon there was the sound of a door being buzzed open and then Lilly walked in, she was waving. Dane's heart was racing now. Finally they buzzed him in too. Now he was walking toward her.

"Hey baby bunny," Dane said, taking a seat.

Lilly pressed her palm against the glass window. "Did you bring me my forty bucks?"

"Yeah," Dane responded uncomfortably.

"Good. So, how are you?"

There was something in Lilly's eyes. Something strange.

"I'm good. How about you?" he asked, not letting her see his reaction to the presence in her eyes.

"Not bad. Fuck, I'm sick of being in here and I've only been here a couple of days." Lilly's eyes were smouldering.

"Listen, do you think that you could do me a favor?" Lilly asked.

Dane thought that Lilly looked positively evil.

"What favor?" he asked, not letting his reaction come across in his voice either.

"Umm . . ." she was moving closer to the window now, so as not to be heard. "Do you think that you could smuggle in two new ones and a point of smack when you come for the conjugal?"

Dane thought that Lilly was crazy. Was she out of her fucking mind?

"Have you seen the metal detectors on the way in here?" he asked.

"Yeah, I know, but if you tape up the syringes, the machine won't go off."

Apparently Lilly was delusional, too. Either that or she didn't give a fuck if he got caught.

"So you won't do it, then?" she asked, as if threatening to boycott the remainder of their visit if Dane did not comply with her demands.

"Lilly, are you aware that if I got caught, I could go to jail?"

"Yeah, but that's just it. You won't get caught," she said.

Dane was beginning to contemplate the possibility that Lilly might have brain damage.

"Look, are you gonna do it or not?" she lamented.

"Absolutely not," he said, staring into her face.

"Then fuck off, then," Lilly said, knocking over the chair that she had been sitting on.

"Visit's over," Lilly called out to one of the screws as she walked away from her boyfriend and disappeared into the corridor. Dane heard a door being buzzed open and then Lilly was gone just like that.
Danes heart was doing leap frogs and his eyes were red and tearful. He had never felt as hurt or betrayed before in his life.

It was 7:10 p.m.

Two hours later, when David Dane reached the door to his apartment the phone was ringing on the other side. He quickly unlocked it and ran inside to answer the phone. Lilly was on the other end. Her tone began as apologetic.

"I'm sorry," she began.

"Yeah," Dane responded, nonplussed. "Why would you . . . ?"

"Because I'm not feeling well in here. I'm sick and there's a girl in here who wants me to have something brought in."

"So fucking what. You're willing to watch me go to jail for that?"

"Yeah, but you wouldn't get caught," Lilly whined.

"I can't believe this," he said. "You need to develop some common sense. Some fucking jacked-up bitch tells you to get your boyfriend to mule shit in there and you tell her that it's no problem? Are you torched in the head?"

"No . . . You won't get caught."

"Won't?"

"So you're really not gonna do it?" she asked angrily.

He felt like twisting her fucking head off. "Have you heard a fucking syllable that's come out of my mouth?"

"You're making me look bad in here!" she yelled.

Dane wondered what Lilly's IQ was. Dane had met horses . . .

"How about a dime bag?"

"What the fuck is a dime bag?" he asked, more out of curiosity than anything else.

"It's a ten-dollar bag of weed."

"Are you listening to yourself?" Dane was moving around the room with the phone in his hand now. The cord was dragging not far behind. "You're talking about me mueling dope into a prison like it was some Oreo cookies, and you're . . . ."

"People do it all the time. One of the girls in here had her mother do it the other day."

Dane couldn't believe what he was hearing. Where did Lilly think she'd be if he went to jail?

"So, are you gonna do it or not?" she demanded.

"Holy fuckin' Christ. Are you hard of fuckin' hearing, Chicoine? NO!!!"

And with that she hung up.

The following morning at nine a.m., Lilly was back on the phone again with the same demands. Only this time the demands were accompanied by extravagant threats. If Dane refused to smuggle in dope, she would not give him her release date. If Dane did not smuggle in dope, she would find a new man. If Dane did not smuggle in dope, yadda yadda yadda. The conversation ended with Dane hanging up the phone.

The next day, Dane made the mistake of a lifetime. He showed up for the visit anyway. In later years Dane would kick himself for this decision and, in retrospect, ask himself how he could have been so stupid.

As soon as he was buzzed through the front door to the prison, Dane was ordered to remove his jacket, his belt, and any money or change that he might have and leave it inside of a numbered locker. Following that, because of the scheduling of his visit, he ended up sitting around for a half hour eating a stale Twix bar that he had bought from a vending machine on the main floor to the left of the stairs. It tasted like shit.

When the time finally came for the conjugal, Dane walked up two flights of steps and through the airport-style metal detector. It did not sound. At the window, Dane left forty dollars for Lilly's weekly canteen that she had requested.

Inside the visiting room there was a series of haphazardly arranged chairs. Shortly after Dane's entrance to the room, Lilly made her appearance, wearing a green jogging suit and white running shoes that were standard issue for most female prisoner across the country.

"Did you bring it?" Lilly asked loudly enough for the attending guard to overhear her. Dane shot a glance at her, as if to ask if she were fucking nuts. "Well?"

"I thought we already talked about this." he said.

"Then why did you fucking come, then?" Lilly demanded spitefully.

"I came to see you," Dane responded.

"Visit's over," Lilly said, waving him off. She then disappeared through the door from which she had come. Again leaving him crushed.

"She's nice, eh?" the female screw commented in a sarcastic tone of voice.

"Yeah," Dane responded under his breath as emotion welled up inside of him.

It always hurt him when Lilly acted like this. There was no one on earth that he loved more. Why did she have to be so void and callous?

"She wanted extra money," Dane explained to the screw who stood opposite him.

On the street ten minutes later, he wondered if Lilly would call him back at all, seeing that she didn't get what she wanted. Of all the girlfriends in the world, he had to get one who acted like this. If it wasn't for bad luck, David Dane would have no luck at all. Now, finally, his luck had become exponentially worse.

Along the way to the metro, Dane stopped and grabbed an ice-cream. Across the way there were two little kids with their parents, the father piggy-backing one of them on his shoulders. Dane wondered if he would ever be in the same position. At least to have a normal life. He could be happy as long as somebody genuinely loved him. Beyond that he needed nothing extravagant at all. Maybe to an outsider that sounded corny, but it was the truth.

On the morning that Lilly got out of jail, David Dane was waiting for her at the main doors. The trade-off, which shouldn't have existed in the first place, was that he bring her a quarter of coke and a hit of smack so that she wouldn't have to go to work right away. However the quarter of coke was likely to lead her back downtown faster that the point of smack would, because it was a stimulant and therefore would make her want to keep going.

But that night, Dane and Lilly sat in the shadow of their apartment for hours watching DVDs of their favorite horror series, Halloween. They made out for awhile before falling asleep in front of the TV which continued to produce images of Michael Myers, Dr. Loomis, and Laurie Strode long after the two lovers were zonked out.

Dane had been a Halloween fan from the time when he was six or seven years old due to the fact that when VHS and Beta first came out, his mother had accidentally brought home Halloween II, only looking at the title. Marilyn Dane had mistaken the infamous horror film for a children's movie and brought it home for Dane to view. Man, how his eyes had popped out of his head when he viewed the images put before him. The soundtrack and legendary score by Halloween mastermind John Carpenter had immediately gotten his attention and he'd been hooked ever since. Halloween, was also Lilly's favorite film.

Chapter 13

Raindrops exploded against the earth on Ontario Street. It was late on a Friday afternoon and a terrible storm had overtaken the inner city, leaving its parks and its gutters overflowing with water.

David Dane and Lilly Chicoine stood on the corner of the stone park holding each other tightly as if they were the last two living organisms on a forbidden planet. No one else seemed to be outside as the treetops dripped with silver and the branches blew about in a high current. The storm had begun in the morning with its engines kicking into full gear as the hour grew later. The day had become dark and shadowy, its lack of light giving the porthole windows of the The Black Domino Tavern across the street a sinister ambiance. Few vehicles made their way through the sea of water that flowed in waves down the street at this hour except for one bus and the odd black-and-white that had been sent out to patrol the area. The occupants of the black-and-whites keeping vigil behind their windshields.

"I can't believe this," Lilly said. "It's freezing cold. It's fucking raining, and here we are."

"When is your fucking dealer supposed to get here?" Dane asked, squinting hard as the rain rolled off his forehead.

"What time is it?"

Two forty-five," Dane answered, glancing at the digital read-out on his watch.

"He was supposed to be here fifteen minutes ago."

Just then a pretty blond girl and her boyfriend appeared out of nowhere. They looked to be no more than twenty-one. The girl was dragging her boyfriend along by the arm.

"We can't call them. We already owe them money," the female was saying to him. There was tension and desperation in her tone.

Their conversation turned David Dane around. They now had his full attention, being the only other people on the street. A car hydroplaned and then drove off.

"Can you get something for us? Please? We're both sick and we owe money. I have twenty dollars but no one will serve us," the girl pleaded. She was addressing Dane, who was listening.

"How much do you owe," Lilly asked curiously.

"Seven hundred," the girl said.

Lilly puckered her lips as if she was about to whistle. "They'll kill you for that," she announced. "If you want me to get something for you, it's gonna cost you. How much are you willing to pay me for the service?"

"Jesus, Lilly. Give them a break. They're already in over their heads," Dane said.

"So what? Why should I care?" This was the heartless side of Lilly that Dane hated.

"Please. We're really sick," the girl begged.

"She's not gonna fucken help us Shannon," they guy said.

"Give me your twenty," Dane said.

"You'll help us?" Shannon asked.

Lilly looked pissed now.

"Why not?" Dane said.

"You're not gonna F-off with our money, are you?" Shannon asked.

"He doesn't use," Lilly proclaimed.

Shannon reached into the pocket of her skin-tight jeans, the legs of which were covered with sequins, and retrieved a twenty dollar bill. "Here," she said, turning it over to the boxer.

"Shannon and . . . ?" Dane asked, waiting for an introduction.

"Mike," he responded to Dane, "and you are?"

"Not too happy to be out here, you know," said Dane sarcastically.

"No seriously,"

"My name's David Dane. This is Lilly," he said in a voice that was both deep and flat.

"You don't use? For real?" the blond kid asked. He looked impressed.

"Absolutely."

"Do you mind if I ask why not?"

"Because I was an athlete."

"What kind of athlete?"

"I was a fighter and I did some bodybuilding too."

"Wow. That's fucking cool."

"Yeah," Dane answered modestly.

"Here he comes," Lilly said. Looking down the street.

"It's Max," Dane said.

"Ohhhh, fuck! Don't stand here," Lilly said to Mike and Shannon. "If they see you, they might not serve us."

Shannon eyed Dane nervously, praying that he wouldn't steal her money.

Dane gave Max Shannon's twenty as the younger couple disappeared around the corner. Max put a half-point of smack in Dane's hand. Lilly then paid Max thirty in tens and got a point.

"Okay!" Dane called into the air after Max was gone.

Mike and Shannon reappeared and Dane gave them the half-point.

"Thank you, honey," Shannon said.

"C'mon, let's go. I wanna do this," Lilly said, in a hurry.

"Alright," Dane said, squeezing Mike's hand. "Hey, nice meeting you guys," he said.

"Let's go," Lilly said.

It was 2:59 p.m.

Later on during the same afternoon, in the shadows of the rain, David Dane and Jenny walked down Ontario Street in the direction of Frontenac Metro Station. Jenny wore a red leather jacket over gray ski pants that fit her ass like a mold in the shape of a heart.

"You like these pants, don't you?" Jenny asked, licking off the end of a plastic spoon as she turned to smile at Dane who was walking just behind her.

"Well, I don't hate 'em," he said, gently scratching his left temple with his first finger as his head rolled to one side. He was wearing black cut gloves, a black leather jacket, blue jeans and a black Nike sweatshirt.

"I thought you'd like these," Jenny said in a luscious voice.

"Have you seen Lilly anywhere around here over the past hour?"

"I saw her at Guardian earlier," she answered

Lilly had gone to work after doing her point and had not yet returned.

"Because I haven't . . . ." But before Dane could finish his sentence, Lilly appeared out of nowhere carrying a schoolbag over her shoulder. She wore a plaid, maroon shirt over skin-tight blue jeans that hugged her sexy curves from the waist on down. Dane thought that Lilly looked beautiful. She was walking toward them, eyes turned toward the ground.

"Hey Baby Bunny". Dane greeted.

"I wanna get high," she said. "I need to make some money. Fuck, it's not gonna be easy. There's no traffic and it's raining," Chicoine said. "I'll be standing out here for hours."

There was a swishing sound as a red Camaro drove past them, its tires cutting ditches in the rainwater. Jenny stood by, listening to them talk

"You want me to wait while you work?" David asked.

Lilly looked around, squinting hard. "I want you to do whatever you wanna do," she said.

"I don't mind waiting, he said

"I'm gonna take off," Jenny said, looking in Dane's direction.

"I'll see you later," Dane responded humbly.

"We have to wait for Angel," Lilly said. "She went to use the washroom in the McDonald's. She'll be out in a minute."

Angel, who was a friend of Lilly's, was nearing her forties and Lilly had once stolen her boyfriend. Dane remembered the name of the guy, too: Francois. Dane, in his heart, believed that Angel still harbored resentment over the issue, and probably rightfully so. It hurt to have your best friend steal your lover. He had been there once many years ago himself.

At that moment, Angel appeared from around the corner. Dane thought that she looked a little weather beaten, with her brown-blond hair stuck to the top of her head from the rainwater.

"Hey!" she said, greeting Dane before going to join Lilly who was several feet away.

"I have a half," Angel said. "Carl fronted it to me. I'll spit with you if you have ten bucks."

"I'd prefer coke right now 'cause I need to wake up, but alright."

Money? She didn't have any money.

"Dane, can you pass me ten bucks?" Lilly asked, turning to look back a few feet.

"Alright," he said, going after what he had in his pocket. He fished out a ten and gave it to her.

"Thank you, baby," Lilly said before pecking him on the cheek.

"Here," she said, passing the ten to Angel. "Where can we go to do this?"

"I know a place a couple of blocks down. It's across from La Fleur. Angel responded

"Then let's go," Lilly agreed.

"You want me to carry your bag?" Dane asked Lilly. She paused for a moment, looking at him. "Here. You got the job," she said, loading her schoolbag onto his shoulder.

Angel gave Lilly a disapproving look. She did not appreciate Lilly's attitude toward Dane sometimes.

The three of them walked about three and a half blocks before stopping under the badly chipped overhang of an elementary school.

"Hey, there's kids around here, Lilly," Dane said. "You guys can find someplace better than this."

Lilly was now squatting down with her sleeve rolled up. "Don't worry, we'll clean up after ourselves," she said.

Danes puppy-dog eyes went in one direction and then the other before stopping on Lilly. He did not like the idea of them doing their hit on the grounds of a grade school.

The rain was pitter-pattering above their heads now, then running off the roof and splashing onto the ground. Lilly poured the remainder of Angel's half-point into her syringe.

"Fuck! Where's my water," Lilly demanded. "It's in my bag. Give it to me," Lilly ordered, having answered her own question.

Dane dropped the bag on the cement next to her. Lilly opened the zipper and then went fumbling around inside. Soon enough she pulled loose a small portion of water that was contained in a clear plastic tube with measurements on it.

"Here we go," she said, mixing the liquid with her drug. "Just about ready," she said, shaking up the contents of the needle as she held down the plunger with her first finger. Lilly looked around for a moment to make certain that no one was coming before finding a vein and puncturing it with her needle. As the drugs began to work on her, Lilly's eyes began to close, her body feeling the effects of the heroin. "Mmmmm, that's better," she said in a warm and fuzzy voice. "That's fucking Heaven."

It was 4:00 p.m.

221

Light and fog on Ontario Street.

Dane and Jenny walked down a short ramp and through an open doorway that led into the bowels of Notre Dame Hospital. Outside, night had fallen. It was past the witching hour and the streets stood empty and dark. Smoke rose from smoke stacks of an unknown origin and sailed into the Devil's sky over Ontario Street. Vapor lamps fought to maintain their glow against the inky blackness of the seemingly endless night while whispers rose from corners of darkness and then died down to even, settled ash. Dane and Jenny, who were now walking down one of Notre Dame Hospital's long and winding corridors, were looking for a quiet room. Jenny wanted to do her hit and Dane wanted to talk. Soon they found a lavatory with sparkling sinks and an open door. There were no people in this section of the hospital to shadow them.

Silence and darkness amidst gurneys and pale yellow light. Their presence seemed a lonely afterthought in the deep twilight-lit nocturne around them that was also punctuated by an ominous energy.

"So I'm gonna do this," Jenny said.

"Yeah, no problem," Dane said, watching her from behind as she walked into the washroom.

"I'll leave the door open so that we can talk," she said.

Images of the black sky outside ran through David Dane's mind.

"So, how are things between you and Lilly?"

"Okay, I guess," he replied.

Jenny bent over the sink pushing her ass out. "Do you guys still fuck?"

"From time to time," said Dane.

"Yeah . . . ?" Jenny said, as softly as she could.

"Yeah," Dane echoed flatly, looking down the hallway.

Jenny rustled around inside of her purse. "I need a condom," she said.

"It's rare that I hear a woman say that," Dane joked.

"No, I mean for a *garro*". Jenny said, readying her syringe.

Somewhere close by, computer screens glowed behind the windows of black rooms

"I'm so hungry," she said sensually.

Dane's temptations were being pushed to their limits. He did not know how much longer he would be able to control himself. In his heart he did not want to do anything that would hurt Lilly.

"Can I ask you something?" he said. "How did you end up on drugs?"

"You wouldn't believe me if I told you," she said.

"Try me," he replied.

"My dog died." The needle was in her arm now and the blood was running everywhere. She was trying to stop it with a Kleenex.

"Did he have a name?" Dane inquired.

"His name was Buster. He was the only person in the world that loved me."

"I find that hard to believe," Dane said, looking at the gorgeous woman.

"It's true. My parents didn't want me, and then I ended up living in this shitty room with blood on the ceiling. My life's not exactly a fairy tale."

"Yeah, mine neither," he said. "Someone told me that you were part Russian," he said, changing the topic.

"My parents are Russian. I was raised here," there was silence for a moment. "And you?"

"I'm Irish and Scottish. I was raised in Nova Scotia."

"Okay, I'm done my hit," she said. "Let's get out of here before somebody notices us."

In a matter of minutes, they realized that they were lost. They were circling the basement of the hospital and there seemed to be no way out. Dane and Jenny walked up a flight of stairs and around a corner which led to an abandoned lounge that was shrouded in darkness. If they kept going, they would likely end up here again.

"Where the fuck did we come in?" Dane asked.

"I can't remember."

"Maybe we outta go back downstairs," he said. Dane began to walk and Jenny followed. They went back down the stairs and came out in the corridor that they had been in only moments earlier. They were no further ahead than they had been only five minutes earlier.

"Shit," Jenny said. "How the hell do we get out of this place?"

Dane tried the handle on a door. It was locked. "I don't know," he said. "Maybe we're locked in. If they saw us on a monitor then they might have called the police."

"It's not beyond the realm of possibility," Jenny exclaimed nervously.

"So, what do you wanna do?" Dane asked.

"I don't know. Oh, fuck. I hope that the cops aren't coming," she said.

"Let's just keep walking," Dane said, leaving his position and moving forward. They were almost out of the corridor when they ran into a security guard.

"Can I help you?" he asked.

"Ah, yeah. We're lost. We just wanna find our way out," Dane said.

"Right this way," the young guard said, leading them to a door. He carried a flashlight in his hand and Dane wondered if they had been the reason for it. They would never know.

"Thanks," Dane said, exiting the building with Jenny behind him. They walked back out into the night and disappeared.

It was 1:18 a.m.

The next morning as fire-like crystal winds blew accross Ontario Street, Dane and Lilly stood in an alley under a fire escape sweating out bullets in the sun's lethal heat. They were not alone, however, because as the sun rose that morning they had found Mike Phillips and Shannon Edwards standing on the sidewalk in front of Frotenac Metro Station with nowhere to go. They had ran out of money about a week earlier and had been booted out of their apartment shortly thereafter. Dane had felt bad for them and offered to let them stay at his place with Lilly and him for a couple of weeks until they could figure out what to do. Now, though, all of them except him were waiting for a smack dealer named Gus.

"You guys must be starving," the ex-fighter said.

"Yeah. I mean this is worse than being in the pen, and I almost never ate in there," the big blond kid said.

"You look pretty buff for a guy who didn't eat," David Dane said.

"I lifted weights inside and, by the way, I didn't wanna say anything before, but I did some boxing, too."

"I didn't know that they had a program for that". Dane said.

"No, they don't, but I met a guy in there who used to fight and he did some work with me."

"Have you ever competed?" Dane asked.

"No, but one day I'd like to," Mike said. "Say, how many fights did you have?"

"I had forty-seven of 'em."

"Did you win them all?"

"I got my hand raised forty-three times," Dane said.

"Wow, that's incredible. We should spar sometime."

"Yeah," Dane responded flatly.

"There's Gus," Lilly said.

"Let's rock," Shannon followed.

Gus approached Lilly and put something in her hand as he watched his own reflection in the lenses of her shades. She handed him three twenties and smiled at him before he walked away.

"I'm ready," she said. "We'll do our shit here and then we'll go home for a while. I'm tired. I need a break. Is that okay with everyone?" she asked. Mike and Shannon nodded in agreement.

Lilly, Mike and Shannon did their hit and then the three of them packed up and prepared to follow David Dane down the hill toward the metro. They only got about three feet before Holly Briggs came out of nowhere wearing a pair of sunglasses. Holly was a friend of David Dane's who worked the street in another part of town, a part of town that Dane had nightmares about. It was called The Heights.

"How you doin', sweetheart?" Dane asked, stretching out his arms to hug his friend who immediately hugged him back.

"I'm good. As well as can be expected, I guess," she said. "I got robbed this morning on the way over here by a fucking cab driver."

"Someone actually had the balls to rob you?" Dane asked.

"Yep. Believe it or not."

"How's The Heights?"

Holly looked off to one side. "As usual," she answered with a sexy drawl. "It ain't paradise."

"Yeah, you can say that again."

"C'mon, let's go," Lilly yelled.

"Just wait a second," Dane said to Holly. "Lilly, come here for a minute. I want you to meet someone."

Lilly turned, approaching them.

"Lilly, this is Holly. Holly, this is the love of my life, Lilly Chicoine," Dane said, making the introductions.

"Hey," Lilly said in greeting. Holly vaguely waved in return.

"Okay, now that everyone's met, we gotta leave," the fighter said with a warm smile. "Holly, it was really great to see you . . ."

"Yep," she said before he could finish.

"Alright, I'll see you around," he said, his smile evaporating into sadness. He hadn't meant to hurt anyone.

"Okay Lilly," Dane said, looking back over his shoulder.

Mike and Shannon grabbed their bags and hustled them onto their backs.

It was 9:09 a.m.

About one hour later, having walked the distance at a slow pace, David Dane, Lilly Chicoine, Mike Phillips and Shannon Edwards walked through the door to Dane's apartment and set their bags down on the floor.

"Hey listen, you're gonna have to go to work later on to make sure that we have enough shit for tomorrow," Phillips said to his girlfriend in an unpleasant voice.

On the other side of the room, Dane's eyebrows raised. He hadn't liked the comment that was just made. What was Phillips? Her pimp?

"Hey look, Mike, everything's fine. I mean you and Shannon just got here," Dane said. Lilly stood silent behind her sunglasses that she had not yet removed.

"Yeah, okay, I'm sorry," Mike said politely.

"Hey, you know, you guys have never tasted my pasta. Well, Lilly has, but that's a different story."

"You're a good cook?" Shannon asked.

"I personally think so," Dane said smiling. "What do you think, Lilly?"

"You're not bad," she said, walking the perimeter of the table and entering the kitchen.

"I love you, Lilly," he said, kissing her on the cheek as she opened the cupboard doors. Inside was a jar of protein shake, a box of soda crackers, some spaghetti in a box, and half a bag of Aero bars.

"Oh, look. This is a picture of my best friend on earth," Dane said. "This is Hunter," he said, proudly displaying a picture of the handsome K-9 to Phillips and Shannon.

"Ohhh, he's so cute," Shannon said.

"Yeah, that's a nice dog," Mike said in a voice that Dane could not read.

"He has the biggest heart on earth, and he'll give you all of it for a ham and cheese sandwich," the boxer said smiling.

Mike Phillips was smirking but Dane, who was still staring at the framed photograph of Hunter, did not notice.

"Baby, do you want me to start boiling the water?" Lilly asked.

"Hey, that's okay. I can handle it," he responded.

"Can I use your washroom to wash up?" Mike asked.

"Sure, go ahead," Dane said.

At that moment there was a knock on the apartment door. "Who's there?" Dane called out.

"It's Bill," the voice said.

"Hey, yo, Billy," Dane said, opening the door. "I can't believe he's here," the fighter said as Bill Ramirez walked in carrying several bags of newspapers in his hands. This was one of Bill Ramirez' fixations. He would read every newspaper that he could get a hold of, from cover to cover.

"Alright, first of all, Bill, you remember Lilly," Dane said, gesturing toward his girlfriend, "and this is Mike and Shannon . . ."

"Hi," Bill said, greeting Lilly. "Nice to meet you," Ramirez said, shaking Shannon's hand.

"Hey," she said.

"Oh, and this is Mike Phillips," Dane said, as the big blond kid came out of the washroom.

Bill's smile seemed to diminish. "What's up?" Ramirez said, greeting him without emotion.

"How's it going?" Phillips asked, his eyes full of sarcasm.

"Say, Bill, how would you like to stay for dinner?" Dane asked.

"Sounds good to me. What are we having?" he asked.

"I'm gonna cook some pasta, if that's okay with everyone else," the boxer said.

"I'm starving, fuck!" Lilly exclaimed

Dane put a pot of water on the stove and cranked up the dial.

They were a half-shady, half tough-looking crowd, Bill thought, but they were Dane's friends and if they were friends of Dane's, then they were fine by him.

"Hey Billy, Can I talk to you for a second?" Dane asked, leading Bill out into the hallway.

"Yeah, no problem, eh?" he responded, following Dane into the corridor.

"Listen, I just wanted to give you the forty bucks I owe you, but I didn't want Lilly to know because if she knows that I have money, she'll want it for drugs," Dane said, handing Bill four tens.

"Thanks, eh. Where did you find this blond guy?" Bill asked. Just then there was a yelp from behind the apartment door. It was not Lilly.

When Dane and Ramirez rushed back in, they found Shannon Edwards lying on the floor in a heap with blood pouring out of her mouth. Phillips, who had dropped her, was standing over her with his fists clenched as if her were waiting for her to get back up so he could knock her down again.

"I told you not to talk back to me," he hollered at her on the ground. Dane immediately grabbed Phillips by his shirt tails with both hands and forced him out the door.

"Get the fuck outta my house!" Dane shouted as Mike back-pedaled into the hallway. "Go!"

The fighter paused for a second after Phillips vanished, waiting to make sure he was gone. Then he turned to survey Shannon, who was being tended to by Billy and Lilly. "What the hell happened?" he asked intensely.

"He told her to go to work and she said no," Lilly explained.

"He hit her face pretty good," Dane said.

"That fuckin' BASTARD!" Shannon cried.

"It's alright, sweetie," Lilly said, comforting her.

"Does she need a hospital?" Bill inquired.

"I don't know," Lilly responded.

"I'll call an ambulance," Dane said.

"No don't," Shannon said. "It'll be alright. He's hit me before," she sobbed.

"Are you sure?" the Scotian with the shiny head asked.

"Yeah, yeah. Thanks, though."

"But, ah, he might bump into you again," Bill said with reservation.

"Trust me, I'll be fine."

"I wouldn't necessarily say so. You got a mean boyfriend," Dane said.

"No, really. I'm gonna be alright," Shannon said as Lilly squatted next to her with a cold washcloth in her hand.

"You can stay here for as long as you want," Lilly said, dabbing at the cut on her friend's lip.

"Yeah, absolutely. We got plenty of sheets," the boxer seconded.

"Now I'm gonna have to go to work later and he might be down there," Lilly said. "Fuck!"

"See, I'm causing trouble already," Shannon said apologetically.

"No, honey, you're not," the other girl said, reassuringly.

"Look, here's what we'll do. I'll go with Lilly to work and you can stay here with Billy Beat," Dane said. Billy Beat was Dane's nickname for Bill. It had no significance.

"Not a problem," Bill agreed.

"So what's gonna happen when I get sick?"

"I'll take care of your dope for tonight. No sweat," Lilly offered.

"Are you sure?" Shannon asked.

"Yeah, I'm sure," Lilly said.

It was 10:21 a.m.

He was trying to revive her, trying to start her heart again, but the CPR wasn't working. Now there would be questions. By morning, the fucking police would be all over the place going over everything with a fine-toothed comb. If only he had used the proper amount of GHB—the date-rape drug—instead of just pouring it into her drink. Now she was going to die here, right in the middle of his gym, right on the floor in front of the windows. What was it? Three or four a.m.? Fucking Jesus. What was he going to tell the pigs? They would find drugs in the autopsy anyway, so it didn't really matter. After all the prostitutes that he had murdered he was going to go to jail for an accident, a stupid childish accident? No way. He would get rid of the body. He would just make her disappear, and then his problems would be solved. Kristen would be a missing persons. Nothing more. And the cops would never even know about him. The name Bobby Troy Edmonds would never have to reach their ears. He would get some blankets from the trunk of the Land Rover and carry her out back under the cover of darkness. Then he would drive her out of town and bury her body. That's what he would do. Then his dilemma would end.

3:44 a.m.

David Dane woke in the middle of the night to find Lilly sleeping and Shannon gone. The covers were pulled back and the futon was on the floor where she had left it. On top of Shannon's pillow there was a note.

Dear David and Lilly,

The first thing that I want to say is thank you for trying to help me, but I know that my life is not your problem. You tried to do a great thing for me and I appreciate it, but I've already been a burden to enough people and I won't allow myself to be a burden to the two of you. I want to keep your friendship, not lose it, and by becoming a burden to you, I'm afraid that's what will happen. So take care of each other and don't worry about me. Lilly, you've got a great boyfriend and I hope you know it. Dane is everything that I wish Mike could be. He's special. And Dane, please protect and take care of Lilly.

All my love and thanks,

Shannon

Over the next few days, David Dane and Lilly Chicoine lived with a lot of anxiety and depression with Lilly going to work sporadically with Dane as her shadow. They scoured Ontario Street looking for Shannon Edwards, but they could not find her. It was as if she had left their apartment and vanished into thin air, leaving no trace. When they returned to two thirty-five Leopold Heights, they found the ground floor of the building under construction, with maintenance men and contractors occupying the first floor as they converted the Tuck Shop where Ahmed had worked into a twenty-four-hour grocery store with an adjoining Subway restaurant, adding huge bay windows and a small seating area with tables and chairs.

"Lookin' good, guys," Dane complimented the crew of workers as he careened his head over the back of his shoulder to survey the work. "At least we'll be able to eat here soon," he said to Lilly who was walking a foot in front of him. "I hope that they let Ahmed keep his job."

"I hope so, too," she said.

It was 12:45 p.m.

As the weather grew colder, Dane began to go to work with Lilly less and less. His body simply could not adapt to temperatures in the range of minus fifteen to minus twenty. Dane had never liked winters. Most nights he would stay in their darkened apartment, the only illumination being the glow of the television set, and he'd wait for Lilly to call from downstairs to come and open the door for her. Usually he would rush to the elevators with butterflies in his stomach and watch as the elevator climbed eight floors to come and pick him up. When he reached the first floor, he would take a left before using his building key to open the door to the grocery store and Subway restaurant. Once inside, his eyes would dart around for a moment until he saw Lilly. She was usually in one of two places: either on one of the two pay phones in the foyer of the grocery store or standing at the counter paying for her carton of cigarettes. If she was on the phone, that meant that she was calling her dealer. Strangely, seeing her like this at the phone in the restaurant would be one of his fondest memories of Lilly.

One of the first employees to get hired on at the grocery store was a young guy with red hair named Ben Sconing. Dane had first met him one night when he'd come into the store to get Lilly, and he found the two of them standing face to face in the foyer smoking cigarettes. Ben was a great guy. Top of the line, as they'd say back home. He had always been loyal to Dane, and he respected Dane's relationship with Lilly. For that, Dane was eternally grateful. It wasn't often that you met people with that kind of integrity.

Most of the time, after Dane came downstairs to let Lilly in, the two of them would go back up to their apartment and wait for Lilly's dealer to call. After Lilly got her smack, she would do it in the bathroom, change into a pair of gray jogging pants and a t-shirt, and then the two of them would get cozy in front of the TV, where they would watch horror movie after horror movie until they fell asleep in each others arms. Dane would always cherish this memory of the two of them together.

Chapter 14

Bring Me To Life

Around Easter, when everything was quiet, Dane walked Lilly down to the front doors of their building and kissed her goodbye before she went to work. It was a Sunday afternoon and the two of them had spent part of the day watching a horror flick called Poltergeist III.

"How long will you be?" Dane asked, holding the glass door open with his shoulder.

"I don't know. It's Sunday afternoon so I probably won't catch that fast."

"I love you, Lilly," David Dane said.

"You too," Lilly responded, her lips connecting with Dane's one more time.

Dane looked up into the sky. It was beginning to rain as Lilly walked away and disappeared. This would be the beginning of a two-week long odyssey that would leave Dane desperate and afraid. Days went by without Lilly returning. Dane waited for a phone call, but none came. The rain outside would not subside and, looking back, Dane would always remember the black radio sitting in the shadows of their living room playing, the song "Bring Me To Life" by Evanescence over and over again.

Around the fourth or fifth day, Dane put his jacket on and headed out to Ontario Street that was flooded by a sea of silver rain, the words from the Evanescence song playing themselves over and over again in his head, giving memorable ambiance to his journey.

"Wake me up, wake me up inside,
Call my name, and save me from the dark.
Bid my blood to run, before I come undone.

Amidst hissing rain, the streets were empty. Dane walked along the edge of the sidewalk toward Frontenac Metro station. Silence and the downpour. Dane turned to his left on Fullum and crossed the street into a small, shadowy diner. Inside, he found a familiar figure dining at one of the tables. It was Haitian Claude. He wore a two-piece denim jean suit over work boots.

"Where's Lilly?" Dane asked in a guarded voice.

Claude cleaned his lips with a napkin. "At my house. She's sleep now," he said.

Dane was gonna fucking kill him. "Oh yeah. You better go get her now before my temper gets the best of me." Dane said.

"No. No, I no get Lilly," he said.

"You go get Lilly before I . . . ."

"Not in here," the small Lebanese man behind the register warned.

"I'll be waiting outside," Dane said, before exiting.

Ten minutes later, the hunched-over Haitian reappeared. This time he had a beer bottle in his hand. He quickly raised it and shattered its lower half against a steel post that was rooted in the ground.

"You want fight? You want fight for Lilly?" he asked, pointing the bottle's jagged in David Dane's direction.

"Put the fucking weapon down," Dane hollered from across the street.

237

"I am no afraid for police."

"Yeah," Dane retorted, heading towards a surprised-looking Claude. They were face to face now.

"Go ahead," Dane said, raising his head to expose his neck. "C'mon! Cut me!" he said, taunting.

Claude looked surprised for a moment, holding the bottle in place before huffing and dropping the remainder of the bottle to the ground. "No. No Lilly. She's not in my house," he said.

"She's not in your house?" Dane asked with a twist of bewilderment and amusement.

"No Lilly. Lilly is never go in my house," the hunched-over Haitian said.

If there was a camera present, Dane would have looked toward it now as if acknowledging an audience that he was not supposed to know was there.

Claude turned now, walking down the street and turning up a staircasing into his building. Within minutes he returned with an antique-looking bicycle. He placed its tires on the square asphalt parking lot across the street from where he lived and began to ride his bicycle around and around in circles.

It was 4:07 p.m.

About an hour later, after Claude went back inside, Dane found Tiffany-whose-ID-said-Dale-Frost standing at the foot of Claude's building across from the brewery. She wore a blue jean suit with a cupcake bodice under it that hugged her huge breasts and her sexy bubble butt in a way that would make any man struggle to find his breath.

"What's up Dane?" she asked the bodybuilder who hadn't finished looking her up and down yet. "Do I get a hug?" she inquired, reacting positively to the attention that she was getting.

"If I don't blow up, first," Dane responded, pulling Tiffany toward himself and embracing her.

"Have you seen Lilly?" the fighter asked.

Tiffany shook her head, gazing into Dane's eyes as if she wanted more than just a hug.

"You're gonna drive me crazy," he said, backing away from her. "Claude told me an hour ago that Lilly was upstairs sleeping."

"He's playing with your head, honey. She's not up there."

"How do you know?" Dane asked with a fixated expression on his face. The thought was still bothering him.

"Because she never goes up there anymore. She hasn't been up there for months."

"You know that Claude came at me with a broken bottle earlier," Dane said with a mild smirk on his lips.

At that moment a car stopped at the curb. The driver was obviously looking for Tiffany's services.

"I gotta go. I'll talk to you later," Tiffany said, reaching for the handle of the passenger door. "I'll tell Lilly that you're looking for her if I see her, though," she said, getting into the car.

Dane nodded as the two drove off. "Yeah," he said to no one.

Upon further investigation of the area, Dane realized that Lilly was nowhere to be found. Back at two thirty-five Leopold Heights, the fighter walked into the brightly lit grocery store / Subway and approached Ahmed, who was standing behind the counter.

"Uhh, good. Very good," the big Moroccan said, showing Dane a photo of a naked woman with a cock in her hand.

239

"Listen, if Lilly comes in here, please call me right away," the fighter said, passing Ahmed his card.

"She not here? No good," Ahmed said.

"I'm sorry Ahmed. I'm just not in a very good mood right now," Dane said, walking away. He approached the three people working at the Subway and made them aware of the situation. The three staff members nodded, accepting Dane's business card.

Later that night, around twelve o'clock, David Dane's phone rang. At the other end was one of Lilly's friend from jail. Her name was Lee Ann, better know to her friends as Lee Lee.

"Can I come up?" she asked. "I'm only two blocks away."

"Yeah, why not? I'm sick of being alone anyway," he said on the other end.

"I'll be there soon. I'll call you from my cell phone to come downstairs and open the door," Lee Ann said before hanging up.

Dane looked around at the cold, dark apartment where he and Lilly lived. It felt like a sad place to him now. He had told Lee Lee that Lilly was missing right off the bat, but she had wanted to come over, probably to use his stove to cook rock, he thought.

In ten minutes the call display on Dane's phone lit up. Lee Ann was downstairs. Dane went to the closet in his bedroom and pulled on a Gators Gym sweater and jeans before grabbing his keys and heading for the elevators. Downstairs, Lee Ann was waiting in the foyer between the doors.

"I'm glad that I didn't wake you up," she said, greeting Dane as he let her in.

"I can't sleep with Lilly gone," he said.

"How long ago did she disappear?" Lee Ann asked, following Lilly's boyfriend into the elevator.

Maybe a week, he responded, pushing the button for the eighth floor twice.

The elevator was ascending now.

"I don't know why she keeps taking off," the stocky girl with the brown hair said. "You obviously love her a lot."

"Yeah, well, that doesn't seem to faze her," David Dane said. "She does what she wants and she doesn't care who she hurts."

The elevator parked itself, jolting to a halt at its destination.

"She should realize how much you love her. Fuck, at least she should call," Lee Ann offered as they stepped out into the bright corridor with the green carpet.

Dane opened the door and turned on some lights as they walked into the big apartment where Lee Ann had only been once before.

"Do you mind if I puff?" Lee Lee asked, fishing a crack pipe from her purse.

Dane nodded his head. He had correctly assumed that this would be on her itinerary. Soon the apartment was thick with the sweet, pungent smell of crack cocaine.

"Can you open a window?" Dane asked Lee Lee who was sitting in a rocker by the balcony door.

She obliged him. "So you don't use drugs at all?"

Dane shook his head.

"What about this killer who's been in the papers?" Lee Ann asked.

241

"I try not to think about it. About him, that is."

"How do you know that it's a him?" she asked.

The darkness was blowing in through the open door now on the heels of the breeze.

"In all likelihood it's a he," Dane said. "Most of the cops on Ontario Street know Lilly. She's well known. If this piece of shit stabbed Lilly, I would've heard from the pigs by now. My name and number are on Lilly's file. It wouldn't take them a New York minute to show up at my door."

"That's a bit callous," she replied.

"So is taking off for five days and not calling," Dane said.

She *is* a drug addict, you know," Lee Ann said kindly.

"She's not stupid, Lee. Believe me, she knows better."

"Most people would have given up by now," the girl said, rising to her feet and approaching Dane, who was standing in the light. "You've done well," she said, resting the tips of her finger on his heart.

"I just wish she'd come home," the fighter said, tearing up. "My heart's empty without her."

It was 12:49 p.m.

About a week later, after Dane had finished his workout at a club called The City Gym, the ex-boxer came through the door to the sound of a ringing phone.

"Hello," he said.

"Hey baby. It's me," a raspy voice said on the other end.

Dane burst into tears. It was Lilly. "Where are you?" he half asked, half cried.

"I'm on Ontario Street. Can I come home?"

"Of course! Where were you?"

"I was coke tripping. Listen, can you pay me a cab? I have no money left and I'm fucking starving. I wanna come home now," the exhausted girl said.

"Yes, baby, I'll pay you a cab."

"Will we have enough money left over for food?"

I have sixty bucks on me," Dane responded. "We can eat at Subway."

"Okay, I'm getting in the next cab," Lilly said.

Ten minutes later, Dane walked out the front doors into the darkness and rain. He watched as car after care swished by in the remnants of the fallen downpour. Soon he saw a minivan taxi with tinted windows pull up at the curb, the side door closest to Dane sliding slowly open as Lilly Chicoine stepped out onto the slick sidewalk and into his arms as the ex-fighter burst into tears for the second time in an hour.

"I love you, Lilly," he said.

"I love you, too," the girl wearing the fisherman's hat said.

"I wouldn't have recognized you in that hat," he said, putting an arm around her shoulder and leading her back inside. He wondered if she had been using the hat for just that purpose.

"Hey buddy!"

Dane turned around to see the cab driver waving to him, ushering him back to the cab.

"I almost forgot," Dane said, pulling a twenty out of his pocket with half a glove on.

"Here you go," he said, approaching the short Italian cabbie with the cap on.

"Thanks," the driver said.

Back inside the building, Dane and Lilly entered the Subway restaurant/ Couche Tard to a round of applause from the staff members. They were happy to see Lilly back home.

"Very good," Ahmed said, his big palms slamming together.

"Thanks," said Dane humbling, waving toward the small crowd that was gathering around them now, as if to return the gesture of only moments ago.

"I'll have an Italian Sub with lettuce, hot peppers, pickles and onions on it. Two chocolate chip cookies and an Orange Crush," Lilly said to one of the Subway employees.

After they were through ordering their food, and there was a lot of it, Dane was handed a torn-up receipt and told it was on the house. That night, Lilly Chicoine and David Dane ate like starving rabbits before going upstairs and falling asleep together in the darkness.

It was 9:09 p.m.

Stretching her arms out above her head, Lilly rolled from side to side on her knees. She had just awoken to the cold sunlight that was filtering in through the open window. It was nine a.m. And already, even after as much heroin as she had done last night before coming home, Lilly was dope-sick as hell.

"Can I have a cigarette?"

"Yeah," Dane answered, momentarily turning his attention from the movie he had been watching on TV. He stood up, reaching for the pack of Players Light King Size that Lilly had left on the black desk top that housed his computer. His joints were stiff and he could hear them cracking as he got up to move.

"Where are my matches?" the girl asked, accepting the cigarette that Dane offered her.

"I don't know. Where'd you leave them?"

"I don't remember. What's this?" she asked, pointing to the image of Jim Belushi and Louis Gossette Jr. on the screen. This was one of Dane's favorite movies.

"The Principal," he answered.

"Fuck, baby. I'm sick. Can you pass me twenty bucks?"

"Nope. That's all the money that I have for food."

"But I'll pay you back double when I go to work tonight. I promise," Lilly begged.

Lilly was probably not going to pay him back at all.

"No. We've been through this. You know the rules."

"But I would do anything."

"Lilly, I'm not in the mood for this shit this morning, as heartless as it sound."

"Pleeeeease . . ." she begged.

He felt bad for her when she was like this, and sometimes he would give in and let her have whatever little money he had, but this scenario was becoming all-too regular. Plus, he was starving and it was just after nine o'clock in the morning. By this time tonight he would be passing out if he gave in.

Pleeeeease, baby."

"Can't you get a front from Jeff or Marcus?"

Noooo. I owe them money."

"How much?"

"Forty each," she said in an exasperated voice. "They will not front me when I owe that much. You have to help me."

"No, that's it. You got yourself into this mess, you get yourself out of it. How? I don't know."

Lilly reached for the phone, picked up the receiver and began dialing.

"Martin? It's Lilly. Listen, I need a favor." Martin was the boss.

"Yeah. Yes, I paid Marcus back last night," she said, responding to whatever he was saying.

"How much did you pay him?" Martin asked with an accent.

"I pay him forty dollars. Forty bucks . . ."

"I don't see anything written down here," Martin said. "Let me check it and I'll call you back."

Lilly's eyes were wide now.

"What's wrong?" Dane asked.

Lilly inhaled. "I lied to him and now he's gonna find out about it."

Two minutes later the phone rang.

"Hello," Dane answered. "Uh-huh. Uh-huh. Yes, she's right here," he said, handing over the phone to Lilly. Dane was slightly humored by all of this.

"Hello," Lilly said, now puffing away furiously on a cigarette. She had apparently located her matches.

"Lilly, you fucking bitch, you lied to me!" Martin yelled so loudly that Dane could hear the voltage of his anger coming through the phone lines.

"Pleeeease Martin. You have to help me. I'm sick. I cannot get out of my bed. I pay you back double, I promise," she pleaded in absolute terror.

This served her fucking right, Dane thought.

"Don't ever call us again," Martin shouted before hanging up in her ear.

She immediately hung up and called him back again, dialing more feverishly this time.

"Yeah, Martin . . . . Please don't . . ." She was crying now.

This exchange of him hanging up and her calling back went on for about the next twenty minutes or so before Lilly retired to her mattress and hid underneath the blankets.

Dane now truly felt badly for her but giving in to her meant that this was going to happen probably another hundred times.

Fifteen minutes later, Lilly sat up, the covers rolling off her naked form. Now she tried calling Martin again.

"Hello," Martin said on the other end.

"Martin, wait. Don't hang up. I have money."

Oh fuck, Dane thought.

"Okay Lilly. I'm gonna send Greg, but you better have money. And after this, lose our number."

"Okay, okay," Lilly said, a bit winded but agreeable.

"And if you call again before he gets there, then I'll tell him not to come."

"Alright. Thank you, Martin." she said as she hung up.

"What the fuck was that? You don't have any money," Dane said.

"I know, I know. That's why you have to help me. Pleeeease . . ."

"N-O. No! You got yourself into this mess, you're going to get yourself out of it," said Dane.

Lilly had a fistful of blanket now, still sitting on her knees. Her eyes were watering, moving out of exhaustion more than anything. She turned around momentarily, looking at him with those sad puppy-dog eyes that were reserved for moments just like this, waiting, hoping that he would weaken and fork over the twenty bucks. But on this morning, not out of spite but out of necessity, out of a need to eat, he would not give in. His resolve in these situations had become too strong. He was to some degree hardened to her antics.

"But I would pay you back . . ." she sobbed.

"No, Lilly. You wouldn't."

"Yes I would!" she begged, breaking down for real.

She must be sick, he thought. But if he gave in, which is surely what she wanted, then these situations would never cease. This predicament would repeat itself over and over again like a drunk with wounded pride.

In seconds she was on her feet and headed into the bathroom which, right now, was black lit.

"What the fuck are you gonna do with that?" Dane asked as Lilly filled a syringe with her own blood.

"I'm gonna do whatever I have to do," she said.

"Which is?"

"I'm gonna hold somebody up."

This was a whole new level of desperation for her. Or it was at least from Dane's point of view. This was terrorism. Give me what I want or I'll do something horrific. She was headed past him now, wearing a sweatshirt and jeans that she had pulled on after capping the needle and stuffing it into one of the large pockets on the leg of her Levis.

"Lilly, where are you going?" he asked, reaching for her elbow as she opened the door onto the hallway. He was considering giving her his twenty bucks, but if he did that then this would never stop, and he knew it.

They were in the corridor now, just walking. His heart was racing. The natives in his head banging on their drums. The elevator doors slid open on their rails and the two of them stepped inside. Lilly in first and Dane second. They were not alone. There was an older woman inside with them. She had white hair, highlighted by the remnants of black. She was surely in her late fifties or early sixties. She was not carrying a purse of a handbag. A thought that eased Dane's anxiety somewhat.

Lilly eyeballed him with a warning.

"Don't even fucken . . . .". Dane warned her back in a whisper.

On the first floor, the door opened and the three of them walked out with the old woman taking the lead ahead of them.

"She had no purse or I would have done it," Lilly said, taking a drag of her smoke.

"Have you lost your fucken mind?"

249

"I don't give a fuck. I want my hit," Chicoine said as they walked out under the cold sun.

Dane was looking back at Lilly now, who was leaning against the stone wall that served as a perimeter for the planter in front of the building. She was looking around now, keeping vigilant. No victims in sight, yet. The sidewalk was almost empty.

Soon a small white caravan with brown siding and rust spots the size of bullet holes pulled up at the curb. The driver was "Greg," a small foreign guy with a tanned complexion and black hair.

"Fuck! It's him. It's Greg," Lilly said. "I'll be right back."

The guy behind the steering wheel eyeballed Dane nervously as Lilly slid across the passenger seat and slammed the door shut behind herself.

They're gonna end her, Dane thought.

There was soon an argument behind the windshield, with a cell phone being passed back and forth. It had started with Greg, the phone ended up on the floor, was picked up by Greg and forced into Lilly's hand. Martin had to be on the other end. Now there was yelling so loud that Dane could hear it even with the van windows closed.

Lilly: "But I pay you back."

Greg: "No Lilly. You don't fucking pay us back. When you need a front, you call us. When you have money, you call who? I don't know. Get the fuck out of my van."

Lilly: "No! I won't get out."

Greg: "Get out or I'm gonna drag you out."

Lilly: "Fucking try it, you cocksucker."

Now Greg was getting out and walking around to the other side of the van.

"Lilly! Open dis goddam door!" he said with a heavy accent. Lilly had locked her door.

"No! Go fuck your mother," she said stubbornly before taking another drag of her smoke.

Greg was yanking on the handle for all that he was worth, with Lilly trying to keep the door closed from her side.

This was unbelievable. Greg was winning the tug of war on the curb.

"Get dee fuck out goddam Lilly," he said, as if that was proper English. "You are big crying bitch".

The passenger door was open now, but Lilly was fighting to close it again. Finally, with Lilly still aboard, Greg walked back around to the driver's seat and got behind the wheel.

Lilly was being polite now. She had found solace in his words and was "Mmmm-hmmm-ing" him. A few more seconds passed before negotiations ceased and Lilly stepped back outside, under the sun with something in her hand.

"I got it," she said.

There was the sound of an engine starting. Greg then pulled away from the curb and was soon gone.

It was 10:08 a.m.

The next Tuesday morning at sunrise, David Dane and Lilly Chicoine stopped at the corner of Ontario and Papineau to wait for a light. There was a group of punks across the street and they were eye-balling Lilly in an obvious manner. One of them in particular.

"That's prime fuckin' meat, right there," a tall blond guy with a pinch called out. He looked like football player-turned-pro wrestler Darren Drozdoff, Dane thought.

"What the fuck did you just say?" Dane hollered back. "I'll put you in a fucken casket," the fighter's voice echoed eerily.

There were six of them and of one of him, but Dane didn't care. You didn't ever, ever, say anything like that around Dane's girlfriend. Street hooker or not.

"C'mon, baby," Lilly said as the light turned green.

They were headed for the field by the highway now where Chicoine would shoot up. When they got there, Fred and Esther, the squeegees, were sitting on the grass under some trees, preparing two hits, one for each of them.

Dane could already feel the morning heat on the back of his neck. It was blazing. Lilly stood over Dane, her face going into spasms as she injected into her arm the coke that she had purchased earlier. She was silent when she was like this. Turned off. Attempts to reach her verbally were in vain. The coke immersed her in a world of her own and turned her catatonic.

Traffic was bustling onto the bridge now, at Dane and Lilly's back, the horns and engines creating a sound that was abhorrent to Dane at this hour of the morning, like rugged thunder while you were trying to sleep.

Lilly's elbow was up in the air as she watched, wide-eyed, as the blood from her vein ran in steady streams down her arm and onto the back sleeve of her red leather jacket.

Another vehicle hollered around the bend behind them and headed onto the big steel bridge to join the rest of the traffic. It was a silver Honda with four doors, its only occupant was a white male who looked to be in his mid forties.

"I wanna do a B an' E," said Fred, his eyes and lips twitching under the influence of drugs.

"That's a lousy fucken passtime, Fred," Dane said. "You should try something more pleasant like knocking off little old ladies."

"Does anyone have a Kleenex?" Lilly asked, coming down.

"No, baby, I don't. You might have some in your purse. I think I saw some in there earlier when I was looking for your straps." A strap was another word for a *garro*.

Fred and Esther were leaving now.

"Fuck, it's gonna be hot outside today, huh?" Lilly commented and questioned at the same time.

"Yeah, no shit," said Dane.

"Let's go," Lilly said, picking up her stuff and placing it back in her purse. "I don't wanna stay here too long. Fuck, I don't need to get arrested this morning."

When Lilly was done packing up, she shouldered her purse with the blood from her vein still running down her arm and continued to walk back toward Ontario Street with Dane behind her.

"I think I'm gonna try to work," she said.

Dane was disappointed. He was hoping to spend a little more time with her, even if it meant having to stay longer. They had been out here since yesterday and his body was beginning to feel the after-effects of it. It was not putting him in a better mood knowing that trying to convince her to come home would mean an argument. Lilly had a mind of her own, however drug induced, and it was very hard to change it once she had it made up.

"So, what are you gonna do?" Lilly asked.

"I'll stick around," the fighter said, still mindful of the group of punks that had been eye-balling Lilly earlier.

"Okay. I think I'm gonna try to work outside the bar, so just wait a few feet away so that my clients won't think that you're a cop."

This was the usual and Dane was used to it.

"I'll wait on the bench," he said.

Fifteen minutes later, Lilly came back carrying a twenty in her hand.

"I think I'm gonna do another quarter," she said.

Dane rose up from his seated position, eyelids heavy with the onslaught of sleep. He stood for a moment, pausing before following Lilly around the corner into the alleyway behind Nightlife where her dealer was waiting.

"What's up, Lilly?" the young peddler with the ball hat and the shades asked.

"Not much," she responded, handing him the twenty in exchange for another round of powder.

"Is that David Dane?" he asked.

"Yeah it is," Lilly said of her boyfriend who was standing under a fire escape in the shadows. "You two know each other?"

Abraham was nodding. "Just from around here. He gave hell to a couple of thugs who were pummeling my little brother one night. Your boyfriend's straight Badass . . . . No B.S.," he said, nodding up at Dane in a way that signified respect.

"Later," the dealer said, as Dane and Lilly walked out of the alleyway and back into the sunlight. Back on the sidewalk, Lilly scanned up and down both ends of the street as if checking for traffic.

"Fuck, I don't know how I'm gonna make a client out here. There's no cars."

"Maybe you should steal a stop sign," Dane joked.

"What for?"

"Well, that way you could hold it up . . ."

"Ha, ha, hah. Very funny," Lilly responded. "Okay, I'm gonna try to work now."

"All right. I'll be around," Dane responded.

An hour later, when Lilly was alone, Bianca came out of nowhere and ripped Lilly's purse off of her shoulder. "You owe me money. Hey little bitch?" she screamed, dragging a fallen Lilly off the ground and tossing her back down again.

"Fucken cunt!" Lilly yelled. They were at the corner of Ontario and Dufresne, close to Frotenac Metro, just across from Haitian Claude's house.

Lilly rose up only to be floored again by Bianca. This time with a fist to the jaw. "This time, stay down or I'll beat your fucken head in," Bianca yelled.

Bianca lifted Lilly's purse, turning it over. Needles, condoms and water came flying out, but no money. Dane's girlfriend was left lying in a pile on the ground, having lost to the much stockier Bianca.

"The next time that I see you, you better have my money," Bianca shouted, delivering one more blow to Lilly's jaw, this time with her boot.

Ten minutes later, Dane showed up just on time to see Lilly walk into the foyer of Claude's building and close the door. What the fuck was she doing going in there? Was she seeing him again, or what?

Bianca now stood two feet away from David Dane, aware of the past conflict between him and Claude.

"I told you, she's a little bitch!" Bianca exclaimed.

Dane did not know what in the hell to think. His heart was pounding in his chest and his glands were secreting sweat. What the fuck was Lilly doing up there?

He was sleep deprived and his nerves were gone, and this situation was not serving as a catalyst to calm them. He stopped for a moment and thought as Bianca walked away from where she had been standing, her hands shoved into the pockets of her painted-on Levis. There was only one way to solve this shit and he knew what it was.

Just then, Lilly walked by the upstairs window in a green robe with a towel wrapped around her head.

"Lilly!" Dane called out. She did not answer, unable to hear him through the closed window.

Dane was fucking fuming now as he crossed the street. He walked through the door and went up the stairs to the foot of Claude's apartment that stood open onto the most opaque blackness that Dane had ever seen. And there, standing in the center of the living room, wearing only beige safari shorts, was Mr Rastaman himself. He addressed Dane calmly.

"Lilly is go. Back door."

Dane, who was not taking his word for it, stormed past the short Haitian and proceeded to throw open every door around him, exposing two bedrooms and a bathroom.

"She's not here," the boxer said.

"Like I said: she's go."

It was 10:35 a.m.

The ashes from Lilly's cigarette were glowing through the darkness behind the window of Claude's apartment and, standing outside on the street looking up, that's all that David Dane could see of her. She had gone back there, obviously. Maybe her sudden departure of yesterday morning had been more a way of avoiding him than anything else. Or of getting rid of him.

He would wait, forever if he had to, even sitting here on this wooden divider that surrounded the parking lot that sat across the street from Claude's building. But inside, patience was not his virtue. There was only rage, anger and jealousy. There was pent-up frustration and hostility like he had never felt before. It could only be described best as a driven, primordial frenzy. He wanted her dead. Not to mention Claude alongside her. Two caskets, he thought. One for each of them to rest in, and he would be the one who put them there, with a gun. No, he would use a knife and he'd sear into their flesh.

Fuck! He was so enraged.

About twenty minutes later, Hedia put in an appearance. She needed to use the pay phone that stood next to him in the darkness.

"She went back there again, Hedia," Dane said.

"She's a scam, honey. How many times do I have to tell you that?"

"Once more". Dane remarked, flat as a pancake.

"Look, honey," she began, abandoning the phone booth and her twenty-five cents, "Lilly is a street girl. Plain and simply. She's never gonna be the way that you want her to be. Let her go."

"And what's the deal with the witch doctor in there? When the fuck did Lilly decide to practice voodoo?"

"You don't listen to me, honey," she paused. "You're hard-headed too, like Lilly. That's probably why you two don't get along half the time."

"I love you, Hedia," he said. "You're not the only one around here who's an addict."

She kissed him on the forehead before giving her surroundings a quick once over.

"I wanna get high," she said with a thick German accent.

"Have fun," he said. "I'll see you tomorrow."

It was 11:45 p.m.

Chapter 15

It began with the menacing glint of the cars parked at the far end of Ontario Street long after sundown. A short wind whistled quietly through the treetops and then ebbed like a candle flame being blown out as Dave Dane stood on a street corner staring across at a place call the Demon Club, that, in reality, simply did not exist.

Once inside, driven by unseen forces, Dane looked over and saw Lilly standing in the shadows. She was dressed in a sequined top with matching pants and there was a man to either side of her, both of whom were looking Lilly up and down as if she were a piece of meat, and it didn't look as if she minded. She was returning their gaze with a promiscuous smile and sleazy body language, not unlike the body language that she would use if she was working. On the walls there were what could best be described as incantations from the Devil, to fit the club's theme, and the busboys, who were dressed in black, wearing aprons, looked filthy and dirty. They looked more like hardcore junkies than table staff.

The first of them, Dane thought, he had seen some place before, selling stolen watches and jewelry from an old briefcase. Dane remembered that the guy had given him the creeps, with his greasy blond curls and his twitching left eye. His hands, Dane also recalled, were covered in black and blue bruises from shooting up. What the fuck was this place? Dane wondered, inside and out. He looked around, back and forth. The curtains, cloaking the club's windows, were black and you could not see past them into the darkness outside. This cover was broken only by wisps of silver light from the street lamps that had found its way in through the cracks, penetrating the otherwise solid shield that the drapery provided.

If all of this was a nightmare meant to frighten him to his core. Then it was working.

"She's not a dancer or an escort, if that's what she told you," the man with the twitchy eye said to Dane. "She's on the junk, and she has AIDS."

Just then, Dane woke up in his bed. There was darkness all around him and rain at the window. His body was perspiring and there were beads of sweat on his forehead.

It was 4:07 a.m.

Eighteen hours later, David Dane found Lilly Chicoine on the corner across the street from Claude's apartment. She was carrying a plastic bag in her hand. It contained over twenty exposed needles that she hadn't bothered to cap earlier that morning before tossing them into the plastic sack that she now held by her side. Most of the syringes sharp ends were exposed.

"Hey," Dane said in greeting, not as angry as he had been the night before.

Lilly simply gestured by raising her eyebrows.

"You stayed at Claude's last night?"

"None of your fucken business," she answered, spacing out her words for effect.

"I'm your boyfriend, Lilly. It is my fucken business."

"Look, I'm not in the mood. If you just came here to bitch, then fuck off!"

"Fuck off? Did I just hear you right?"

She was giving him her profile while she watched the street. Just then, a red Mustang with a white top drove by, its orange headlights shadowing the pavement before it. The driver and the passenger both looked to be girls in their mid to late twenties with the driver wearing a scarf.

"Who the fuck takes care of you, Lilly? Who loves you no matter what?" he reminded her.

"I said, I'm not in the mood for this, now FUCK OFF!" she yelled, whipping the bag full of needles in his direction.

"Hey! Watch out! There's needles in there," Antoine who was a friend of David Danes called out. Antoine was a neighborhood regular. He was sitting behind them on the wooden divider next to the dimly lit phone booth wearing shorts, a polo shirt and a pair of prescription glasses.

Again Lilly whipped the bag at him, to which Dane simply stepped aside.

"Mother Fucker!!" Lilly hollered, out of frustration once more, whipping the bag in his direction.
Again she missed, and she retreated onto the road, screaming back at him at the same time.

"Go FUCK YOURSELF!" she yelled, just as the bumper of a red Toyota connected less than gingerly with her left leg and at the same time, knocked Lilly to the ground.

"Oh, fuck!" Dane shouted from the curb. Antoine was stunned, using exactly the same language.

Being hit by a car did not seem to faze Lilly any. She simply stood up, limping a bit and walked onto the sidewalk across from the two men who were watching her.

"Lilly. C'mon, let me see your leg," Dane said, walking across the street to meet her.

"No!" she said with a hint of softness in her voice.

"Lilly, come here, baby."

"No. Go away. I don't wanna be around anyone right now."

Dane stopped in his tracks, letting her go. He didn't want to risk a second battle. Not tonight and not next to Antoine who had just been joined by Angela O.

"Where's the driver?" Dane asked.

"He took off. It was her fault. She's the one who ran out."

"What happened Dane?" Angela asked.

"Lilly did more coke today than Tony Montana sold in Scarface," Dane replied. "She's damn full up."

Just then a police cruiser rolled by them.

"You have to be careful. She's crazy when she's like that," Angela O. said.

"Swinging those fucken needles around. She's psychotic. She shouldn't be on the street anymore, One of these days she's going to hurt someone badly," Antoine remarked.

"Lilly is a stupid bitch sometimes," Angela remarked.

"Yeah. She needs to clean up. There's no question about it," the fighter said.

"Why were you two fighting?" Angela asked Dane.

"Because she stayed at Claude's last night."

"That's where she stayed for a while last winter. She was sleeping outside on the bus stop when he found her, but she's not in love with him." Angela informed him. "They're not in love." she re-inforced. Well, maybe he's in love with her, but I don't think that she's in love with him. Lilly can't love anybody because she doesn't love herself. Do you think that she loves herself? She can't. She's a prostitute, and a junkie."

Dane raised himself from the wooden beam.

"I think I'm gonna go home. Thanks for the talk, guys," he said.

"Anytime," Antoine said.

"Take care of yourself, Dane," Angela said lovingly.

"I'll try," Dane responded.

It was 10:49 p.m.

Lilly came home around two o'clock the next afternoon. She had a bad limp and was extremely dope sick. There was a twenty dollar bill on the dining room table and Lilly quickly noticed it.

Can I have that?" Lilly asked.

"No," Dane responded. He was standing in the kitchen wearing only a pair of gray sweat pants.

He was stirring spaghetti which he planned to mix with Ketchup, chopped Bar-B-Que weiners and Taco Sauce. A David Dane original.

"You're still mad at me," Lilly exclaimed.

"No, but I need that twenty. We're out of toilet paper and soda."

"Oh come on!" Lilly said, wrapping her arms around him from behind. "I can't make a customer like this. Fuck, I can hardly walk," she said turning him around to meet her lips. She kissed him slowly, but he lightly brushed her away. "Oh, what? You don't wanna make love to me anymore?"

"Lilly, I don't mind making love to you, but not when there are strings attached."

"That's not why I was doing it," she said.

"Yeah, and i'm the Walrus of Goo-Goo Kitchoo," he said, returning to the pasta on the stove.

When he turned around again, the twenty dollars was missing from the empty table behind him.

"Lilly, where's the fucken money?"

"I didn't take it," she said without blinking.

Dane looked her up and down, from her white sneakers to her black jeans to the brown shirt that she wore over a white t-shirt, all the way up to her white ball cap, and she had not moved.

"Lilly. Give me the twenty bucks."

"I can't give you what I don't have."

The nerve of this woman. Did she really believe that he was this stupid? Proof positive that the drugs had taken a toll on her brain.

"Lilly, you obviously . . ."

"I swear I didn't take it."

"Ah, yeah. That makes everything better," he said. "Lilly, give me my fucken money. Listen, if you just admit that you have it, then you can keep the lousy twenty bucks."

"You promise?"

"Scouts honor."

"I hooped it."

"Hooped it?" Dane asked. He had never heard the term before.

"I shoved it up my twat."

"Now why didn't I think of that?"

"Can I still keep it?"

Dane gestured with his hand in the affirmative. After all. He was a man of his word.

It was 2:15 p.m.

"Hello?" David Dane asked in a gravelly voice. The ringing phone had awakened him.

"Ya know that it's ten a.m." the voice on the other end asked said.

Dane looked at the digital display on his cable converter terminal. His uncle was right. It was ten a.m.

"Haven't heard from you in a while. My mother said that you were in some foreign country," Dane said.

"Yeah. I was overseas. They wanted top military brass and whatever and whatever and whatever."

Dane's uncle was a high-ranking military commander who had spent more than thirty-five years in the armed forces. There were also rumors of his work in counter-espionage, not to mention being a terror analyst for The Middle East. During his tenure, Thomas Wallace (aka The Shepherd) also worked as a top-level bodyguard for Prince Charles and Lady Diana, and also, at one point, for former Prime Minister

Pierre Elliott Trudeau, who had chosen him personally. He had more decorations than a Christmas tree, Dane recalled. He had seen photos.

Tom Wallace had been close to Dane ever since Dane was a baby, always showing the same concern for him as if Dane were one of his own kids, and he had three. Their names were Thomas jr, Lorraine and (Will) who has attained the rank of "Captain" in The Canadian Armed Forces.

Lilly moaned from underneath her blankets on the floor. She had fallen asleep there and hadn't bothered to get up and move over to the mattress that was only feet away. Nonetheless, she was sound asleep and cradling two teddy bears by the names of Teddy and Junkie. Teddy wore sun glasses and a hat. There was also a small white bear next to her that she called "Pepsi" because she had once spilled half a can of it on him.

"What's this I hear about a drug-addicted girlfriend and a Serial Killer?" Tom asked.

"My mother told you about Lilly," Dane stated plainly. *

"Just briefly. Her and your father haven't yet met her yet."

"That's not my fault. They're the ones with the frequent flier miles. You've probably earned a few yourself by now."

"Aye, aye," Wallace said, choosing a term from his Scottish ancestry to respond.

"Have you talked to your mother?" Dane inquired in reference to his Grandmother.

"For a minute. Poor Mum, she just sits there and stares at the TV all day."

"Can she still see it? Last time I was home her sight was worsening. She wears tinted glasses now."

"She can't see people's faces. She can only see around."

Thomas's Mother, Dane's grandmother, had been a war bride. Her name was Doris Wallace, wife of Tom senior, and daughter of Acadian Mary Le Blanc. Doris had met her Scottish husband in Canada, but had then returned to Scotland during the war. She had even crossed the Channel later on in the war with her husband on a military transport. She had had her fair share of air raids and dropping bombs. She was now, today, legally blind.

"So, someone's killing girls?" Thomas asked, going back to the original subject. "Boy, I'll tell ya. That girl that you're in love with, Lilly, she had better be careful," he said seriously.

"Yeah. Try telling her that. She thinks that she's Evil fucking Kneivel," Dane said.

"Well, what can you do about it?"

"Nothing."

"Is she interested in rehab?"

"Do bears wear silk shirts?"

"Not at all, eh?"

"Nope."

"Jesus Christ," Thomas said. "I'm gonna try to get out there at some point. I've gotta fly to the United Arab Emirates tomorrow, but I'll call you when I get back. Love ya, son," the commander said before hanging up.

It was 10:12 a.m.

Etienne Armena worked at Santino Video, but on this wet and rainy Tuesday night, Etienne was not at work. Rather, he had just returned from playing the cello for a local symphony and was now standing in a park off of Ontario Street talking to David Dane. The two had known each other now for about a year, having met at the video store during the wee hours of the morning on a Friday. Even though the two were from completely different worlds, and had little in common, they had managed to become as thick as thieves in no time.

Dane liked Etienne. He was trust worthy and loyal, and he had a helluva big heart. They didn't come anymore honest or genuine and, for a small guy, Etienne was a damn big person.

"So I told Bill, the next time that thug, Yves, comes in here you will have to call the cops, because I won't get murdered for ten bucks an hour. I will find another job," Etienne said with a French accent.

"I told Bill a long time ago that Yves had to go," Dane said. "He's bad for business. Not only that, but the staff doesn't wanna work there anymore. He's a thug, and Bill has students for staff. Not cops.

The rain was coming down harder now, accelerating. Dane had one foot up on a bench with Etienne standing in front of him. They were both getting drenched.

"Yves' way of thinking is, 'You will be my friend, or I will kill you.' He is that way with everyone, except you," said Etienne.

The shrubbery around them was lined with silver from the downpour and the wind was blowing in gusts, cutting moats and canyons around them in the darkness, giving ambiance to an otherwise moodless night.

"I can't believe that. I've been waiting all this time and Lilly still hasn't come back yet," Dane said. "It's very discouraging."

"I don't think that it's the first time that she's done this," Etienne remarked.

"Yeah, and I don't think that it'll be the last either."

"How long have you been waiting?"

Dane paused. "More than enough time for her to do what she had to do and come back."

I am not surprised," said Etienne.

"What brings you to our quiet little town tonight anyway?"

"I am living here now. Close by, on Wolf."

"You live around here?"

"For maybe six months. The rent is cheap and it's close to everything."

"Yeah, you can say that again."

Just then Lilly walked into the park with a fist full of money.

"Okay! I made a hundred bucks. Let's go," she chirped, anxious to call her dealer.

"Okay. I will say goodnight, then," Etienne said.

"All right, Etienne. You take care of yourself. Be careful of the neighborhood."

He was carrying his cello case. Dane thought that he would be lucky to make it home alive.

"Let's go, Lilly," the boxer said.

It was 11:47 p.m.

One week later there was a knock at Dane's door, and when he opened it, he got the surprise of a lifetime. It was Mike and Shannon standing side by side, looking at him anxiously.

"Yeah, how you doin'?" David Dane asked, turning to glance over his shoulder at Lilly who was standing behind him.

"I'm okay," Mike said. "We just wanted to come by and apologize."

"Well, I don't really think it's me that . . ."

"I know, I know," Mike said. "Well, what I did to Shannon was awful."

"Uh-huh."

"Especially in front of you guys and your buddy Bill. Look, if it makes any difference, I'm off drugs now, and so is Shannon. We were just wondering if you'd be willing to give us a second shot . . . I mean chance," Mike said, realizing that 'shot' was a lousy choice of words.

"Well, I don't know if . . ."

"Please, Dane," Shannon pled. "If we could just stay here for a short time. We can't go back out on the street. We'll end up on drugs all over again, and we've worked so hard . . ."

"Alright, alright, alright. Yeah, I guess . . . if Lilly doesn't mind," Dane said soberly.

Dane was looking over his shoulder again at Lilly who was nodding softly in agreement.

"You guys can sleep in the living room on the cot," Chicoine said. "I'll get it ready."

"Thanks. Is there any place in particular that we can put these things down?" Mike asked of their bags.

"Ah, maybe right over there," Dane said, cheering up a bit. He was always willing to give people a second chance, plus he felt badly about Shannon's predicament.

Mike laid their bags down on the floor and then whispered something into Shannon's ear.

"I can make some pasta or some hot dogs if you guys are hungry," the boxer offered.

"Yeah, sure. Why not?" Phillips said.

"I'll put the water on the stove," Chicoine said.

"So, where have you guys been? I mean we haven't seen you downtown," Dane inquired, thinking of the scare that Shannon had given them.

"We were in rehab, but those few days after we got back, we were up in The Heights," Mike said.

"Oh, yeah?" Lilly said cheerfully, taking an interest in the conversation.

"You know The Heights?" Dane asked.

"Well, a bit. Yeah. I mean, not real well or anything, but we've been there a few times in the past," Mike responded.

"Baby, what's The Heights?" Lilly asked.

"It's a bad place," Dane responded.

"What's so terrible about it?"

"It ain't Ontario Street. Up there, if a girl owes money or if she doesn't wanna work, she gets tossed into a circle by a bunch of pimps and then they beat her until she either passes out or bleeds to death. I've known girls that it's happened to," Phillips said, nonchalantly.

Dane's head was lowered.

"Then I'll never work up there," Lilly said.

"Yeah. You got that right," Dane exclaimed, looking up.

"I mean, it's not so bad if the girl does what she's told. Shannon worked Aryl Street for over seven months and she had a pimp."

"Yeah," Shannon said sheepishly.

"Can we change the subject now?" Lilly asked.

David Dane took a pull from his can of Diet Pepsi.

"So, Mike, are you interested in coming to the gym with me tomorrow?" Dane asked, setting the can down.

"Well, I mean, I don't really have any money."

"Hey, that's okay. You don't need any. I work over there," Dane said sympathetically.

He trains people," Lilly interrupted proudly.

"Oh yeah? Which gym do you train at?" Mike asked enthusiastically.

"I prefer Iron Gym. Of course, I'm a little biased . . ." Dane proclaimed. "My friend owns the place. You'll meet him. He's great," Dane said, matching Mike's enthusiasm.

"Hey, maybe someday I could get a job there. I lifted weights in jail."

"It shows," Dane responded.

"I used to train," Lilly said cheerfully.

"Lilly puts on muscle easy. You should have seen her the last time she came out. You looked beautiful," Dane said. "Well, you always look beautiful. You're my Lilly. The most beautiful woman in the world."

Lilly looked happily pleased with her compliment.

There was subdued mockery on Mike's face.

"Thank . . . you," Lilly, the little orphan said.

"I love you, ya know. You're always welcome," Dane said genuinely.

"So, how long have you been lifting?" Phillips wanted to know.

"Maybe too long. I'm in pain a lot."

"How many years did you fight?"

"Five."

"Do you know how to fight outside the ring?"

"I'm a product of Chris Markem So. Yeah. I know how to do that."

"So your coach taught you how to fight bare knuckled as well?"

"Chris taught me a lot more than that. If I'm dangerous in the ring, then I'm lethal on the street," Dane said.

It was 10:56 p.m.

"I know I'm no one to talk, but this guy's a bit questionable, eh?" Lilly said later on, after Mike and Shannon had gone to bed.

"Yeah, you could say that. Look, I have no illusions about Mike Phillips or what he's capable of, but we all deserve a second shot. You should know that better than anyone." said Dane. "Hey, look, a lot of people in my life never even gave me a first chance, and I wish they had."

"Yeah, but believe me, this guy's not you. He could never be you," Lilly said.

"Look. Let's give them a place to stay until they can afford a place of their own."

"And when will that be?"

"Let me talk to Bobby in the morning and see if he'd be willing to give Mike a shot."

"What if Mike starts hitting Shannon again?"

"I ain't gonna let that happen, all right? You have my word."

"I love you, baby," she said.

"Alright," Dane said.

It was 11:07 p.m.

Manning Robar fancied himself as a big-time pimp, and to the low-lifes that he hung around with, that's exactly what he was. As a matter of fact, Manny Robar had been a pimp for so long that he could hardly recall a time when he wasn't in The Game. To Manning, living off women was second nature and, toward most of his girls, Manny Robar showed no mercy, never once sparing the rod. Women were simply a commodity, a source of income, and if he had to put one under, there would be another one right around the corner to take her place, sometimes on the same day.

Tonight, however, Manning Robar was cruising Ontario Street in his chauffeur-driven limo, searching for women to add to his stables.

Now, by and large, most of the women who worked Ontario Street were addicts and of no consequence to Manning, but every so often you found a rare gem. After all, it was on Ontario Street that Manning Robar had met his current main squeeze, Latisha Haines, a light skinned black girl with nice features, big breasts and a round butt. Just the way that Robar liked them.

A traffic light turned red and the limo stopped.

"Look what's up on the stroll," Manning said in a deep, rasping voice.

Franco responded by glancing over his left shoulder at whatever his boss was looking at.

"Pull the car over. I'm gonna let that little Latin bitch suck on my dick."

Following orders, Franco pulled the limo out of the lane and parked by the curb in the darkness.

"Roll my window down," Manning said, folding up a hundred.

"Wanna get high?" Robar asked, flagging Chicoine over with the creased C-note.

"Yeah," she responded, bending to get eye level with him.

"Get in."

Lilly opened the door and climbed into the back seat next to Manning.

"Wow, fuck. This is a nice car, eh?"

"You think I'm gonna give you any money, bitch?" Manning growled. "You gon suck my black dick, then you gonna come and make me some money!" he yelled, yanking on the back of her neck and forcing her head into his crotch.

Manning was foaming at the mouth now, like an animal with rabies.

"Come on, bitch. Get all up in it."

"Fucken scum-bag!" Lilly yelled, all at once breaking free from Manning and running out of the car. It's door was still open onto the night.

Manny was cursing out loud as he reached out to try and pull Lilly back into the car but she was to far gone.

"Shiiit"!!!!!!!!!!!!!!!!!!!! Robar exclaimed.
It was 9:00 p.m.

Bryan Ferry's "Don't Stop the Dance" echoed loudly over the speakers inside a nearby car as David Dane met Lilly at the front doors of their building.

"Some fucken asshole tried to stick his dick in my mouth!" Lilly exclaimed.

These were things that David Dane would rather not hear, but usually ended up hearing anyway.

"He looked like a fucken pimp."

The lights were on in Dane's eyes now. He looked taken aback. Pimps were not allowed to try and work the girls on Ontario Street. It was an un-written rule.

"When was this"?? he asked.

Maybe an hour ago," Lilly said, leading Dane about two feet ahead through the glass doors and into the foyer of 235 Leopold Heights.

Dane's angst was burning now, stirring his adrenaline. He had a mind to make an unscheduled appearance on Ontario Street.

"Fuck, he didn't even pay me anything."

The crimson light in Dane's head was flashing now. Somewhere demons roamed.

"He was in a limo. It looked expensive. Fuck!" she said.

"Have you seen Mike or Shannon tonight?"

"Ah . . . I think I saw Shannon on Delorimier when I was with a client," Lilly remarked. "Where's Mike?"

"I took him to the gym with me this afternoon. He met Bobby. I think he left after that. Bobby seemed to like him pretty good. No bad vibes you know". Dane said, scratching his temple.

"Sooo . . . . is Bobby gonna hire him?" Lilly asked.

"Yeah, but I don't think that it's gonna be in the capacity of a trainer. Mike's gonna be like an equipment maintenance man. It pays ten bucks an hour, so at least that'll give Mike and Shannon some income."

They were on the elevator now. When they reached their floor, Mike Phillips was waiting at the door to their apartment.

"Hey, Mike. How you doin'?" Dane asked.

"Where's Shannon?" Chicoine wanted to know.

"She's not coming back for a few days," Phillips said sheepishly.

"Well, . . . why not?" Dane questioned with lethal overtones in his voice.

"Well, Shannon has this client, and every so often she goes and turns for him for a few days. It's good bread, though," Phillips said, letting a slight cackle escape his lips.

Dane shot a glance across at Lilly. She was already monitoring his response.

"Well, when will she be back?" the fighter inquired.

"Maybe six, seven days," Mike responded, his tone leaving him on the last word.

Dane unlocked the door to the apartment and the three of them went inside. Mike sat down first and turned on the lamp that sat next to him. There seemed to be a grimace on his face that was there and then gone.

"Can I ask you a question?" Phillips asked.

"Yeah, sure. You can ask me anything you want, my friend," David Dane responded.

"You think you could get me more than ten bucks an hour from Bobby?"

Dane was taken off-guard.

"Ah, I don't know. I can try, but Bobby's kind of strapped for cash right now."

"'Cause you know it would really help me and Shannon."

Lilly had evaporated into the darkness of the bedroom.

"Hey, Mike. I'll see what I can do," Dane said affably.

There was a knock at the door.

"Who is it?" Dane hollered.

"It's Bill," Ramirez said.

"Can I get a beer?" Phillips asked.

"Oh, yeah. Sure," Dane responded affably.

"Hey Billy," the fighter said in greeting as he held the door open for his tall, weathered friend.

"Man, I'm sorry I didn't call first. I had to run by the store to pick up some groceries. I was out of toothpaste and bread."

"That's a bad combination," Dane remarked slyly as he scratched his temple.

"Hey Dane, so, you'll talk to Bob tomorrow?" Phillips asked.

"Yeah, alright," Dane responded peacefully. "I'll see what I can do," he said.

Manning Robar stepped left foot first out into the blackening night, his pimp's staff sparkled and shimmered at its devil's head. He was in The Heights. The coiling madness of its streets were all around him now. Nightmares in cold reflection flashed and gleamed in his eyes. He was by most definitions a wicked man with an evil heart. He was callous and cruel, and to most, his soul bore not a shred of compassion or sympathy, even to those who stood close to him and knew him well.

Latisha Haines exited from the right back door of Robar's limo with a six-foot tall street soldier at her side.

"I wanna get good and high," the pimp's girlfriend said, handing a fistful of cash to Manny's soldier.

"I want that Latin bitch. I'm gonna break her in. Call our contact downtown and tell him no later than the end of the week, if he wants his money."

Manning's soldier nodded in response to his boss's demand.

"Look up," Robar said, pointing to one of the upper-floor windows of his sprawling estate. Above his circular driveway there were eight windows, each of which represented stables for each of his girls. On this night, though, there was one named "Lacey" that he had been waiting for for a long time. Compared to most men in his profession, he was well off, if not affluent. He had come up from nothing. A low-level street hustler.

"I called him, Boss. He's not answering. His mobile phone's going into voicemail," the bodyguard said.

"Keep trying," Robar ordered, rounding the back of his limo and heading into the house.

The first floor consisted of two living rooms, three bathrooms, each with jacuzzis and a two-level kitchen and master bedroom.

Manning Robar had done very well for himself indeed.

Chapter 16

Mike Phillips' beeper went off just after nine p.m. It was Shannon. He made a quick walk to a pay phone and dropped a quarter inside. Soon Shannon was on the other end. She sounded groggy and fucked up, as if she'd been tripping for a day, which, in fact, she had.

"Where are you, baby?"

Shannon sniffled once before answering. "I'm in The Heights. Listen, there's hardly any minutes left on my phone, so I have to be quick, okay? I talked to Latisha late last night. Manny wants to see you."

"Did he say what for?"

"He wants a specific girl. He didn't say who."

"Well, when does he wanna see me?"

"Tomorrow at two. At the house. He says he's not paying you if you don't show up."

"Alright. Tell him I'll be there." And with that Shannon hung up.

Just as Phillips hung up the phone, he turned to see David Dane standing in the shadows behind him.

"Who were you talking to?"

"That was Shannon."

Dane's face was long and expressionless.

"Tell who you'll be where?" he asked with no emotion in his voice.

"Oh, I have a business meeting."

"Oh, yeah?" Dane responded ominously. He did not trust Mike Phillips.

"Hey, don't worry about it, buddy . . ."

"Hey Mike, you're living under my roof. Don't lie to me about nothin'."

"I have business to take care of . . ."

"From now on, all of your business concerns me. Don't bring people into my life that I'm gonna have to hurt to get rid of. You understand me?"

"Yeah. So, did you talk to Bob for me?"

"Yeah, I did," Dane answered, his tone softening.

"And. What did he say?" Phillips asked impatiently.

"He doesn't have anymore payouts right now."

"'Cause I ain't workin' for ten bucks an hour, man."

"Beggars can't be choosers," Dane replied. "No offense."

"You can't even get me five bucks more an hour?"

Dane cocked his head to one side. "Not right now."

Soon Lilly was upon them. She looked more than a bit fucked up.

"Alright, Mike. I gotta go right now," the fighter said, walking off with his girlfriend.

It was 9:15 pm.

The Heights was a series of post-apocalyptic looking buildings, seedy crack joints, sleazy bars, and strip clubs that had not been kept up in years. It was also a busy place for police patrols.

On this afternoon, the very stench of semen, decay, and other incomprehensible odors was streaked across the air.

Across the street in an old tavern, Mike Phillips sat across from Manny Robar and two of his henchmen.

"Michael, I need you to do something for me," Robar began, just before snorting a line of coke up his left nostril.

"There's a girl. She's Latina. Her name's Lilly. I want you to bring her to me with her teeth in her mouth."

Phillips was suddenly aware of the predicament that he was in. He could hardly believe that Manny had just asked for Lilly.

"I know that you live with her because Sweet Shannon told me. Are you following along, Michael?"

"Yeah," Phillips said with an indecisive look on his face.

"You know, I've kept Shannon up for years. I've let her slide. I've let you slide too. There's a lot of money to be paid back, and the two black eyes that Shannon is wearing right now out on that curb are a taste of what I might decide to do if my investment in you both doesn't start to pay off. I want her not later than next week or you don't get paid at all. Today, I have a car full of girls that needs to be driven across town to one of my houses. Can you do that?"

Phillips nodded.

"Here's some candy for your nose," Robar said, tossing a small, tidy bag of white powder across the table.

Phillips' eyes were wide now, and he was smiling.

"With her teeth, Michael."

Soon Phillips was out the door.

It was 2:14 p.m.

The vapor lamps that usually glowed ominously over Ontario Street were shut off, leaving nothing but blackness in their wake. Somewhere in the shadows there had been a power outage and now he was given the power to watch without being seen. He was the Devil over this earth, his pulse thundering and pounding harshly with every moment that he had to wait. He could smell their scent, that heavy pungent odor of perfume and cover-up mixed together. Soon his jagged army blade would sear another heart, stopping the algorythms of life.

Somewhere in the distance, red lights glowed atop a yellow ambulance while two uniformed attendants unloaded a stretcher and unfolded its undercarriage. There was no patient in sight.

He could hear her now. The one that he would take from this world tonight. She was coming toward him from someplace in the shadows, her heels clicking against the stroll. His eyes began to close. He could taste her presence now, feel her pulse in his head. Soon. It would be time.

It was 1:00 a.m.

Down the street from where Bobby Troy Edmonds stood in the shadows with his knife, Lilly Chicoine and David Dane stood in the blackness, waiting for one of Lilly's smack dealers.

It was quiet tonight. The traffic had ebbed and Lilly's dealer was taking a lot longer than usual.

"C'mon, fuck!" Lilly exclaimed. "They're usually a lot quicker than this. Is it because of the blackout that they're taking so long?"

"Isn't this the guy that you owe eighty bucks to?" Dane asked.

"I owe everywhere."

Soon there was a blood curdling scream from somewhere in the darkness. Dane turned, his eyes locking on the murky shadows in the distance.

"It's happening again," Dane said horrified, his soul taking a tumble. Something terrible moved through him. A morbid air. That sixth sense that made his heart race when trouble was near.

"Where is it coming from?" Lilly asked.

"Close to Fullum."

Dane could hear sirens in the distance and soon flashing red and blue a short distance away. The unveiling of Hell would be soon. Soon.

"The body that was pulled away from the coiling shadows of Fullum Street's seedy depths was that of Shannon Nicole Edwards, twenty-four. Our senior reporter Raoul Damon will have further news at eleven," Deborah Taylor said, her words ominous and lingering, as the abyss of late-night television droned on.

David Dane turned to embrace Lilly Chicoine whose tears glistened in the heat of the night air that was pouring in through the screen door in massive waves. She was broken now, with more emotions than Dane had ever seen in her face before, exploding amidst cries and sobs of terror for her fallen friend. If Lilly was a body of water, right now she would have been a tidal wave.

"Did I even say goodbye?" Lilly cried. "I mean, I don't have very many friends," she said. "Why would someone do this?"

"This is someone's dark fantasy," Dane answered, using the palm of his left hand to wipe the sweat from the back of his neck.

"What do you mean?" Chicoine sobbed.

"Someone, or something. This is the way that their tortured mind lives out a fantasy. You know that moment when you're dreaming and you don't know whether you're really awake or not?" Dane asked in a low gravelly voice.

"Yeah," Lilly responded, again through sobs.

"Most serial killers live their whole lives in that moment," he said. "It's like consecutive acts in a play or a nightmare, except the killer is the playwright or the Sandman," he said.

"Do you think that Mike knows yet?" Lilly questioned, darkness framing her face now.

"I don't know," David Dane answered.

The phone was ringing now.

"It's my Uncle," Dane said as the call display flashed in and out.

"Hello?" Dane said.

"Are yeh there son"?? Commander Wallace began, "I just happened to be on the phone with a friend of mine that works with The Police down there. I was watching your news broadband at the same time".

"This is a local broadcast. How the fuck . . . ?"

"I've ways, . . . I've ways," Thomas said, avoiding the longer terminology.

"She was a friend of ours. What can you find out about this?"

Dane knew that Thomas could find out about just about anything if he really wanted to."

"You let me handle it. Okay, son?" Thomas said, half ordering.

"This girl is special. She and her boyfriend were staying with us. Michael still is."

"I have a few friends in your area. I'll try and reach at least one of them tonight. How's your girlfriend?"

"Terrible. She never had a chance to say goodbye to her friend. She really liked Shannon." Dane said.

"Stay close to the phone. Your mother's been trying to call you."

"I'll leave my cell on."

It was 3:07 a.m.

Mike Phillips was in handcuffs. He had been picked up on the same street where Shannon was murdered shortly after they lifted her body out of the shadows. Now he was up shit creek without a paddle. He now had no money and no source of income either. With Shannon gone, the perils of his situation were deep, if not abysmal. Manny would be furious. Enraged. And there was little that Phillips could do about it.

If he got out anytime soon, if they granted him bail, he would do exactly as Manny had suggested. He would do what it would take to put Lilly to work for the pimp, even if that meant betraying David Dane.

The big clock on the debriefing room wall ticked away. It was getting late. Phillips was pacing the room now like a caged animal. His eyes were deep and dark in the shadow of the bright debriefing room lights.

He was angry. Powerfully enraged. He would leave David Dane lieing on the pavement in a pool of his own blood if he had to. Soon. He would find him, and show him who THE MAN was . . . .

It was 3:10 a.m.

Chris Meagher was true blue.

Dane had known the man who was stepping off the plane into the Montreal heat since childhood.

He was as loyal a friend as you could get in today's day and age, and his heart was always in the right place. He had the same passion for bodybuilding as Dane, only Meagher had seen more profound results, pumping iron like an obsession until he was bestowed with the nickname "Little Arnold." That alone was not all that David Dane and Christopher Meagher had in common. Their appearance, some said, made them look like brothers, both sporting shaved heads and neatly trimmed pinches that ran in square around their lips. Meaghers eldest brother, Michael Meagher, had assisted in introducing both Dane and his own younger brother Christopher, to the regimen of bodybuilding many, many moons ago.

Both families had grown up only a block from each other. Chris had two brothers, Michael, the eldest, and PJ (Patrick Jason), the second eldest. The siblings in the Meagher Family, Michael, Pat and Christopher had made their living in the field of Security. The youngest of the Meagher clan, Christopher, now owned his own company.

The parents, James (Jimmy) and Alexis were also life-long family friends. Both Marilyn Dane and Alexis Meagher sang together in the local choir. Christopher's father, Jimmy, was a man with a big heart and great compassion who worked at the post office for many years and had recently retired to his favorite pastime of relaxing and taking it easy, often soaking up the rays on his favorite sun chair in the family's back yard.

"This is Christopher Meagher," David Dane said six hours later in the same a.m.

"Nice to meet you," Lilly said, extending her sun-blasted hand.

"Just put my bags anywhere?" Meagher asked, addressing Dane with an obvious comfort and familiarity.

"Anywhere," Dane confirmed. "Give me a hug, you bastard," the boxer said, embracing his life-long friend. "How was the flight?"
"Rough. Alotta turbulence,"

Lilly was preoccupied in the other room.

"How are Jimmy and Alexis?" Dane asked.

"Not bad. Not bad," Chris said, adjusting his ball cap.

"Lilly and I lost a friend last night."

"Fuck! What happened?"

"Shannon was murdered.We have a serial killer on the loose."

"Serial killer!!" Meagher exclaimed. "This is like a fucken movie."

"I swear to God I'm gonna write a book about all of this one day."

"She's still out there working?"

Dane was nodding.

"Lilly's crazy," C.M. said, his voice dipping so as not to be overheard.

"You want a beer or a soda?" Dane the host asked.

"I'll have a soda."

"That's good," Dane smiled, "because we don't have any beer."

"Oh. I forgot to mention. I saw Mark Bernard before I left. He said to say "Hi".

Mark Bernard, who was thirty two years of age was a life long friend of David Danes aswell as Chris Meaghers. He was born and raised on some of the toughest and meanest streets of Nova Scotia, and he carried an attitude along with a very well honed natural gift for both MMA and Martial Arts. Mark had been an avid fan and student of Bruce Lees from the time he could crawl, also admiring and patterning himself after The Gracies. Particularily his favorite Gracie "Royce". His natural gift for the fighting arts had gained Mark a reputation for being a hardcore Badass on the street aswell as an African American Role Model to the youth of his community. He was by his peers, well liked and well respected.

"I'm going to work," Lilly said matter-of-factly. "Fuck, I need smack."

Meagher looked like he had just been struck by another wall of turbulence.

"I'm gonna go keep an eye on her," Dane said. "You can tag along if you want."

"Ahh . . . . I'm kinda beat. Is it okay if I just crash"??

"Make yourself at home". Dane said, ending the conversation.

11:00 a.m. had arrived.
That evening over dinner at Star Of India Restaurant Lilly Chicoine, Chris Meagher and David Dane discussed the possibility that The Ontario Street Killer could be a regular who had turned angry at one or more of the girls who worked the stroll for something that may have been done to him. Meagher had in his line of work seen his share of psychos. Even one who had drawn a gun on him and almost fired before he had had a chance to wrestle the Walter PPK away from him.
"What's on the menu"?? Chicoine asked shifting in her seat.

"These people in my opinion serve the finest Cuizine in Montreal"
David Dane said to Lilly who looked absolutely elegant and stunning in
her black cocktail dress and deep rouge lip stick.

"Do you know the people who work here"?? Lilly asked.

"Most of them. Jamil, Syed, Pinku, Manjure, and Joynal". Dane listed.

"These people are friends of mine. The food is addictive. You've never
eaten a damn meal in your life until you've tried The Chicken Jalfrazzi
and Nan bread".

"It's good to see you brother. Everyone misses you back home. Mum
and Dad send their love".

"Make sure that you let them know that I do to".

"I gotta be back at work the day after tommorrow right. So this'll be a
short visit".

"Bad news. When are you leaving"?? Dane asked the heavily pumped
Meagher.

"Later tonight".

"Make sure that you come back soon".

Lilly was pouring spices on her food.

"Cheers." Dane said lifting his glass against his friends.

"Cheers". Christopher Meagher said.

It was 8:34 P.M.

Mike Phillips stood beneath the glow of a white vapor lamp in an alley
just off Ontario Street. The police had released him after six p.m. that
night, having nothing to hold him on. As well, those badge-wearing
fuckers* shouldn't, he thought. After all, why would he have slaughtered
his own cash cow?

It was dark now. Around ten thirty or ten forty. The darkness swelled. The
winds over an invisible cauldron seemed to change course somewhere
in the outstretched blackness.

Phillips wanted to know where Lilly was. She would be his new source of
income, even if it meant betraying or physically punishing David Dane.

About fifteen minutes later, Manny Robar's limo rounded the corner
onto Ontario Street.

David Dane fished into the pocket of his black leather jacket and pulled out Lilly's matches with one of his gloved hands.

"Here you go, Baby Bunny," Dane offered, lighting up Lilly's cigarette with his right fingertips.

"Thanks. Fuck, it's getting cold outside, eh?"

"Hey look. It's Mike," Dane exclaimed as Phillips leaned out the window of Manny Robar's limo.

"Whose is that?" Dane wondered aloud.

Mike Phillips and Manny Robar stepped into the street around Lilly Chicoine and David Dane.

"I know this guy," Lilly said of Robar in a weakened voice.

"How you doin', Mike?" Dane asked the man in the blue, yellow, red, and white track suit.

Phillips said nothing as visible air rose in swirls from his mouth.

"You wanna make some real money?" Phillips asked Lilly. Ignoring David Dane.

"Hey, Mike!" Dane shouted at the man two feet away from him. The boxer's eyes looked like smouldering heaters now. His fists were clenched and the mucles in his jaw were tightening. Dane could feel the fuse of his temper burning to its wick.

David Dane clenched his left fist inside of his cut glove and swung at Phillips opening him up just below the right eye.
David Dane and Mike Phillips spilled onto the stone park as a number of The Ontario Street Originals looked on. Tiffany-whose-ID-said-Dale-Frost screeched as David Dane opened up the larger Phillips further with a series of blows, blood flowing freely now from Phillips' nose and

mouth. Ann Marilyn roared into the street, knocking Latisha Haines flat on her ass as she tried to exit the limo to hand a crowbar to Mike.

Mike Phillips threw a hard right, almost knocking Dane off his feet. He was staggering backward now.

"Fuck YOU!!" David Dane said, regaining his balance, with Tiffany-whose-ID-said-Dale-Frost, Angela O. and Sheryl at his back.

Mike's face was dripping crimson now as Dane split Phillips open above the eye with a left hook. The crowd moved backward in a roaring wave, the streetlights overhead bleeding into the center of the semi-circle formed by the crowd.

"C'mon David!" Sheryl cheered.

Lilly eye-balled Latisha Haines as the mulatto prostitute rose to her feet as if to retrieve the steel bar.

"FIGHT LIKE DAVID"!!!!!!!!!!!!!!!!!!!!!! Chris Markems voice echoed from somewhere within the recesses of Danes mind. "KILL THIS FUCKEN MUTANT"!!!!!!!!!!!!!!!!!!!!!! Markems voice ordered authoritatively.

"I'll try." Dane responded, as Manny Robar stole into his peripheral vision momentarily.

Phillips was on him again, engaging him with a barrage of wild blows that Dane answered with a blistering right hand followed by a left uppercut that left Phillips reeling.

"DO EM IN"!!!!!!!!!!!!!!!!!!!! Chris Markems voice echoed once more through the fever of Dane's mind as Lilly's left foot kicked the crowbar from Latisha's reach.

"C'mon David! This is your show!" the sexy Alyssa M. yelled.

Phillips was back-pedalling toward Robar's limo now as Dane hit him with two stone cold rights that sent Phillips head first into one of the limo doors and then to the ground.

"Like I said, my friend," Dane said addressing the fallen Phillips, "Blood runs when the time comes."

Lilly was approaching her boyfriend now.

"I love you Lilly . . . . I love you," Dane said, lifting Lilly into his arms.

It was 11:45 pm.

The street roared on.

DAVID!!!!!!!!!!!!!!!! DAVID!!!!!!!!!!!!!!!!!!!!!!!!!!! DAVID!!!!!!!!!!!!!!!!!!!!!!!!!!!!
!!!!!!!!!!

Chapter 17

"Son, listen. I've kept a routine watch over the people that you've associated with over the past several months. Last night I got a page at about four o'clock in the morning from a guy that I know who's with The Montreal Police. Phillips is dead. Word has it that it was Manny Robar's crew. He got two bullets to the back of the head, execution style. He must have pissed off someone in Robar's organization," Tom Wallace reported to Dane. Then the personal side of him kicked in.

"My concern is this, this girlfriend of yours is gonna lead you into serious trouble, and those fucken dealers that she knows. Boy, I'm telling you, most of them have wrap sheets longer than both of your arms, one in front of the other."

Dane tugged on the zipper of his black leather jacket. He was standing under the canopy of a convenience store, trying to stay out of the rain.

"Yeah, Manny Robar got Lilly in the back of his limo once. The guy's a total fucken scumbag, even for a pimp."

"This Phillips guy has been to your house on numerous occasions. I'm tellin' ya, son, these fucken lowlifes are bad news."

Dane paused for a second.

"I don't know how the fuck you know all of this shit, but your people are good."

"Yeah". Thomas responded flatly. "This Robar character, he served ten years for raping and pimping out a minor. If I had my way, he'd get his fucken skull cracked," Thomas said.

"Yeah. I'm not a fan. He did something to Lilly that I don't even wanna discuss. Where are you now"??

"I'm in a hotel room."

"No, I mean where?"

"Across the water from you," Thomas was being his usual evasive self.

"Gotta go. Love ya, son," he said, then hung up.

"Fuck," Dane said lightly to himself.

The rain was coming down now.

The next morning at 8:30 am, Lilly called David Dane. She was screaming.

"I'm in some guy's car!" she proclaimed amidst sobs. "He drove me out of town and he won't bring me back."

Dane felt as if he'd just been slammed in the cranium with a brick.

"Alright, baby. Baby! Calm down. Whose phone are you on?"

Dane heard dead air for a second followed by the horrific sound of a dial tone.

She was gone.

Dane quickly ran into the other room to examine the call display. It registered only an unknown number.

"Oh, JESUS!!!!" Dane exclaimed, trying to recover his faculties. He quickly lifted the receiver and dialed 911, telling them of his predicament. The operator on the other end did little or nothing to soothe his nerves.

"Sometimes people in her profession play these games, sir. Did she give any indication as to where she was?"

"What? NO!!!!!!!!!" Dane yelled.

"We'll see if we can trace the call, but it may take several hours."

"I don't have several hours!" Dane protested.

Several hours? Lilly could be a corpse by the time these assholes got back to him. Dane lifted the phone as he stood up, accidentally dropping it back on its cradle. He had lost the call.

"Fuck!!"

He was dialing Bill Ramirez now, who he wanted to enlist to help him in his plight.

"Okay, okay," Ramirez responded sympathetically. Ramirez had once told Dane never to call him before noon unless it was a life and death emergency. Well, lo and behold, here was one.

Ramirez could tell by the panic in Dane's voice that he was frantic. Poor guy.

"Bill, I'm gonna call my mother. Let me call you back in five," Dane said.

Soon Marilyn Dane was on the phone. She, too, was frantic.

"You didn't hear anything in the background?" Dane's mother asked.

"Nothing. I'm gonna hit Ontario Street. It beats sitting here waiting. I'll forward my land-line to my cell."

The first person that Dane encountered on Ontario Street that morning was Claude F. He was decked out in a black nylon tracksuit and a black ball hat with the frontal mirror, the kind that gangster rappers wore in videos and, as usual, he sported a sand-colored moustache.

Dane told Claude about the phone call that he had received earlier on from Lilly. His hands had not yet stopped trembling. He did not know if Claude noticed or not.

"She has not come here today," C.F. said honestly.

"SHIT"!!!!!!!!!!!!!!!!!!! Dane exclaimed. First Phillips, and now this.

"I will tell Sheryl if I see her." Claude said. Claude had seen Dane fight the night before. He thought the boxer looked exhausted with darkening circles around his eyes. He thought that Dane should sleep.

Leaves blew about in a shadowy wind at the feet of both men.

"Call my cell if you see her."

"I am go now," Claude said, ending their talk. As usual Claude was a man of few words.

It was 10:44 a.m.

Dane stood and pondered his situation for a moment after Claude left. Did Lilly have a death wish? What other possible scenario could have existed for her to live her life this way? Someone had once suggested that Lilly was spiritually ill. Could this be a possible explanation for why someone would volunteer to live their life in this fashion. Because to David Danes psyche. This was fucking un-believable.

"Dane?"

"Angela. How you doin', angel? Thanks for being in my cheering section last night."

Angela O. smiled in response.

"Where's Lilly?" she asked. Dane quickly explained the situation to her.

"I don't believe it. She's up to her games again," Angela O. theorized.

Dane looked one way and then the other.

"Let Lilly know I'm around if she turns up. Love you," Dane said, pecking his sister figure on the cheek.

"You too, Dane," the girl said. "Try not to worry, alright?"

"I'll try," Dane said.

"You are look for your wife"?? The man standing in the car port between two buildings asked.
"Yeah. Do you know where she is"?? Dane asked. "Hey. How do I know you"??
"Because, because. The girl who are always go here always tell me that you are search for your wife". The man with the grey/black hair and the white painters cap said. His name was Francois. And Dane would one day come to think of him as more of a Brother from another Mother than a friend.
"Do you know where Lilly went"?? The Fighter inquired. "All this walking's killing my feet."
"Not now. But maybe for two hours ago she was go to The Bar to see the dealer. But for now I don't know". Francois said in his trademark dry, raspy tone of voice.
He was very likeable. Dane thought.
"I am now maybe look for the work". Francois commented with his hands on his hips.
"Work. What do you do"??
"I am do maybe the painting for a month But now . . . ." Francois said letting his arms drop slightly as if to signify that he was doing nothing.
"You ever work in a Gym"??
"No. But I am do painting, repairs, anything for the work" The Frenchman said.

"I have a friend who owns a Gym. Drop me your digits, and i'll call you if anything comes up. Things are slow right now but if Bobby needs a Painter or wants some repairs done i'll definently see to it that he calls you". Dane said honestly.

Francois took Danes cell phone and keyed in his number.

"Okay. You just can reach me at this number". Francois said.

"Alright." Dane said as Francois returned his phone to him.

The hot glare from the sun above seemed to expand for a moment before returning to it's regular ball of orange flames.

"I have to go catch Lilly" Dane said looking one way and then another before crossing the street

It was 2:15P.M.

The following night, Lilly reappeared on the stroll as if nothing had happened. Dane didn't know whether to be furious or relieved. In stark contrast to what he was feeling, he chose to display the latter. However the question remained. Where had she been all this time? Even her make-up was properly applied. He would ask her for details when they got home later on. Right now, all he wanted to do was get Lilly back to their apartment.

It was 7:43 p.m.

"Where the hell have you been. And don't tell me about some guys car either". Dane began, with shades of night in his voice. "Lilly?" he continued, unwillingly ominous.

Lilly turned from her position in the kitchen to face her lover.

"This guy drove me out of town, then he wouldn't bring me . . ." Dane was already shaking his head in disbelief. ". . . then I . . . ."

Dane lifted a hand as if to silence her. "You showed up downtown. You were seen hours before I found you walking around. Your make-up was flawless. You never even attempted to call and tell me that you were all right. EVERYONE—EVERYONE!—was worried sick!"

"Fuck off! I can't take this shit. I'M GOING BACK TO WORK!" she shrieked back at him.

Dane could feel his adrenaline pumping, feel his exorbitant rage boiling over.

"Lilly . . ." It was times like this that David Dane could not understand why Lilly couldn't just come clean and tell the truth. What the hell was wrong with her?

"TELL ME THE FUCKIN' TRUTH?" he shouted at her.

As Lilly headed for the door, Dane grabbed her wrist.

"Let GO of my fuckin' arm, mother fucker!" Chicoine said, slapping Dane across the face.

"Lilly. I wanna know where the fuck you went and who the fuck you were with."

There were blood-tones in Dane's voice now and Lilly thought he looked like a viper about to strike.

"NONE OF YOUR FUCKIN' BUSINESS?" she yelled, turning the handle on the door to let herself out.

As soon as she was gone, Dane was plagued by the same fear that he was always plagued with after they had had one of their fights. The fear that Lilly would not come back.

8:49 pm.

The next morning Dane's fears were quelled when, after responding to a knock at the door, Lilly strolled in with eighty dollars in her hand. He immediately embraced her and told her how much he loved her.

"I made a customer this morning," she said happily.

"We're going to my Parent's place for Christmas," Dane said. "My mother's sending me money for two tickets."

"Oooh! When are we leaving?" Lilly asked while preparing her hit.

"Close to Christmas. Maybe a day or two before," he said.

"I'll have to make sure that I have enough smack on me to tide me over."

"How much?"

"Two grams, maybe?"

"Mike Phillips is dead," Dane said.

"Fuck off. When?"

"A couple of nights ago. Up in The Heights. We think that Manny Robar's people hit 'em up."

"How did you find out?"

"I can't tell you that."

"Ahhh . . . . It's a secret!" Lilly said, leaning into the couch with her knee.

"Have you called Max yet?"

"Nope. Smack isn't open yet." Selling heroin had become something like running a Walmart, Dane thought.

"What time is it?" Lilly asked.

"Nearly 8 a.m. You got a kiss, baby?" Dane asked, leaning in close to Lilly who pecked him on the lips.

8:00 a.m. had come.

"I'll rock your world" Sharon "Sugar Bear" said approaching David Dane from about three feet away.

"With those bad ass curves it wouldn't surprise me" Dane responded.

"You got a light"?? Sharon asked producing a cigarette.

"Nope".

"You got fifty bucks"??

"I don't do that".

"Do what"?? The Gorgeous brunette asked.

"Pay for sex around here. Besides. I think that would upset Lilly".

"Who's Lilly"?? Sharon "Sugar Bear" who resembled actress/Super Model Hilary Swank asked.

"My Girlfriend". David Dane answered.

"Yeah. But she's not here".

"No. But she will be. She works out here".

"Oh. Fuck. I didn't know that". Sharon said. "Where you from"?? She asked trying to change the subject.

"Disneyland"

"No really"

"Nova Scotia" Dane responded.

"Holy shit. Me to"

"What part"?? she asked.

"Halifax".

"I'm from Shelburne".

"Oh my God". Sharon said throwing her arms around Dane. Clearly she was excited to have met one of her own out here.

"You certainly didn't get cheated in the looks department did you? And you smell good to". Dane said pressing his lips into Sharons dark, sexy, main of hair to give her a quick kiss.

"How long have you been working out here"?? The Fighter asked.

"Long enough".

"Listen. I have to go. Lilly's here". Dane said spotting Lilly on the other side of the street.

10:00 P.M. Had come.

The pro wrestler standing to one side of the room with a flock of women surrounding him was Eddy Dorozowsky, better known as "Sexxxy Eddy." His appearance was reminiscent of a Techno Club male dancer with his dark hair, squared pinch, leopard skin vest, red bow tie, skin tight blue jeans and snakeskin boots. Dane and Eddy had met about a year earlier at Santino Video through the owners son, "Tony".

Tonight Dane and Eddy had both stopped by a mutual friend's house to wish him a happy birthday and to take part in the festivities.

Dane looked up from his standing position between two blond exotic dancers who had also stopped by to wish the same friend a happy birthday. He wore a shiny black hoodie and a pair of expensive shades, designer jeans and black Nikes.

"You wanna drive home?" Sexxxy Eddy, aka "The Sex Express," asked Dane, looking over the flock of women who stood before him.

Dane, who was on the opposite side of the room nodded. "Fuck, E, are you drunk?" he asked. "E" was Dane's nickname for Sexxxy Eddy.

"Not yet," Eddy responded, now approaching Dane.

One of the dancers turned to watch their exchange as she nibbled on a square of birthday cake.

"Let's go," Eddy said, walking past Dane who was now saying his goodnights to both of the dancers. Dane gave the bustier of the two blonds a squeeze on the ass before following The Sex Express to his shiny black sports coupe out front.

"You wanna drive, D?" Dorozowsky asked, tossing Dane his set of keys over the hood of the car. Eddy knew that Dane had no license.

"If I do then neither of us will have a career," Dane said tossing the keys back to Eddy who was smiling. "Too bad. I thought we could've come up with a behind-the-wheel brand of hardcore tonight. I'd do it, but I need my license to get to the arenas."

Just as Dane was about to get in on his side of the car someone shouted to him from the window of the house.

"Whatchoo chattin up my bitch for?" the mulatto bodybuilder asked.

"What the fuck? Is he serious?" Dane asked aloud. Eddy's smile had evaporated now. He was not impressed by the fucking clown in the window with the red vest and 22-inch guns.

"Yeah, you. Wait there," the roid-head said.

Soon after, the mulatto dude and his big blond white buddy appeared on the sidewalk in front of David Dane and Sexxxy Eddy.

"Whatchoo chattin up my ho for?" the mulatto dude asked.

Dane turned quickly to glance over his left shoulder at Sexxxy Eddy, as if to foreshadow what he was about to say and do.

"You know, I'll tell you. I was talking to . . . Yeah, her," Dane said comically pointing at the blond dancer who was peering at them out the door. "When she told me that she had always heard that black men had big dicks and that that's why you really surprised her . . . ."

At that moment both of the monsters lunged. One for Dane and one for Eddy. The blond dude completely missed Eddy who had already stepped back two feet before drop kicking the blond guy in the skull.

"Yeah, fuck you too!" Dane hollered rhythmically before hammering the mulatto dude with a pair of left jabs followed by a right cross that shattered the punk's nose, in seconds soaking his face in blood.

Eddy was now dragging the blond guy back to his feet, his upper lip now pouring with blood.

"Yo Dane," Eddy said, "watch this." The wrestler shouted as he savat-kicked the blond dude on the chin in much the same fashion as Eddy's idol and mentor The Heartbreak Kid Shawn Michaels would have.
As a Pro-Wrestling Fan Dane had always been partial to Canadian Icon Bret "The Hitman" Hart having idolized "The Hitman" for years.

"Careful E., you're going to fucken paralyze him," Dane hollered.

"Fuck him. He started it," Eddy replied getting ready for a grand finale. He was on the roof of the sports coupe now, in swan dive position.

"Eddy. JESUS CHRIST!!" Dane yelled as Sexxxy Eddy did a 450 Splash onto the semi-conscious blond roid-head.

Dane heard the blond guys ribs crack.

And he did this for a living, Dane thought.

"Let's get the F' outta here before the cops get here," Dane said.

Eddy pulled himself to his feet. His arms were grazed and bleeding and his heart was drumming in his ears. The mulatto guy was sprawled over the curb face down.

"I should've given him a fucken smiley," David Dane said. "Get the keys. You dropped them on the ground."

"Fuck!!!" Eddy said trying to catch his breath.

Half an hour later Sexxxy Eddy's black sports coupe purred to a stop in front of 235 Leopold Heights.

"Helluva fucken night," Dane said.

"At least the food was good."

"I think we worked that off."

"You got my digits?" Eddy asked.

"That I do."

"Goodnight. Take it easy, bro," Eddy said.

Dane nodded as he closed the passenger door.

Soon the sun would be up.

The next time that Lilly went to jail and came out, she had a friend with her. Her name was Tracy. She was white with long flowing red hair and two missing front teeth. Dane thought that she looked a bit like a jack-o-lantern. Two hours later, Tracy, Lilly and Dane himself went up to the apartment as another man got out of a cab in front of 235 Leopold Heights. His name was Nick Monroe, and he was Tracy's pimp, as well as her boyfriend.

"I'm Nick Monroe. We met on the phone," the African-American said as he gripped Dane's hand. The two men had talked on the phone via a three-way call while the girls were in lock-up. They'd become good-humored fast friends. Dane recalled his ribs nearly cracking with laughter when Nick had asked Tracy: "Tracy? Tracy? Did you do your little sit-ups today? 'Cause I don't want no big-bellied woman, you know."

Dane picked up one of Nicks bags and the two boarded the elevator together.

"This is it, 802," Dane said, fishing the house keys out of his pocket. Nick smiled as the door creaked open and Tracy threw her arms around him.

"Okay, okay," Tracy began, speaking with a lisp, "okay, you front me two rocks. I mean, for now, and I bring you a brownie later on."

"Rock," was slang for crack and a "brownie" was just the same for a hundred dollar bill. Nick was also a drug dealer.

"Okay, listen Tracy. Dane wants to order a pizza. He hasn't eaten all day," Nick replied.

"And Lilly wants to go out to work for coke," said Lilly speaking of herself in the third party.

"Awww, Jesus Christ!" Dane exclaimed. "Can't this wait until after dinner, baby?"

"Nooooo . . . ." Lilly whined. "I wanna go to work for coke now!"

"David, if I had a QT on me, I'd front her myself," Monroe said.

"I know, I know," Dave Dane said.

"You and I can stay here and Tracy can go with Lilly," Nick suggested.

"The offer's appreciated," Dane said. "I'll go to work with Lilly. You guys can chill out here while we're gone. Nick, you can order a pizza and I'll order a second one when I get back."

"We'll wait," Monroe said graciously. That was his nature. Despite his occupation, Nick had a big heart and always proved to be a good friend. No one who met him on the street would otherwise know what Nick did for a living.

"Let's go," Lilly exclaimed."

It was 8:45 p.m.

Minutes later Dane was only a few feet behind Lilly, walking down Ontario Street, Lilly dressed in a red halter-top, blue jeans and white running shoes. The air was dark and moist with humidity. As Lilly went to stand at the edge of the stone park, she quickly made a client who put his arm around her waist in plain view of a maniacal, angry David Dane.

As Lilly and her client headed down a shadowy side street to the motel, Dane followed closely behind, his eyes smouldering with anger and jealousy.

Lilly turned occasionally to glance angrily over her shoulder at her boyfriend who wasn't far behind. This was their psychotic relationship.

As Lilly and her client turned the next corner, they disappeared into the cheaply lit Champlain Motel.

It was 9:20 p.m.

Dane and Lilly sat in a dark corner behind some houses just off of Ontario Street. The hour was late, and the picturesque inner city lay quiet and still at this hour. There was blackness all around them now, rippling in invisible waves that momentarily shifted Dane and Lilly's view of each other. The two sat a few feet apart, Lilly smoking a cigarette with one hand while massaging her bare, swollen feet with the other.

"I don't think I'm gonna be able to walk out of here," Lilly said.

"If you can't, I'll carry you," Dane answered.

At that moment, a fluffy white bunny-rabbit appeared out of nowhere and ran underneath a fence into a yard that was bathed in crimson red light of an unknown origin. In a few days time, this event would take on a significance of its own, as it would remind Dane of a story that he had heard from a pro wrestler named Jake "the Snake" Roberts years earlier. The story, The Rabbit and The Snake went something like this.

Once upon a time there was a rabbit and a snake. The rabbit met the snake along a dark and shadowy road. The snake was wounded and the rabbit offered to take the snake home and nurse him back to health. And the snake said, "Oh no, Mr. Rabbit, you can't do that. I'm a snake. I'm a snake. You can't do that" But the rabbit insisted. He said, "Oh, but Mr. Snake, I'll take you back to my den and nurse you back to health." And the snake said, "Oh no, you can't do that. I'm a snake. I'm a snake you can't do that".

But, against the snakes warning, the rabbit took the snake back to his den, and, slowly but surely, the rabbit nursed the snake back to health. One day, the rabbit went out for food. He came back. The snake was gone. He turned around, AND THERE WAS THE SNAKE HISSING AT HIM!!!!!!!!!!!!!!!!!! And the snake said, "Mr. Rabbit, I am going to eat you." And the rabbit said, "Oh no, Mr. Snake, I'm your friend. I'm your friend, you can't do that." And the snake said, "In the very beginning. I told you that I was a snake . . ."

"Tracy! Tracy!" Nick Monroe began, the next morning. "Did you get me my money?" he asked in a comically rhythmic voice as if he were half serious, half joking.

Tracy stood up from the glass table where she was seated.

"I'd like to welcome y'all to the Nick Monroe Show," Dane interjected.

"Okay, Nick," Tracy lisped. "Okay, you can front me two rocks . . ."

"Tracy, I fronted you two rocks last night and you haven't brought me my money yet."

Dane was smirking at this humorous exchange.

"Okay, okay, Nick," she began again. "You front me one rock so that I can go to work and make two brownies."

"No, Tracy," Monroe said, rising to his feet in protest. "Go to work and get me my money. Dane and I have things to do."

Dane and Nick were going out for burgers.

Tracy was resigned. "Okay, I'm going to work now. Lilly's going to work, so I'll go with her."

Lilly was in the shower.

It was 11:45 a.m.

"Judy, this is David Dane," Monroe said as he introduced the forty-something year old black female with the wire-rimmed glasses to his friend. They were standing in Dane's living room.

"Can I smoke here?" Judy, aka Suzy Q asked. "You don't mind if I puff, do you?"

Nick had just sold her a rock.

Knock yourself out," Dane responded. "Just open a window. I don't want that shit reaching the hallway".

"Yeah, no problem. No problem," Judy/Suzy Q said.
"So. You're Lillys Boyfriend"?? Suzy asked.
"I am".
"Well. I'm from the same place as you are. I'm a Scotian woman. And you know what they say about us Scotians"??? Suzy/Judy asked between puffs. "We don't play"
"Tell me about it". Dane said.
"Well. I hope that Lilly treats you well cause. You're the one that takes care of her".
"Yeah. That point doesn't resonate real well with her sometimes".
"Well. She better smarten up then or i'll have to whip some of that good Scotian sense into her. I don't fool around with people, and i'm very loyal to my own kind". Judy said raising the glass pipe to meet with her mouth. Smoke trailed into the air.
It was 2:00 pm.

Two days later, Tracy came through the door. Lilly was not with her. It was first light and not seeing Lilly's face was beginning to worry David Dane.

"Where is she?" Dane asked Tracy.

"I haven't seen her since last night."

"Tracy, Tracy," Chris began rhythmically. "You go down there and get that stupid girl right now. Doesn't she know that Dane frets when she doesn't call or come home? He's worried sick," Monroe said. "Look, here, take twenty bucks out of the money you just brought me and go get Lilly and bring her home. NOW, TR-ACY!!!!!!!!!!!!!!!!!!!!!!" Nick demanded.

When Lilly walked into the lobby twenty minutes later she looked, for lack of any other word, bizarre. Her mascara was running and her demeanor was strangely despondent. She wore a pink neon top with bursts of purple over blue jeans. Her hair was tied up in a ponytail.

When they came through the door to the apartment, Tracy quickly double-backed out and returned to work. Nick was still there.

"You found her," Nick exclaimed.

Dane looked at Nick with a frown, as if to signal that something was wrong. Monroe stopped smiling, respectful of the situation, whatever it was. Lilly disappeared into the bedroom and disrobed. In moment she returned to the living room. Naked.

Chris gave no response. He knew what was coming.

"Lilly!!!!!!, Go put some clothes on," Dane said with subdued fury in his voice. "NOW"!!!!!!!

"Oh! So you're calling me a SLUT?" Lilly yelled spitefully.

"No, but I want you to at least put a robe on."

She disappeared into the bedroom. Dane followed. She was bouncing up and down on the bare box-spring now.

"What the fuck is wrong with you?" Dane demanded.

"You FUCK-ING BASTARD!" the girl shouted at Dane, in response to nothing.

At that moment Lilly lifted a glass HP steak sauce bottle from her purse. It was broken with jagged edges around the top. It had been painted up with an Easter Egg-type design, as part of an arts and crafts project at

Guardian. She wound up and whipped the broken bottle at Dane's skull, grazing the back of his ear as he ducked to avoid injury.

"ARE YOU FUCKING CRAZY"?????? he yelled, rounding the corner, retreating back into the living room.

Nick sat forward. "What the fuck . . . ?" he shouted.

Dane made a bee-line for the balcony to avoid getting hit by Lilly's second attempt at catching him with the broken bottle, a decision that would prove nearly fatal. As his feet reached the cement balcony surrounded by the iron railing, Lilly took one more throw of the bottle, from inside the apartment, shattering the big glass window directly in Dane's face.

"GO!! GO!! Get out of here!" Dane heard Monroe holler at Lilly through a fog as he stumbled back into the apartment, blood-soaked. He just barely caught a dreamlike glimpse of Lilly vanishing into the hallway. Nick looked horrified, his face a mask of terror.

"That girl has NO sense!" Monroe yelled. He would later tell Dane that he was certain that Dane's left eye was gone.

There was blood everywhere. The apartment looked like a murder scene, there was so much of it. Even the drapes were now crimson with fluid.

Dane stumbled past Nick and walked into the bathroom to survey the damage in the mirror. His face was a crimson mask. There was no telling what was what.

"Call an ambulance," Dane yelled to Nick.

Monroe lifted the phone and dialed 911.

Soon the ambulance boys responded. They bandaged Dane's head and taped gauze over his left eye. Then they took him out front and loaded him into the ambulance, its red lights flashing through the shadowy morning underneathe the clouds that promised rain.

On the way to the hospital, Dane's head swam and he hallucinated. He felt like he was somewhere else dreaming of all this. This blood-drenched nightmare. At the hospital the two attending police officers asked David Dane if he wanted to make a statement. At the moment he said that he did, not knowing that making a statement constituted pressing charges. He told them what had happened. They wrote it down and Dane, in his panicked and freaked mind, signed it.

It would be a week before David Dane would hear from Lilly Chicoine again, and this time it was by phone. Lilly screamed at Dane, blaming him for their fight while periodically lamenting that the cops were probably looking for her now. They were, and Dane regretted this. He still loved Lilly. She screamed some more and then hung up.

"Uh-huh?" Dane responded after dropping the phone back on its cradle.

"Was that . . . ?" Nick asked.

"That was Lilly. She's gonna need a lawyer," Dane said.

"Are you gonna get her one?"

"Probably."

Dane wondered if he could do that. They'd already told him that he couldn't drop the charges because there was violence involved.

"You'd feel differently if you'd lost your eye," Monroe said adamantly.

"I can't live without her, Nick," Dane responded. "The sun rises and sets with her".

"That woman has NO SENSE!" Monroe continued. "She has no sense. What if you'd lost your eye. Then what Dane. Then would you want to get her a Lawyer"??

"I wish things were that simple yeh know, but they're not. I have to help Lilly fight her way out of this mess".

"Dane. You don't have to help Lilly fight her way out of anything. That stupid woman almost cost you your sight".

Dane looked at Nick for a moment.

"Thanks Nick" Dane said genuinely.

9:32 P.M.

Lilly called again. This time she was in jail. They had pressed charges against her for assault on Dane, and upon her arrest. The Police had been rough with her. This information only served to make David Dane feel worse. He hadn't wanted that to happen to Lilly. She was still the love of his life. No matter what.

"Will you talk to the prosecutor for me? Please, baby," Lilly asked.

Dane agreed to be in court the next morning.

The following morning, David Dane appeared in court. Lilly was quickly tried and at the recommendation of the prosecutor, who had spoken to Dane in the corridor, she was sentenced to only twelve days in jail, which to Lilly was like twelve hours. Court was adjourned and Dane went home.

When Dane arrived back at 235 Leopold Heights, an unscheduled, unauthorized gathering was taking place. There, in the confines of his living room were Alyssa, Nick and his friend Vince, Tracy, Judy/SuzyQ and Tracy's twenty one year-old crack slinging, gun-toting son, Brian.

"Jesus fucking Christ, Nick. How the fuck did all of these people get into my house?" Dane asked.

"The door," Monroe said lightly.

"Of course you had nothing to do with that?" Dane asked, smiling and taking a seat at the same moment.

"Of course not," Monroe responded.

Alyssa came over and wrapped her arms around Dane's neck. She quickly pecked him on the lips before seating herself again. Brian was waving a loaded .38 around the room. Dane's smile evaporated.

"Put that away," Dane ordered, pointing at Brian who he was only meeting for the second time.

"Brian. Dane doesn't like guns and for that matter. Neither do I. Put the toy away," Nick seconded.
"Don't you know that I'm locked and loaded?" Brian asked, jesting. A question that would one day be laced with an evil wickedness as a threat against both Dane and Monroe.

"Fucken' prick," Dane said grabbing a handful of the gun's barrel. "Give me that," he said with a smirk in his tone. Brian complied.

Nicks eyes switched back and forth between Dane and Brian. Tracy was on her feet now.

"Okay, okay, Nick. You front me two rocks. Okay? Two rocks," Tracy began.

"Tra-cy, Tra-cy," Nick responded. "Did you scrub the kitchen floor like I asked you to?"

"No. Not yet," she lisped. "But I will. I promise. Just pass me one rock."

"Do you have any money, Tra-cy?" Nick demanded.

"How long did Lilly get?" Alyssa interjected.

"Twelve days, sunshine," Dane answered.

"They only gave that senseless woman twelve days?" Monroe asked.

"I talked to the prosecutor. I asked her for a reduced sentence."

"You'd feel differently if you'd lost your eye!" Monroe protested.

"That girl could have taken your sight?" Judy protested. "I need to have a talk with that woman. She needs to show some more respect for you 'cause you're the one that takes care of her," Judy said with harsh sincerity.

"She doesn't treat you right," Alyssa said seductively as she wrapped her arms around David Dane from behind. Her chin was resting on his shoulder now. She was sexy, and as tempting as Hell is hot.

At that moment the telephone rang. It was Lilly. And she wanted everyone out of her house. Now.

Dane held the phone up for everyone to hear. Lilly was on an adorable yet adamant tirade.

"I want everyone out, out, out of my house," she demanded in a small bunny-ish voice.

Everyone began to filter out except for Nick, Tracy and Brian who stayed there.

"Out!" said Lilly.

The next afternoon, Dane ran into Jenny on Ontario Street. She was with Fred and Esther the Squeegees. Jenny's skin was very pale and her blue eyes were deep. Foreboding. Dane couldn't put a finger on it, but there was something wrong with her. She wore her trademark red leather jacket over a long black dress. As was always the case. Jenny looked like a fox.

"Walk with me," she said, taking Dane by the hand. "I'm going to see a friend."

They walked to a series of white apartment buildings that were just up two blocks. The sun was low, as if preparing to drop below the horizon.

They were standing in an alley now, facing each other. Jenny embraced Dane tightly.

"I love you," she said, holding onto him.

This would be the last time that Dane would ever see Jenny. He would hear of her one last time, about a year later. Dane was told that Jenny had died of heart failure due to an overdose. But this was never confirmed.

His last words to her were, "I love you too, angel."

When Lilly came home twelve days later, the apartment was in a complete shambles. Not that Lilly had ever contributed to it being otherwise. There were used syringes on the tables, crack pipes on the sink-board, and clothes literally piled up so high in the bedroom that it would take three snow shovels and one whole day to clear them all away.

"Holy FUCK!" Lilly shouted. "Who did all of this?" she asked.

"Well, some of it was Tracy, then there are about twenty-five others," Dane responded.

They were home alone at this time.

Just then the phone rang. It was the concierge downstairs. "There's a girl down here with red hair. She says she lives here, but she looks drunk and she might be on drugs. Should I let her come up?"

"Jesus fucken' Christ," Dane said, clutching his bald head. "NO!" he barked into the phone.

"Where's Nick?" Lilly questioned.

"I have no fucken' idea," Dane answered. "He's gonna get us evicted."

"We're never gonna be alone in our house again," Chicoine said.

About a minute later there was a loud knock on the door. It was Tracy. She had evaded Claude the concierge and was now wobbling around out in the hallway.

"FUCK!" Dane yelled. "Go away!"

The knocking persisted.

"C'mon, let me in!" Tracy demanded.

"I'm gonna kill her," Dane said.

Now the phone was ringing again. It was Claude downstairs. "I call the police," Claude explained.

"Awww, fuck," Dane said, beginning to stress. "Call them back and tell them not to come," Dane said.

"I can't," Claude said. Then he hung up.

"Tracy, the cops are coming. Get outta here," Dane warned. "GO!"

Silence on the other side of the door.

Tracy was gone.

Brian had a scheme, but in order to pull it off he needed a bank account. That account, in the long run, would end up being David Dane's. Worse still than that was the fact Dane's account was a joint account that he shared with his Father. On this late afternoon, Brian had walked through the door with two full bags of groceries and a third bag containing a woman's purse. In that purse, David Dane would soon see, was a wallet. In that wallet was a piece of ID with the woman's name and work affiliation on it. It read, in bold lettering, Department of Justice.

"What the fuck is this?" Dane asked.

"I held up some bitch outside of an office building," Brian answered casually, as if he was talking about stealing a can of beer from the liquor store.

His face was perspiring. Sweat dripped from his eyebrows as he pulled out the earpiece that belonged to his cell phone.

"You car-jacked a woman?" Dane asked incredulously, convinced that Brian was crazy, mindful that the little bastard was carrying a gun.

"Yeah," Brian said, removing his red t-shirt and toweling off.

If Brian wasn't strapped, Dane would have already beaten the fucking little punk so badly that Tracy wouldn't recognize him. Then again, considering the state that she found herself in half the time, she might not recognize him anyway.

Dane stared down at his own feet. He couldn't believe that the little motherfucker had done this and then had the nerve, not to mention the balls, to show up at his house.

Brian had rolled something and was now smoking it.

It was all that Dane could do not to try and take the gat (gun) from him and then beat him to death with it.

"There are two microwave dinners in the bags. You want one of 'em?" Brian asked.

The only thing Dane wanted to nuke was Brian.

It was 4:45 p.m.

Chapter 18

"Brian is a cold, miserable bastard. I made him that way. That's the side of him that I like," Tracy was quoted as saying of her son.

Doing this favor for Brian hopefully meant getting him out of the house once and for all. This would be it, and then the little bastard would hopefully go follow a yellow brick road someplace else.

"Just put the envelope in your account and withdraw the money when you're done," Brian said. He licked the envelope and then he handed it to Dane who was about to fall victim to the oldest trick in the book.

"The check inside is for a thousand dollars," Brian lied. "I need you to simply cash it for me."

Dane deposited the envelope and then withdrew a thousand dollars in cash which he would later regret handing over to Brian at all. Brian then pocketed the money before the two of them stepped back out into the warm night air. Dark outside now.

"I owe Sniper money, but I wanna keep all of it, so I'm just gonna tell him that I got robbed," Brian explained. "He'll believe that."

Sniper was Brian's Boss and a supplier in the crack cocaine business. Dane had heard of both Sniper and his brother Shoot to Kill. They were infamous gunmen from an area known as Burgundy.

"Dane, I'll give you two bills if you come with me to meet up with Sniper," Brian said, handing two brownies to Dane.

"Where are we going?" Dane asked as he pocketed the cash.

"Black Lace," Brian said.

"I think I know the place. It's an exotic dance cabaret, right?"

"Yeah. I have to meet Snipes there by eight thirty."

Dane was well aware of the danger that Brian was in, trying to rip these dudes off, but he decided to let the piece of shit learn his own lesson. If they decided to drag him into an alleyway and then make sure that he was one and done then that was Brians cross to bare.

Stepping inside the bar, Dane felt the cool air from the ceiling fans glide across his skin. The break from the heat outside was like Heaven. There was one dancer on stage and about ten of them working the room in hopes of gaining clientele for a private dance throughout the night. Most of them caught Dane's eye.

"Call 'em," Dane said. "See if he can put in an early appearance."

Brian punched up Sniper's number on his cell phone. "He's on his way now."

When Sniper arrived, he and Brian moved to a booth away from David Dane. Dane watched them talk for a few minutes before Brian returned to the table where Dane sat.

"What'd he say?" David asked.

"He said that we have to make that money back."

The stage dancer licked her lips before fastening her eyes on Dane.

"You should call Nick. See if he's home yet," the boxer suggested.

"I already talked to my mother. She said Nick won't be home until after nine."

"Give 'em a call anyway. Ask 'em where the fuck he is."

Brian dialed Nicks cell phone. "It's busy."

"Aw, fuck," Dane said. "Let's blow this joint."

"Crack Down" by Murderous Heat played on.

"That money didn't belong to him. It belonged to us". Marilyn Dane exuded.

"I'm gonna call The Police on him.

"No, don't do that, because they'll see me on the bank surveillance tape, too."

"Prick" Marilyn Dane said.

"I agree."

At that instant Monroe walked through the door.

"What the hell happened?" Nick asked Dane after he hung up the phone with his father.

Dane explained the situation.

"David," Nick began, gesturing with his hand, "you just fell for the oldest trick in the book!" There was the faintest hint of a smirk on Monroe's face, more out of irony than anything else.

The phone that Dane had just hung up was now ringing again. It was Brian.

"You lifeless bag of shit". David Dane said. "Where are you and more importantly. Where's my goddamn money"??

"Don't you know that I'm locked and loaded?" Brian asked.

"HEY! HEY! You greasy fuck!" Dane shot back. "I'm gonna break your fuckin' neck!"

There was a click at the other end of the line, followed by a gunshot.

"You hear that, big boy?" Brian sneered. "That was for you."

With that, Tracy's son hung up.

The next day Tracy and David were alone together in the apartment. Tracy sat in her usual chair at the table fiddling with her crack pipe. Nick had told her the story.

"Brian is a cold, miserable bastard," Tracy lisped. "That's the side of him that I like. I made him that way."

"Tracy. Get the fuck outta my house," Dane yelled, pointing towards the door.

"I'm not going anywhere. I'm staying here with Nick."

"Do you understand what I'm telling you to do?" Dane asked curtly. "I want you outta this house, you miserable sack of shit. Not when Christ comes gets back. Not some other time. NOW!"

"No!" she retorted.

"Get out or I'll throw you out on your ass. You were only here because Lilly wanted you here. Now I want you out. Get up. Get your shit together and GO!"

"I told you I'm not . . ."

"I mean business. You've got ten seconds . . ."

Tracy stood up, straightening herself. She paused. Before spitting in Dane's direction. Dane moved, avoiding the flying saliva by an inch.

Just then, through the unlocked door a six-foot tall, dark-haired female warrior of a woman burst into the living room. In the years to come she would become a dear friend to Dane. One he would never forget.

"Did you hear him, BITCH?" Emanuelle asked, locking her huge palm around Tracy's jaw. "He said GET OUT!"

Tracy looked shocked and then frightened.

Emanuelle took a fistful of Tracy's red hair and dragged her to the door. "OUT!!" she hollered as Tracy fell into the hallway, Emanuelle slamming the door shut behind her.

"Jesus. Wonder Woman," Dane said, his face a mask of surprise. "I'm David Dane. You sure as hell handled Tracy," he said. "I'm sorry, I don't believe we've met."

Emanuelle introduced herself. "I'm Nick Monroes friend," she said. "He sent me here."

"Well, any friend of Nicks is a friend of mine," Dane said, turning to glance quickly in the direction of the door and then backward at Wonder Woman. "Except Tracy, that is," he said. "Have a seat. Would you like something to drink? OJ? A soda?"

"I'm okay," Emanuelle said kindly.

"So, you know Nick?"

"For years. He talks about you a lot. He likes you."

"Well, I like Nick, too," Dane said in all honesty.

"You have a nice apartment," Emanuelle complimented.

"Thanks. It needs some overhauling, but one day we'll be happy with it again." Then Dane asked, "Listen, by any chance did Nick say when he'd be back?"

"Maybe tomorrow night. I'm not sure. He went out of town to see someone. Do you have a light?" Emanuelle asked, producing a cigarette.

Dane handed her Lilly's red lighter.

"Do you mind if I puff here?" Emanuelle asked, fishing a glass pipe out of her bra.

"Yeah, why not?"

"I have to got to work soon, but I can come back. It'll take me two hours."

Dane lifted a pot from the cupboard and set it on the stove.

"Listen, if you happen to see Lilly at work, tell her to get the hell home. Christ! I don't know what the fuck she's been up to for the past two days. Hey," he suddenly realized, "Do you know Lilly?"

"In passing. Yeah."

Emanuelle finished her rock and then stood up. She walked into the kitchen and kissed Dane's neck from behind. "Okay, sweetheart. I'll be back," she said.

Dane would not see Emanuelle again for about a month.

Brian phoned David Dane the next night. He was downstairs in the lobby and wanted to talk to Dane alone. Dane obliged him, meeting him to the left of the elevators in front of the mailboxes. Now there was tension between them so thick that you could cut it with a knife. And had Dane had his way. He would've.

"What do you want?" Dane asked the gun-toting little prick.

"I want you to know that I'm locked and loaded," Brian said, pulling the shiny black .38 from the waistband of his jeans and pointing it at Dane.

"Put the gun down, Brian." Dane ordered in an ominous tone.

The twenty one-old gunman did not comply.

"I want more money or you're gonna be so full of lead they'll think your a pencil."

"Brian. Put the gun down," Dane warned once more, his eyes smouldering in the heat of the threat. Again, Brian did not comply.

"We're gonna see what can be done about you getting me some more money."

"First of all, I'm not giving you anymore money, and secondly, you better put that piece away before someone gets off the elevator and sees you with it. You're gonna end up dead or in prison kid. And neither one is a place you wanna be."

"We're gonna see what can be done".

"The only thing that'll be done is you". Dane responded in a low voice.

"I'll be seeing you soon". Brian said.

And with that, he casually slipped the gun back under his waistband and walked around Dane, disappearing out the front doors and into the darkening night.

It was 9:45 pm.

"Your son is a loose cannon, Tracy!" bellowed Monroe at Tracy who was sitting on Dane's couch. "Pulling a gun on Dane!"

Tracy looked nervous.

"He needs to be dealt with, Tracy!" Monroe continued, his open black dress shirt rippling under the force of the breeze that was blowing in through the open balcony door.

"Last night was an example of just how messed up your kid is!" he said.

Dane was pacing back and forth behind Nick, letting him deal with his own woman. At this point, Dane couldn't have given a shit if both Brian and Tracy were murdered right in front of him. One was as bad as the other.

Nightfall had come hours ago and Lilly still wasn't back yet. It had been four days.

"That kid. Let me tell you. He's gonna use that fucken' burner to off somebody and he's gonna go to prison for twenty-five to life," Dane added.

Monroe turned. Grimacing. "Never mind prison. He oughta be shot," Monroe said.

Tracy's eyes were wide with tension and fear now. "Look, Nick ... David, I'm not the one who did any of this."

Dane's expression was unforgiving. "Yeah, but you made him that way though, didn't you?" Dane responded. "You said so yourself."

A hint of a smirk crossed Tracy's lips.

"Bitch," Dane said, under his breath.

It was 11:33 pm.

The next afternoon when Dane was alone, Lilly showed up. She was wearing a red sweater and a tight pair of black jeans. Dane thought that she looked edible.

"Fuck! They kept me in jail overnight," Lilly said, resting a brown paper bag on the dining room table. "I'm exhausted. Give me a kiss, baby," she requested.

Dane obliged her.

At that moment there was a hollow metallic knock on the door.

"I'll answer it," Dane said.

"Jesus Christ!" he said, looking through the peephole. "It's Brian. He's got a gun in his hand."

Lilly sat down on the floor.

"Call 911," Dane said.

"If you're calling the cops, I'm leaving. Fuck! I just got out of jail."

"Was Lilly deaf, or crazy? Now he had her to contend with on top of Brian. It was against Dane's nature and his principles to involve the cops in anything, but under these circumstances what other option did he have?

"Lilly! Give me the fucken' cell phone," Dane demanded.

She balked at his request. She was going to put up a fight. No 911.

The knocking came again.

"Jesus, Lilly!"

"If you call the cops, I'm leaving."

She was leaving? What if the little bastard decided to plug her? Dane had no choice. He restrained Lilly with one arm and dialed 911 with the other.

"911 operator, what is your emergency?"

"Yeah, my name's David Dane. I live at 235 Leopold Heights, apartment 802. I've got a gunman knocking outside my door and, in his own words he says he's locked and loaded."

"There is someone outside your door with a gun?"

What was this woman doing, watching a soap opera while she was taking his call?

"Yes! There's someone outside my door with a gun!" Dane yelled.

"Okay. We have units responding," the 911 dispatcher said.

Lilly was squirming on the floor, to no avail.

In moments the hallway outside their apartment was swarming with police officers who had their guns drawn. They quickly announced their presence with a hard knock and the standard command, "Open up. Police!"

For once, and only once in his life, Dane was happy to see the Cops.

"Where is he?" Dane asked.

"We don't know. We didn't see him leave and we've got officers all over this place," one of the uniformed cops told Dane.

Lilly had stopped squirming.

"How do you know this kid?" the cop asked, looking down at Lilly.

"Friend of a friend," Dane lied.

"Okay. Do you have a phone number for this Brian person?" the officer asked.

"I have his cell number," Dane responded.

"Okay, because we're gonna get you to call him. Does he trust you?"

"At this juncture, I would doubt it."

"Okay. So try it. Call him up and tell him to meet you out front."

"When?"

"Half an hour," the cop said.

Dane dialed Brians number and Brian answered. The cops around Dane were listening intently.

"Look, I know there's been bad blood between you and I lately and I'm sorry about that. All I wanna do now is just put all of this behind us and move on."

"Are the cops there?" Brian asked.

"No, fuck! Why would you say that. This is between you and I."

"And you're not lying to me?"

"Look, you're a friend of mine, for better or worse," Dane said, cringing at his own words.

Listen, can you meet me out in front of my place in thirty?" Dane's eyes were shooting back and forth. "We need to resolve this situation".

"Okay, I'll be there."

In thirty minutes the police and David Dane were in position. The sting operation consisted of about ten different officers in plainclothes circulating in close proximity to Dane. The two that Dane knew about stood behind a white planter pretending to converse as one of them was merely there to meet Brian face to face and then they would have to take him down.

Time ticked away. The clock drew past an hour. Brian was a no-show.

"Okay, we're gonna pack it up, but we'll put an APB out for him. We'll find him," The officer assured Dane.

Lilly had waited inside the apartment for things to culminate.

It was 12:49 pm.

The next afternoon around two p.m., Dane's phone rang. It was one of the officers who had responded to the call the night before. "We got him," he said.

Dane breathed a sign of relief. "Where is he?"

"We caught him on the way outta town. He was driving a stolen car. There was a loaded .38 on the seat and a bag of crack. We also have him for robbing a woman at gunpoint. She worked for the Department of Justice, so he'll be facing several tumultuous charges. Anyway, he's off the street and in our hands, so he won't be bothering you for at least a few years."

"I thank you, man," Dane said.

"Well, he's gonna get whatever time he has coming to him," the cop finished.

David Dane would never see or hear of Brian again.

The next morning Dane told Nick what had happened and suggested that Tracy find out in her own time. Nick agreed not to tell her.

"Look David, Brian got what he had coming to him. He used that gun to try and intimidate me one time when we were out in the woods. He said, 'Don't you know that I'm locked and loaded?'"

"Yeah. He likes that line."

"I wanted to jam him up for that," Nick said. "If he wasn't Tracy's son, I'd have put that punk under a long time ago."

"Now he's gonna be someone's bitch," Dane replied. "He'll probably even get a surprise up that wise little ass of his."

"And you wanna know what, Dane?" Nick offered. "He'll deserve every single inch of it."

Some time later, in the darkness on that night, David Dane went to Ontario Street in search of Lilly Chicoine. When he found her, she was standing in the park on St. Alexander talking to a young Italian guy with black hair.

"Lilly!" Dane called to his girlfriend as he approached both of them. She looked way out of control.

"Look, just stay out of it!" Rico ordered, flagging Dane away with one hand.

"Excuse me . . . . ?" Dane began.

"He's my boyfriend," Lilly said of Dane, who might otherwise have slaughtered Lilly's comrade.

"I'm sorry," Rico apologized.

"No problem," Dane said, kissing Lilly full on the lips. He thought his girlfriend looked adorable in her pink neon top with the bursting purple clouds on it over red jeans. She also wore a fisherman's hat and brown shoes. To Dane, she was gorgeous.

As Dane and Lilly began to walk underneathe a trellis, Rico followed. In the end he would turn out to be a very nice guy, and Dane would come to greatly appreciate his friendship and support.

"Hey, nice to finally meet you," he said. "Lilly's told me a lot about you."

Dane turned, extending his hand. "I'm David Dane," the fighter said.

"Rico," the Italian said. "Hey, you have a cigarette?"

"Nah, sorry, I don't smoke. Lilly's lungs are turning to charcoal. Not mine," Dane said, smiling.

"Oh."

"I'm going to make a customer now," Lilly said.

"You're leaving already?" Dane asked.

"Yeah, fuck. I wanna do a quarter."

"Don't you see that you're hurting your boyfriend?" Rico asked.

Dane looked pleased by Rico's consideration for his plight. This guy had a heart.

"He's used to it," Lilly responded, slightly put off by Rico's empathy for Dane.

"I'm not used to it," Dane said. "I love you too much to get used to it."

"See? You're hurting him. Like I was telling you earlier. You need to get clean."

"Fuck, I need to make a client," Lilly said, ignoring them both and walking the curb.

When her first client stopped, he got out of the car and solicited Lilly directly. He wore a black T-shirt and black jeans over a well-muscled frame. He had a black Englishman's golf hat and brown suede boots. He looked like a pro athlete. Dane's fervent jealous streak was rising to the surface now.

"Then I'll chase your customers away," Rico told her. "Ah-ha! Look at the perverted john!" Rico mocked, pointing at the guy.

Dane was damned impressed with Rico. Just then, Ann Marilyn walked by with a bewildered look on her face. She waved to Dane who was too busy to wave back.

The john was headed back to his vehicle, scared off by Rico's taunts. Good for the motherfucker, Dane thought.

About ten seconds later Lilly disappeared into another client's car and was driven away.

"Shit!!" Rico bellowed.

"You can't keep her from it for long. I appreciate the concern though. Thanks, Rico," said Dane.

"She shouldn't be out here," Rico said. "I used to be heavy on the shit, too. She's not just hurting herself, she's hurting you, too."

"Yeah, no kidding," Dane responded. "I live this with her every day."

"Have you tried getting her into therapy?"

"She has other ideas," Dane said. "Like not attending."

"She's a beautiful girl. I don't know why she's trying to destroy herself," Rico said.

"That's what I've been asking myself ever since I met her. I love her very much. I just wish she'd love herself enough to get some help."

About twenty minutes later, Lilly popped out of nowhere with a bag of French fries in her hand. She looked happy.

"I'm gonna go now," Rico said. "My roommates have been waiting for me all night."

"You're welcome to stick around," Dane said, inviting him.

Lilly offered Dane some fries. She had a gesture of kindness in her eyes and, at that moment, Dane felt that Lilly truly loved him.

About half a mile down Ontario Street, now minus Rico, Lilly and David ran into a blond woman in her early forties who was accompanied by a Labrador on a red leash. She wanted Lilly to cop eighty bucks worth of powder for her and at the same time be present to ensure that Lilly wouldn't fuck off with her money. The woman regarded Dane for a moment, in his light colored denim blues with his pinch and his bald dome. It was as if she were appraising him for what was to come.

"I can't take my dog with me," she said. "Can your boyfriend watch him for me?"

Brandy the dog eyed Dane for a moment, as if looking for a sign of friendship. Dane immediately thought of his own dog, Hunter, whom he missed even more with each passing day that they were apart.

"He loves dogs," Lilly said. "He'll watch Brandy for you."

Dane leaned in and extended his right hand for Brandy to sniff. Instead, Brandy placed his paw in Dane's palm and the two shook hands in a token of new-found friendship.

"He won't steal my dog, will he?" the woman asked.

He's not gonna steal your dog, honey. He has one his own."

Dane and Brandy were following behind Lilly and the blond woman now, Brandy trotting happily at Dane's side as if he had known Dane all his life and was used to being there.

Brandy paused for a moment, sniffing something on the ground. Dane looked down. Nothing there.

They walked a few more feet and the foursome stopped. They had reached their destination.

Okay, Brandy," the woman said. "Mommy will be back soon," she said, pecking the Lab on the forehead.

"We'll be okay. We'll probably grab a couple of beers and watch the game or something," Dane joked.

"Cute," the woman said, smiling.

"Okay, baby. We'll be back in five minutes or so," Lilly said. And with that, she and the woman disappeared into a well-lit alcove past a green door.

Dane and Brandy took stock of one another for a moment.

"So, you drink Molson or Canada Dry?" Dane asked. "No? You want a soda?"

Brandy reclined his neck to look straight up at Dane as if to signify that he got the joke and was playing along.

"So, you watch TV? You have a favorite show?" Dane continued.

Brandy barked, as if giving a response.

"I've never seen that one. Hey, you guy's have cable?"

Just then Lilly and the blond woman returned.

"Thanks for watching him," the woman said, smiling.

"No, hey, my pleasure," Dane replied. "He even told me the name of his favorite show."

"Which is?" the blond asked.

"He likes The Sopranos, but he's also a big 24 fan."

"Okay . . ." the woman said, taking Brandy's leash from Dane who was petting the pooch on the head now. "We watch ER a lot. Did he mention that one?"

"No, he didn't say anything about that," Dane went on, keeping up the joke.

"Thanks" the woman said, addressing Lilly. "How much do I owe you for the service?"

"Twenty bucks," she said.

The woman reached into her purse and fished out a twenty which she handed to Lilly.

Just then a very pissed off looking Barbie and J.P. passed them by on the street.

"She thinks I stole her shit," J.P. stopped to tell them.

Dane laughed heartily.

"This wouldn't be Ontario . . ." he started, but J.P. was already shadowing Barbie, reading her the riot act from about ten feet away.

"Let's go," Lilly said.

Dane turned to look over his shoulder. Brandy and the blond woman were in the distance now.

"Cute canine," he said. "You know, we should have Hunter sent out here to us. I'm concerned about him getting on a plane, though. He doesn't like heights. Maybe if he wore a suit they'd let him ride in first class."

"I doubt it". Lilly mumbled.

"Of course, we'd have a limo pick him up at the airport. Hey. Hunter looks good in an Armani . . . ."

It was 12:01 a.m.

One week later, when Hunter got off the plane, he looked slightly worse for wear. They had rejected his request to sit in first class, and Hunter looked pissed about it. Nonetheless. He was taken off the aircraft in a miserable cage, looked around for a moment, yawned and then made a beeline for his owner who was awaiting him. Emotional, Dane lifted Hunter up as if he were still a puppy and kissed him on the snout.

"Ladies and Gentlemen. My homeboy," Dane announced, borrowing a lyric from a "Limp Bizkit" tune.

Hunter licked Dane furiously, happy to see his owner. He barked a Hello. His tail wagging furiously.

Dane had not seen Hunter this happy since he had confiscated two ham and cheese sandwiches from the counter-top of Dane's parents' kitchen back home and woofed them down, undetected . . . at least for about fifteen minutes.

"I love you, dude," Dane said fastening Hunter's leash onto his collar. Again Hunter barked cheerfully in response. "And I brought you a treat."

Hunter's ears pricked up. The last word in Dane's sentence was one he knew very well, the best word in the English language.

"Your favorite," Dane said, producing two squares wrapped in aluminum foil.

Hunter sat now, as if to show his very best behavior.

"Two handmade, hand crafted, delectable ham and cheese sandwiches," the boxer said, unfolding the aluminum in sections. Dane kissed Hunter on the top of his head and presented him with his favorite meal, to which Hunter graciously licked his master's cheek. His way of saying "Thank you."

"Bon appetit," Dane said as Hunter attacked his favorite dish.

After Dane's dog had finished with his sandwiches, Dane crumpled up the foil wrapper and tossed it into a nearby trash can. It was getting late, Dane noticed, as he flipped his cell phone open

Outside, a friend of Dane's who owned a minivan was waiting for Hunter and his owner. Dane and Hunter quickly crawled in to the back seat and were chauffeured away.

Darkness had fallen over the twinkling horizon of the city. Traffic ebbed, and there were fewer and fewer people on the downtown city streets. Most commuters had already gone home and turned in for the night.

Two hours later, as Dane unlocked the door of his apartment to let Lilly and Hunter inside, Nick and Tracy were gone. They had left a note saying that they had found a sublet nearby and would be in touch as soon as they were settled in.

"This is a surprise," Dane said, handing the note to Lilly.

"Hi! Nice to meet you," Lilly said, cradling the dog's head and kissing it.

Dane walked over to one of the end tables by the couch and turned a lamp on by its switch.

"Welcome home, dude," Dane said, looking toward Hunter who was now on tour.

"I'm gonna go in the bathroom and do my hit. I bought two quarters," Lilly said.

Dane hoped that Hunter would not pick up Lilly's habits. He didn't believe that they had drug rehab for dogs.

"If you sniff anything in this house, it had better not be what Lilly's sniffing," Dane said to the dog, smiling.

Hunter flopped down on all fours and used his paws to cover his eyes. Dane was laughing out loud now.

"Oh, you're a fucken' riot and a half," he said jovially.

"I heard that comment," Lilly said from behind the bathroom door.

"Good," Dane said, grinning. "Whaddya want on your pizza?" he asked her, flipping on the TV at the same time.

"The Mexican shit. Pepperoni and hot peppers."

The volume dial was rising on the television now. On the screen there was a young female reporter standing in the shadows in front of a familiar-looking six unit apartment building that had been cordoned off with police tape. She looked sullen.

". . . a slaughter-house, when three bodies were pulled out of two upstairs bedrooms earlier this evening. All were known to police and are believed to be local sex-trade workers."

"Fuck," Dane mumbled below his breath.

"Lilly! LILLY!" Dane shouted, turning his head in the direction of the closed bathroom door.

No response. The coke had obviously overtaken her already.

"Oh my God!" Dane exclaimed.

It was 11:45 pm.

Early the next morning before first light, Dane followed Lilly beneath a nightmarishly-lit toll bridge well known to most commuters of the city for its historic relevance. It was extremely dark outside, yet the bright harbor lights atop the bridge cast an eerie glow over this early morning scene, making Dane wince against their impenetrable glare as he followed Lilly underneath the shadows of the overpass toward a darkened filling station.

"Fuck! Smack doesn't open for another two hours," Lilly said.

"Do we have to stay out here that long?"

"I have no choice. I wanna do smack," Lilly protested.

"Can't we go home and call from there?"

"The guys who sell China White won't come to our area."

China White was the purest form of heroin you could get on the street.

"Jesus, Lilly, you are my favorite motherfucker," Dane said sarcastically.

"I know," she said.

By the time they arrived back on Ontario Street the sun was piercing the clouds and a light fog hung in the air. It was otherwise cool outside.

"Good morning, Nadia," Dane greeted the sexy blond in the tight gray dress.

"Where's my twenty bucks?" Nadia asked.

"What twenty bucks?" Dane asked, a frown building on his forehead.

Lilly was looking toward Nadia now. The three of them were standing in front of a big church that overlooked a park.

"What the fuck?" Dane questioned, looking now towards Lilly.

"Dane stole the twenty bucks that fell out of my shoe," Nadia complained.

"Do you have her twenty bucks?" Lilly asked, turning to look over her shoulder at her boyfriend.

"No," Dane responded.

"He doesn't have it," Lilly said.

"Yes he does!" Nadia insisted.

"No, really, do you have her twenty bucks?" Lilly asked Dane.

"No, baby. I don't have Nadias twenty bucks." Dane responded.

"Give me back my twenty bucks," Nadia ordered.

"I don't have your money Nadia," Dane protested.

"Yes you do!" Nadia insisted.

"If my boyfriend says that he doesn't have your twenty bucks then he doesn't have it," Lilly said.

"I know he has it."

"Nadia, look, I have no idea what happened to your twenty bucks, but I don't have it!" said Dane, trying to control the boiling rage within.

"Yes you do!"

"Jesus, look. I'm not gonna stand here all day and fight about this. I already told you . . ."

"FUCK! HE DOESN'T HAVE IT" Lilly yelled.

Dane was proud of the way that Lilly defended him. He had never seen her stick up for him like this before. It was a first.

"He has it," insisted Nadia. "That was my smack money."

"I don't have your fucken' smack money," Dane said.

"You're calling my boyfriend a thief!" Lilly shouted. "If he says he didn't take your twenty bucks then he didn't take your twenty bucks."

"YES HE DID!" Nadia shouted.

"FUCK OFF! He didn't take your money!" Lilly yelled, spoiling for a fight.

"Let's go, baby," Dane said, towing Lilly in his direction. But Lilly wasn't giving in.

"Don't call my man a liar!" Lilly went on.

"He took my money!" Nadia shot back.

"No he didn't!" Lilly screamed. She was totally enraged.

"Hey baby. It's okay," Dane said pulling Lilly away.

"No, it's not okay," Lilly yelled.

"Okay, okay . . . Maybe I lost it . . ." Nadia conceded.

"Ah . . . eh?" Lilly said, backing away. "Let's go, baby."

It was sun up.

Chapter 19

It was nearing the end of December. Finally. Thanks to Dane's parents, he and Lilly would be heading home for Christmas. Or at least Dane was going home, and he was taking Lilly with him.

Hunter, on the other hand, had made earlier travel plans. He had already been chauffeured back to Halifax in the confines of a minivan driven by a female friend of Dane's who was an animal rights activist. He had already been home for two weeks.

It was dark outside. Flakes of snow blew about in a crisp wind as traffic ebbed and flowed in line-ups across the city.

"Lilly, we have a train to catch in two hours and you haven't even run your bath yet."

Lilly preferred to take baths rather than showers. Sometimes she'd sing "Teddy Bears' Picnic" as she splashed around and nearly emptied the tub all over the bathroom floor. Other than having to mop up the floor, Dane found this to be one of Lilly's most adorable habits. He loved her, and, despite some of the heinous shit that she did from time to time, he always would.

"Fuck, c'mon! Where the hell are they?" she lamented, wondering where her smack dealer was.

It was getting late, and Dane knew that if they missed their train they would also miss spending Christmas in Hali.

"Call Max again. See where the fuck they are," Dane said.

Lilly picked up the phone and dialed her drug dealer's number.

"Fuck! Now they're not answering," she said.

Dane was really beginning to panic now. They were late. And it was on account of Lillys dealer.

Finally, exactly an hour before their departure, Max showed up downstairs. Lilly quickly pulled on her brown winter jacket under which she wore a two-piece beige jogging suit and hurried downstairs with Dane in tow. Outside the building Lilly hurried around the corner and hopped into the front seat of Max's green Toyota. The car rounded the corner once and, in minutes, came back, as was the usual routine.

Dane was waiting on the curb. After Lilly got out of the car carrying two grams of H, the two hurried back upstairs.

"Baby, you're gonna have to skip your bath."

Nooo . . . . I wanna take a bath first," she moaned.

All this and bronchitis, too, Dane complained to himself. For three days he'd hardly been able to breathe. His luck was astonishing.

"Sweetie, we have to go. You smell great."

Lilly finally conceded and the two grabbed their suitcases and hit the elevator to go downstairs.

"I love you," Dane said on the elevator, kissing the gorgeous Lilly Chicoine on the lips.

Once outside they loaded their suitcases into the trunk of a cab and took off for Via Rail. When Dane and Lilly finally barreled through the doors to the train station it was 12:01 a.m. And, save for a couple of janitors and desk workers, the station was empty. Nonetheless Dane and Lilly made a beeline for their gate.

When they arrived at Gate 16 there was only one female attendant there. She eyed Dane up and down inquisitively. "Can I help you?" the attendant asked.

"Yeah, we have reservations on the midnight shuttle to Halifax, Nova Scotia," Dane explained, way out of breath and wheezing.

"I'm sorry, sir, the midnight shuttle has already left," the attendant said.

"What?" Dane asked desperately. Suddenly he thought he might vomit.

"Well are there anymore trains tonight?" he inquired frantically.

"Ohhhh . . . . this is all my fault," Lilly proclaimed.

"No, I'm sorry sir. This is Christmas Eve. There are no more trains until four p.m. tomorrow," the woman said. "But I think there's a bus leaving Terminus Voyager at one a.m."

"Can you refund our tickets?" Dane asked, now with a spark of hope in his voice.

"Yes, I think I can," the woman said, focusing on her computer terminal. "Just give me one second," she said punching something up on her keyboard.

"Yep," she paused, before refunding the full transaction via debit card.

"Here you go," she said, handing Dane a receipt.

"Let's go!" Dane shouted to Lilly, grabbing both his suitcase and Lilly's, and heading back out the door to the underground cab stand.

Snow poured in under the cement canopy as Dane and Lilly loaded their cases into another cab. Danes heart was drumming so loudly between his ears that he thought his head might explode.

David Dane Wallace

This time they would get there. This time they would make it, Dane hoped optimistically.

"Terminus Voyager," Dane said as he and Lilly slammed the cab doors shut.

Once at the bus station, Dane paid the driver and closed the door behind him

"Let's go," he said, lifting both of their cases from the snow laden concrete.

"I love you, baby. Merry Christmas," Dane said, quickly pecking Lilly on the left cheek.

"I love you, too, boo," she said. 'Boo' was street slang for boyfriend.

At the gate Dane quickly paid for two tickets. There would be lots of gifts waiting for Lilly in Hali.

Dane had told his mother not to worry about his own gifts this year and to concentrate on Lilly instead. He wanted her to have a beautiful Christmas.

On the bus, Dane peeped out of the smoked windows into the night. The glare from the overhead vapor lamps made everything look dreamy and surreal as if from a darkly majestic fairy tale with the light zigging and zagging in parallel L shapes and bouncing narcotically off the bus windows and onto the ground.

"Lilly, I'm gonna make damn sure that this is the best Christmas that you've ever had," Dane promised. He loved her more than words alone could ever tell. Especially now, here, on this cold Christmas eve. She was the love of his life. Dane was sure that he would go to his grave feeling that way. Lilly Chicoine owned his heart.

The cabin was now dark. The driver had shut the lights off for the long ride to Halifax.

"I think I'm gonna do a little hit as son as we're on the way," Lilly said.

This would be the first sign of disaster to come.

Ten minutes later they were on the road and Lilly was in the bathroom shooting up. The bus turned the corner, out of another parking lot, and onto an empty street. Blackness inside the bus and at the windows now. Total darkness. Dane could hear Lilly in the bathroom moaning from where he was sitting near the front of the cabin. He wondered to himself where her consuming her H. on the bus would lead.

Reflections washed over the windows and landed in Dane's lap. They were still on the edge of downtown. Still in the city passing by tall buildings with night beyond their windows. It was Christmas Eve, and everyone had to get home to be with their families and loved ones.

Again Dane could hear Lilly moaning. "I need a drink!" she blurted out.

"I'll give you something to drink," some tall dark-haired goof responded.

"What did you fucken say?" Dane asked. But he wanted to get home for Christmas. If he did what he wanted to do, he would be spending the holidays in jail. "That's my girlfriend," Dane warned ominously.

When Lilly finally returned to her seat she had completely lost touch with reality, having consumed all two grams of smack that were originally supposed to last her the next three days. Now, as he was acutely aware, Dane had a major problem on his hands, one that, in this predicament, he had no idea how to handle.

"Hey baby bunny," Dane said to Lilly as she slipped into the seat beside him.

"All gone . . ." Lilly said, beginning to moan as she nodded off.

Dane's bronchitis was worsening. The tubes in his throat were really constricting now, producing blocked airways and greatly reduced breathing. There was that and now Lilly might go ape shit right here on the fuckin' bus.

"Are you all right, baby?" Dane asked Lilly who had changed into a heavy brown wool sweater and black jeans.

Lilly moaned loudly in response, a combination of sleep deprivation and all the smack she had taken.

Someone got up to go to the bathroom, noticing Lilly's odd behavior even under the cover of darkness. The bus had made it onto the highway now and was moving under the orange vapor lamps at a rapid speed, charting a course bound for Nova Scotia.

Dane stood up, fishing a white pillow from the overhead compartment and placing it behind Lilly's head. With any luck, she'd simply fall asleep. That wasn't to be the case however, as Lilly's moaning persisted. Dane wondered what it would be like to walk to Nova Scotia carrying both the suitcases and Lilly.

The first stop on this ride through the bowels of hell came at a small diner at roughly three o'clock in the morning. Dane and Lilly stepped off the bus and made their way inside, shadowed by the plethora of the passengers. It was a small, quiet little eating establishment with red table cloths and flowery centerpieces. Because the restaurant was so small, Dane and Lilly were forced to sit at a table with two other men. The four made idle small talk, Lilly reasonably coherent now. Lilly had some toast and Dane was too sick to be bothered eating at all.

As the passengers and crew boarded the bus some sixty minutes later, Dane's breathing had become worse. Lilly was exhausted next to him, ready to pass out. Soon the engine started and before long they were back on the snow-dampened highway. Lilly was soon slipping down underneathe the seat, her eyelids falling shut. Her moaning had become worse, more noticeable, its sound beginning to attract attention.

"Fuck!" Dane said under his breath.

Their second stop of the night was at a Tim Horton's coffee shop. Dane bought four jelly doughnuts and woofed them down on the bus.

At around four thirty a.m., Dane thought that his bronchitis might claim him. His tubes had become so constricted that it felt as thought he were breathing through a straw, and all that he had for meds were the Halls cough drops he had purchased before leaving home. Somehow. He did not believe that would be enough.

At the next stop at a terminal in some town, Dane and Lilly would run into trouble. Someone had reported Lilly's strange behavior.

As they went inside to use the washroom, Dane and Lilly were confronted by two security officials as well as the driver of the bus himself.

"Yeah? How you doin'?" Dane asked. Lilly was moving around a bit.

"Look, we know that there's something wrong," the older security officer said. "If you need help, now's the time to get it."

Dane was now as nervous as he'd ever been.

"Noooo . . . I'll be fine," Lilly explained softly. She was still dancing.

"Well, you don't look fine," the guard said.

"She's fine," Dane said, and promised they'd be good. And that was that.

The next morning, at first light, the bus made a stop over in Truro, which was two hours outside of Halifax. Lilly got off to have a smoke, leaving a deathly ill, slumped over David Dane inside of the bus. When she returned, she was talking to a blond guy who apparently sold shoes. He was about average build with below average looks. He was obviously putting the moves on her.

351

At one point, when Dane was hunkered over, re-tying his shoe lace, he overheard the guy make a remark to the effect that he would like to have Lilly give him and his friends blowjobs. "We can all get blowjobs," he said. Then he asked, "Where's your old man?"

"He's right here," Lilly said, pointing toward and into the seat in front of her. She was standing up. Dane would forever believe that all involved, except Lilly, were the luckiest bastards alive, because had they, Dane and Lilly, not been under close scrutiny on that bus, and had Dane not been deathly ill, he would likely, would have without a doubt hospitalized the Shoe Man and his friends with life-threatening injuries.

When the bus finally arrived in Halifax two hours later, Jonathan and Marilyn Dane were waiting for an excited, exhausted and starving Dane and Lilly. Marilyn greeted Lilly first with a hug and then a kiss. She then followed suit with Dane himself.

"My goodness, you must have had a rough ride," Marilyn said, looking at the sad shape that they were both in.

Jonathan Dane already had a head-start, having lifted their suitcases into the trunk of the car.

"I feel like shit," David exclaimed.

"Wow, I like your hair," Lilly said to Marilyn.

"Yeah, I just had it done so that I'd look good for you guys when you came home."

Lilly yawned. "Oh . . . ! I'm tired," she said. "Merry Christmas."

"We've hardly eaten," David Dane said. "We should stop and pick something up."

When they stepped outside into the brisk morning air, Lilly immediately noticed Jonathan Dane sitting behind the wheel of an expensive-looking ice blue, four-door, fully loaded Nissan Infiniti with a spoiler on the back.

"Wow . . . that's your Mum and Dad's car?" Lilly asked. She was obviously very taken with the automobile.

"In the chrome flesh," her boyfriend answered, opening the back left door for Lilly climb in, to which he followed suit.

Soon the carload of the four of them was on its way to Dane's parents' house. Dane and Lilly were both starving, hungrier than either of them had been before in their lives.

Half an hour later and two floors off the ground, Hunter slid excitedly across the kitchen floor to greet Dane and Lilly as they entered the house where they would spend Christmas. He was wearing a red Santa hat with a white pom-pom. As always, Hunter was dressed for the season.

"Hi!" Lilly said. "You're such a Mister Cutie-Petutti!" she exclaimed, patting hunter on the head.

Dane reached down and hugged Hunter. "I love you, baby," Dane told him. "Merry Christmas."

When the trio entered the living room, the first thing that they saw was the huge Christmas tree that was bright silver with bulbs, tinsel, ornaments and decorations. There had to be a hundred presents stacked underneath. This was Dane's Christmas miracle. Being here with Lilly and Hunter. This was the Christmas miracle that he had dreamed of. More than anything, he wanted Lilly to be happy and to have a family. He knew how much she had always wanted a mother figure and he was hoping that maybe his own could fill the void.

"I love you, Lilly," Dane said, wrapping his arms around his girlfriend.

"I love you too, baby," she replied.

At that moment Dane's live-in grandparents came up from downstairs.

"Lilly, this is Tom and Doris Wallace," said Marilyn.

"Merry Christmas," Tom said, handing Lilly a gift that was from both he and his wife.

Hunter was looking upwards at what was transpiring, his tongue handing out.

"Merry Christmas, Lilly," Doris said, hugging the brunette that she had just met for the first time.

"Thank you, guys," Lilly said.

Soon Dane and Lilly were unwrapping Christmas presents together as Hunter did everything that he could to turn wrapping paper into an edible commodity. Of course Christmas morning itself would not end before Hunter opened a few of his own presents. He was happy sitting there before the big shiny tree wearing his Santa Claus hat, attempting to shred Christmas paper into one million pieces.

Dane reached over and kissed Hunter on the snout. "Love you, buddy," he said.

Marilyn Dane had gone out of her way to spend money on gifts for Lilly this Christmas. She had managed to buy Lilly everything from perfume to clothes to stuffed animals to DVDs. This Christmas was Dane's one-day paradise, never to repeated or duplicated ever again.

"I love you, Lilly, so much. So much," Dane repeated, holding Lilly in his arms in front of the big pine tree. And it was true. She was the love of his life. Never before had he met anyone who had consumed his heart the way that Lilly Chicoine did. She was to him, his sunrise.

Soon after, David Dane and Lilly Chicoine, Dane's parents, Brother* and grandparents sat down at the Dane's expensive dining room table, under which Hunter presided over his new squeaky toy along with some gourmet doggy treats.

On this Christmas day, Dane and Lilly would eat like kings and queens, eating plateful after plateful of turkey and stuffing, followed by a triple-layered jello dessert topped off by whip cream and cherries.

Hunter on this special day was also a special guest at the table, dining on a two-course meal of turkey and stuffing sautéd in gravy along with his favorite snack: a ham and cheese sandwich. He devoured it all leaving only crumbs on the floor.

That night, in the quiet shadows of the guest bedroom, Dane and Lilly made love.

Morning.

At sunrise, Dane and Lilly piled into the back of his parents' Infiniti for a fourteen hour drive back home.

Hunter and his chauffeur would soon follow, with a twenty-four hour delay.

They had received an eviction notice* before leaving for Christmas, so, upon returning, Dane, Lilly and Hunter would be moving to a new location further west from their former abode.

Chapter 20

Ten days after returning from Halifax, Dane and Lilly moved into their new apartment on Brook Street, and, not long after, Lilly vanished into the night and did not come back. She had dressed for work at 8 pm on a Tuesday night and left around nine o'clock. When she failed to return after two days, Dane became concerned. And after seven days, he was worried sick. It had been cold outside for weeks, with temperatures reaching all-time sub-zero records. Now more than ever, there was reason to panic.

The first two people that Dane phoned were Star and her sugar daddy, Marcel. Marcel, who was in his mid sixties, a short, dark-haired Frenchman with an accent, had been keeping Star and her drug habit going for over a year. He and Dane had become good friends as well as confidants in a very short period of time, having their women's situation as an interest in common. Marcel had a jealous streak that put Dane's to shame. Talk about explosive. The usually kind hearted, gentle Marcel could quickly become a nuclear bomb.

"Hey Marcel". Dane greeted with the phone resting on his shoulder.

"Oh, David. Hello," Marcel said, greeting the boxer.

"Have you or Star heard from Lilly? She's been missing for seven days."

"Star?" Marcel asked, clearly turning to look in the opposite direction at Star who was seated behind him. "David cannot find Lilly. Did you see her when you went out on Jolicoeur or Ontario Street?"

"She's missing again? Jesus Christ, Marcel," Star began. "Doesn't that bitch know any better by now?" the sexy, tattooed blond asked.

Apparently not, Dane thought to himself.

"David, Star hasn't seen Lilly. It is sure that she has not tried to call here," he said.

"Marcel, can you pick me up and drive me down there to look around? I'll pay you for the gas. I'd walk but it's colder than fucken' hell!"

"Oui," responded Marcel in the affirmative in French. "It will make two or three hours before I can be there."

"Thanks, bro," said Dane.

When Star and Marcel showed up in Marcel's black Ford Tempo it was close to the witching hour. Star, as usual, looked like a blond haired, blue-eyed sex bomb. At least Dane thought so, and it was pretty damned certain that Marcel did too.

.

"Hey, baby," Star said, kissing Dane fully on the lips. "You look handsome," she said. Marcel must have loved that, Dane thought. If this continued. There would definently be trouble soon.

"David," Marcel said in greeting, with now a slightly jealous look.

"Hey Marcel," Dane said in return greeting. He knew that Marcel was probably pissed off at him now.

Star was thirty five. Marcel was in his sixties. It caused problems.

"Oh, David. Hello," Marcel said. Dane could hear the jealousy in his voice.

"Let's roll," Star said.

As soon as the engine turned over, Dane could smell heavy gasoline fumes.

"You might wanna get that gas smell checked, dude. If someone lights a match, we're gonna go up in flames," Dane remarked.

"Oui. Sevre. It's true," Marcel responded. "I am a crack-pot". He said proudly beaming from ear to ear. It was an image, and Marcel wore it well.

When they reached Ontario Street, everything was cold, silent and dark. There was hardly a single passer-by. Ontario Street on this night was an eerie sight, sitting forlornly in the blackness. Still, white and frozen.

"Somehow I don't feel like Lilly's down here," Dane commented.

"What the fuck happened? Did you and Lilly have a fight or something?" Star asked.

Dane shook his head in response, a way that Star could see him in the rearview mirror. He was too busy peering through the windshield at the darkness and cold white pavement ahead of them.

Regardless of the occasional jealous tension between them, Dane loved Marcel. He was to Dane like a brother. A crazy brother, but a brother nonetheless. Marcel was like Dane, a writer and poet by nature. He had penned several works in his lifetime.

"We're not gonna find her out here," Dane said.

"I mean in this cold, where the fuck could she be?" Star asked. "What about Tanguay?" she asked.

"No. If she was in jail, she would have called, but if by some bizarre chance she is in jail, I'm gonna take a field trip out there tomorrow and talk to them, even if I have to tell them that she's missing."

Snowflakes flanked the windshield now.

"Have you maybe missed her call?" Marcel questioned.

"Nope, my phone's always on. I haven't missed one call," Dane answered.

"Marcel, put the high-beams on," At Stars request.

Marcel obliged her.

High beams and falling snow.

By dark the following night, Dane had exhausted both Tanguay Pen and Ontario Street in his quest to locate Lilly. Where the fuck was she?

It was getting blacker outside and a light snow had begun to fall.

None of this made sense, Dane thought. It was well below zero outside. The temperatures had hit nearly their maximum drop. It was freezing. Where the hell could she be?

Dane had made a checklist of regular visiting spots that Lilly frequented, but nothing had turned up. Less than zero. It was mind boggling. How could it be that not a single lead had surfaced?

Dane paused for a moment, his eyes stopping on a pair of Lilly's jeans. Something willed him to fish into one of the back pockets. Inside was a small piece of torn paper with a name and phone number on it. First came the name "Joe" and then the number. Dane dialed the seven digit local number. A recording said, "Hi. It's Joe. I'm in the Metro. Leave a message."

Dane left his name and number, never believing that he'd hear from the guy, but lo and behold, five minutes later he got a call.

"Yeah? This is Joe. Can I help you?"

By the voice, Dane assumed that Joe was young, maybe in his early twenties and was likely a low-level dealer.

"Joe, my name is David Dane. I don't care who you are or what you do. I'm interested in finding my girlfriend. Her name's Lilly. She's been missing for a while . . . ."

"I know her. I haven't seen her for about two weeks, but yeah, I know her."

"Joe. I need to know where you saw her last and who she was with. Please," Dane said, trying to keep his tone level.

"Yeahhh . . . I think it was outside Frotenac Metro. With some dude with a buzz cut. He was tall. Kinda goofy looking."

"FRED!!!" Dane proclaimed. "Listen, Joe. I can't thank you enough. If you see her, will you ask her to call home?"

"No problem."

Hunter gulped inquisitively as if to take part in the revelation. Soon after he lifted himself up and came to sit next to Dane.

"Fuckin' Fred!" Dane said out loud to himself.

Six hours later Dane found Fred standing outside in the cold. He was across the street from the Jolicoeur Hotel. Dane quickly stepped over the curb and grabbed Fred by the scruff of the neck.

"Where the fuck is Lilly?" Dane demanded.

"She's not with me."

"Two weeks ago she was. Out in front of Frontenac Metro. Then what?"

Fred looked genuinely puzzled. There was a frown on his tanned face. A frown that didn't bare a shred of dishonesty.

I haven't seen Lilly for over a month," Fred said. "We don't really spend that much time together. We used to trip, but that's it."

Dane believed him. He could tell by what was in Fred's eyes, or by what wasn't that Fred was telling the truth. "Fuck!" the boxer said, releasing his grip on Fred. He felt bad that he'd done this at all. "Well, if you see her you let me know, alright?" Dane said, ending the conversation, slipping him his business card.

"Yeah. Yeah. Alright". Fred said.

"FUCK"!!!!!!!!!!!!!!!! Hollered Dane out of frustration as he trapsed back across the street.

White snow and silence.

When Dane arrived home late that night, he felt empty and cold inside. Somehow betrayed. The night seemed to surround him. For a moment it was as if he didn't have a sense of the room. Evil had a way of hiding the truth and Dane believed that that was what was going on now. Where could Lilly be? Was she dead or being held captive? Had something other than one of those two scenarios happened. He did not know. But he did know what he was going to do. He was going to wave some heat Joes way.

Dane fished into the phone directory that sat by his computer. After scanning about six names Dane dialed a number.

"Yeah. Vincent. It's me. Listen. Can you drop by within the next quarter hour.

On the other end Vincent agreed that he could.

A bright light flashed through the darkness outside the window.

A few minutes later the phone rang phone. The call display was private. Dane lifted the receiver to his ear, standing in the shadows.

"Hello?" he said.   361

"Yeah. I'm downstairs. Open the door". Vincent greeted.

Vincent, via his Family, had some "Well Organized Connections", and he and Dane had known each other for years. The two had met at an After Hours Bar through a mutual aquaintance many, many summers ago.

When Vincent arrived on the floor. Dane let him in, and the two immediately embraced.

"What's going on"?? Vincent asked making himself comfortable on the couch.

"There's big fucken trouble in little China". Dane responded. "I need you to call a guy for me".

"What is he"??

"He's a low level dealer. I've only talked to him once, but I think he fucken knows where Lilly is. I want you to see if you can get the truth out of him".

"Christ. Shit because of this stupid girl again? She should be hung. Pass me the phone".

Dane handed Vincent his cell with Joes number already dialed.

"Hello" Joe muttered.

"Joe. My name is Vincent. You probably don't know me, but i'd be willing to bet that you've heard of my Family. I'm only gonna say this once so pay close attension. My friend Mr. David Dane has a girlfriend that he'd very much like to find. Now. Given your considerable time in the street, and what you do for a living, i'd be willing to bet that you can tell me exactly where she is. And I want the truth, or you're gonna be one and done". Vincent commanded in a sleek baritone voice that was silk in inflection.

Alright. Alright. She's with Mathieu. She's been with him the whole time. He told me not to tell David before because he said he'd make trouble."

Vincent cupped the mouth piece with his hand.

"She's with Mathieu". He said.

Dane felt his pulse accelerating. She'd left him like this, all this time. Afraid. Terrified. And all this time she'd been with Mathieu??

Dane grabbed the phone from Vincent.

"Joe. Do you have a number for Mathieu?" The Boxer asked.

Joe broke off the number.

"He doesn't know that I told you. So please don't tell him."

"You have my word," David Dane said.

"Okay, thanks."

"Joe. Where abouts is Mathieu staying"??

"With another friend of his. I think his name's Mathieu to".

"Thankyou". Dane finished and hung up.

"Thanks Vincent". He said.

Dane was dialing a second number now.

The phone on Mathieus end rang five times before Mathieu Logan picked up. Dane would keep his word, he would not expose Joe.

"Yeah, hello?" Mathieu said on the other end.

It was just like a familiar voice echoing through a bad dream, Dane thought.

"Mathieu . . . . Logan". It's been a long time, Dino Machino," the fighter said. "It's David Dane."

"First of all, how did you get this number? And second, this isn't my house. I'm living with friends, so you can't call here this late. I . . ."

"Mathieu. Lilly's missing. I haven't seen her in weeks. Do you know where she is?"

"I have no idea. And I told you already, you can't call here this late."

See, look, if I don't hear from Lilly, sooner rather than later, I'll have no choice but to call the police. I have a responsibility because Lilly's a resident of my home. If something terrible has happened, the pigs are gonna point a dirty finger at me."

"Yeah, well, Lilly's a survivor. If there ever was one. I'm sure . . ."

"Not good enough," Dane said.

"Look, you're harassing me,"

"Harassing you?" Dane said, his blood beginning to boil. If Mathieu didn't start talking, Dane would hunt him down and kill him. Fuck the harassment!

"You know, for a guy who claims to care about Lilly, you're not showing much concern."

"Look, do you have any idea how late it is?"

"Mathieu, I need you to listen. You can talk to me or you can talk to the police. It's up to you."

"Let me call you back," Mathieu said in a voice that was now back-pedaling. Then he hung up.

"I should've put you on the phone with him to". Dane stated.

"Call him back".

"Nah. I'm afraid that whoever he's staying with might call The Police".

"Let em. He'll find out who the real sharks are". Vincent said.

"She's gonna call. You wait". Dane exclaimed.

It was 11:38 P.M.

The next night around six, the phone rang. It was Lilly. Mathieu was saying something in the background.

Star was in the room with Dane. His only savior in this wicked reality.

"I'm gonna get a fucking GUN!" Lilly began.

"Oh Yeah. And what the fuck are you gonna do with that"?? Dane began. He had a basic understanding of where this was going. Lilly, living on her planet of one, saw herself as "not accountable" for any of this and was thus threatening his execution. He had forced her to be accountable, something that Lilly loathed, beyond all else. This was typical Lilly.

"Well, it's nice to hear from you, too, Baby Bunny," Dane retorted, but inside he was so hurt that words could not describe it. It was as if his soul had been deflated.

"Tell him that I'm sending people over to get your stuff," Mathieu piped up in the background.

Dane wanted to put a bullet in him.

"Why did you leave me?"

"Because I'm sick of it," Lilly retorted spitefully.

"What's she saying?" Star asked from the background, licking chocolate pudding from a wooden spoon. She was dressed in a green silk robe that stopped just below her hips.

Dane turned, waving Star off.

"I'm sick of it," Lilly repeated.

"Sick of what?" David Dane asked.

"Everything."

"Here, let me talk to her," Star suggested, taking the phone from the bald-headed boxer.

"Yeah, Lilly?" Star began. "You're some little bitch," she said. "you've had Dane and I worried sick."

"Oh, so you're fucking my man, now?" Lilly demanded.

"Which one?" Star asked. "You treat him like shit. You disappear into the night without telling anyone, and now you're with Mathieu."

"None of your business," Lilly answered.

"You're some little bitch . . ."

Dane gingerly took the phone from Star who turned to walk in the other direction.

"So, now you know where I am?" Lilly said before hanging up in Dane's ear.

A tear fell from Dane's cheek.

"I've never been so abused by someone I've treated so well," Star remarked.

"Yeah. You and I both."

"I'll stay tonight, if you want. Marcel knows I'm pissed at him, so . . ."

At that moment Dane walked over to Star, grabbed her head and kissed her passionately on the lips. Soon they were both naked on the floor where they spent the next few hours making love.

Star left Marcel and moved in with David Dane. It was an expected turn of events since Marcel had been a sugar daddy to Star and in her eyes nothing more.

Now it was three o'clock in the afternoon, and it was raining outside. It almost looked like a tropical rain storm, like something from a movie. Dane was thinking as he surveyed the clothes that Lilly had left behind. All this time, and all the history that the two of them had, but it didn't take even two minutes for Lilly to walk out on him. What had made Lilly such a callous person. Why was she so void of emotion and humanity? So completely fucken empty on the inside.

Star had gone to a doctor's appointment to renew her prescription for methadone. Mandatory, once a month.

The silver outside was building. It wasn't long before lightning accompanied the rain. Dane looked over Lilly's jackets and designer jeans. Where the fuck had he gone wrong? What act had he perpetrated to deserve this. All of these questions served as a disturbance in his mind.

Soon Star was back. She was carrying two wet shopping bags.

"Hey, I bought some bagels. They were on special," she said.

At that moment Hunter rose from his corner on the floor and came to join David Dane in the bedroom. He looked inquisitive. Somehow puzzled by all that was going on.

"Hey, you," Star said, stealing a kiss from Hunter Woof.

"Are you gonna throw those out?" Star asked in a more serious tone. She was looking over Dane's shoulder at some of Lilly's clothes that were lying on the bed.

"Yeah. When I get around to it," he said.

"She didn't deserve you, hun."

Hunter burped between them and they both laughed.

"Hey! Say excuse me," Dane said. "Bark, at least."

As if understanding, Hunter did just that. Then he went into the living room and climbed onto the couch.

"He probably speaks ten different languages," Dane said.

Star chuckled. "Yup," she said.

Just then there was a flash of lightning outside as Star began to seductively lift David Dane's shirt over his head. "You look nice". Star said trailing David Danes muscular chest with her finger-tips.

"I'm not the only one". Dane said lifting Star up by the ass.

Soon they were on the bed having sex as the rain blasted away at the earth outside.

A week later Star called from a private number. She had been picked up for prostitution and was back in jail. This would be the beginning of everything going totally haywire. Soon Star was having erratic mood swings that of which Dane could not comprehend. To make matters worse, Lilly had phoned and left a message saying that she wanted to come home and would soon be in touch. Now Dane was torn. He was still in love with Lilly. There was no denying that. He had been with her for five years, despite her routine wickedness. And where was Mathieu?

This too was an unanswered question. One minute she was with him, and now she was coming back to Dane.

That night, while Dane was in the gym talking to a gorgeous blond bombshell named Vania, he received a cell phone call from Lilly. She had been living at the hotel and had been kicked out with all of her stuff.

"It's raining outside and I have nowhere to go. My stuff is in some bags under the porch behind the hotel. Please, baby. Can I come home?"

"I love you Lilly," Dane said. "I don't understand why you left me, but I love you."

"So, you'll come get me?"

"I'm coming," Dane said, flipping his phone shut.

When he got to Ontario Street, Lilly was waiting on the corner of St. Alexander. The street was sleek and black with rain and there was hardly a car in sight.

"Oh, I love you, baby," Lilly said, running toward Dane with open arms. "You're always there for me when I need you.

Dane felt strange, but it was a feeling that he could not describe. His vision seemed to tremble a bit. As if his inner self were calling out, sending a message. A message that Dane could not understand. Lilly's soaked arms were around him now.

"I missed you, Baby Bunny," Dane said, burying his lips in her hair.

"Me too," Lilly said.

"Let's go get your stuff," Dane said. He had no idea what he was going to tell Star. Lilly was his true love. There was no denying that.

They walked down the street one block in the darkness and rain, and took a right.

Rain fell in gusts from the eaves behind the Jolicoeur Hotel. It was cold outside.

Lilly pulled a stuffed blue bunny rabbit from the depths of one of her bags.

"See. When you wish something on a bunny's heart, it comes true," she said, cuddling the stuffed rabbit and tweaking its ears.

Dane adored Lilly. He loved her totally.

"Okay, let's get these bags into a cab and go home," Dane said.

Back on Ontario Street, Dane and Lilly hailed a cab and piled Lilly's bags into the trunk. They held each other all the way home in the rain-spattered taxi never for a second letting go of one another.

Dane used his elbow to push open the door to his apartment. He could hear Hunter stirring somewhere. As if he'd been awakened by the sound of Dane's key turning in the lock and had gotten up to see what all the commotion was about.

"Oh where are you, Mister Cutie-Petutti?" Lilly called out to her furry friend. Hunter ran to the door, wagging his tail.

"Hey, dude," Dane said, petting his best friend on the top of his head.

Hunter was making a big fuss over Lilly now, jumping all over her. He was very happy to see her home. Dane left Lilly's wet bags on the kitchen floor as he removed his own wet clothes.

"Baby, can you hand me a towel?"

Lilly obliged him by passing him a fluffy while linen. Just then there was a knock at the door.

"Yeah, who is it?" the boxer asked, discarding the towel.

"Mr. Dane?" the friendly, familiar voice responded. It was Yves Gabriel, the building manager.

Yves Gabriel, in his early fifties, was a tall, wiry man with a gray-black beard and short hair. He was a true gentleman and David Dane called him a friend.

"C'mon in, dude," Dane said, holding the door open.

"Sorry to bother you so late," he said.

"It's alright. How you doin Evil Yves?"

"Ah, I'm fine. An envelope accidentally ended up on my desk today. It has your name on it," Yves said handing Dane the bulky yellow package. There was no return address on it.

"Everything is under control?" Yves asked smiling, looking towards the bathroom.

"Reasonably," Dane answered flashing a quick grin.

"Alright then, Mr. Dane. Have a good night". Yves concluded, pulling shut the door behind himself.

"Have a good night, brother," Dane said, preoccupied by the anonymous piece of mail.

Lilly was in the bathroom now, busy with her quarter.

Dane used a letter opener to unseal the mysterious yellow package. What he saw inside caused his heart to race. It was a series of photographs. All of them were of Lilly, taken at different places on Ontario Street. Lilly did not seem to be aware that she was having her picture taken. No note of explanation accompanied the snapshots.

Dane looked across at the closed bathroom door. He would have to alert Lilly of what he presumed to be imminent danger.

Somewhere down the hall the song "The World is Mine" by David Guetta played behind someone's door.

Hunter paced about for a moment and then lay down on the pink Venetian rug.

The witching hour was almost upon them.

PART III
The Endless Night

"This is Richard Dees, for Up All Night," the radio disc jockey's voice flowed hypnotically over the airwaves as the sun rose against the paneling of a house somewhere on Ontario Street.

"This morning in our studios we have a very special guest. For those of you out there who frequent the Ontario Street area, you may know him just by the sound of his voice. His name is David Dane, and he's here this morning to discuss some of the grisly murders that have taken place in the Ontario Street neighborhood over the past number of months. Our guest this morning has a very personal stake in the slayings because the love of David's life is one of the addicted who roam the shadows of Ontario Street after hours in search of hardcore street drugs. David, what would you like to say to our listeners this morning?"

"My name is David Dane. I wanna speak to the person or persons who are responsible for these slayings. I wanna speak to you because I know that you've targeted my girlfriend, and because i'm powerless to stop her from doing what she does to get her drugs. I know that you've targeted Lilly because I got the series of photos that you sent to me along with the photo of Bethany "Torrid" Katman's postmortem. I want you to alter your target package. I want you to come find me instead. That is, unless you're not up to facing a worthy adversary. I know how you like games. And i'm willing to play one with you, or do you only hunt defenseless women whose minds are fogged by drug use. If this is a sport to you, whoever the hell you are. Then i'm willing to play. If it's hunting human beings that you desire, then I'm offering myself to you. I'll be on Ontario Street every night until you come find me. All that I ask is that you leave Lilly alone, and make me your prey instead".

Dane sat frozen for a moment in the studio, his expression fixated and obsessive.

"Thankyou". He said addressing Richard who sat beside him before removing the mini-mic that was attached to his sweater.

That night in the coiling blackness, Lilly Chicoine stood below the mist of a vapor lamp on Ontario Street. David Dane was watching her from afar, his eyes crazed and vigilant as they darted back and forth in the absence of light where he stood. His heart seemed to be pumping pure adrenaline, not for fear of his own safety, but for Lilly's. He had shown her the photos to which she had, as he expected, reacted stubbornly, as if the photos hadn't been shown to her at all.

A car stopped for Lilly. Dane watched her reach for the door handle and get in. The adrenaline pumping through Dane's system was causing his heart to palpitate. Somewhere inside him demons danced as if jubulant at the hold that they had over him.

Somewhere in the distance an orange bulb glowed under a slight canopy.

Across the street a sexy, dark-haired working girl named Christine walked the stroll. Dane remembered her once telling him that she was from Ottawa. He had met her late one night after eating at Subway. She had been with a tall nerdy looking guy with brown hair.

It was coming close to the witching hour as Dane flipped open his cell phone to check the time. Around him the night sparkled and shined like a fused ocean of black sequins. To his far left, Dane could see Lilly's close friend Mikhail coming toward him. Asking the good-looking mulatto chick with the glasses to keep watch for Lilly would be useless though, because Mikhail spoke only French and not a single syllable of English.

"Fuck," Dane breathed.

"Heyyyyy," Mikhail greeted him, smiling.

Well, she had picked up one or two syllables of English, obviously.

"Christ! Where are you, Lilly?" Dane asked no one.

Mikhail hugged the fighter and pecked him on the cheek. "Hey, sweetie," Dane responded.

"Ahhh, Lilly? . . . Lilly?" Mikhail asked, displaying her enticing smile.

"No," Dane responded, hoping to get his message across by pointing at a passing car.

"Ahh . . ." Mikhail responded as if signifying that she understood. Then she walked away.

Soon a red car pulled up and Lilly got out. Dane's pulse slowed to a regular pace.

"Now can we go home?" the boxer asked.

"I just wanna make another forty bucks for a point and cigarettes."

Dane's heart started to speed up again.

Just then a yellow Jaguar sports coupe with tinted windows purred into the shadows.

"I'll be back soon. I promise," Lilly said approaching the yellow car and getting in.

Dane could not see the driver.

"Was that Lilly?" Christine asked as the coupe sped off.

Dane turned. "Yeah, that's Lilly," he answered in a voice that was fueled by obsession. "You okay, Diamond Doll?" he asked.

She gave him a flattered smile. "You look good in those jeans," Christine complimented him, biting her lower lip seductively at the same time.

Dane did not respond. He was too preoccupied with the empty street before him, as if watching it would somehow produce Lilly.

Christine leaned in so that Dane could kiss her cheek. "Thank you, sweetie," she said as he pecked both sides of her face, one after the other.

Another hour passed without Lilly's return. The worst part of it was that Dane's nerves were on such shaky ground that he could hardly think or act. His physical movement was almost frozen. He needed sleep, but could not afford it. He had been on his feet for maybe a total of forty-eight hours, give or take, and now that lack of rest was taking its toll.

Down the street, Dane could hear sirens, and see red lights flashing under the black shadow of billowing treetops. Commotion and a cluster of noise had broken the still silence of the otherwise peaceful night. As Dane made his way toward the mess of ambulance and police vehicles, he heard a wispy voice mention something about six bodies. The official vehicles and three coroner's cars were sitting in various directions in front of a white rooming house with gray wooden steps that was now cordoned off with police tape. Dane knew it to be a place where several working girls lived.

"Jesus Christ," Dane whispered as the first of six bodies was carried out of the luminous entryway of the the three-story building.

Where was Lilly, he wondered desperately. Ten seconds later, Dane's phone lit up. It was a local area code but Dane did not recognize it.

"Hello?" Dane said.

"Dane. It's Alyssa. I'm at the hospital with Lilly," she said.

There was a news crew in a white van in front of the rooming house now as the second corpse was pulled out of the shadows. Dane's nerves had just gone into overdrive.

"I don't understand," Dane said. "Why is Lilly at the hospital?"

"She was stabbed a whole bunch of times," Alyssa said. "I found her."

"What?" Dane fumbled, his mind racing. "But I was just with her . . . What the fuck happened? What hospital did they take her to?"

"St. Alexander's. We're at emergency. You better hurry!"

"FUCK!" Dane yelled, slamming his phone shut and pocketing it.

"I need a cab," he yelled to an old white haired cab driver who was standing outside of his car.

"Get in," The Cabbie ushered.

"Where to?" the driver asked as soon as Dane was in the back seat.

"St. Alexander's Hospital. Emergency,"

At the front doors of the ER, David Dane paid the driver and exited the cab. Inside, Dane pushed his way through a crowd of hostile patients and overworked medical staff until he came to an administration window. Somewhere along the way a security guard had tried to grab for him. Now the team of one had multiplied to three.

"Alyssa!" Dane hollered as soon as he saw the short-haired girl standing idle at the end of the waiting area. She immediately turned and ran toward Lilly's boyfriend, throwing her arms around his muscular frame.

"Where is she?" Dane asked out of breath.

"She's with the Police. She's conscious," Alyssa responded through a river of tears.

"Freeze! Security!" one of the guards yelled.

Dane turned away from Alyssa masking his expression.

"Wait. We wanna talk to him," a police officer said. He had just appeared through some swinging doors from the patients area.

The security guards immediately aborted mission, realizing they were outranked.

"You're David Dane, right? The victim's boyfriend?" the officer asked.

Dane nodded with his hands resting on his hips.

Okay, come with us," the cop said. His partner, a white-haired man with glasses, had just appeared.

"Where are we going?" the fighter asked.

"Follow us," the older man commanded, leading Dane into a small, dimly-lit office.

"Have a seat," he said.

Dane obliged him.

"Okay. We spoke to your friend Alyssa. We also spoke to Lilly. You're girlfriend's a tough woman." the young officer said, taking a seat opposite Dane. The older officer remained standing.

"Your girlfriend was drugged tonight before she sustained the sharp force trauma to her lung and her kidneys. She managed to give us a pretty good description though. We think it's the same guy that's been killing girls in this area for sometime."
"The Ontario Killer" Dane exclaimed without expression.

At that moment a black Chevy Impala pulled up at the corner of Ontario and Dufresne. The man behind the wheel of the vehicle sported a thick black beard and a matching head of black hair. He wore a dark blue leather jacket over black jeans and cowboy boots.

"I'm looking for my nephew," Commander Tom Wallace said to Christine. "His name's David Dane." He said offering her a folded twenty.

"He's probably at St. Alexanders Hospital with Lilly. She got stabbed tonight." Christine said pocketing the twenty. "Do you know how to get there, because I can show you".

"It's alright." Thomas said, then sped away from the curb, burning rubber.

The range lamps on the ninth floor of St. Alexander's Hospital bled ominously into the still, silent darkness of the corridor. It was well after midnight, and most of the staff had already been dispatched or had departed to other parts of the hospital on rounds, or for other emergencies.

Lilly woke alone in her private room with shadows and rain outside the window. Loneliness and fear immediately engulfed her along with faded images of being stabbed earlier on in the night. Right now, there was no one at her side, a feeling that brought her no comfort and caused her insides to sear with a sharp, nauseating pain beyond that which they normally would have, even in the morphine-quelled aftermath of such a blatant, sharp-force trauma.

Looking to her right, Lilly immediately noticed the IV bag that was emptying into one of the veins in her right arm. Morphine was indeed the first word that registered with her. Her head was swimming now, and although afraid, she still felt very weak and tired. For a moment Lilly could hear the wind whistling outside. Then she closed her brown eyes again and went back to sleep.

Outside in the inky dreamlike blackness of St. Alexanders Hospital Parking Lot. Tom Wallace stepped out of his dark-colored Impala and deposited the keys in his jacket pocket. Inside, he hoped to find his nephew and maybe speak to The Police whom he felt should have collared the killer long before this night had they not been completely fucking inept.

As he crossed the parking lot, headed for the main doors, a yellow taxi almost hit him as it rounded the bend and parked in front of the main doors.

"Jesus," Wallace muttered under his breath.

At Emergency, Thomas found his nephew standing in front of a vending machine drinking a cup of coffee. Thomas thought that his nephew looked spent with gray black circles ringing his eyes like a raccoon. It was obvious that he had not slept in quite some time.

"Hi, son," the commander said, embracing Dane tightly.

"Good to see you," David Dane said.

"Yeah. You talk to the cops yet?"

"Earlier. Lilly got a half decent look at him. He's black, over six feet, maybe two sixty with a way above-average frame. He's killed six people tonight. They think that she knows more, but that's all they got before she passed out again."

"Where is she now? Do you know?"

"They have her somewhere upstairs, but they won't let me see her."

"Uh-HUH" Thomas acknowledged. Stressing the last part of the two word phrase.

"When did you get here"?? Dane asked.

"Not long ago. I flew in with Secret Service."

"First class". Dane exclaimed, downing the rest of his coffee.

"Are you David Dane?" a young police officer suddenly interrupted them, his voice urgent and out of breath.

"Yeah," Dane answered, crumpling up his styrofoam cup.

"There's a yellow sports car outside that matches the one that you gave us a description of. We have it surrounded. The guy the car's registered to matches the description of The Ontario Street Killer".

Dane and Thomas followed the police officer out the main doors and into the parking lot. Thomas had now drawn his 9 mm Beretta and it was discretely at his side.

"David Dane?" another officer asked, resting his palm on David Dane's shoulder.

"That's me".

There's a woman in the suspects car who says she want to talk to you. We pulled her ID. It says Carol Edmonds. Do you know her"??

"What"?? Dane wasn't sure what he had just heard. It was as though he'd just been punched in the gut by an eight hundred pound gorilla. He simply couldn't find his voice for long enough to respond.

Dane's face was a mask of astonishment and confusion as he approached the circle of cops with their firearms trained on the yellow Jaguar coupe, the rain exploding on its outer ceiling. The front passenger door was open and Carol Edmonds sat inside the car. There was silence, aside from the rain. To Dane it seemed as if he was in a trance walking through the line of police officers toward the woman he had known for years who also was the longtime girlfriend and wife of his employer and close friend.

"David," she said as he faced her.

"Son," Thomas said from three feet behind Dane, his gun now also trained on Carol.

"What's goin on Carol?" Dane asked with tense seriousness on his face.

"I'm dieing, David. So is Bobby," Carol went on. "We took one of your sick little friends home with us one night and had a threesome. Bobby didn't protect himself. I went for a blood test eight months later. A week later I got the results back. That's when I found out that I had AIDS. It's cuz of Bobby. I got it from him," she sobbed.

"So that's when you decided to do this?" Dane exclaimed, tears welling up in his eyes. "Bobby did this. And you did this through Bobby".

"Where's Lilly"?? Dane asked suddenly, turning to one of the cops.

"I don't know," he responded. "Where is she, Sarge?" he asked, glancing over his shoulder while at the same time keeping his pistol trained on Edmonds.

"Ninth floor," someone with a badge whispered to Dane.

"There's no guard at her door. Someone should look in on her," an older cop suggested.

Dane had already left heading back towards the doors through which he came.

"Hey!" one of the cops called to him over his shoulder.

Somewhere among the twinkling black shadows of the ninth floor, Bobby Troy Edmonds pushed a syringe full of coke into his vein. It was quiet, and the only sound that could be heard were the sound of oxygen pumps pressurizing in several of the rooms. The floor was still and there would be no interruption from anyone at the nurse's station. Edmonds had already seen to that by cutting the throats of each of the female staff members, one by one, in a single smooth motion.

Now there was only Lilly to tend to.

As Bobby made his way down the shadowy corridor, he stopped to look at the outline of his face in the reflection of a shiny black window of a wooden door with an overhanging range lamp. He recognized but did not react to his own twisted reflection in the nocturnal panel. He could see the lines, the wrinkles of expression, the images, but he was indifferent.

Somewhere from an ocean of darkness, behind him, he heard a familiar voice.

"Bobby."

As Edmonds turned around, he saw the face of David Dane.

"The police are downstairs. They arrested Carol."

Edmonds said nothing. His black eyes pinned and high.

"Put the knife down or they're gonna kill you for it". Dane said genuinely.

Edmonds' black leather glove tightened on the grip of the bowie knife now.

"Give me the knife Bobby." Dane said reaching out, his voice echoing through the surreal reality of this nightmare.

Dane saw Edmonds' face twist before the knife came toward him.

At that moment five loud gunshots exploded out of the darkness and Edmonds fell to the floor in a heap, blood exiting his body from several wounds.

"Son," Thomas said, shooting a concerned glance at his nephew while still holding the 9mm. that killed Bobby Troy Edmonds. Thomas's gun was still trained on Edmonds, but the gun was lowered.

Dane reached down on one knee and checked for a pulse.

"He's gone," he said. "He's gone."

Epilogue

On Christmas day, 2005, Lilly finally decided to call her family, after ten years of being estranged from them. They were shocked to tears to hear from her after long believing that she had died on the streets.

On April 30th 2006, Lilly's parents came to get her on a warm and sunny Tuesday afternoon. On that day, after briefly meeting Lilly's parents, Lilly left David Dane for good. She said she had agreed to go into rehab in T.O. under her parents' supervision, and that one day she hoped they would be together again.

This would turn out to be the last of Lillys lies, for although Dane would speak to Lilly several more times by phone. He would never see Lilly face to face again.

Dane and Lilly embraced one last time on the curb in front of his apartment building. Dane thought that Lillys hug was distant and cold. Two minutes later. Dane and Hunter watched Lilly and her parents drive off into the mirage of the afternoon heat. Dane's final image of the girl that he had loved and taken care of through the dark night of the soul would be that of her waving "Goodbye" to him from one of the cars rear windows.

Tragically.Hunter passed away on Sept.13th. 2006 due to complications stemming from Cancer. He was ten years old. He is intensely missed by his Family and friends all of whom still love him very much and miss him more with each passing day.

Commander Thomas Wallace was the second to come in this pair of tragic losses as he died due to a short and sudden illness on May 31st. 2011. He will be forever missed by his Family and friends, and he has one nephew who will never forget him.

On the street, in reality, David Dane is better know as Von. Some call him, Von "The Icon".

End

* * *

Postscript

Saturday, September 9th, 2006. 3:07 a.m.

For Hunter

The Kingdom

Once upon a time, in a majestic land far, far away, there was a Kingdom. And in that kingdom there lived a Knight who had a dog, and his name, coincidentally, was Hunter.

During his many years in the Kingdom, Hunter was loved very much and had many, many friends. The closest of which, aside from the Knight, was a very, very big bunny who, by the way, was insinuated into this story for very auspicious reasons.

The job of the very big bunny was to entertain the Kingdom's precious K-9 by making Hunter happy everyday. So the bunny would go out into the forest that surrounded the castle and all of its occupants, and plan big parties with all of the other animals in the majestic woods. He would bring squirrels and chipmunks and even raccoons, which Hunter would greet at the door each day. For that was Hunter's job at the castle; to welcome all who went there.

And Hunter, in all his years of service, never met a guest at the castle that he didn't like. And, in turn, Hunter was loved by all.

But one day, the big bunny returned from the afternoon haze of the woods to find that Hunter was sick and was not eating his food. So the big bunny, the Knight, and all of the people who loved Hunter came to surround him in his hour of need. They told Hunter how much they loved him and how he had stolen all of their hearts. They told him how much he meant to so many people and how much happiness he had brought into all of their lives. In his darkest hour, Hunter had become a hero at the castle, and people traveled from all over to see him. They had come to wish him well and to bring him food in hopes that he would eat, in hopes that one day Hunter would once again become the beloved and happy canine that everyone at the castle had always known.

His legend would never be forgotten, and neither would he.

The End

Murderer in Lingerie

Crisp clean winds off the night ocean.
Woman in a sequined dress.
Shadows wash accross faces of secrecy.
Angry whispers under a night of veils.
Somewhere the sounds of a downed sun.
Woman in the shadows removes her dress.
Watch reflections move in mirrors of darkness.
Her eyes meet the ocean as she draws a blade of shining silver.
Walk slowly through the blood smeared night air.
Bare witness.
Shadow falls to the ground at the foot of the ocean.
Evil with no boundaries reveals itself.
Sounds from above the surf again.
Sea gull grazes the sands before taking off again.
Breach of faith.
Ends of trust.
Burst of fire.
Waves lap the shoreline.
The breeze.
Angels dance.
Souls rise.
Eyes meet.

Von "The Icon"